Avanti Chr

Corin's Chance

$\rightarrow\hspace{-0.3em}O\hspace{-0.3em}\leftarrow$

Hannah Walker

Avanti Chronicles:

Corin's Chance

>O€

Posted to some stars awful cruiser, Dr. Corin Talovich hoped to serve his time quietly and get on with his life, but fate stepped in and decided otherwise.

Crashing into an unknown planet was the last thing Corin expected. With only his friend, Lieutenant Commander Tate Riven, by his side, they face the unexplored world and new enemies bravely, leading them to the Derin Clan, where they're welcomed by the leader's son.

Kel isn't sure about the strange men, but he isn't about to send them away, especially when the bond between Corin and himself is something he can't ignore.

When another clan wages an attack, Kel is forced to make some hard choices which nearly costs him everything he holds dear. Together, with their allies, Corin and Kel fight, focusing on the future they desire, knowing failure not only dooms their love, but also those around them. Side by side, they work to destroy the evil threatening to keep them apart and becoming the family both men desire.

May your journey be swift and uneventful, may you all get one step closer to your truemates and may good triumph over evil. Remember love conquers all.

Copyright

———————— ➤O€ ————————

Dedication

———————>O<———————

This book is dedicated to my father. I would not be the woman I am today without him. He taught me so much. I will be eternally grateful to him for passing on his love of the written word. It's thanks to him that I have a love of Sci-Fi and Fantasy, of epic stories that transport us to another time and place, of heroes who inspire us to be so much more than we ever dreamed of being.

He taught me to never give up, have faith in myself and to reach for the stars.

Pops, you're my hero.

I'd like to take this opportunity to thank two very special women, who I am privileged to call my friends, Nicole Colville and Emma Marie Leya. These two authors reached out to help me when I started on this incredible journey. They have supported me every step of the way. They are incredible mentors who have guided me through all aspects of writing, editing, and publishing. They are awesome beta readers whose comments have inspired me, made me laugh and smile. Our plot discussions have given me inspiration and they have been the best cheerleaders a writer could ever hope for.

You're both amazing, and I wouldn't be writing without your help and your encouragement.

To my last beta reader, Laura Raven. Thank you. You helped catch things that slipped us all by.

My editor, Jessica McKenna. Thank you for having so much patience with me, it has been a pleasure to have you as my teacher.

www.facebook.com/JessicaMcKennaLiteraryEditor

liteditor.com

My cover designer, Kellie Dennis. I am truly amazed at the incredible work she does. She took my rambling thoughts on a cover, descriptions from the book that I sent her, and created this incredible cover. It is a perfect representation of how I see the world I have created. I recommend her to anyone who is looking for that extra special something. One look at her website and you will see why.

Cover art by Kellie Dennis @ Book Cover by Design

www.bookcoverbydesign.co.uk

www.facebook.com/bookcoverbydesign

Table of Contents

$$\longrightarrow O \longleftarrow$$

If. By Rudyard Kipling

If you can keep your head when all about you
Are losing theirs and blaming it on you,
If you can trust yourself when all men doubt you,
But make allowance for their doubting too;
If you can wait and not be tired by waiting,
Or being lied about, don't deal in lies,
Or being hated, don't give way to hating,
And yet don't look too good, nor talk too wise:

If you can dream—and not make dreams your master;
If you can think—and not make thoughts your aim;
If you can meet with Triumph and Disaster
And treat those two impostors just the same;
If you can bear to hear the truth you've spoken
Twisted by knaves to make a trap for fools,
Or watch the things you gave your life to, broken,
And stoop and build 'em up with worn-out tools:

If you can make one heap of all your winnings
And risk it on one turn of pitch-and-toss,
And lose, and start again at your beginnings
And never breathe a word about your loss;
If you can force your heart and nerve and sinew
To serve your turn long after they are gone,
And so hold on when there is nothing in you
Except the Will which says to them: "Hold on!"

If you can talk with crowds and keep your virtue,
Or walk with Kings—nor lose the common touch,
If neither foes nor loving friends can hurt you,
If all men count with you, but none too much;
If you can fill the unforgiving minute
With sixty seconds' worth of distance run,
Yours is the Earth and everything that's in it,
And—which is more—you'll be a Man, my son.

The Barin Alliance

In the year 2435, light years from New Earth, The Barin Alliance is a dominant force. A vast network of planets and systems, it is controlled by a senate of planetary leaders.

The Alliance is supposed to lead the Seven Universes to the betterment of all Starkind. Their ideals that all of citizens deserve equality and liberty are met with contempt by many. Some simply believe that over time the Alliance has become increasingly corrupt.

In 2368, to help ensure peace, The Alliance created the Avanti, an elite division of warriors. They are the last line of defence and the first to wade into any battle. They fight to protect both the innocent and the citizens of the Alliance. Drawn from all quarters, races, and planets within the Alliance, these warriors are the best of the best.

A group of Avanti, led by Commander Daxin Rydoc, is assigned to the Karinski Quadrant in the Delta Sector. Filled with the dregs of society, it's a tough, thankless job. On a routine transport Dax and his men encounter Captain Corin Talovich. One of the most brilliant surgeons within the Alliance's Medical Corps, he becomes friends with Dax's squad. The Avanti Chronicles are their stories.

Chapter One

>O€

Captain Corin Talovich studied his new medical bay with a contemptuous look. It was so far from the standard of what he was used to, and he wondered how anyone could treat people in here. The stock cupboards were beyond depleted and barely held even the minimum needed for minor emergencies, let alone anything of a more complicated nature. He was relieved he brought his own supplies to this rust bucket of a battlecruiser.

His assignment to the Barin Alliance Cruiser (BAC) Delphini was still a contentious issue for him. While he preferred it over the posting at the Cassini, it still left a lot to be desired. The Cassini was a research outpost, with a sum total of seven civilian scientists who were studying anomalies in a radio pulsar. Apart from their regular health checks, there would be virtually nothing for him to do. No, as depressing as the Delphini was, it was still preferable to doing nothing. With a heavy heart, he started unpacking his supplies and creating the medical field packs that were nowhere to be found. His own surgical pack was the first he assembled, containing a full complement of all the possible surgical tools he might need, various medicines, portable scanning devices and treatment packs. Next, he readied the packs for medically trained personnel, followed by the basic first aid kits he would need to station around the battlecruiser.

When he finally looked up from what he was doing with a weary rub on aching muscles, his stomach growled and he remembered how many hours passed by since he last ate anything. He wished he could postpone going to the mess hall. Even though he knew he needed to face the crew sometime, they would not be receptive to him. After all, who would want a medical officer who was assigned to a posting as a punishment?

As he dragged himself towards the mess, he thought back to one of his favourite quotes. It was actually a poem from Old Earth and had been his grandmother's favourite.

If by Rudyard Kipling
If you can keep your head when all about you
Are losing theirs and blaming it on you,
If you can trust yourself when all men doubt you,
But make allowance for their doubting too;
If you can wait and not be tired by waiting,
Or being lied about, don't deal in lies,
Or being hated, don't give way to hating,
And yet don't look too good, nor talk too wise:

It was the way he tried to live his life. He trusted in himself enough to know the decisions which brought him here had been the right ones. Admiral Car'velac was fuelling the rumours about him, implying he refused to treat anyone that fateful day. The Admiral was deliberately stirring up hate, both amongst the enlisted men and officers within the fleet. Corin wouldn't descend to that level of hate and engage in a war of words— he would carry on as himself, for better or worse, facing each challenge as it arose.

His footsteps took on a slow, methodical beat as he made his way through the corridors to the mess hall. With a deep, steadying breath, he opened the door and was greeted by a myriad of different looks. Hostility, disdain, and disapproval were written across almost every face there. He briefly wondered exactly what stories were circulating about him before he noticed a group of soldiers sat off to one side. They hadn't noticed his arrival and were engaged in a lively conversation amongst themselves. Maybe not everyone would be against him, he hoped.

The food, if you could call it that, was standard space fare. Nutritious, but completely unappetizing. Still, he loaded his plate and was about to find somewhere to sit when the squad he saw laughing earlier beckoned him over. Walking closer, he noticed these were no ordinary soldiers— they were, in fact, part of the Barin Alliance's group of elite warriors, The Avanti.

One of them spoke as he dipped his head in greeting. "Doc, it's good to have you here." He gestured towards the others. "Ignore those idiots. They don't know the full story."

"And you do?" Corin challenged in a slightly gruff voice.

"That we do. It was one of ours you saved that day, Doc. We know the Admiral was pissed as hell you ignored his broken leg in favour of treating someone else, but the guy you saved, he was from one of our top squads. You have the loyalty and support of the Avanti anytime you need it."

With those words, the squad of Avanti stood as one, and with clenched fists held over their hearts, they dipped their heads and spoke in unison, "This we pledge as truth to thee."

Corin, floored at the gesture, realised silence once again reigned in the room. As he glanced around, he noticed shock, confusion, and questioning looks on many faces. The pledge the Avanti just gave made him an honorary member of their Core, able to call on their support at any time with no questions asked.

"I thank you all," Corin responded formally. "I didn't expect this, nor did I choose to ignore the Admiral's order to get your support. I did what anyone would have done. The Master Sergeant was seriously injured—waiting even two minutes could have cost him dearly. I could not, would not, ever ignore someone injured. No matter the circumstance. No matter what I'm ordered. No matter the cost to me personally."

"You're wrong, Doc. So many people would have treated the admiral first, too scared of the costs. You're one in a million..." Dax held his hand out to Corin in greeting. "I'm Commander Daxin 'Dax' Rydoc. This here motley crew is Lieutenant Commander Tate Riven, Lieutenant Bellan 'Bell' Nimeri, Lieutenant Braylen 'Bray' Dasthor and Lieutenant Hunter Escedas."

"I'm Captain Corin Talovich, but as you guessed, most people just call me Doc." He grasped each of their arms in turn in the traditional greeting of the Alliance. "So, what are you guys doing on this rust bucket? Can't imagine this is your usual mode of transport."

Dax laughed. "Nah, we're hitching a ride to Karinski station. We're supposed to be picking up our new medic there, then on to a new assignment in the Delta Sector."

Corin grinned at the guys as a feeling of immediate acceptance and friendship washed over him. "Bet you're looking forward to going, huh? Delta Sector's quite some holiday destination they have you going to."

Corin grimaced even thinking about it. Delta Sector was known to be populated by a lot of gas giants. The whole sector was heavily polluted due to all the mines extracting everything from metals to chemicals. The few habitable planets in the area were often used for resistance and terror networks, mostly due to the fact the Alliance tended to ignore the outer reaches of their empire.

Tate grabbed Corin in a headlock and playfully started punching him in the stomach, laughing as he did it. "Oh, sure, and when all we smell of is rot and decay, it's you I'm coming to snuggle up to!"

"No way, you're sexy as hell and all, but damn, no one is good enough to ignore that smell," Corin jokingly replied before suddenly realising what his words meant. He froze, eyes wide and darting from one face to the next before looking down and away from them, wondering what they would say. While he felt immediately at ease with these guys, he did have to wonder how they would react to him basically announcing he liked guys, not women.

"Hey, it's cool, Doc. You're kinda sexy yourself. We're not into women either. You're in good company here." Hunter winked at him as he spoke.

"The Tarin people do not put labels on sexuality the way many in the Alliance do," Bellan added. "We believe in our fated mates and that love is love. You will never have anything to fear from my people. We accept people for who they are. We do not prejudge, instead we determine the mettle of a person through our interactions with them. And you, my friend, have earned my respect and friendship." Bellan smiled at Corin as he spoke.

"Mmm, I can just see you in bed, Doc." Dax whistled as his gaze roamed over Corin's figure, taking in the toned body encased in his medical jumpsuit. He was neither tall nor short at five feet eleven.

Corin wasn't heavily muscled like them, but there was a fine amount of definition and a healthy bulge in front of his jumpsuit, coupled with what looked to be an exceedingly sexy bubble butt. His hands appeared elegant, yet small calluses dotted his fingers from years of scalpel use. His gunmetal grey eyes were bracketed by laugh lines, a slight contradiction to the worry lines creasing his forehead. He had plump lips and the stubble gracing his face added to his overall appeal. All this was topped off with rich, chocolate brown hair, which appeared as though Corin constantly ran his fingers through it.

Blushing, Corin returned the favour, checking out each of the men in turn. Dax must have been six feet three, his strong body covered in muscles, especially visible in the tight workout shirt they all wore. The training pants did nothing to hide the power in his legs. His thighs were bulging as he sat casually with an arm draped over the back of his seat. His head was shaved close as was common in the Avanti. His arms were covered in ink.

While Corin himself possessed some tattoos, it was nowhere close to the amount covering Dax's skin. Corin could spend hours studying the designs etched into his skin and still not see all the intricacies of each piece. Dax's eyes were such a dark brown they almost appeared black, yet at the same time, a vibrancy shone from them. There was a collection of scars covering his left shoulder. The surgeon in him knew they were the result of concussive forces from an explosion. His lips were on the thinner side and cocked up into a smirk as Corin studied him.

Moving on, Corin studied Braylen. He seemed the quietest of them all and had the appearance of being the most serious. His eyes seemed to take in everything around him, cataloguing it and filing away for future reference as needed. His olive skin was smooth and unblemished. The only defining features were the subtle ridges running down the side of his neck, darker than his normal skin tone, which indicated his Dunfrainian heritage. His eyes were a soft emerald green, and his hair a rich burnished copper in colour.

Hunter was the smallest of them. His body was much leaner than the others, yet solid at the same time. His features were softer, giving him a youthful appearance. His eyes, though, held a world of strength and determination in them. His irises swirled in the unique way of the Haverian people. The purple hues were mesmerising, drawing you in as they seemed to peer deep into your soul.

Bellan was the most unusual of the group. He was from one of the planets which had recently joined the alliance. He was of Tarin descent. He was a pale blue in colour with long golden hair tied in a plait down past his shoulders. While he wasn't wearing the traditional pleats, which were akin to kilts the Scottish warriors on Earth wore, he still kept to his heritage by wearing the gold bands over his biceps. They were engraved with what Corin knew to be his family crest. His face was more angular than others within the Alliance, his lips thinner, his physique more graceful. He radiated an aura of strength and power, no doubt coming from his inner beast. He was a feline shifter from a very rare race of warriors who lived high in the mountains of Tarin. Darker blue spots were just visible underneath the hem of his training top.

Tate was busy flexing his muscles at Corin, pulling outlandish poses, all the while fluttering his eyelashes and blowing kisses at Corin. Tate was around six feet and was solid with muscles. His shoulder-length, wavy hair was so dark it was almost as black as liquorice and, unusually for such colouring, his eyes were a vivid blue and dimples graced his cheeks. He could tell Tate was the joker of the group, especially when Tate dropped to his knees in front of him, clung onto his legs and started to declare his undying love for Corin. The other guys were laughing at the picture they presented as Tate kept trying to drag him down for kisses.

Shocking all of them, Corin retaliated by hauling Tate to his feet. He wrapped his arm around Tate's waist, dipped him and kissed him. His tongue swept tantalisingly over Tate's lips before he pressed tiny kisses all over his face, then swung him back up to standing. Turning to face the other guys, he took a long, low, sweeping bow. Laughing, they all settled back down to their food and quiet conversation.

Braylen finally spoke up, "Seriously, Doc, I went to the academy with Vasiliy, the guy you saved. He's a great man and the Alliance would have been poorer without him in it. You're an amazing man to do what you did, and to carry on doing it even after the Admiral threatened you."

"I wouldn't change anything," Corin vowed. "I've never been someone who could ignore anyone in need and certainly not when I've been in a position to help them. It was Admiral Car'velac who got pissed and you know how up his own ass he is. Even the Commander in the room was shocked at how he behaved, but, hell, what could anyone really say? He's not just an Admiral of the fleet, he's on the Alliance Senate. No matter what threats of dismissal from the medical corps or reassignments he bellowed at me, I was not going to stop treating Vasiliy."

"You know, Doc, your quick actions didn't just save his life, you saved his arm and therefore his place with the Avanti," Braylen pointed out. "I heard he'll be back in the field in a couple of moon turns. I know he's desperate to meet you."

"Thanks, Braylen. I wondered how he was doing, but a lot of people in the medical corps are avoiding me at the moment in case they get treated as guilty by association, so I've not been able to find anything out about him. I'm glad he's doing well." Corin's face lit up with a smile as he spoke.

"Well, Doc, you better get used to us real quick. You're one of us now, and as for those idiots," Hunter gestured over his shoulder at the room. "Fuck 'em."

Corin's lips quirked slightly before morphing into a full blown grin. He realised having these guys around would mean that life would never be dull while they were on-board. He was looking forward to getting to know them better. They seemed like the type of men that would be both good friends and staunch allies.

Chapter Two

Corin was working out in the training room assigned to the Avanti. He and Tate were currently working on self-defence training. Or rather, Corin was practicing getting his ass whupped. He'd lost count of the amount of bruises, scrapes and general aches and pains he'd suffered over the last two weeks. Corin had grown increasingly close to the guys, settling into a routine of training with them, as well as spending his down time alongside them. He was beginning to think that they were attempting to prepare him for something, as well as just enjoying his company. They had already schooled him in weapons training, combat tactics, and the art of survival and adapting to whatever environment he was in.

He was getting hints about joining them as their medic rather than the one they were on route to pick up. They kept asking if he would ever consider going back out into the field. He would have said no, after everything that happened with the admiral, had it been anyone else suggesting it. However, Corin knew without a doubt if they actually offered him the chance he would grab it. Anything would be better than a life on this rust bucket or on some backward research colony. The chance to be with these guys, who he now considered friends, that would be just about perfect.

"Come on, handsome," Tate taunted him with a wiggle of his eyebrows. "Pin me down and I'll make it worth your while." Grabbing his crotch, he joked, "I'll even let you give me kisses. You can choose which part of my body."

The other guys who were training near them burst out laughing.

Corin was smirking as he teased Tate right back. "Yeah, yeah, Tate, we all know you fantasize about my lips wrapped around your cock. Come on, just admit it, nothing to be scared about!" He'd worked out early on in their friendship to meet fire with fire. At this, the other guys were almost crying they were laughing so much.

"Oh, it's on now. You're going down, Doc." That just set the guys off even more. Once Tate noticed what he'd said, he swore, "Oh, for fuck's sake, you lot. Ya bunch of bastards!"

Just as Tate started to charge at Corin, sirens blared out all around them, sounding an alarm. A split second later, Corin was propelled across the room before slamming painfully into a bulkhead. His ears were ringing from the concussive forces of whatever the hell had just impacted the cruiser. Despite the blood that trickled down his forehead, he hauled himself to his feet, trying to see through the haze of dust which still permeated the air.

"Report!" He heard Dax call out.

"I'm okay," Corin coughed out.

"I am beside you and uninjured," Bellan responded.

"Here," Braylen groaned quietly from somewhere to his left.

"I'm pinned, but uninjured," came from Hunter in what sounded like the far corner of the room.

Apart from the klaxon still going, there was silence as they waited for Tate's voice.

"Tate, check in," Dax demanded.

Still there was no response.

"Goddamn it, spread out and find him," Dax bellowed.

"Wait, he must be near me." Corin was sure of it. "He'd just started to charge me as we were hit. Shit, can anyone run to the med bay and get my med bag? I have a feeling I'm going to need it."

"You go, Bray. Bell, and I will help here," Dax commanded.

Dax, Bell, and Corin all started scrambling around, feeling their way amongst the mass of twisted metal and wood.

"Hunter, can you free yourself or do you need help? And are you sure you're not injured?" Dax queried.

"I've cleared most of it, just one big piece left that I'll need help with. No serious injuries, a couple of scrapes and what I reckon is a broken wrist. Just get to Tate." Worry for Tate was evident in his voice.

"We will," Dax vowed, conviction rang true in his voice.

They were getting more frantic in their efforts to find Tate when Corin suddenly touched what felt like Tate's foot. "Here!" he cried.

It took five painstaking minutes before they uncovered Tate's body enough to see how injured he was. He was unconscious, with a large gash on the side of his temple which was bleeding profusely. Corin wasn't too worried about the gash at present; head wounds bled like a bitch even if they were minor wounds. He was more worried about any internal injuries and crush damage. Just as they lifted the largest piece covering Tate's torso, Braylen ran back into the room.

"I didn't know which one you wanted, Doc, so I just grabbed the largest of your bags and two others," Bray gasped as he took in the scene before him. "Oh shit, is that a bloody spike piercing his stomach?"

There was no response to Bray's question. It was clear to all of them just how much trouble Tate was in. What looked to be a shard of metal from one of the internal bulkhead panels was piercing his body in his lower left torso.

"Bray, give me the largest bag." As soon as the bag was in his hands, Corin started yanking out equipment, immediately setting up a monitor to measure Tate's vitals. As he was setting up a sterile set of cloths to clean Tate's wound so he could see what he was doing, he heard the guys freeing Hunter.

His focus was fully on Tate as he examined the extent of his injuries. He was scanning the large wound with his portable scanner as the guys joined him. Corin breathed a small sigh of relief as he watched the results scrolling across the screen.

Hunter immediately dropped to Tate's side and gently stroked the hair from his face. "Come on, Tate, we need our funny man back with us. Come on, buddy, open those baby blues and I'll make sure Corin smothers you in those kisses you're so desperate for!"

"Fuck you, Hunter, you're just jealous of my sexy lips," Tate's voice quietly rasped as his eyes fluttered open. "What the fuck just happened?"

"Lay still!" Corin commanded. "I'm going to have to stabilise your wound, then operate to remove this shrapnel. You're one lucky son of a bitch, Tate, it's missed everything major. I think it's nicked an artery, but at the moment the metal is stopping it from bleeding out into your stomach."

"Aw, fuck man. Why's it always me?" Tate groaned.

Bell smiled at him, although his smile didn't quite reach his eyes. Those were filled with worry. "Because you, my friend, are simply a trouble magnet. You only have to remember the Pelanas incident to know we speak the truth."

"Shut it." Tate glanced down his body, trying to take in his injuries. "How was I supposed to know half-pint was some secret baby ninja! I swear I wore his bruises for weeks." Quiet laughing broke some of the tension in the room as Tate grumbled at them.

Corin gave Tate one last, quick scan, just to make sure he hadn't missed anything. He put the scanner aside and refocused on Tate. "I've stabilised what I can. We need to move him from here so I can work on him properly. Bray, grab the portable stretcher from the side of the large bag. Do you know how to assemble one?" Corin glanced Bray's way as he spoke.

"Yeah, Doc, I went through grade one field medic training. Want some help with Tate? Or do you want me to check the other guys out?" Bray wished his training was greater, but he would do what little he could to take the pressure off his friend.

"Start with Hunter, then move on to the others. I'll shout if I need help with Tate, and thanks, Bray. We need to make sure the guys don't have any hidden injuries."

"No worries, Doc. That's what I'm here for."

After the stretcher was assembled, they carefully moved Tate onto it, strapping him down to prevent any further damage occurring when they moved him. Once he was clear of the mess of twisted metal, Dax took a minute to truly look around as the dust had finally cleared.

"Shit, this is bad. Look at the bloody hull." He whistled in shock.

They all followed his line of sight to the hull, or rather, where the hull should have been. The internal emergency force field must have been triggered because the hull bore a gaping hole. The size of it was stunning in its magnitude as the force field pulsed around it. Beyond the field, they could see the ship's shield. It was sparking with bolts of electricity firing off in different directions. They could see fissures were already forming in its integrity.

"We need to get out of here and fast," Bell gave voice to what all of them were thinking.

Just as Bell spoke, the klaxon changed from the slow, methodical tone of an attack alarm to three rapid beeps.

"Fuck me! The evac alarm. We've got to move." Dax swore as he grabbed one of the smaller med bags and passed the other to Hunter.

Corin ignored the equipment dotted around him and found his large surgical med pack, shouldered it and grabbed an edge of the stretcher as the other guys all fell into place around it, each taking a handle, even the injured Hunter. There was no way he wouldn't help carry his friend and teammate out of there.

Working together, they lifted Tate and started to move as fast as they could, while keeping him as stable as possible as they worked their way to the escape pods. The corridors were a hive of activity. Flight crews and soldiers were running back and forth, some to the escape pods, others to the fighter decks or control centres. The only focus of the Avanti, though, was to get the hell off the cruiser. Rounding the last corridor into section B's escape dock, they saw all the large pods were already gone and almost everyone had left.

"Shit. We're going to have to split up." Dax ran a frustrated hand over his head. "Doc, you obviously have to go with Tate. Bray, you go with Hunter so you can patch him up. Bell and I will take a third pod. Programme the pods to take you to the closest inhabitable planet. I've no idea where the fuck we are, but with our training, I don't see it as too much of a problem. Hopefully we can get the emergency comms working, well, that's if the pods are actually stocked properly. Stars knows if that's the case on this goddamn pile of space junk. Hunter, and Bell, you guys go and get our pods started up. Bray and I will help Doc get Tate strapped in."

The guys split up, running to get their assigned tasks done. Once they got Tate securely strapped into the pod, Dax found a suitable destination and Bray encoded the flight plan into the computers. With a terse good luck to Corin, as he strapped himself into the control chair, Bray and Dax sprinted for their own pods. Corin hit the command keys Dax had programmed into the console. He had just finished strapping himself in as the pod was released by its docking clamps and blasted through the escape hatch.

"Talk to me if you can, Tate. You need to try and stay conscious for me. I need to know if anything changes. As soon as we are away from the cruiser, I'm going to unstrap you, remove the shrapnel and fix you up, okay?" Corin spoke as he grabbed Tate's hand, holding tight.

"Doc, focus on getting yourself out of here. Forget about me, there's too much damage. I won't make it."

"Oh, fuck no, Tate, don't you dare talk like that. I'm a bloody Gold Rank Surgeon. I can fix you up no problem, but you have to stay with me for a few minutes until I can finish. You get me?" Corin squeezed Tate's hand, hard, forcing him to focus on his words.

"Alright, Doc, but you've got to promise me to leave me be and save yourself if it comes to it." Tate squeezed back.

"Not a chance, Tate, and you bloody know it. We make it together or we don't make it at all."

"Stubborn bastard," chuckled Tate as Corin shot him a wink while he worked the controls on the pod, seeing what destination Dax was sending them to.

Corin tried to lighten the tense atmosphere surrounding them. He didn't want Tate's blood pressure to rise any higher than it already had. "Okay, our holiday destination for today is a class G3 planet. We lucked out, Tate, Dax chose well. An inhabited planet with perfect atmospheric conditions. It's not part of the Alliance. Instead, it's listed as neutral. So we shouldn't encounter too many hostile forces. At least I hope we won't."

Corin quickly set up a sterile environment to operate on Tate. "I'm sorry, Tate, but I can't knock you out. It's too risky without all the equipment I need. I'm giving you as many painkillers as I can, but you're going to have to get through it somehow. I'm not going to lie to you— this is going to hurt." He injected as much painkiller as he could safely give him.

"Do it, Doc." Tate locked eyes with him and took a deep breath as Corin slowly pulled the metal free. A grunt was the only sign Tate let show he was in any pain, although the pale, clammy skin and shudders wracking his body were clear signs of the stress and pain he was enduring.

Working as fast as he could, Corin removed the shrapnel and immediately started sewing the small tear in Tate's artery. Trying to balance the effects of the pod's movements, he finished off the first stabilizing line of stitches. It wasn't pretty, but it was secure and effective. Grabbing the mouldable silicon graft he laid out earlier, he trimmed it to the right size before wrapping it around the artery he'd just repaired. He sprayed the activating agent over it and watched as it moulded itself securely to the uninjured points on either side of the tear. Cleaning the area, Corin waited, watching in case there was any blood leaking out. Satisfied the repair would hold, he reached for the needle and thread again, intent on sewing up the layers of muscle ripped apart by the shard.

"Doc, you're going to have to hurry. I can see the planet approaching." Tate grunted through the pain.

"Stars, that was fast. Okay, this is going to be fast and so not pretty, but at least most of it's inside you."

Corin's hands seem to fly as Tate looked on amazed at the speed and precision with which Corin worked. "Damn, Doc, you have some serious skills there."

Corin looked up briefly, smiled at Tate then carried on weaving an artificial mesh into the rips in the layers of muscles, knitting them back together with structural support. His entire focus was on his work, ignoring their descent through the layers of the planet's atmosphere. Tying the last stitch in place, he looked up, a gasp leaving his throat as the stunning vista in the viewport caught his eye.

The planet before them reminded him of his home, Earth Centari V. Landmasses littered the planet, ranging from small to one seemingly covering half the planet. There was plenty of water visible and barely a cloud in the sky. Mountainous ranges seemed to be concentrated on one large landmass to the left of his view. The pale pink tips gave the appearance of snow, but he had never seen pink snow before. Realising just how close to the surface they were getting, Corin packed the wound, turning to Tate as he did so.

"I don't have time to finish sewing up the external wound site before we hit, although I've finished everything inside you. I need to pack away these sharps or we could have problems when we hit. I'm packing your wound tight and wrapping it up securely. I'll finish it off once we've landed safely."

Corin worked fast, securing Tate back onto the reclining seat he was laid on and packing away his instruments. The last thing they needed were more injuries. He felt the pod's landing thrusters desperately trying to slow their descent. The low pitched whine and grinding noises coming from the engines were a testament to just how hard they were working. The front of the pod was bathed in such intense heat it shone vibrant red as the engines worked against the gravitational forces battering them.

He was just strapping himself back into his seat harness when they hit the surface. The impact tore the last buckle from his hand, ripping it along his bicep, leaving a ragged gash in its wake. Without the last restraint in place, the other parts of the harness tore apart with the stresses they were under. For the second time in a couple of hours, Corin went slamming into a bulkhead. The last thing he heard before passing out was Tate screaming his name.

Chapter Three

Corin slowly became aware of a dripping sensation on his face and ringing in his ears. He could hear muffled noises behind the ringing and it was tugging at his consciousness. He tried to open his eyes, barely managing more than a flutter of his lashes, before pain ripped through his skull. He groaned at the onslaught. He felt the stab of a needle in his arm and the pain suddenly started to ease.

"Doc, Corin, come on, buddy. Wake up for me, please?" A voice was begging him. "Come on, open those gorgeous eyes for me. You can do it."

More dripping accompanied those words. The anguish behind them tugged at his resolve to go back to sleep.

"Doc, please, I don't know how else to help you, other than give you something for the pain. Come on, open those eyes for me. I need you to open them, buddy."

With a Herculean effort, Corin opened his eyes to see a face peering down at him. In a rush, the events of the last few hours came back to him.

"Damn, Tate, what the fuck happened now?" He finally managed to groan out.

"We crashed. You didn't get strapped in on time and went flying. I couldn't stop you or help you. It's taken me ten minutes to get to you. I am so bloody sorry. I did manage to engage the pod's cloaking device, but it's not going to matter for long. Can you feel the heat?"

It was only then Corin understood the drops he was feeling were sweat from Tate's face, dropping onto him as he tried to wake him up. Taking stock of his body, he realised Tate had managed to wrap the gash on his arm tightly, stopping the bleeding. Small scrapes and a decent sized bump littered his head. He was pretty sure he was dealing with a mild concussion, but that was going to be the least of his worries if the pod was still this hot. They were going to need to get out of here. He was pretty sure his wrist was damaged as well. Unbidden, another section of his favourite poem sprang to mind.

If you can force your heart and nerve and sinew
To serve your turn long after they are gone,
And so hold on when there is nothing in you
Except the will which says to them "Hold on"

He needed to do that now. He fought to clear his head, trying to shake the fuzzy feeling away. Looking at Tate, he tried to assess if his stitches were ripped open or if he was suffering from further injuries sustained during the crash.

"How are you feeling, Tate? Is everything holding okay? Any other injuries?"

"I'm better, more worried about you."

"Ok, we're going to have to work together. I'm going to finish stitching you up, then talk you through sorting my arm out."

"I take it we can't wait?" Tate asked. As Corin shook his head, Tate continued, "Shit. Okay, we'll fix each other up and then we need to get out of this bloody oven. It looks like the pod was fully stocked, which is a bit of a surprise considering the state of the rest of the cruiser. Anyway, we have plenty of rations and equipment. That's something. I also need to try and rig something up to boost our comms device signals. I'm not getting any response when I try to raise the others. I'm going to try a couple more frequencies just in case."

"Right now our priority is getting you fixed up, Tate. You're still badly injured and I can see the strain it's putting you under. You should have left me." As he spoke, Corin managed to haul himself upright, holding on to one of the control panels to steady himself when he was hit with a wave of dizziness. He was studiously ignoring the look Tate was sending him, but he sure felt the intensity of it.

Looking around, he could see the damage inside the pod wasn't actually too bad, but the hull was another matter entirely. Corin could see jagged rips in the metal. Other parts were buckled from the intense heat they had been subjected to during descent. Cracks ran like a web across the viewport. How it hadn't shattered was anybody's guess. It looked like they had crash-landed on the edge of an expanse of emerald green grass.

"From what I can see there are trees on the other side of us." Tate continued to rapidly cycle through the frequencies, getting increasingly frustrated when nothing happened... All he was getting was static. "It should help provide us some cover when we leave here. I'm pretty sure I saw what could have been a rocky outcrop or something similar just before we hit. We should probably aim for those rocks when we leave here— it will provide us the best protection. I'm not really in any condition to fight. I will if I need to, but it will be tough. Best to avoid it if we can."

Now that was something Corin could fully agree with. Neither of them were in any fit state to fight, but he also understood Tate's background with the Avanti would have him defending them through any means necessary.

Corin rolled his eyes as Tate guided him back to his seat— stubborn man was worse off than he was. Grabbing his equipment again, he set up to finish stitching Tate back together, making sure he gave him shots for both the pain and to prevent infection first. With gentle fingers, he unwrapped the dressing and probed Tate's wound. Feeling around, he could tell the mesh was intact within the layers of muscles. He was thankful the gravitational forces of their impact didn't rip it apart again— it could have gone disastrously wrong. Gently moving the muscle out of the way, he ran his fingers along the graft of the damaged artery. It was just as he left it. He couldn't help but sigh in relief. He hoped it was the start of things going better for them.

After withdrawing his hands, Corin picked up his needle and thread with one hand whilst drawing the skin together with the other.

Bending his head, he set to work. Delicate stitch followed delicate stitch. While the inside may not have been the prettiest job he'd ever done, he would not scrimp on time fixing the outer wound on Tate's abdomen. He would make it look as good as possible.

"Damn, Doc, the Admiral really was a prick. You're an incredible surgeon. To try to relocate you the way he did has denied the Alliance one of their best infield surgeons. I'm not complaining, mind you! I'm certainly reaping the benefits of Admiral Arsehole's actions."

Corin smiled at Tate as he drew the needle through his skin for the last time. Knotting the thread in place, he drew back before bathing the site in Battlegel. The Battlegel was designed to deliver slow release infection control, draw out any impurities still left in the skin, provide numbing to the area and provide a waterproof cover. Corin firmly believed it was one of the best medical inventions created within the Alliance over the last couple of decades. The amount of lives it was already responsible for saving was incredible.

He started to prepare another set of wound control for his own injury. As he briefed Tate on what he was going to have to do, they cleaned out the wound between them. He was thankful it appeared to only be surface damage.

"Doc, I don't think I can do this." Tate's fingers trembled again Corin's skin. "What if I fuck it up? I've faced armies with no more than a squad of us Avanti, but this? This is fucking scary. I don't want to hurt you. I won't be able to make it look anywhere near as good as you do. I wish I could though."

"Put the needle to my skin, take a deep breath then push the needle through. The first one is always the hardest. You can do it, Tate, but honestly, we have no choice. I can't sew it up myself, well, not easily anyway. I don't care what it looks like as long as it does the job. Once you've done the first one it will get easier, I promise."

Expelling a deep breath, Tate pushed the needle through Corin's skin. His fingers were still trembling slightly, but he tried to ignore it. He started to sew the two sides together. To distract him, Corin started to talk.

"Did I ever tell you about the Korsavian ambassador I met at headquarters?" Tate shook his head, so Doc carried on. "Damn, that man was absolutely beautiful and he didn't know it. His features were delicate yet masculine. Every movement he made was sensual and his butt… Damn, it was a work of art, pure perfection. It was a butt to be jealous over, to drool over. It was just the right amount to grab onto, all round and firm. Man, you could fantasize for weeks about it and never get bored."

Tate burst out laughing. "Really, Doc? You're trying to distract me with stories of men?"

"Is it working?"

"Stars yes!" Tate laughed even harder.

"Good." Corin shot a wink at Tate. "Now hurry up and sew me up or I'm going to have to start talking about just how skilled he was with his lips, and I'm not talking about his skill as a negotiator!"

"Damn, Doc, maybe I should take my time. I kinda want to hear this story."

"Urgh, you, my friend, are sex mad."

"You say that like it's a bad thing." Tate smirked at the eye-roll Corin sent him.

"So tell me, Tate, is there really no one special you have your eye on? Or are you a man in every dock kind of guy?"

"In the past, I was a man in every dock kind of guy. Now? I just want to settle down. I want the kind of epic love affair people talk about. I want to lock eyes across the room with someone and know it's the man fate designed, just for me. My one and only, my soul mate. I know that makes me sound weak or maybe girly, but I have to believe the life we're living as Avanti can be offset by something pure and full of love."

"It doesn't sound girly and it damn well isn't weak, Tate. You're not the only one looking for love. I want to have someone to come home to, someone to share the good and bad with. As stupid as it sounds, I want someone to curl up with at the end of a long day. To just enjoy being in their company, even if we aren't doing more than just watching the newsvid. I want a family as well. I want kids." Corin shrugged. "It's not likely to happen, not impossible, but not likely. Aside from the fact I've yet to meet the man of my dreams, I'm hardly in a position to offer anyone anything. My career is in ruins aside from anything else."

"Well, Doc, here's to us both finding what we want. Right now, though, it's time to try to get moving." Tate smiled as he finished placing the last stitch into Corin's skin. After covering it with Battlegel, he finished packing all the medical supplies away.

Both men groaned as they got to their feet and started to prepare to leave the pod, gathering everything they could use together. Thankfully, there were sets of new military uniform in the pod. Both of them were in the tattered remnants of their training gear and it would have offered no protection in the unknown environment they were facing outside of the pod.

Once dressed, they both began filling the pockets up with their gear. Corin made sure both packs contained basic first aid equipment and rations, while Tate sorted out the weapons and other survival supplies. Pockets bulging, they moved on to the backpacks. Corin added some more survival gear to his medical pack, another weapon and some rations. Tate's backpack soon contained the rest of the weapons, comms equipment, rations and some extra water.

"Tate, you can't carry all those. It's going to pull too much on your abdominal muscles. You're going to have to pass some over to me. It's going to be hard enough for you to walk, let alone be carrying so much stuff."

"Doc, you're injured as well."

"So not the point, Tate, and you damn well know it! You're far worse off than I am. Now stop being a stubborn bastard and pass me some of your gear over." Corin held out his hand.

"Doc." Tate sighed, frustrated because he knew Corin was right.

"Nope, not listening to any excuses you have, Tate," Corin interrupted. "Think about it for a minute, will you? If you get worse, there is no way I can manage both bags, you, and cope with the unknown environment. I know I've done some training with you guys, on top of what I did through basic training, but I'm in no way capable of doing all this without you. Please, Tate, pass me the gear?"

With a fierce grumble, Tate complied. Corin understood he wasn't happy about it, but it really was the only sensible solution. Stars, as it was, there was no way Tate should even be out of bed, let alone attempting what they were about to. But what choice did they really have? As it was, Corin recognised he would be supporting Tate sooner rather than later. He could see Tate was already struggling with the pain, and they hadn't even left the pod. Corin worried about what he would do when Tate couldn't carry on. He could only hope they made it to shelter before then. With a last look around to make sure they left nothing they would need behind, or could easily take with them, they left the pod.

Turning to look at the damage, they both cursed.

"Fuck, man, how the hell did we actually survive the impact?" Tate whistled.

The outer hull of the ship was completely missing over three quarters of the pod. Debris was littered all around them. What little of the pod remained was buckled and warped from the intense heat and gravitational forces it endured during descent. Scorch marks crisscrossed the twisted and pock marked hull.

Taking a further step back, they could see how the cloaking device was flickering in and out. It wouldn't be long before it failed completely. While this world was supposed to be neutral as far as the Alliance was concerned, it didn't mean they wouldn't encounter hostile forces. What happened on a global political level often had little impact on the ground. A lot of the worlds in this sector were divided amongst clans. These clans were often more focused on fighting amongst themselves, and many were not impressed with the Alliance's sometimes pushy tactics.

Digging into their reserve energy levels, they both took the first weary step to refuge. Slowly and methodically, they started to make their way through what looked to be a small forest. The trees kept drawing Corin's attention. The trunks were massive, the branches thick and covered in blue and red leaves. The vibrant colours seemed to almost pulse at times when the light from the white sun, high up in the sky, hit them. They could hear animals moving throughout the trees.

"Let's hope they steer clear of us," Tate spoke quietly. "I don't want to have to kill something if it attacks purely because we startled it. What's more, I don't think I have the strength."

Corin hummed in agreement, but his mind was elsewhere as the doctor in him registered the increase in wheezing coming from Tate. His colour was starting to pale further, the sweat on his face increasing and his steps slowing.

"Tate, we should take a break. You're not looking too good."

"Not feeling good, Doc, but we need to keep going. I saw rocks through the trees when we crashed. I'm hoping we can find some shelter there."

Corin sighed, knowing Tate was right, but not liking it. He was so torn. His eyes caught a branch on the ground. It looked thick and sturdy enough to support Tate's weight as a walking aid. He grabbed it, passed it over to Tate and raised his eyebrow. A silent challenge, followed by a battle of wills occurred. With a groan, Tate grabbed the branch and used the curved end under his arm to help him both support his weight and walk. Within a couple of steps, he understood just how much help it gave him. He looked at Corin out of the corner of his eye and mock growled at him.

"Doc, don't you dare say I told you so."

"Would I do a thing like that?"

"Yes!"

"Yeah, you're right, I would." Corin laughed. "But I promise I'll be good."

"The twinkle in your eyes tells me otherwise, Doc."

Tate kept laughing, but his laughs were turning wheezy. He started to sway and Corin made a desperate grab for Tate as he suddenly collapsed. He was just in time to prevent him from crumpling to the ground.

"Damn it, Tate, you stubborn bastard, you should have told me it was this bad." Corin cursed, but Tate was unresponsive. Lowering him to the ground, he ripped open his pack, digging through it for his portable vitals monitor. Watching the screen made Corin curse even more creatively. Tate's vitals were weak and thready, before they suddenly stopped. He had simply pushed himself too far.

"Fuck!" Corin swore at himself. "You stupid bastard, Corin, you should have overridden him. Look what's happened now."

Corin slammed his fist down onto Tate's chest in a desperate attempt to kick-start his heart again. Pumping out a rhythm of compressions, he fed air into Tate's lungs, breathing for him. Time seemed to slow as he fought to keep Tate's heart pumping blood around his body. He could feel tears welling in his eyes, but could not pause for even a moment to wipe them away. He silently willed each breath he gave Tate to be the one which brought him back. He kept up a punishing rhythm, refusing to stop. Corin felt liquid fire racing along his arm as it struggled to cope with the stress he was putting on his wounds.

Still, he would not stop.

Minutes passed as even the nature surrounding them seemed to hold its collective breath. Suddenly, he felt a soft gasp against his lips. Brushing his fingers against Tate's neck, he searched for a pulse, elated to feel a slow *bump bump* against his fingertips. Breathing a small sigh of relief, he grabbed for the Battleboost injector. It would deliver a shot that was a mix of painkillers, artificial stimulants and adrenaline. It would keep Tate stable while he continued to work on him. Thankfully the boost would last around an hour, long enough for what he needed to do, he hoped.

Corin watched as Tate's breathing finally took on a slow but steady rhythm. He wondered if the boost would give him enough time to get them both to shelter or if he would have to create something here in the middle of the copse of trees. Looking around, he saw another branch roughly as big as the one Tate already used. Grabbing the portable stretcher from the side of his pack, he quickly assembled it before shifting Tate onto it and strapping him down securely. Spying some rope in his pack, he grabbed it and started twining it around his belt and through the handles of the stretcher. He was going to have to move slowly, but he could pull Tate along. Too fast and he would both tire himself out and probably cause Tate further injuries.

Corin kept up a steady pace as he trudged out of the copse of trees using the two branches as walking sticks, helping him push off the ground with each step. It wasn't long before he saw the rocky formation they discussed earlier. It was an impressive array of outcrops and what looked to be caves. A cave would be ideal for them. It would provide shelter, safety, keep out the weather and keep them hidden from anyone nearby. He picked up the pace as best as he could, but his legs were getting heavy. He was flagging with the added weight of both Tate's backpack and Tate himself. Pain was flaring around his stitches and he briefly wondered if they were pulling loose. It didn't really matter as there was nothing he could do about it right then.

Reaching the bottom of the rock formation, he studied it, trying to scout out the best location to give him easy access, whilst simultaneously panicking about how much time was left before the booster he gave to Tate would wear off. Deciding it was safe to leave Tate on the ground and make his way up first, he untied him. Checking there was no one around, he made sure both bags were securely strapped to his back before working his way up to the cave. Thankfully, it was an easier and quicker task than he thought it would be. Scrambling the last few feet, he looked over his shoulder to check on Tate. He was still safe, and by the looks of things, his condition hadn't changed.

Looking around the cave, he realised there were, in fact, two sections to it. One was much darker and almost completely hidden from view. The only reason he even discovered it was because he tripped over a rock on the ground in his weary state and saw it as he pulled himself back up. Peering into the second part of the cave, he noticed they would be completely hidden from sight if anyone happened upon the cave. Stepping in and looking around the second chamber, he noticed there was an opening leading even deeper into a much smaller chamber. He had to wonder if this was a natural formation, or, if it was carved out by someone in the past. It was far too conveniently hidden. As much as it piqued his interest as to the history behind the caves, there was far too much to organise to pay attention to it now. The only thing he really cared about was the cave giving them as much security and protection as they needed. Dropping the bags on the ground, he hurried to climb back down to Tate.

Tate was just starting to groan as Corin reached him. Looking from Tate to the rocks, he realised the stretcher wasn't going to work. He unstrapped Tate, dismantled the stretcher, and started to jam the parts into his various pockets. With a deep breath, he bent down and manoeuvred Tate onto his shoulder. With a huge grunt, he slowly came up to standing. His arm was protesting every second and he felt a huge tug on his stitches before feeling a wet trickle run down his arm. Glancing at the dressing, he saw a patch of blood was slowly soaking through it. Choosing to ignore it, he balanced their combined weight and started the climb.

It was much harder with Tate over his shoulder and he wished he had secured Tate to him before starting out. Yet another thing he was failing at. He was bent over almost double to balance the extra weight and his hands looked like he had jabbed them repeatedly into a bed of needles. He finally hauled them up over the lip of the cave and staggered through the first, and then the second cave, before finally getting into the small chamber off to the side.

Gingerly lowering Tate to the ground, he immediately started grabbing things out of the packs. Setting up his torch to give him a greater amount of light to work with, he washed his hands using the minimum amount of water possible from one of their water cans. He unwrapped his arm to see the stitches were split open over half of his wound. Having no time to focus on himself, he grabbed the surgical glue and drew a line down the join between the two pieces of skin. He counted to a minute, then let go, pleased to see the glue held the wound closed. Rewrapping it quickly, he rewashed his hands and turned his focus to Tate.

After a thorough inspection, Corin was pleased to see Tate's stitches were stretched slightly, but they didn't need repairing and he could see no further injuries. It meant Tate's condition was most likely deteriorating due to the added stresses placed on his body with the trek from the pod, and the shock he was no doubt suffering from. Corin was thankful they didn't have a repeat of what happened in the trees.

He quickly set up a combined transfusion of blood replacements, painkillers, anti-infection meds and stabilizers to combat the shock. It would help regulate Tate's body's reactions while he rested. There was certainly no way they could leave the cave for a while. Any further attempt to move Tate for at least the next two days would likely kill him.

Corin made a makeshift bed on a fairly flat bed of rocks using the stretcher as a base and prepared some survival blankets before he hefted Tate up one last time, laying him down before strapping him down securely. He certainly didn't need to deal with further injuries because he wasn't being careful enough with his patient. He hooked Tate up to the vitals monitor so he could easily track any changes.

Slumping to the ground in front of the ledge, Corin let out a deep sigh. His body was wracked by pain. His head was still pulsing from the crash, he was bone weary, and his vision was starting to go black at the edges. He realised he was clammy to the touch and hoped it was just from exhaustion and he wasn't developing a fever.

Wrapping himself in one of the survival blankets, he forced himself to reach into a pocket and dig out a ration pack. The puree inside had never looked appetising, but his stomach churned even more than normal at the sight of it. Forcing himself to eat it, even as bile rose in his throat, he looked around to keep his mind off what he was doing. He was debating with himself as to whether he could risk a fire for warmth when his eyes started to flutter, before they finally stayed shut and he slipped into a dreamless sleep.

Chapter Four

As Corin slowly came to, panic set in. He didn't have any idea how much time had passed or if anything happened to Tate. Scrambling over to Tate, even as his muscles protested the movement, he was relieved to see Tate had settled in his asleep. His skin wasn't so cold or clammy to the touch. His breathing seemed a little easier and his vitals appeared to be much steadier.

"Thank the stars," he exclaimed. He would never have forgiven himself if something happened to Tate while he'd been passed out.

Seeing as Tate was still deeply asleep, he took the time to sort himself out. Grabbing the med pack, he prepared himself a booster. He was still in a lot of pain, but needed to make sure his own wound didn't become infected. It was a bad doctor who neglected his own health. He unwrapped his arm and realised he should have dealt with it earlier, before passing out.

Dried blood was caked onto his arm and interwoven through this were the stitches, some of which were snapped or stretched. He sighed as he slowly set about removing the temporary glue, cleaning up the wound, and then carefully unpicking the remaining stitches. Bracing his arm against his legs, he gingerly started to sew up his own skin. He was thankful it was his less dominant arm that was injured. He didn't think he would have been able to treat himself otherwise. It was tough enough to do as it was. Once he finished, he smothered the site in Battlegel, and then wrapped it back up in a bandage.

Slumping back down, he realised even using that small amount of energy left him feeling weak. He wasn't entirely sure why he was so hungry, but it made him wonder just how much time had passed while they both slept. Grumbling, he grabbed another ration pack, knowing he needed to keep his strength up to care for Tate. He was thankful this ration pack didn't taste nearly as bad as the last one.

While it wasn't pleasant, he wasn't retching the entire time. His concussion had probably been more serious than he believed.

He slowly got to his feet and cautiously explored the cave system they were camping in. He was incredibly lucky to have discovered this cave system. They could certainly stay here while Tate recuperated. Peering out from the mouth of the cave and into the sky outside, he realised it was night-time m. Judging by when they landed, he calculated they'd either been asleep for a couple of hours or well over a full day—his money was certainly on a full day. With an audible gasp, he looked up.

He was used to Earth Centari V, where there was so much air pollution and it was almost impossible to see the stars. Here, however, there were no such restrictions. The sky was littered with stars. The way some were clumped together, others not, and the occasional shooting star that was visible gave him the impression of a giant celestial playground. The stars varied in intensity and colour that just increased the beauty of such an incredible visage.

Turning slightly, his jaw dropped as he caught sight of a nebula to the left of the cave. A deep purple in colour, there were swirls of pink winding itself around the outside of the nebula, almost like a snake coiled around the branches of a tree. To the north of the nebula, he could make out a pulsar throbbing. He could almost see it expanding and shrinking with each pulse. Despite it being night time, the visibility was high. He was sure it was due to the presence of three moons. They formed a slightly off centre triangle.

The largest was brilliant white and appeared to be smooth. The two smaller moons were duller and pock marked, a testament to a violent history. Perhaps these two smaller moons acted as guardians to the large moon, bearing the brunt of all meteorite impacts, keeping the blemish free moon safe. Taking one last lingering look at the beauty this planet offered at night, he turned and made his way back to Tate.

He set up everything he would need to check on Tate. Then, as he was pretty sure there was no one around, he made a stone circle and set about making a fire. Once it was going nicely, he used one of his portable containers and made some Tarmuk Tea. It was known on its planet as being a boost to health. Other medics within the Corps often looked at him with derision when he used things like this. However, he had long since believed it wasn't just advances in medicine which mattered in patient care. Sometimes the old ways provided more help than even the newest and most advanced treatments. It was completely natural and would certainly do no harm. Sitting in front of Tate, he gently brushed the dark locks back from his face and tried to wake him up.

"Tate, Tate, I need you to wake up for me. I need to see how you're doing, buddy. Come on, you can do it." He watched Tate's eyes flutter open as a groan escaped his lips. "I know it sucks, but we need to check on things."

"Hey, Doc," Tate rasped out. "Water." As the water can was pressed to his lips, he let out a low groan, taking slow, steady sips. "Thanks, Doc. What happened? Where are we?"

Corin moved behind Tate, cradling him in his arms as he held the tea to his lips. "Here, drink this and I'll explain."

As Tate sipped on the remarkably sweet tea, Corin filled him in on what happened from the moment Tate collapsed until now.

"Shit, Doc, I owe you, big time."

"No, you don't. We look after each other. It's what friends do, Tate." Corin smiled. "I'm just thankful you're back with me. It was incredibly close there for a while. I was pretty worried about you."

"Sorry, Doc, but you're not getting rid of me quite so easily." Tate's lips kicked up into a small smile that ended in a groan. "Damn, I feel like I've been transformed into a training dummy and the guys have let rip."

Laughing, Corin smirked. "Sounds about right, and I'm sorry, but it's time to check on things."

"Ah, come on, Doc, do we have to?" Tate threw a pout in Corin's direction.

"Your pout isn't going to work on me, handsome. I'm immune to your charms and you know it!"

"Ah, but you think I'm handsome, Doc." Tate fluttered his eyelashes at Corin. "Besides, you can't blame a guy for trying."

"No, you can't. Now lie back down and let me check you out."

"Hell, Doc, give me the best offer I've had in weeks, why don't you? Planning on checking out my package, huh?"

Corin just rolled his eyes at Tate as he got up, settling Tate comfortably back down on his makeshift bed.

"Damn, Doc, your tea was pretty good. Feeling a little bit better here."

"Good, isn't it?"

"Yup, I think I'll be carrying some in my pack from now on. Alright, Doc, have at it while I don't feel so bad." Tate spread his arms slightly, but soon stopped as his body protested the movement.

Corin unwrapped the wound on Tate's abdomen and was relieved to see it was already starting to heal. Cleaning it up, re-applying the Battlegel and covering it back up, he kept his focus on the monitor measuring Tate's vitals. He was pleased to see things looked much better than before. His heartbeat was steady and strong. Not at strong as it should be, but it was a definite improvement.

"So, what now, Doc?"

"Well, we can't move you for at least a day or so or we're just going to make things worse. So we stay here, recuperate and see how things go."

"How long were we out and have you heard anything on the comms?"

"I think around a full galactic day, but I passed out myself so I'm not entirely sure. As for the comms? Nothing. Although, seeing as we were both pretty out of it for a while, we could have missed something. I didn't really think about it when I came to. I just wanted to make sure you were alright first. I'm sorry."

"No worries, Doc, I'll look into it in a bit if you can bring the gear over here. I don't think I can move yet."

"Nope, and you aren't allowed to either!" Corin smiled as he set Tate's pack in front of him.

As he did so, Tate noticed the damage done to Corin's hands. "Oh fuck, Doc, your hands!" A look of horror was etched on his face.

"They're not too bad. It will heal," Corin assured Tate.

Tate just hummed, vowing to himself to keep an eye on them as he started to work on the comms equipment they had brought with them. As he worked, Corin cleaned up the supplies, packing his med kit back together. The last thing he needed was not being able to find something in an emergency because he was too tired to pack it properly. Just as he finished cleaning everything up, Tate let out a huge sigh.

"Nothing, Doc. It's working, I know it is, but there is no response from any of the guys. It could mean something as simple as their comms are broken, or something far more serious, but there is nothing else I can do." Tate massaged his temples as he spoke.

Corin smiled sadly as he ran his good hand through his hair. "We just have to hope their landings were better than ours."

"No shit, Doc!" Tate laughed.

"We better get some more sleep while we can. I doubt we got as much rest as our bodies really needed under the circumstances. I'm going to snub the fire out. No point in drawing more attention to us when we aren't alert." Already Corin could feel his body slouching and his mouth stretching wide in a jaw-cracking yawn. He banked the fire before they both settled down to sleep. Corin was on a makeshift bed below the ledge Tate rested on. It wasn't long before both slipped into a deep, dreamless sleep.

"Doc."

Corin woke to Tate whispering his name urgently and his hand shaking him gently. He had no idea how long they had been asleep. "Whatisit", he mumbled, his words merging together.

Tate placed his finger to his lips, motioning for Corin to be quiet, then beckoned him closer. As he bent down, Tate whispered into his ear. "I can hear something in the other part of the cave. Sounds like we have company."

"Hostile?" Corin rubbed his neck as he spoke.

"I'm not sure, but I could swear I heard a young girl cry out in pain a minute ago. It was followed by male voices laughing." A vein was throbbing in his neck as his eyebrows lowered into a scowl.

"Shit. That doesn't sound good. I'll go and have a look." Corin put a restraining hand on Tate's upper chest as he protested and tried to get up. "Seriously, Tate, you're in no condition to go. Let me check this out. I won't get caught."

Letting out a frustrated breath, Tate shook his head even as he agreed. "Alright, Doc, but at least take a weapon with you and pass one to me. It's better to be safe than sorry."

Once both of them held a gun and a knife, Corin slowly made his way to the edge of the chamber. With a quick movement of his head, he scanned the second chamber before turning towards Tate signalling the room was all clear. Moving on, he quietly made his way to the edge of the second cave. Waiting for his eyes to fully adjust to the change in lighting, he then gingerly peered around the edge of the rock he was hiding behind. A rage consumed him with righteous anger. Fists and jaw clenched tight, he studied the scene before him.

A young girl, probably no older than three of four years old, was tied up with rags stuffed into her mouth. Tears tracked down her face, her skin muddy and raw. Her bloodshot eyes were a testament to how long she must have been held like this. His gaze moved on to where he could see two male humanoids asleep around a fire.

He had never seen humanoids like this. They appeared to have a thick skin, which was a mottled brown. Brilliant white hair stood out on their heads like a beacon. Their faces were angular with hard planes. A third figure, the same as the other two, sat in front of what looked to be a dead body. At least he hoped it was a dead body. It was heavily mutilated and his heart grew heavy at the thought of what the young girl was made to watch. He could tell whoever it once was, it was female, but he could go no further in the identification process. He wondered if the little girl was related to her. The third humanoid looked to be revelling in the fact he was a killer.

He watched as the male grabbed something from the floor and sauntered over to the girl, yanking her head back by her hair before he roughly blindfolded her. Corin's fist flexed at his side over the harsh treatment she was enduring. When the man had finished securing the girl, he stalked back to the fire and dropped back down, settling back in to staring at the fire.

A few minutes later, the male suddenly stood up and joined a human man who was just walking into the cave. This man was tall and thin, his face weather beaten with jet black hair framing it and flowing down his back. He was dressed in an elaborate outfit. It seemed totally impractical for the situation. The sapphire blue tunic was studded with gems that seemed to twinkle in the light from the fire, sending pinpricks of light bouncing off the walls of the cave. The two figures seemed to be arguing, but the elaborately dressed man definitely appeared to be the one in charge. Anger was pouring off him as he paced in front of the humanoid.

Corin was wondering how he could take them all out before the other two woke up when he sensed movement beside him. Turning, he nearly cried out. He huffed out an exasperated sigh while glaring at Tate, who moved to crouch beside him. Motioning Tate to go back and rest, he scowled when Tate's only response was a shake of his head. They once again locked in to a silent battle of wills, their eyes seemingly able to communicate everything they were thinking and feeling. In the end, Corin simply sighed, raising his hands in supplication. There was no point arguing it out now. Tate was already up. Any damage was already done. Maybe now they could find a way to rescue the little girl. There was absolutely no way he was going to leave her in this situation.

Movement caught both pairs of eyes and they turned as one to watch the man leave the cave, with the humanoid trailing behind him. With a smile, they looked at each other. This might be easier than they had hoped. If those two stayed away, they could rescue the girl and leave them none the wiser as to where, or how, she escaped.

By mutual whispered agreement, they waited five minutes, although it felt like an eternity to Corin. Each passing second seemed to make him feel more anxious, more desperate. He understood waiting gave them a better chance at getting out of this without bloodshed, however, knowing something and accepting it were two different matters entirely.

When they realised neither of the males were coming back, Tate leaned in close. "You go and grab her. I don't want to risk this wound any more than I have already. I know it was stupid of me to come out here, but I couldn't cope with the worry of what was going on. I'll keep guard while you get her. Be as gentle as you can, Doc. We don't want her crying out." His fingers were busy tapping out a rhythm on the butt of his gun as he spoke.

Corin nodded and slowly inched forward. As soon as he reached her, he gently placed his hand over her mouth, feeling a whimpered breath against his palm. He pulled off the dirty rag from her eyes and ran his hand down her face and smiled. The smallest of whimpers escaped her lips as a tear rolled down her cheek. As soon as he caught the girl's eyes, he put his finger to his lips, silently urging her to keep quiet and removed his hand from her mouth. Wide eyed, she looked at him and nodded. He could see her shaking, but he was in awe of one so young displaying such strength in staying quiet and not drawing any attention to them.

Crouching, he scooped her up into his arms, thankful she was so light. Slowly stepping backwards, refusing to take his eyes off the sleeping forms in front of the fire, he made his way back to Tate. Tate's hand landed on his shoulder as he guided them back to the safety of the cave wall. Tate immediately moved in front of them, taking on a protective stance as he motioned him to go back to their chamber. Corin stood, turned, and quietly walked away.

Tate took a turn walking backwards. His eyes were trained on the small opening between the first two caves. As his back hit the inner wall, he raised his hand to trace the edge as a guide before he slowly disappeared around it and on into the small cave, breathing out a sigh of relief. This inner chamber was so well hidden in the back corner of the second chamber, he was sure that even if these hostiles discovered the second cave they would not find the inner chamber they were hiding in. Still, he would stay alert and keep watch so Corin could focus on the little girl they rescued.

Corin settled the girl onto the makeshift bed and removed her restraints. His movements were slow and steady while he quietly talked to her in a reassuring manner. "It's alright, little one. Do you understand me?" She nodded slowly. "Good." Corin smiled. "I'm Corin and that's Tate over there. We've got you. You're safe now, okay? We won't let anything happen to you, but we still need to be quiet, alright? Those bad men are still out there and we don't want them finding us."

Tate smiled and waved at her when she looked over at him.

Once her arms were freed, she flung them around Corin, her little face burrowing into his chest as quiet sobs wracked her little body. Gently, Corin ran soothing hands over her arms and back, willing the blood flow back into her muscles. He could feel her tears soaking into his shirt. He could feel her trembling, coupled with silent, deep, heavy sighs, escaping her lips. He reached over, grabbed a cloth and wet it. Gently lifting her head, he smiled at her and washed her face, exposing elfin features and wide eyes of a soft blue that had been hidden under a layer of grime.

"What's your name, sweetie?"

"Eliya," she whispered.

"Do you speak Galactic Standard?" Corin smiled when she nodded. "Well, Eliya, sweetie, can you tell us why those men tied you up? Where is your family?" He made sure to speak softly so as not to upset her further.

"Bad men took me 'n my nonnie when we was coming from the water. They was mean to Nonnie. They hurtied her. I scared. I want my Papi and my Kel." Her bottom lip quivered even as it jutted out.

"I know, sweetie, but we're going to have to find them first. Do you know where they are?"

"At home." Eliya solemnly nodded.

"Do you know where home is?" Corin couldn't help but smile at her answer.

Eliya dipped her head to one side, her face scrunched up as she thought. Corin smiled. She looked adorable. A pang settled in his heart as he hoped someday he would be graced with a daughter as cute as her.

"By the big rock," Eliya whispered. "Papi said ifs I gots lost I should walk the water till I gots to big water and saw the big rock."

Corin looked over to Tate, who was listening intently while he kept guard. "Please tell me you noticed something similar as we were coming down?"

Tate smiled. "I think so. There was what looked like a small mountain bordering a lake. It should be to the west of us from here."

"Eliya, did you hear what Tate said? He knows where it is. So we are going to get some rest, wait for the bad guys to go, and then see about getting you home and back to your Papi."

The smile Eliya gifted them was blinding. She jiggled in happiness, causing both men to smother a laugh. Corin continued cleaning her up. She was covered in dirt and he did his best to wash her as he checked her out for any injuries. Blessedly, there were no injuries larger than simple scrapes and bruises. While they were no doubt painful, he was relieved to see they were all that was wrong with her.

He reached into his bag, digging about until he came up with one of their spare shirts. He helped Eliya into it, both of them giggling quietly at how she was swamped in it. Taking some leather cord from his pack, he fashioned bindings to act as a belt and wrapped some lightly around each arm to hold the excess material up. Ripping apart another shirt, he wrapped the material around each leg, before again binding it in place with the soft leather. It was far from ideal, but at least it would help keep her warm. He was just thankful she still wore shoes. He wished he could give her some tea, but they couldn't risk a fire. Instead, he opened up a ration pack and watched as she devoured it.

Over his shoulder, Corin heard Tate chuckling. He turned and raised a brow at him in question even as he shook his head, smiling. He watched Tate's body shake, he was laughing so hard.

"That has to be the first time I've ever seen anyone quite so happy to eat one of those packs. She must be bloody hungry as those things really are disgusting."

Corin joined in the chuckling. It was good to have something to laugh about. The stresses of the last two days lifted slightly with the lighter, happier mood around them. It was nice to think things were starting to look up again. Suddenly, an almighty roar echoed throughout the cave system. Eliya whimpered, curling in on herself as her body shook. Corin grabbed his gun and joined Tate at the entrance to their little bolthole. The roaring continued and was swiftly followed by the sounds of fighting. Grunts and yelps of pain came thick and fast. The two men looked at each other. Tate nodded his head in the direction of the cavern between them and the hostiles. Seeing it was empty, they both crept forward to the wall that separated them from the first chamber. Crouching low, they both peered around, taking stock of the activity going on.

It became obvious the humanoid who left the cave earlier had returned and discovered Eliya was missing. The other two males were up now and all three of them were fighting. The two men watched silently as a blade suddenly severed the head of one of the two sleeping humanoids. They continued to watch as the fight raged on. Both the remaining humanoids were oblivious to their audience. They landed crushing blow after crushing blow on each other. The impacts were so hard they were being flung around the chamber, knocking rocks loose from the walls. Green blood sprayed across the chamber in a gruesome fountain as claws came into play. The second sleeping male was a mass of deep grooves, inflicted by those claws. The gouges were harsh and uneven, the slimy green blood oozing from them.

Tate saw he was losing the battle fast. He watched as with a last, desperate lunge, he grabbed the blade which had severed the head of his friend. He turned and swung out, slicing the other man across the chest, tearing through skin and muscle to the heart beating beneath them. At the same time his sword struck, the clawed hand pierced his chest, driving into the gaps where Corin presumed the ribs should be and likely piercing his heart. Neither male could stop their momentum, and Tate looked on as both of them collapsed to the ground, writhing and gasping for air, their chests ripped open to the elements.

Corin felt the medic in him war with his feelings at not going to help the injured and dying. Never before had he ignored someone in need. He knew he couldn't, knew they were just as likely to turn on him, and that ultimately their injuries were fatal. Besides, by going, he would give away what they had done. It didn't stop the guilt from forming in his chest however. He felt Tate's arm restraining him, a look of compassion for Corin's feelings shining in his eyes. When all movement finally ceased, both men crept quietly forward. Wary eyes stayed trained on the bodies in front of them, alert for even the slightest sign of movement, however unlikely it seemed. When none came, Corin checked each body in turn for a pulse. He turned to face Tate shaking his head.

"It's for the best, Doc."

"It doesn't make it any easier though."

"I know." Tate threw his arm around Corin's shoulders, giving him a one-armed hug. "Come on, let's get back to Eliya."

Corin walked straight up to Eliya, scooped her up, and hugged her tight. "It's ok, sweetie, it's over. They've gone. You're safe."

Tate joined them, smoothing Eliya's hair back from her face and smiling at her. "So here's what we are going to do, little one. We're going to rest for a bit, then we're going to take you home."

"Back to Papi and Kel and—"

Tate cut her off with a laugh. "Yes, little one, back to everyone." He laughed even harder when she performed what looked like a happy dance while in Corin's arms. They put her back onto the makeshift bed and watched as exhaustion pulled her quickly into a dreamless sleep.

"How far do you think we need to travel?" Corin hoped it wasn't too far. He was seriously worried about the physical effects on them all.

"Actually, I think it will be no more than a day's walk. Once we get past this rocky bit, I think it's fairly gentle terrain. It's probably best for us to follow the river, even if it might take us slightly longer. I know we will be more exposed, but if Eliya was told to go that way, then we are more likely to meet a rescue party. Although, I guess we have no idea how long she has been missing." He shook his head, then massaged his temples, trying not to let his frustration get the better of him.

"Still, I agree, it's the best idea we have, Tate. So let's get hunkered down, sleep, and all being well with your wound, we should be able to leave here tomorrow. You're healing well, you know. I'm really impressed by just how well, and how fast," Corin assured Tate as he softly lay down next to Eliya.

"Doc, my healing speed has more to do with your skill than anything else." They simply smiled at each other before they both watched indulgently as Eliya trustingly turned and burrowed into Corin's warmth.

Both settled in, weapons at the ready, and they slowly slipped into a light, refreshing, dreamless sleep.

Chapter Five

Corin woke first and smiled to himself as he listened to the light snores coming from Eliya. Looking at her, there was a peacefulness to her face. Her innocence shone through in her sleep and he hoped her experiences did not tarnish her joyful innocence. He was drawn to the little girl, felt protective and nurturing emotions he'd never really felt to such an extent before. He wasn't used to young children, having been an only child. He was deeply loved by his mother and gamma, but he missed a fatherly influence in his life. He was at peace over the fact he was likely a product of an accident, but part of him still wished he had met his father. Certainly, he wished he knew more about the man. His mother kept everything from him, never saying a word to him about the man, right up until the day she died. Through it all she maintained it was better he didn't know. It often made him wonder just what she was hiding and why?

Shaking off memories of his past, he quietly rose, retrieved his weapon, and went to check on the other parts of the cave, hoping there was no one else about. It would be good to get some tea into both Tate and Eliya, particularly with the long trek they were going to be facing. Worry about how both of them would cope was his constant companion. He wasn't sure he would be able to manage if their situation deteriorated any further and he was desperate to get them all somewhere safe.

Seeing the smaller chamber empty, he gingerly crept to the main outer chamber. Peering around, he saw nothing different from earlier; it still resembled a battlefield. Dried green blood was sprayed across the walls and floors in some horrific parody of paint. Puddles were encrusted around the severed body parts littering the floor. He would have to talk to Tate, quietly, about how they were going to take Eliya past it. Surprise shone in his eyes when he saw the fire was still going strong, even with no one tending to it all night. A small smile rose to his lips as realisation dawned he would be able to start his own fire and use this one as cover. If anyone detected the smoke, this was what they would find upon investigation, not them hiding in the other chamber.

As he got back to his two sleeping companions, he saw Tate was in fact starting to stir, a slight grimace on his face. Letting him wake naturally, Corin set about building a fire, preparing the tea and warming up some rations. Digging around, he found some breakfast grains packs. They would be a good option for breakfast, especially as it would help keep their energy levels up.

"Morning, Doc. If it is morning," Tate quietly whispered.

"It is. You'd better get some tea and food inside you before I check over your wound."

Once Tate was settled, Corin raised his worries about going through the main chamber. They both pondered their dilemma as they sipped their tea and ate their grains.

Tate went to throw his cup down, before stopping himself and setting it down gently. It wasn't a good idea to spill the tea that was helping him. "What about if we cover her head as we walk through? We're going to have to think of a way to get through this trek with her anyway. She's too small to make it very far. I would offer to carry her, but I don't think I'll be able to manage." Frustration laced Tate's voice. He was unaccustomed to feeling weak.

"Maybe we can find some way to strap her to me? Similar to how you see mothers carry their babies," Corin suggested. "I don't know if it's possible. While she's still small, she's a lot bigger than a baby."

"I'll see what I can put together. What about your pack? How can you manage both? Maybe I should try to take more of our gear."

"Tate, I'll manage. The whole point of me taking her is because of your wound." Corin huffed out a frustrated breath at his friend. He really was a stubborn man.

"But you're injured too, Doc."

"Not as badly and you know it."

"Fine." Tate pouted, eliciting a gentle laugh from Corin.

It was enough to wake Eliya who stumbled over to them and immediately climbed into Corin's lap, burrowing into his warmth. "Have something to eat, little one," he gently told her. "Tate has some nice warm food for you."

She gifted Tate a brilliant smile before climbing back off of Corin and sitting by the fire to eat. While she was occupied, Corin redressed both their wounds before packing away all their supplies. He was beyond thankful Bray had grabbed his full surgical pack back on the Delphini. It made him wonder how the other guys were doing, and whether they carried enough supplies with them. Despite his worry, he knew there was little point dwelling on it. He could not affect their outcome, only his own. Still, it didn't make it any easier.

Once they were all finally packed away and fed, Tate came up to him with a makeshift sling. It would tie around Corin's back and make a pouch at the front for Eliya to lay in. They agreed Eliya would walk to start with, taking naps as needed. It would give his muscles a break from carrying her, while at the same time, not force her to cope with having to stay in place when she was awake. After getting his pack on, he knelt down in front of her.

"Sweetie, listen to me, we are going to have to go through the caves first."

"But the bad men are there," she whimpered as her lips trembled.

"It's ok, sweetie, they can't hurt you anymore. But, maybe if you hug me and keep your eyes closed until I tell you it will be best. Then you don't need to think about it or see anything. Okay?"

"O-okay." She trembled.

Making sure her eyes were covered, they made their way through the cave system. Corin wished he could have done something for the woman who had been with Eliya, but it was just not smart to take the time. It would only lead to a greater chance of them being discovered by the wrong people. Still, as he passed by her, he sent up a thought to the stars wishing her spirit peace. The climb down the rocks was slow going. It wasn't an easy job for Eliya, but she was remarkably brave and strong willed, refusing to be carried and wanting to play a part in her escape.

As they walked around the base of what had been their home for a few days, they finally discovered the river. Smooth and gentle, it meandered through a vast delta of green. The sky was bright, the sun shining more vividly than either man could remember from when they crashed. Neither was sure if it was truly brighter, or just the effects of them having been in the cave for days. They kept up a slow and steady pace as they walked. The peace surrounding them brought a calmness to Corin that he'd not experienced in a long time. Not just since the Delphini, but back to before his run-in with the Admiral. He couldn't understand what was going on, but he was drawn to both Eliya and the planet. They were calling to something in his soul.

It wasn't long before Corin noticed Eliya was tiring, her steps slowing and dragging. Gently, he lifted her up and swung her into the sling.

"I'can do it," she mumbled, even as she let out a massive yawn.

"I know you can, sweetie, but you don't need to. Let me carry you for a bit."

"Mkay."

"How's she doing?" Tate whispered a few minutes later, not wanting to wake her.

"She's sleeping, but restless. It could be nightmares, but I hope not."

"It's going to take time for her to recover from this. Let's hope she has plenty of love and support to go home to. I'm slightly worried that whoever took her has done more. There could be so much more to this than a simple kidnapping. Maybe it's just me being an Avanti, but something about this is bugging me. It seems off." Tate shook out his hands, trying to relieve some of the tension he carried. He realised all his senses were on high alert, his eyes constantly scanning the horizon.

"Hopefully we won't encounter any more problems before we get her back to her family."

"We can only hope."

As they carried on slowly making their way through the vast open fields, they quietly talked about everything and anything. Since meeting the Avanti, Corin had got on exceptionally well with Tate. He was perhaps closer to him than any of the others. He found himself sharing more of his hopes and dreams than he ever had before.

"So, you want young ones for yourself, then?" Tate could see Corin with children, and he was sure he would be a fantastic father.

"Yes, but it's unlikely. First, I would have to find someone to love who I would want children with. Realistically though, my life at the moment is far too unsettled to have them. Who knows what's going on up there?" He nodded up to the stars hidden above them. "I mean, why was the cruiser attacked? Has the Alliance even looked for us? You... maybe. Me? I doubt it, not if the Admiral has anything to do with it."

"He really is a prick! I've been wondering about the cruiser myself. We were in neutral space, in an old cruiser and not in a battlegroup. It's not like we would have looked particularly threatening. Besides, the hit seemed far too precise for my liking. Even a cruiser as out of date as the Delphini should have been able to withstand a more severe battering before the shield integrity was compromised. I imagine Dax will have a better idea, if, and when, we meet up." Tate spoke with a heavy heart, the worry about his teammates written all over his face.

"I'm worried too," Corin whispered with a sad smile. "We just have to keep the hope alive."

"Easier said than done." Tate sighed.

There was not much left to say then, even if either man wanted to. Both of them were lost in thought until Eliya woke. Deciding it was as good a time as any, they took a break for some more rations. Corin took the time to make sure all their wounds were healing, pass out some cold tea from earlier, and to dose Tate up on more pain killers and medicines.

It was an hour later when Eliya cried out, making both men jump. "I see the big rock! We nearly home." A wide smile split her face as she bounced up and down.

"Where is home once we get there?" Corin prompted.

"At the top, in the big place. Salin and Frenkie stand outside to say hello to me when I go in." She seemed happy at the prospect of seeing them.

"You think she means guards?" Corin wondered.

"Probably."

Both men scanned the horizon, registering the mountain in the distance. Tate figured it would take another hour or so for them to make it. It would be hard, but it was just about doable without breaking for the night. They would be tired and bedraggled once they got there, so he hoped they would receive a warm welcome. He didn't want to think about what would happen if the reception they received was hostile. Even another night's sleep would help if that were the case. Despite this worry in the back of his mind, he refused to share his concerns with Corin. Corin was dealing with so much already, especially as Tate had been so out of it. He deserved not to have more stress added to the burden on his shoulders.

As night started to descend on them, Eliya once again started to flag. Her little shoulders were drooping, her steps slowing; she was no longer chatting about anything and everything. Tate looked at Corin, they both nodded at each other, and once again, hopefully for the last time, Corin bent down and lifted her into the sling. There were no protests this time. Instead, her eyes shut instantly and she dropped into a dreamless sleep within seconds.

As they approached the mountain, they could see a town nestled into the base. It appeared to be well fortified and yet welcoming at the same time. They could see lights dotted about, and a large structure was nestled at the back, higher than the rest of the buildings. It seemed like the village was growing up onto the mountain rather than sweeping out before it. Darkness had fully descended by the time they made it to the outskirts. Walking along the cobbled streets, they were the focus of attention from some, while others simply ignored them. Feeling protective of Eliya, Corin wrapped his cloak around him, covering her completely, and away from prying eyes. He wanted to have time to explain before being confronted by angry relatives. Despite being relieved to have made it to what, Corin was sure, was actually a castle, they approached the guards at the entrance with trepidation.

Both guards locked eyes onto Corin and Tate as they stepped forward. They were clad in what appeared to be some sort of leather trousers with leather crisscrossing their bare chests. Their hands were resting lightly on swords at their sides.

"Who seeks entrance?" The guard on the left demanded in Galactic Standard, eyes locked onto Tate.

"We are looking for Kel." Tate was calm, thankful everyone appeared able to speak in the universal language. Not all neutral worlds used it.

"It's Laird Kelin Tharn of the Derin Clan to you, stranger."

Tate's eyes shot to Corin as he mouthed the word "Laird?" *What had they got themselves mixed up in now*, he wondered?

Chapter Six

"My apologies, we were only given the name Kel as a guide. No offence was meant," Tate apologised, hoping to ease any tension before it started.

"Wait here," was the terse response as the guard left, leaving the second guard to watch them closely. Shortly, another guard joined them, presumably replacing the guard who had left.

Tate moved closer to Corin whispering softly, "So what's going on, do you think? Is Kel her father?"

"I don't know. She mentioned her Papi as well as the name Kel, so I'm guessing Kel is someone else."

"Shit, Corin, this is a bit of a clusterfuck. The last thing I want is for us to be accused of kidnapping her."

"We just have to hope they believe us and Eliya backs us up. Although it raises the question as to whether they will believe her."

Both of them fell silent, well aware they were not completely out of earshot of the guards, no matter how quietly they were talking. The guards were certainly keeping a close eye on them. After a few minutes, the original guard came back, insisting they follow him indoors. He led them to a small room just inside the entrance.

"Sit. Wait," the guard barked at them.

A few minutes later, they were joined by another man whose gaze raked over them both in a calculated and assessing manner.

"I am Carn Dibren, Master of Laird Kelin Tharn's Guard. For what purpose have you sought an audience with him? Why did you only refer to him as Kel? Even Offworlders are expected to know who the clan rulers and leaders are and how to address them." The man narrowed his eyes at them both as he took in every aspect of their appearance.

Tate stepped forwards, positioning himself in front of Corin and Eliya. Standing tall, he made sure to look as strong as possible. He was too well trained to show any form of weakness, especially in such an unknown environment.

Corin placed a calming hand in the centre of Tate's back and dipped his head slightly towards the man in front of them. "We must apologise for the error. As we told the guard, we were only given the name Kel as a reference, and a building to go to. It is extremely important we meet with him."

"And again, I must ask for what purpose?" Carn reiterated with little patience.

"It is about a young girl called Eliya." Corin hoped her name would be enough information until they got to meet this clan leader Kel.

As soon as Eliya's name left Corin's lips, Carn gasped and turned to the guard who raced out of the room. "Follow me," he barked.

With a quick glance at each other, they got up and followed him as he led them through a maze of corridors, past various people, all of whom cast them wary glances; some paused in whatever tasks they were doing to turn to companions and whisper. The further they walked, the more guards they passed. Some stood with feet braced, claymores held in front of them and hands clasped around the hilts. Others stood with spears and shields. Not one of them moved a muscle, other than tracking the group's progress with their eyes. Eventually they came to a set of double doors. With a nod to one of the four guards at the door's entrance, Carn led them into the room. Following behind him, they walked right up to the massive table sat at the end of the room. Around the table were stood six men, ranging in age from late teens to mid-sixties. They all looked weary and haggard, their bodies drooping where they stood. Maps, paperwork and cups littered the table in front of them.

One of them turned to Carn who was standing at the front of Corin's group. "Damn it, Carn, I told you we weren't to be disturbed for anything. I don't care who the latest bloody delegate from the

Alliance is. Now is not the time." A huge frown accompanied the man's words.

"Laird Kel, these aren't delegates. I think you are going to want to hear this. They came asking for you as Kel, saying it was about a young girl named Eliya." Carn cautiously spoke, wary of upsetting any of the men around the table.

All around them heads shot up from what they were focused on. Suddenly every pair of eyes in the room was focused on them with a laser-like intensity.

"What do you know about Eliya?" the man named Kel demanded. Corin's eyes watched as he stalked towards them. His movements, while predatory, were graceful. He was close to seven feet of solid planes and hard muscles. His skin was a golden bronze which seemed to glisten in the lights around him. His hair was a mid-blonde, and flowed to just past his shoulders. Leather bracers covered his forearms while smaller leather circlets were wrapped around each bicep. Leather trousers were moulded to his thighs. Corin's heart began to beat faster. Never had a first glance at someone affected him as it did now.

Laird Kelin was rugged in appearance. While still young, his face had a slightly weathered visage which was likely due to many hours spent outdoors. His eyes were both brown and green, with the green bleeding into the brown on the outer edges. He had a strong nose, coupled with a square jaw, and a dusting of facial hair that just added to his overall manliness.

Corin felt his cock go from soft to rock hard and aching instantly. Damn, this was a man he would happily have under him, over him, inside him. In fact, he would take him any which way he could. Tate shot Corin a questioning glance and Corin realised he hadn't been able to hide his reaction from his friend. Shooting a glance at Tate and shaking his head, Corin stepped forward.

"I need to know who you are to Eliya before I can say anything," Corin boldly stated.

A second later, one of the other men stood around the table jumped over it and was hurtling towards Corin with a look of murderous intent on his face. Just as he got to Corin, he threw a punch that never landed. Instead, Tate stepped between Corin and Eliya, who was still asleep in the sling, and this new man. The punch hit him square in the abdomen. The pain was instantaneous, and he staggered back, all the air gone from his lungs. Tate could feel his stitches rip open from the impact. Trying to suck in a deep breath, he called on all his years of training with the Avanti and pushed the pain into the recesses of his mind and forced his body back to standing whilst simultaneously pulling his knife from the sheath at his side.

"Make another move towards him and I'll kill you. You want him? You have to go through me first, and I promise you, I. Will. Win. You have no idea what you nearly did there." Tate growled at the man, his stance wide, both aggressive and defensive at the same time.

"Do you know who I am?" the new man demanded as he bared his teeth at Tate.

"No," Tate replied. "And frankly, I don't care. Now. Back. The. Fuck. Off."

They watched as the man named Kel placed a restraining arm across the other man's chest. "Leave it, Tir, let me deal with this. I mean it. We won't find anything out if we beat them. They came to us willingly. Give them a chance to explain."

They all watched the man called Tir run his hands over his face before he gave a small nod and took two small steps back.

Kel raised an eyebrow at him, sighed and then turned back to Corin. There were several emotions swirling through his gaze, but his voice was calm when he spoke again. "I am Laird Kelin Tharn, son of the Chieftain of this clan, and Eliya is my niece. Laird Tirathon Tharn is her father. She was kidnapped two weeks ago with her nurse when they were walking the grounds. We have heard nothing since. There have been no ransom demands, no sightings, nothing. We have searched and searched and no trace has yet been found. The entire clan is grief stricken. As you can see, my brother is barely holding it together. Now. What. Do. You. Know." His voice rose slightly as he struggled not to let his impatience show.

Corin looked at Tate, his eyes registering the fact the Tate looked clammy once again. They nodded to one another and Corin reached up to slowly untie the cloak from around him. He gently lifted the sleeping form of Eliya from the sling before looking up at Kel and quietly asking, "Is this her?"

Gasps echoed all around. A choked sob came from Tir's direction before he quickly lifted her from Corin's arm, tears streaming down his face. Smiles shone around the room as a small voice whispered, "Papi?"

Quickly, a group surrounded the reunited father and daughter, cheers echoing around the room. A wave of happiness ran through the chamber and out the doors as word passed from one guard to another. Shouts of joy could be heard from the hallways as the news spread. A soft whimper from beside Corin saw him snapping his head to look at Tate.

Chapter Seven

"Doc…" Tate managed to gasp out before all the blood drained from his face and his knees buckled.

Corin looked on in horror at the blood covering Tate's shirt. A vibrant red dribble was escaping from his mouth and running down his chin.

"Oh, fuck no, Tate, no." Corin grabbed Tate and lowered him to the floor as Tate descended into the embrace of oblivion.

Corin yanked the pack off Tate's back as he lowered him. Throwing off his own pack, he all but ripped it in a desperate attempt to get to his equipment inside. Uncaring of what was happening around him, he yanked up Tate's shirt, looking at the damage the punch had done. As his training kicked in, the first thing he did was give Tate yet another dose from the Battleboost injector, followed by a shot of pure adrenaline. Never had Corin been more thankful for the chemical reaction inside the injector. It meant, in time, the compound replenished itself. The last thing he wanted was to run out of it. He didn't want to have to rely on whatever medical options were available on this planet, especially as he didn't know how good they were.

Fully easing open the wound, he lifted the muscle out of the way to give him a clear view of the artery. His heart missed a beat as he saw his previous patch was damaged beyond repair. Removing the artificial implant, he worked quickly to stitch the artery back up, all the while struggling to keep the area clear of blood. The volume of blood pooling was making things slippery and harder to deal with. It was at times like these he wished for a surgical aide and his full operating theatre at his disposal. He worked as fast as was possible, conscious of the fact Tate could not afford to lose any more blood. Once the stitching was complete, he attached a new implant, watching to see if it held after it was activated. He couldn't detect any further damage to the artery, but with the dim lighting available to him he hoped he hadn't missed something. Just as he was pondering his dilemma, Carn moved a light closer to him.

"Does this help?" Carn asked, and when Corin nodded his thanks, Carn continued, "Is there anything else I can do?"

"Can you find something to raise his head a little, please? I don't want blood pooling in his throat."

Carn quickly undid his own cloak, folding it and gently placing it under Tate's head.

A sudden scream of "Tate!" rent the air before Eliya raced over to sit by Tate's head. "Tate, please be ok. Please, please, Tatey, you're my fwiend." She sobbed.

Eliya's actions caused the focus of the room to shift back onto Corin and Tate. Tir tried to move Eliya out of the way, but she was having none of it. "No, Papi, NO!" She screamed, one little hand beating on her father's arm as she refused to let go of Tate who she held tight in her other hand.

Kel dropped beside Corin before quietly speaking. "I'm sorry, we didn't see. We didn't realise he was hurt. I've called for our doctor."

"I am a bloody doctor and he was fine until the bloody punch reopened his wound," Corin muttered, his focus fully on Tate.

Kel sighed as he quietly sat and watched the man beside him perform surgery right there in the middle of the war room floor. He was stunned both at the level of skill displayed and the speed the man was working at. He hoped the surgery was a success. His brother would be devastated if he killed a man with a single punch in a fit of despair-filled anger, especially one who had been instrumental in rescuing his daughter. Kel's focus, however, remained on the doctor. There was something about the man he found intriguing. He couldn't place his finger on what it was, he just wanted to get to know the man. A man who could ignore everything around him and fight to save a life. A stranger who appeared to have gone out of his way to return a lost child. This was someone he wanted to know more about.

He heard his father call him and went to join him slightly away from what was going on.

"I know they brought Eliya back to us, but we need to be careful. It could all just be an elaborate plot to infiltrate the clan."

"I'm sorry, Father, but I just can't believe that's the case. I mean, look at them. It's obvious they are both injured, one of them seriously, even before Tir made it worse. You would have to be a special kind of crazy to try to infiltrate somewhere in the condition they are in. Besides, you heard what Eliya told Tir. They saved her. We can't ignore what they have done for us. I *won't* ignore it. Yes, I will get to the bottom of what went on, but I will do so while extending them our hospitality and treating them as honoured guests. Shame on anyone who thinks it should be otherwise."

"And if you're wrong?" his father asked.

"Then I'm wrong and I'll admit it. I'm sorry, Father, but my instinct is to trust that this situation is exactly what it looks like. If I'm wrong, I'll take full responsibility and deal with it myself." Kel calmly faced his father down.

"Fine, so be it." His father turned, and walked away, leaving considerably less tension among the Derin still in the room.

Turning his focus back to the men on the floor, Kel sighed. It had been a long two weeks since Eliya was taken from them and for some reason he was sure life wasn't about to calm down anytime soon. After all, if these men had indeed rescued Eliya, it still left them not knowing who was responsible for taking her in the first place, or why. While he was talking to his father, the man, Corin, had set up more equipment and a very soft, slow beat was quietly coming from it. If it was indeed a heartbeat, it sounded too slow to Kel's ears.

Corin's eyes remained focused on the rhythm coming from the vitals monitor. Tate's heartbeat was too slow for his liking. There was no choice but to give him another booster shot. It would take Tate close to the limit for adrenaline, but he didn't see any choice in the matter. He was pleased to hear Tate's heartbeat get stronger and faster as soon as the shot hit his bloodstream. Shifting back to focus on repairing the external stitches, Corin could feel sweat forming on his forehead. His hands were busy so he had neither the time nor ability to wipe it clean, despite how much it was starting to annoy him. Suddenly, a cloth was gently wiped over his face. He quickly flicked his gaze to see the man, Kel, was the one to help.

"Thank you." He smiled softly.

Kel gently brushed his fingers over the back of Corin's hand as he spoke. "You are most welcome. Tell me if there is more I can do. Please, let us help you."

"If you have them, some more wrappings would help. I am nearly out."

With a quick clicking of his fingers, Kel summoned a guard and dispatched him off to collect supplies. He continued to wipe Corin's face clear as he worked. He was surprised to find his fingers trembled slightly as he pressed the cloth to Corin's head. He drew in a deep breath as a subtle scent wafted towards him from the man. His heart sped up with each passing moment.

A few minutes later, the guard returned with both supplies and the clan doctor.

"Move out of the way, idiot, you have no idea what you're doing. I will deal with this, I'm the doctor here," the clan doctor announced as soon as he entered the room and saw what was going on. Kel didn't really like the man. He was arrogant and self-absorbed; he liked to look down on just about everyone.

Kel looked on with amusement at the look Corin shot the doctor. Without taking his focus off his patient, he continued to simply ignore the man. Helping Corin out, Kel prevented the clan doctor from trying to take over.

"Leave him be, Al'Feram, he's a doctor himself, and a damn good one by the looks of things. Let him help his own companion. If he asks for help, then you can assist him. Assist him, mind, NOT take over."

"But I'm the best doctor on the planet!" Al'Feram puffed out his chest in self-importance.

"And I'm one of the best bloody surgeons in the Alliance," Corin shot back at the man, "I'm a Gold Standard field and trauma surgeon, so I think I outrank you here, hmm? What's more, this is my man and my decision."

At those words, Kel felt a twinge in his chest. His mood soured when Corin mentioned the injured man was his man. Were they partners, he wondered? As the thought went through his mind, the feeling hit him again. He recognised it as jealousy, but how could he possibly be feeling it? He didn't even know Corin, much less have any claim on him. As the word claim registered in his mind, it brought on a wave of images.

He could see Corin, naked underneath him as he drove his cock into him, a look of ecstasy on both their faces. He saw them both in the bathing chamber, arms and legs wrapped around each other, their bodies sliding against one other as their mouths were locked into a slow, passionate dance. The two images which affected him most, however, were the ones of them wrapped around each other's bodies as they slept in his bed, a look of pure happiness and contentment on his own face as he slept.

The second confusing image was of Corin taking him, his cock driving hard and fast into Kel. Bodies slick with sweat, Corin's hand twisting over his cock, a look of desperation on his face. He had never allowed a lover to take him before, so why would his mind show him the image now?

No matter how much his mind was confused by the images, his body was not. His cock was rock hard and leaking, his breath shallow as arousal thrummed through him. His body felt tight, itching for relief. Trying to shake his head clear of the images, trying not to think about what they meant, he forced himself to focus back onto what was happening in front of him.

"You alright?" Corin glanced in Kel's direction. "You look pale all of a sudden."

"Fine," Kel managed to choke out, not wanting anyone to realise something was going on with him. He turned back to Al'Feram, who was trying to take over, much to Corin's annoyance. "I said leave it.

It's his decision to make and it doesn't look like he needs help anyway. Just give him any equipment he asks for, no questions asked."

Al'Feram grunted in annoyance. "Fine," he bit out as he stomped off to the side to watch.

As Corin finished stitching up Tate and began wrapping him in bandages, he was pleased to see Tate wasn't as pale or cold to the touch compared to a few minutes earlier. He sent a silent thank you into the universe for giving him the ability to once again save Tate's life.

Corin was thankful to see Tate open his eyes a little. With a groan, he muttered, "Damn it, Doc, I'm cursed I tell you, cursed!"

"Nah, you're not. You're just a giant bloody trouble magnet." He bent down and gave Tate a kiss on his forehead as he ruffled his hair. "Just take it easy, okay? I don't want to move you just yet and we're going to need to figure out where we go from here. Just let me deal with it, alright? I want you to use your strength to get better."

"K, Doc, love ya, man," Tate mumbled as he drifted to sleep.

Kel looked on, seeing the closeness of the two men, his irrational jealousy spiking once again. Although it lowered when he heard Corin mutter,

"Ah, Tate, I love you too, brother."

Those words eased Kel's mind— perhaps they weren't lovers, merely brothers, friends. He couldn't believe how relieved and happy he was about it. Turning to Corin, he spoke. "We have plenty of suites we can move him to. It will give you space to care for him and yourself. I know we need to talk to you. We need to know what happened with Eliya, but please understand we never meant to hurt him, and we don't want to push you."

Kel's breath stuttered as Corin gifted him with an incredible smile. It brought him an immediate sense of peace and happiness, warmth rushing through him.

"Thank you, Laird Kelin." Corin dipped his head slightly, although with such a large difference in height between them, he already felt bowed. "We would be grateful for your help."

"You are more than welcome, and please it's simply Kel to you. I will get some help to move him safely, and get you settled in. I'll get food sent up and anything else that you need." Kel smiled as he seemed to drift unconsciously closer to Corin.

Kel's smile was doing funny things to Corin and his cock swiftly came back to life. He stuttered, "Um, nothing else needed, thanks though. Food would be good and it would be nice to bathe."

Both of them stood stock still. Corin's mind assaulted him with images of them bathing together. His cock grew impossibly hard, and he desperately hoped a wet patch wasn't visible, based on how much he was leaking.

Kel was meanwhile willing his cock to behave. The same earlier images of them bathing together hit him again. So intense was the vision it seemed to take his breath away. Neither of them were aware of the effect they were having on each other. Coughing, Kel turned and ordered the guard to get a stretcher together and dismissed Al'Feram who stormed off, muttering to himself.

"Is he going to be okay?" Eliya sniffed.

Corin moved to sit next to her and she flung her arms out towards him, trying to climb from her father's lap to his. Tir was reluctant to let her go, and to go into the arms of a stranger, even if it was one who had rescued her. She gave him a quick kiss on the cheek before she shuffled out of his protective hold. "Yes, little one, he's going to be just fine. I promise. Remember when I helped him out in the cave and how he got better afterwards?"

"Uhhuh, when we was hiding from the bad men."

"That's right, sweetie. Well, it's the same here. I've fixed him up and as long as he rests he will be fine."

"You pwomise?" Worry was evident on her brow and there were tears in her eyes. "He's my fwiend, he save me."

"I promise, sweetie." Corin hugged her tight. "Now I want to see a smile on that pretty little face of yours, okay? You're back with your Papi and Kel and I know they missed you."

Eliya leaned in close and whispered in his ear, "You think I get some cake?"

He burst out laughing, whispering back to her, "Sweetie, I think they will give you just about any treat you ask for."

Eliya stood up, doing her little happy dance and threw her arms back around her father, her wide eyes staring up into his face, innocence tinged with a hint of mischief on her face as she solemnly asked, "Papi, can I have cake?"

Laughing, Tir hugged her. "Ely, baby, you can have anything you want." He turned to Corin with a sad smile. "I'm truly sorry for my actions. I cannot ever repay your kindness in bringing my daughter back to me. If you require anything, anything at all, please ask, and I will do all in my power to give it to you. I could not have lived if she was taken from me. She is my world."

"She's a wonderful little girl and you should be proud of how strong and brave she was. I hope one day I am blessed to have a daughter such as her."

"Thank you." Tir rose with Eliya wrapped tight in his arms and left the room.

He had never been more relieved than after they got Tate settled and he was able to wash. Yet he was conflicted. He didn't want to leave Tate's side for long enough to take a bath. Kel must have sensed his feelings and offered to watch over Tate. While Corin was relieved, at the same time, he was embarrassed as he lay in the bath. He couldn't stop fantasising about Kel. As his thoughts focused on the image of Kel in the bath with him, his hand drifted down his body. Soapy fingers reached his nipples— already hard, they ached to be pinched. When he succumbed to the desire, a low moan escaped his lips as his hips thrust upwards. One hand stayed teasing his nipples as the other drifted on down his stomach to reach his cock. He teasingly brushed his fingertips over the tip of his cock and down his length. He gently squeezed his balls before giving them a firm tug.

In the next room, Kel sat by Tate's bed, keeping an eye on him. His mind was drifting to the gorgeous specimen in the bath. The more he thought about Corin, the more he wanted him. Mulling over his immediate and fierce attraction to Corin was confusing him. His head jerked up when he heard a moan, thinking Tate was waking up, but he hadn't moved at all. Hearing another moan, his focus shot to the bathroom door. Was Corin injured and no one had noticed? Moving towards the door, he froze mid-step when he heard Corin moan.

"Yes, Kel, yes!"

His cock jerked in his trousers. He was stunned, realising Corin was just as attracted to him. His eyes flicked to the bed, making sure Tate was asleep before his hand grabbed his own cock, the material providing friction, deepening the sensations. The soft moans coming from the bathroom were driving him crazy. He didn't want to be caught if Tate woke up, or if either door opened, and he moved to the window, keeping his back to the room, thankful they were on the fourth floor and no one could see in. Unlacing the front of his trousers, he pulled them open and brought his cock out. A shudder tore through him the second he wrapped his fingers around it. He started a slow up and down stroke, adding in a twist every time he moved over the head. He brought his other hand down to play with his balls, gently cupping them before tugging on them. He was imagining Corin lying in the bath, one hand wrapped around his own cock, the fingers of his other hand teasing his hole. Every time he imagined Corin's finger slipping inside himself, his hips jerked in appreciation.

Corin's fingers drifted from his sac to his hole, pausing briefly to cover them with oil he found beside the bath. He began a slow tease, tracing around the edges, flicking his nail over it then dipping inside. Slowly but surely he slid his finger deeper inside. One finger became two, twisting and thrusting, hips moving in tandem. With each thrust of his fingers, he imagined it was Kel's fingers prepping him to take his cock. He twisted his fingers around so he was constantly brushing over his prostate. He stroked faster and faster, his mind overloaded with images of Kel fucking him. He was so close.

Kel could hear faint splashes of water joining in the moans emanating from the bathroom. His hand sped up, the tugging getting harder, and his hips thrust faster. He was on edge, desperate for relief, when he heard "Fuck yes, Kel..." That was all it took. Ribbon after ribbon of cum exploded from the tip of his cock, coating the wall in front of him. Panting, he smeared the evidence into his skin as he leaned his forehead onto the cool window. He fought to bring his breathing back under control, his mind in a state of shock. He had never come so hard, or fast before, from just his imagination.

Corin was feeling a post orgasmic high. He sagged deeper into the bath, every muscle relaxing as the stress from the last few days melted away. Thinking he was spending too long in there, he dragged himself out, drying off before climbing into one of the most comfortable outfits ever which Kel had left out for him. There was a pair of loose, flowing, wide leg trousers that rested gently on his hips. Alongside them was a loose tunic top made out of the same soft material. It was sleeveless, presumably so he didn't irritate his wound. It surprised him though, as he hadn't mentioned being injured. Kel must he noticed something earlier. His body almost felt weightless, having been carrying all his gear and Eliya for so long. Opening the door, he saw Kel relaxing in a chair by Tate's bed, reading papers. Kel looked even taller than he had earlier, with his long legs stretched out and crossed at the ankles. He looked very relaxed and content, a slight smile playing at the corners of his mouth, a marked change from his earlier appearance.

Kel looked up at Corin as soon as the door opened. He ran his gaze over Corin, taking in his appearance. A thrill ran through him at the sight of Corin in his clan colours.

"How's he been? Any changes?" He fought the blush trying to take hold of his face as he looked at the man who was the star player in his bath-time fantasy.

"No changes, but he does look peaceful." Kel smiled at him. "I'll go and get some food for you. Is there anything else you would like me to bring?" When Corin shook his head no, Kel walked out the door saying, "I won't be long."

Taking the seat Kel vacated, Corin swore he could smell the man and his cock made a valiant attempt to get hard again. Trying to push all thoughts of Kel to the back of his mind, he turned his focus fully onto Tate. Seeing Tate's vitals, he was pleased to notice his heartbeat was settling into a normal strong rhythm. The colour was returning to his body and his bandages were blessedly clear of any traces of blood. Things were finally starting to look up for Tate.

"Hey, Doc," Tate softly spoke. "So what's the damage this time?"

"Tate! You're awake. Good to see it." He smiled broadly at his friend. "Okay, so you're lucky. The punch managed to rip your stitches open and pull the implant away from the artery. I had to go back in and redo everything. You lost a fair amount of blood, but I was able to fix everything."

"Damn, Doc, you're good. So why do I get the feeling there's a but on the end of that sentence?" Tate asked.

"I'm afraid to say there is. While I was able to fix everything, the damage was greater than last time. If it were to happen again, I don't think I would be able to repair it properly and that's if you even survived. You can't risk any more injuries, it's simply too dangerous. So it means you have to be on total bedrest for at least a week, buddy. We just can't risk it."

"Damn."

"Yeah."

"Okay, I can cope with it. I guess, as long as we're safe here. You need to fill me in on everything that's happened since I passed out, Doc. Although if we aren't safe, I'm not sure what I can actually do about it." Frustration rippled through his voice.

"We're safe, Tate, I promise," Corin reassured him before filling him in on everything that happened while Tate was out of it.

"So, a quick snapshot is, the guy really is sorry he punched me, they're all over the moon she's back, the doctor's a prick, they're a pretty decent bunch of guys when they aren't all pissy and I'm guessing the questions are coming soon?" Tate surmised.

"Sounds about right." Corin laughed at Tate's succinct description of events.

"Okay, I get all that, but answer me one question, Doc?"

"Sure, anything."

"Why the hell does this room smell like sex? Something you're not telling me, Doc?" Tate queried with an inquisitive look in his eyes.

Corin blushed like crazy, stuttering as he spoke. "Uh, um, well, I..."

Tate laughed. "You go, Doc, you stud you."

"It's not like that, Tate." Corin sighed, running his hands through his hair. "I don't know what the fuck is going on. Every time I close my eyes all I see is Kel, kissing, touching, fucking, I don't understand it. I've never been so drawn to anyone and I don't just mean sexually. There is something about him that calls to me. I swear, it's like he's calling to my soul. I want to get to know him, spend time with him. It's fucked up, I've never experienced this sort of reaction." Corin got up and paced as he spoke.

"Hey, Doc, stay calm. Don't panic, alright? If it's any consolation, from what I could see Kel couldn't keep his eyes off you either. So I'm guessing whatever's going on, it's not all one-sided."

Corin's lips twitched as though he was about to smile and then thought better of it. "I don't know if it's a good thing or not, Tate."

Tate sighed and held Corin's gaze as he spoke "It is what it is. You're just going to have to go with the flow, Doc, see what happens. There's nothing else you can do but let it happen and enjoy the ride. Oh, now riding Kel... hmm, yum. I'm pretty sure you wouldn't mind doing that." He smirked at Corin, then waggled his eyebrows at him while making smooching noises.

"Yeah, yeah, how is it even when you're this injured you can still talk about sex?"

"It's a talent, Doc." Tate grinned, before letting out a soft groan.

"Well, Mr. Talented, I think it's time for more painkillers for you." Corin had a look of concern on his face as he spoke, especially when all Tate did was to simply nod at him. "Oh, and Kel is bringing food back for us. So after you've eaten, I want you to get more sleep."

"Yes, boss!" Tate smiled at Corin.

Corin simply rolled his eyes in response.

Chapter Eight

Corin kept a constant vigil by Tate's bed. While he was sure, medically speaking, that Tate would pull through, after everything they endured, he needed to keep an eye on him. He needed to make sure. It felt like Tate was the only constant in his life and it was something he wasn't prepared to lose.

Corin spent the first morning of his vigil with his focus firmly on Tate. He was worried about what was going to happen to them, where they would go, would they have trouble over what had happened with Eliya? But he kept pushing those thoughts to the back of his mind.

Kel had been busy asking him questions about what he was doing before he had ended up on the planet. He had to wonder if this was a subtle form of questioning. Was Kel attempting to find out more about him and Tate, or was he genuinely interested, he wondered?

Kel broke the comfortable silence that had descended between him and Corin. He was feeling a compulsion to know everything about this beautiful stranger. "So you are a... what was it? Gold Ranked Surgeon in the Barin Alliance?"

Corin smiled softly, yet proudly. "Yes, a trauma surgeon mainly. Although, I do have extra training in a variety of fields. I've worked with some of the best specialists in the fields of neurology, orthopaedics, cardiovascular, and, of course, internal surgery."

"So that's what? Brains, bones, heart, and your organs?" Kel was amazed at the variety.

"Yes, but I am far from a specialist in them. I just did extra training so that it would make my life easier when treating traumas. It also means I lose less patients, which is always a good thing."

"Still, that's quite a lot of knowledge," Kel mused. He was beginning to understand just how important it was to Corin to be the best doctor he could be.

"Yes, it is. But I have always believed if something is important to you, then you do your best at it." It was something that had been installed in him by his grandmother.

"That's a good way to be."

"It is."

As had been fairly common in the time they had spent together, both men slipped quietly into their own thoughts, the silence around them comfortable. Neither of them felt the need to fill it.

Again Corin found himself wondering what was going on outside of the room they were in. Surely Eliya's father, Tir, was going out of his mind trying to work out what had happened. He was almost certain that was the case, and, if it was, then why wasn't he here demanding all the answers they had? It really was starting to concern him. Had they already decided they were to blame for everything and just biding their time till they worked out what to do with them? To them?

Kel was confused. Everything about this man called to him and yet here he was basically keeping the man a prisoner in this room, a fact he was feeling increasingly guilty about. He had to wonder if Corin had realised it yet or was just ignoring it. He snorted quietly to himself. It seemed as though ignoring things was contagious. He was certainly trying to hide his burgeoning desire and soul deep need for the man. The one thing, the only thing, Kel was completely sure about was the necessity to hide his feelings from Corin. He certainly needed to do it until they were sure these men weren't their enemies, and they weren't the ones responsible for what had happened to Eliya.

However, he was finding it increasingly hard to hide his attraction. It was taking every ounce of self-control he possessed. Firstly, while he knew his father accepted that he was attracted to men, he knew Damron only really believed it was a phase he was going through. His father believed he would eventually settle down with a good woman by his side. Secondly, he had no idea how his father was going to take him being attracted to an Offworlder. His father had never been against Offworlders in the past, but his recent behaviour had become increasingly regressive. He was becoming more like his own father, who had been very stern and determined to maintain the old ways.

Kel didn't want to disappoint his father, no man ever did, nor did he want to disappoint Tir, but he was getting the distinct impression that he was falling in love with Corin. No, it was best all round if he kept his feelings to himself, at least for the moment, and certainly better that he didn't act on them. No. He needed to keep telling himself that word. He needed to keep his hands off this man, no matter how much compulsion he felt to touch the man, to kiss him, to hold him in his arms.

Kel was confused though. All the men he had been attracted to before had been similar in stature to himself. This man, Corin, was much smaller than he was. He wasn't delicate by any means, and he certainly had plenty of muscle definition, yet he would still feel small in Kel's arms. It was already bringing his protective instincts to the fore. His mind was already dreaming about what it would be like to make love to this man, how being with someone smaller than he was used to would change the experience.

Kel was also starting to wonder why his father hadn't ordered the two Offworlders be questioned. Was his father really so ready to proclaim them guilty already? Just because they were Offworlders? Since when had his clan, his father, become so judgemental? Kel simply couldn't see them as being guilty of kidnapping Eliya. Not only had they gone out of their way to bring her back to them, but they truly did seem like good men.

——————————————>O<——————————————

It was a couple of hours later, when he was having dinner with his father, Tir and Eliya that he understood a little more.

"Kelin, I know that you have been spending quite some time with the two Offworlders." Contempt dripped from Damron's voice, his eyes blazing with a depth of fury Kel had never witnessed.

Kel drew back slightly. Since when had his father become such a hateful man? He shared a look of confusion with his brother. "We need to, Sire. We need to know what really happened with Eliya. We must know if they are responsible and, if so, what we are going to do about it."

Damron waved his hand, like he was trying to get rid of a bug that was annoying him. "Of course they are responsible. Who else would do something like this? Someone from a neighbouring clan? Pfft, you're talking rubbish, boy. Kidnapping is something only a traitorous Offworlder would do. No, these men will be dealt with soon enough, don't you worry about that. Now you've gone and put me off my food. I care so little for this conversation. I shall retire to my rooms. See that you leave them well alone, boy. I forbid you to have anything to do with them." With those parting words, he stalked out of the room, his advisors and guards following swiftly behind him.

Tir looked at his daughter, relief etched on his face. "Are you okay, sweetie? Sorry Grampi is in such a bad mood, he's just been worried about you."

Eliya sniffed, raising her watery gaze to meet her father's. "Papi, Tatey and Cori is nice. They helps me. They tooks me from the bad men, they nice. No hurties them please, Papi. They my fwiends." Her lips trembled as she fought not to cry.

Tir's shocked gaze bounced from his daughter to his brother. "Do you really believe her, Kel? Do you really believe the only thing they had to do with all of this is to rescue her? I need answers. I've waited overnight, mostly as I could not bear to leave her side, and there was no way I was taking her with me to get them. But I must know, Kel, I must. I can't ignore this. I won't ignore this. I *will* have my revenge on whoever is responsible, one way or another."

Kel tipped his head back a little, closed his eyes, sighed, took a deep breath, and then dropped his gaze down to meet his brother's.

"Honestly? I don't think they kidnapped her. I believe what Eliya has said to be the truth. I just don't see this as anything more than them being helpful. I would start to look elsewhere, look at what other enemies we have. These men are not responsible."

"You are sure?" Tir's eyes were imploring for the truth.

"Come and talk to Corin. See for yourself."

Tir took a long, measured look at his brother. His gaze scoured over every nuance of Kel's face. "If you are certain, brother, then I will. I will come in the morning. I will give them that long, out of respect to you and Eliya. She may be young, but I don't see her telling lies— she never has before. If she believes they saved her and are good men, then I have to respect that. I will give them till morning, as I find I cannot bear not to have her as my constant focus. I need to keep my eyes on her at every minute. I am so scared she will be whisked away from me again. I'm putting Carn on her detail for the moment, just to make sure. I cannot wait any longer than the morning though, I truly cannot. It matters not what our father says or believes, I need to seek these bastards out. I need to find them and kill them. I need to make it hurt."

Kel rolled his glass around between his fingers, his eyes focusing on some imaginary point in the distance, before he looked at his brother. "I don't know how much information Corin will be able to give us. He is just a doctor, a damn good one, but I can't help feeling that we will get more information from Tate. He seems like a military man."

Tir absentmindedly stroked the hair away from Eliya's face as she ate. He had to smile when he noticed that she was swinging her little legs back and forth under the table. It was a habit of hers whenever she sat on chairs designed for adults, rather than her small frame. "Well, how about we gently prod some information out of Corin first then? If all is as you say it is, then the man who organised this is probably long gone. The trail will be cold by now anyway. So waiting another day or two won't change anything."

Kel nodded in agreement. "We need to stay calm and level-headed. I know you're angry, I'm angry, but angry people make mistakes. Do you really want to make a mistake and hurt the very men who saved your daughter? To make a mistake and lose our only chance at finding those responsible?"

"No, no I do not." Tir sighed. "I will try and stay calm, I will, but it's not easy. I want to rip someone's throat out, but I will keep it tamped down. For the moment."

———————— ꙮ ————————

Corin kept wanting to reach out and touch Kel. The need he felt to do so was a constant, overpowering desire. He was viciously suppressing it. If the need was so strong now, he had to wonder about what would happen if he did touch the man. No, he was going to keep his hands to himself, no matter what. Corin was feeling a compulsion to this man, one he didn't understand. Why? He kept asking himself, why this man? Why now? It certainly seemed to be a very one-sided pull, and he'd not seen the slightest indication Kel was interested in him. As far as he was concerned, this was a very one way attraction, and an unwelcome one at that.

Putting those intense feelings to one side, he was still enjoying having the company as he kept his vigil over Tate. Kel seemed to spend most of the days there with him. He presumed it was so they were not left alone until they had given whatever answers these people were looking for.

It was on the second morning that Kel brought his brother, Tir, with him. It made Corin slightly nervous considering the way that the man had reacted to them at first.

"Corin, I'm sure you remember him, but as a proper introduction, this is my brother, Laird Tirathon Tharn. Tir, this is Captain Corin Talovich."

Corin dipped his head towards Tir, another hulking giant as far as he was concerned. What was it with this planet and its excessively tall men?

"Corin." Tir dipped his head in return.

The seriousness of the moment was broken by Eliya. "Cori!" she screeched from her spot hiding behind her father's leg. Before anyone could stop her, she jumped up onto the chair next to him and clambered across to sit in his lap, throwing her arms around him in her own little bear hug. "I mithed you and Tatey. Why Tatey sleepin? He gots an owie again?"

"He has, sweetie, and he needs to rest. It's the same owie from earlier." Corin hugged her back.

"Tatey be okay?" she asked tearfully.

Corin ruffled her hair. "He will be, sweetie, he just needs to rest."

"Can I hugs him better? Likes my Papi does to me?" She smiled at Tir as she spoke.

"As long as you are careful, then yes."

All three men watched as she climbed down from Corin's lap and tiptoed over to the bed. Grabbing the stool that was beside the bed, she clambered up to lean half on the bed, half off. She rested her little head on Tate's arm, gently wrapped the other arm around Tate's neck, leaned in and kissed him on the cheek. "You gets better, Tatey, then we plays." With another quick kiss, she climbed down, walked back to her father and held her arms out for a cuddle.

Tir happily obliged his daughter, hugging her tight. It was where he wanted her anyway, safe, in his arms. Coughing to clear his throat, he sat down in one of the chairs.

"Thank you for saving my daughter." Tir focused on Corin. "I still want to know everything that happened. I still have a lot of questions. Stars, I'm still angry, but I'm with Kel. I don't see that you are the men who took my daughter. I'm sorry I didn't trust you sooner."

Corin smiled sadly. "Thank you, for saying that. We didn't take her, and I do understand why you reacted the way you did. But please, understand this, we could never hurt a child. Children are to be loved, cherished and protected at all times. They are a gift and to be treasured. I don't know who took your daughter, but I promise once Tate is fully awake we will do everything in our power to help you." He could only hope it would be enough. He had a feeling these were not the sort of men you wanted to get on the wrong side of.

Tir quickly met Kel's gaze with his own, seeing he believed Corin. "I can give you till he is awake, as long as it's not too long. I still need to find out who they are."

"It won't be. Tate is starting to wake more and more. I would guess no more than two days, quite possibly less. If that's alright?"

Tir sighed. "Okay, I can give you that long, but then I really will need to know everything, from the very beginning."

"We can do that." Corin assured, surprised this meeting was going better than he had dared hope for. "I can describe the men for you, but they are all dead, bar one man, and he will be long gone. Tate will probably have a lot more insight than I do— he's the military man." Corin scrubbed a hand over his face. "I can tell you where the caves we found her were. Will that help?"

"It would, we can send a squad to check. Thank you."

"At least it will be a start for you."

"Good. I am thankful, you know. Please, do not, for even one moment, think I am not. You brought my little girl home to me. She is everything to me and there will never be enough words or enough ways that I can thank you for that. We were losing hope that we would ever see her again, there were no traces, no signs, nothing that told us where she was or who had her. If it hadn't been for you…" Tir let his words trail off, unable to complete the sentence.

Kel hugged his brother and niece tight, a solitary tear trickling down his own cheek at the thought of what they could have lost.

Corin had to clear his throat, overcome with the emotion at seeing the pure love radiating from the group in front of him. He could see just how much Eliya was loved. He had to wonder where the little girl's mother was. It made him realise that this family had likely already suffered more loss than anyone should have to bear. He surreptitiously wiped the tears from his own cheeks, choosing to focus on Tate and his equipment as Kel walked his brother out of the room.

—————— ⟩O⟨ ——————

Apart from that small talk he had with Tir, Corin whiled away the hours with Kel, talking about their hopes and dreams, of the past and the future. They traded childhood memories and stories, bringing laughter and sometimes the occasional tear to their eyes. For each hour they spoke, the bond between them continued to grow.

Corin was inexplicably drawn to Kel. Oh, he knew it was pointless, knew it would likely lead to heartbreak, and no doubt his, yet he couldn't find the will, or the strength, to stop it from happening. Every time Kel touched him, it was like an electric shock. He spent the entire time in Kel's company at least semi-hard. Those innocent touches between them sent his pulse skyrocketing, his cock pointing straight up and weeping, begging for attention. While he grew frustrated at the time they spent apart, they were also a blessed relief from the sheer physical ache he constantly experienced whilst in Kel's presence.

When he woke up the next day, he realised just how thankful he was that they hadn't questioned him fully yet, although it would be happening soon. Tir had to be at the end of his patience. There was no doubt in his mind they would want to know everything. Tate was spending most of time awake now. He was in less pain with every passing hour and therefore less med-crazy, which, while it was a good thing, it would no doubt be the cause of the upcoming talk they were facing.

Unbeknownst to Corin, in a room further down the corridor, Kel and Tir were sat talking to their father, Chieftain Damron Tharn.

"We must know what they know and we need to know it now. I don't care how you come by this information, but you will get it. Do I make myself clear?" Chieftain Damron Tharn was livid. Not only had his granddaughter been kidnapped, but his two sons seemed to

84

be blindly accepting the story these two men were telling them. "How can you possibly trust them? I fail to see what you see. They should be prisoners and held in the cells."

Kel and Tir exchanged confused glances. It was only two days ago he was adamant that no one should be questioning them. Kel wasn't going to say that to his father, mind you, not when he was being this volatile.

"Father." Damron shot Kel a look of pure annoyance. "Sire. One of them is seriously injured, the other a doctor. Between them, just what do you think they could do? We aren't in any danger, so keeping them in one of the guest suites seems sensible. They brought us back Eliya, damn it! I think their actions so far ensures they get treated well and given a bit of time to recover." Kel gritted his teeth, knowing it would do no good to get angry at his father.

"You're just thinking with your cock. Don't think I don't see how you look at the doctor, son, even though I told you to stay away. Who knows what's going on inside your head? I find I cannot simply trust your judgement on this. You're compromised."

"Sire!" Kel exclaimed, stunned his father would think he was so easily swayed in this by his libido.

"Father, I stand by Kel's decision." Tir crossed his arms over his chest and stood his ground. "They brought her back, never demanded anything. If we lock them in the dungeon and go to any means necessary to get the information we want, well, it makes us no better than the men who kidnapped Eliya. We are not them and I won't act like them, no matter how much I want to find those responsible." Sighing, he continued. "Look we will go and talk to them. At least let us try this way first."

"Fine. But I want information soon or I will have them moved to the cells." Damron held up his hand as Kel tried to speak "Enough, son, it's my final say on the matter. I suggest you get me the information I want if you don't like it. You're dismissed." Damron waved them away before turning to the advisor at his side.

Kel shot his brother a look and they both swiftly left the room, not wanting to incur any more of their father's ire.

"What's going on, Tir?" Kel demanded as soon as they were out of earshot from their father. "I've never seen him this worked up, this volatile. He's changing, and not for the better. There has to be more going on. What do you know?"

Tir sighed. "He's getting pressure from the other clans. Chieftain Martellon wants his daughter married off and with child. He wants to secure his succession and he wants to form an alliance with us to do so."

"But it would mean, I… it would have to be me. You know Martellon is old school. He isn't going to accept you as his daughter's husband when you're a widower with your own child."

"I know, Kel, I know. It's why I couldn't tell you." Tir shot Kel a sympathetic look.

"But I like men. I mean, sure I always understood one day I would have to find a way to have a child. I accepted what was coming and hoped I could either find my truemate or make some sort of arrangement with a woman to have one. I can't marry her, Tir. My life will be over, and she's a bloody nightmare. The clan has never had a problem with same sex relationships. I know they don't normally end up as mates, just lovers, but still…"

"I know, brother. I wish I could find a way out of it for you."

"Damn it!" Kel cried out, turning and punching the wall beside him. His knuckles split open, blood dripped down his hand and onto the floor before his knees buckled and he sat down heavily. Looking up at Tir with anguish in his eyes, he begged his brother, for what he didn't know. There was nothing Tir could do. "Not now, please, Tir, it can't happen, not now. I finally found someone who calls to my soul. If he weren't an Offworlder, I might almost be tempted to say he was my truemate. I know, I know, no one's truemate has ever been from the same sex before, but, Tir I feel compelled to be with him. Truemates are rare anyway, so we can't really say what the clan would think. Remember there are some same sex matings, not many, but some."

"Oh, brother." Tir sat and drew Kel into his arms as his tears fell. "If he is your truemate, and I don't know if it's a possibility, but if he is, then you have to be with him, no matter the consequences."

"I don't see how I can," Kel cried. "If Father were to find out, I would be banished, and while I could deal with anything he did to me, I know he would take it out on Corin. He would blame him, hunt him, hurt him and set about to destroy him. I can't put Corin through so much pain. I already feel too much for him. I can't let anything happen to him. I don't understand what has been going on with Father lately."

"Then what's the alternative, Kel? Deny him? Marry Teriva? What sort of life would you have? She's evil to the core and far, far, worse than her father. She will make your life hell." Throwing his arm around his brother, Tir pulled him up to standing. "Come on, brother, let's go see your man. What better way to see how he really feels then tell him you're injured?" Tir waggled his eyebrows at his brother, drawing a laugh from him as they made their way to their guests.

Tate was glad to finally be awake. While he couldn't deny the rest was good for his body, he was growing increasingly concerned for Corin. Emotions were playing out on his face and behind his eyes. There was hope, fear, love, confusion, apprehension, worry and anticipation. There was a nervousness to his movements that made Tate wonder what happened while he was resting. "What's going on, Doc?" Tate asked. "You seem off and don't even bother trying to deny it."

"I've fucked up, Tate. I'm so screwed." Corin huffed out a breath.

"Talk to me, Doc."

"I think I'm falling in love, Tate. I can't explain it. I don't understand it. I'm so confused, but it's happening whether I want it to or not." Corin laughed bitterly as he finally admitted out loud what was happening.

"I take it you mean Kel?"

"Yeah."

"Why is it fucked up, Doc?" Tate's forehead furrowed with confusion.

"Because he's all set to lead a clan and I'm a bloody nobody. We crashed on this fucking planet, we have no idea when we will get rescued, or where the other guys are. What happens if we get to leave? If I do fall in love with him, I'm just going to have to leave him? Yeah, that's going to suck, and not in a good way. It doesn't really matter, I guess, as I doubt he's gay anyway."

"Ok. First of all, Doc, you're not screwed, you've not fucked up, alright? Now come here." As Corin sat down, Tate threw his arms around him in a hug. "Secondly, let's just say everything worked out. There isn't anything stopping you staying here. With the way the admiral screwed you over, and is probably going to continue to do so, it might be difficult for you back within the Alliance and the Corps. This place is a neutral world so the admiral can't get you here."

"I hadn't thought about what this being a neutral world would mean. Still, it doesn't matter really. I don't see Kel returning my feelings. There's been no indication he feels anything for me other than someone who helped rescue his niece. I somehow doubt he's gay, Tate."

"I wouldn't be so sure, Doc." Hugging Corin tight, Tate continued, "I've seen the way he looks at you when I'm half asleep and you're not looking at him. I think whatever it is you feel, he's feeling it too."

"Wishful thinking, Tate, wishful thinking."

"We shall see." Tate smiled at Corin, throwing in a wink, making Corin throw a small smile his way.

Just then, the door was pushed open and both Kel and Tir came bounding in. Kel looked like shit and both Corin and Tate shot each other a look.

"Corin, any chance you can take a look at my brother?" Tir requested.

"What happened?" Corin jumped up, his brows curled in worry.

"He got some bad news and didn't take it too well. He got into a fight with a stone wall about it. Bloody idiot! As you can guess, the wall came off better." Tir forced Kel to hold out his hand to Corin.

Corin leapt off the bed, racing over to the other side of the room to grab his med pack. When he was at Kel's side, he gently pushed on his shoulder, forcing him to sit in the chair in front of him, muttering to himself about "stupid bloody macho men," and he set about inspecting the damage.

Tate and Tir exchanged amused glances as they took in the scene before them. Kel was sat there looking like a puppy who was being told off. He was pouting and looking at Corin with a contrite expression on his face. Corin was in turn fussing over him, while cleaning the wounds gently with an exasperated but loving look on his face.

Tir turned to Tate and whispered, "Pretty sure we can say whatever's going on is mutual."

"Yup," Tate agreed, "they can't keep their eyes off each other. If they don't get their fingers out of their own asses soon, we're going to have to give them a nudge in the right direction. You up for the challenge?"

"Definitely. I think Corin is exactly what my brother needs. He'll call him on his shit and challenge him." Tir was laughing heartily at the thought of just how Corin would make his brother suffer and work for his affection.

"And I can see Kel giving Corin the strength he needs. He won't say it, but having to stay in such extreme control in emergencies takes its toll on him. It would be good for him to have someone look out for him and take control when needed."

"I am sorry, you know." Tir spoke in a normal voice now they were no longer discussing the pair of lovebirds.

"For what?"

"For letting my emotions get the better of me. I should never have punched you and I truly am sorry for what it did to you. I was just pissed off and scared, angry and desperate."

"It's cool. I really do understand. I doubt anyone could honestly say they would have behaved any differently." Tate smiled at Tir. "Now how is the little lady? Is she recovering from her ordeal?"

"I would say so. She's being a bit petulant as we won't let her visit you again, especially as you've needed to rest. She's certainly making her displeasure known."

"I don't remember her visiting. When was that?"

"Early yesterday. You were pretty out of it, but she wasn't to be denied. It was easier than dealing with her tantrum."

"Bless her. Your daughter is such a sweetie and I'd be glad to have her company." Tate couldn't repress the grin that appeared on his face as he thought about the precocious little girl.

"As long as you're sure? I don't want to make things hard for you." Tir understood just how much he owed these men. He would never knowingly cause them any more pain, physical or otherwise.

"Absolutely."

They both looked back at Kel and Corin in time to see Kel drag Corin into a tight hug.

"My thanks, Corin," Kel muttered into Corin's hair, but made no move to release him.

Sighing, Corin replied, "It was my pleasure," before hesitantly putting his own arms around Kel. The tension seemed to ease from both of them. It was almost a visible draining of tension from every muscle. Neither of them made any move to withdraw from the hug, and in fact, relaxed deeper into each other. They were soaking up each other's presence and revelling in it. Both of them had their eyes shut, lost in the feelings of simply holding one another. Serenity and a sense of rightness descended around them.

"Yup. The feeling is definitely mutual," Tate whispered to Tir. "Want to help me next door for a few minutes? Give them some peace?"

"Gladly." Tir turned, and in a swift move worthy of a hero in those epic love stories he read to Eliya every night, scooped Tate up into his arms and carried him into the reception room of the suite.

Tate jokingly sighed, "my hero" at him while fluttering his eyelashes.

"Don't make me laugh or I'll drop you!" was Tir's swift response.

Kel pulled back from hugging Corin slightly, loving the way he fit in his arms. It made him feel strong and powerful and brought his protective instincts to the fore. With a trembling hand, he gently cupped Corin's cheek, his calluses scraping gently over the stubble there. His thumb moved to brush softly over Corin's full lips. They opened under his touch with a soft gasp. Corin couldn't believe how big that thumb felt as it grazed his lips.

Corin's eyes shot open and searched Kel's face. He could see a swirl of emotions in Kel's gaze as he leaned down and slowly inched closer as though giving Corin all the time in the seven universes to refuse or pull away. Corin could do neither, instead he pushed up onto his toes to close the distance. A compulsion within him demanded he stay just out of reach of Kel's lips, waiting for his next move, but he certainly felt both their heartbeats racing with anticipation.

Just as Kel's lips touched his, Corin's eyes fluttered closed again. The kiss was achingly slow, tender and romantic as Kel's tongue softly explored his lips. Corin's fingers drifted from Kel's back up to his neck, his arms stretching up more than he was used to as Kel was so tall, softly brushing his fingertips over the exposed skin, making Kel shiver. Corin's body arched into Kel as Kel took the kiss deeper, exploring Corin's mouth, tongue sweeping every part of him like Kel was trying to commit it all to memory. There was no hurried pace, no awkwardness, no frantic jerky movements and no desperation. It was simply a kiss, a kiss that tasted of love and belonging.

Pulling back, Kel rested his forehead against Corin's, taking a moment to simply breathe in his scent, to enjoy the purity of the moment before the rest of the world intruded on them again. There was no doubt in his mind now. Corin was his truemate, Offworlder or not, man or not. He was everything Kel had ever wanted, everything he had ever needed, his one and only, forever.

Caressing Corin's face again, Kel smiled at him. Corin's heart stuttered at the beauty of the smile directed his way. "You're beautiful, Corin."

Corin tried to pull away from Kel, despite how he loved the feeling of being held by Kel, despite how safe and protected he felt being in the arms of the larger man. "Beautiful? What sort of man is beautiful?"

"You are." Kel drew him back into his arms. "Inside and out. The way you care for others, your integrity, your honesty, your determination, your spirit, your compassion, it all adds up to a beautiful package. It was meant as a compliment." Kel smiled.

"Really?" Corin's eyes were full of wonder. "You really see me that way?"

"Really. Can't you tell I'm completely captivated by you? You're in my mind, my heart, my soul. I know it's crazy, I know there are things we need to talk about, but make no mistake, Corin, I. Want. You." Kel punctuated each word with a swift kiss on Corin's lips. "I want you in my life, in my bed, by my side, in my thoughts, in my heart." Kel stared into Corin's eyes as he spoke. "I want to claim you, make you mine." An anxious look descended on his face. "Do you not feel the same? I would understand. It would hurt to withdraw from you, but I would understand. I know I cannot possibly be good enough for you. You deserve so much more than I can possibly give."

Corin tilted his head back and looked Kel in the eyes, getting distracted by trying to work out if they were actually green or blue, before his shock made him burst into quiet laughter, a slightly harsh tone to it. "Not good enough? Stars, Kel, it's the other way around. You're going to end up leading a clan one day. I'm nobody. You're loved by the clan from what I can tell, you're honest, hardworking, respected, you have a core of strength I can only envy, and frankly, you're downright sexy."

Kel's face lit up at being called sexy.

"I've all but got myself kicked out of the Medical Corps, my career is in ruins. What can I possibly bring to you?" Corin shook his head at Kel as he spoke.

"You bring hope, peace, light and love to my life. You are not nobody. You saved a man when no one else would step up, no matter the consequences. You saved my niece. You brought her back to us, risking your own life to do it. You are the most selfless, amazing man I know. Please, Corin, give us a chance. You have to feel this." Kel almost begged as his eyes were beseeching at the same time as he dragged his thumb back and forth over Corin's lips.

Corin shivered at the feelings Kel was producing as he touched his lips. It felt so large, mind you, Kel was so much larger than any man he had ever been with. It made him feel so safe. "There is no way I could ever say no to you, Kel. I'm here, and I won't go anywhere unless you send me away. I may not feel good enough for you, but I'm not strong enough to walk away from this, from you... So yes. Yes, I want to be with you, yes, I want to give us a chance."

Kel's only response was to take Corin's lips in another kiss. It was as though the green light from Corin released a hunger in him. He all but hauled him into his lap. His hands moved down to cup the ass that had tormented him from the moment he saw it. He moaned in appreciation of just how perfect it felt in his hands. Kel was thrilled at how well Corin fit to him. He had been worried the size difference would be too much for them both, having always been with men who were so much bigger than Corin. But it felt perfect, Corin felt perfect.

Corin's passion matched Kel's. He couldn't get close enough to Kel, he shifted as he straddled him, hungry for more. For more contact, more kisses, more touching. Just more. The movement lined their cocks up, and with the first gentle thrust of his hips, both of them moaned in pleasure. Stars, how he loved being wrapped up in the larger man's arms. His hands reached down and worked on unlacing Kel's trousers as he pushed his own down his thighs.

Kel's hands were tracing patterns over his ass cheeks, winding their way closer and closer to his hole. The first tentative brush over his hole saw him cry out. Corin's hand finally grasped Kel's cock and he sighed in pleasure. It was long, thick and slightly curved. Simply touching it made him ache to be filled. He gasped as he ran his hand down the length. Kel's cock was different, with small raised bumps up and down the shaft. It was unlike anything he'd seen before, but he loved how they felt against his palm.

He moaned in anticipation of the sheer size of it, of what those bumps would feel like dragging along his inner walls, what they would feel like across his prostate. Lining his own cock up alongside Kel's, he started a steady rhythm going, twisting as he neared the top. His stroke didn't reach the bottom of Kel's cock, as it was so much bigger, but it didn't seem to matter. They were both desperately thrusting now, searching for more friction as Corin tightened his hand around them both. The kiss was becoming carnal. Kel was possessing his mouth in a simulation of how he would possess his body.

"I'm close, Kel." Corin shuddered as the sensations swarmed his body.

"Then come for me, love. I want to see you, feel you, hear you come." With those words, he gently pushed the tip of his finger into Corin.

That was all it took. Corin came screaming Kel's name.

One look at the ecstasy on Corin's face pushed Kel over the edge, his cum joining Corin's, spurting over Corin's hand and pooling on their stomachs.

Collapsing onto Kel, hand still wrapped around their softening cocks, Corin gently rested his head in the crook of Kel's neck, snuggling deep into the larger man's chest. He slowly let go of their cocks, too sensitive to endure even the slightest touch and wrapped both arms around Kel's glorious chest.

Kel's arms immediately followed suit and wrapped tightly around him as their breathing slowly gentled. Kel was softly stroking

Corin's back. No words were needed, they simply luxuriated in the peace of being in each other's arms.

Chapter Nine

Tir and Tate were sat in the reception room where Eliya soon joined them. She was on Tate's lap against Tir's better judgement. He found he couldn't deny her, though. She looked so happy sat there. He hadn't realised just how worried she'd been over Tate. They really had bonded during her ordeal, and he had to admit, both Tate and Corin were remarkable men. It warmed his heart to know despite everything she went through, she was still the same little girl she had been before, playful and kind with an impish streak a mile wide. Tate was twisted around her little finger it seemed as she was sitting fiddling with his hair, styling it however she saw fit. Tate kept getting revenge on her by tickling her sides, and the peals of laughter ringing out from her warmed Tir's heart.

Their conversation was light in intensity, partly in deference to Eliya being there, partly as they were waiting for the lovebirds to come out of the bedroom. Tir was worried though. He was glad his brother had finally stopped fighting his attraction to the guy, but he knew, based on their earlier conversation, Kel would no doubt feel guilty. Guilty about what he was dragging Corin in to, guilty about the risk they would be taking. Tir was adamant that he would do anything to protect his brother and, by extension, Corin. He was sure once Tate was fully recovered he too would help keep Corin safe. He was going to make damn sure his brother did nothing to throw this opportunity aside.

Just then the bedroom door opened and the two men stepped through. A deep blush stained Corin's face despite his skin tone and Tir couldn't help but laugh. His brother wore a deeply satisfied and happy expression on his face. Corin's hand was clasped tightly in Kel's much larger one and despite his obvious embarrassment he made no move to pull it away.

"Corin!" Eliya cried out, as she climbed gently off of Tate before racing up to Corin and jumping up at him. He caught her and twirled her around.

"Hey, Kiddo, did you miss me then? I mean what it's only been, twenty four hours?" he teased.

"Uh huh." She wrapped her little arms tightly around his neck.

"What about me?" Kel laughed. "Does your favourite uncle not even get a hello?"

Eliya leaned over and planted a wet, smacking kiss on his cheek. "Lub you, Unca Kel"

"As I love you, Ely." Kel ruffled her curls as he spoke.

The two men made their way over and joined Tate and Tir.

"You shouldn't be up, Tate. I'm sorry we made you leave," Corin whispered while his blush deepened.

Tate laughed, softly saying, "Prince Charming over here carried me so it's all good."

"Damn, I'm sorry I missed seeing that."

"No, you're not! Are you telling me you would have rather watched me than do what you were doing?" Tate teased.

Corin pretended to think about it for a moment. "Okay, you have a point there!" He laughed. They hadn't been talking as quietly as they thought and laughter erupted from both brothers.

"Ely, time for you to go back to your lessons." Tir held out his arms to his daughter.

"Oh, but, Papi, I want to stay here with my friends." She whined with an adorable little pout scrunching up her face.

"You can see them later, I promise." He motioned to Naris Vilinx, the head of his personal guard, to take her. They could hear her pouting and moaning at the poor guy as they made their way down the corridor.

The atmosphere in the room grew more serious, all of them knowing what needed to be discussed.

"I am sorry, but we are going to need to know everything now. We've held off as long as we can, but I need to find the men responsible. Please, don't think we don't believe what you have already told us, but we need to go over everything closely. We still need to know why Eliya was taken." Tir ground his jaw together at the mere thought of whoever had taken her.

"We will start from the very beginning. Trust me, we want to find whoever is responsible for kidnapping Eliya as well," Tate vowed.

Over the course of the next few hours, the two of them filled the brothers in on everything. From the first hit on the battlecruiser to the minute they walked into the war room. The two brothers sat in stunned silence for a moment before Tir grabbed the closest thing to him, a decanter filled with water, before hurling it across the room, the crystal splintering on contact with the wall. Tiny shards fell like raindrops, and the water was making them glisten like the dew on the grass in the early mornings.

"I'll fucking kill them with my bare hands. How dare they treat my daughter like she was nothing but dirt?" Tir was shaking with pure rage as he pictured how his daughter had been tied up. His hands flexed as though they were gripping a broadsword, preparing to strike. Taking deep breaths, he forced himself to regain control. However, his eyes maintained their anger and resolve.

Tate wondered momentarily if he should be worried for whomever had kidnapped Eliya, before realising they deserved no sympathy and he was more than likely to join Tir in his vengeance.

Once calm descended back on the group, it was Kel who broke the silence. "Okay, firstly I'm amazed the pair of you have managed to survive as well as you did. What's more, Corin, you have some serious skills to keep Tate alive the way you did. I know for sure there is no way our doctor would have managed it."

"Yeah, well, you know what I think of your doctor." Corin smirked at him.

"Indeed I do, love." Kel winked. "So, the squad we sent found nothing helpful in the caves and there was no trail to follow. Can you describe those kidnappers again for me?"

"Sure." Corin smiled at him. "They ranged in height, but average to me rather than as tall as you guys. Their skin seemed really thick and leathery. It was a combination of browns, all mottled and streaked. They all had brilliant white hair. While the rest of them seemed dirty and unkempt, their hair was clean and well cared for. When they were fighting, they did a lot of it with blades, but when one of them lost his blade he suddenly grew claws where his hands should have been. The blood they spilled was green."

"Sounds like the Tremack people," Kel groaned. "They are a clan of mercenary shape shifters. Over the decades their clan has weakened and their abilities have lessened. Most of them can only do partial shifts. They aren't known for their hard work. They will do anything to take what they can without working for it. It's partly why they are dying out. They hire themselves out for the dirty work no one else will do. It's unlikely we would be able to get any information out of them. They pride themselves on keeping their deals quiet. It's why they are as successful as they are. We would be better focusing on the man who was present."

"From what you have said he must be the man who hired them, then." Both brothers nodded as Tate took over the talking from Corin. "He was tall, certainly the same height as you, Tir, possibly slightly taller. He was thin, almost ill-looking thin, and his face was really ragged and weather beaten. His hair was jet black, framing his face and flowing down his back. It was odd, the clothes he wore were so out of place there. It was almost as if he was called there at a moment's notice. It was the kind of clothes I could imagine someone would wear for high society occasions. It was all gems and soft materials. Definitely not something your average person would wear every day, let alone out in the wilds."

"From your description, I can only limit it down to three clans, it could be any of them." Kel groaned in frustration. "Would you recognise him if you saw him again?"

"Honestly? I don't think I could." Tate shook his head. "I was in so much pain and weak, I can't be sure I would pick out the right person."

"I would." Corin was positive. "I can see him clearly in my mind. There is no way I wouldn't recognise the bastard responsible for doing this to Eliya."

"You're sure?" Tir's eyes were pleading for it to be true.

"Oh, I'm very sure," Corin promised.

"So all we have to do is get Corin in a situation where he can see members of all three clans." Tir mulled over how they could arrange such a situation.

A low growl came from Kel's direction. "I don't like the idea of him being put in danger."

"I know." Corin smiled at him. "But I'll do it anyway and you'll let me, for Eliya's sake."

"You will have protection at all times, babe, I insist," Kel grumbled. Corin simply nodded. "Not one word, brother, I mean it." Kel growled as he caught Tir laughing at him.

"Babe?" Corin cocked his head.

"Uh, too soon for you? Because it feels right to me." Kel's gaze was looking anywhere but at Corin.

"No, actually, I don't know why, but it feels right to me too. I like it." Corin's face lit up his smile was so bright.

Kel's gaze shot straight to Corin's smile. "Good." His eyes glittered with happiness.

The next few days were spent with Kel and Tir trying to arrange how they would get Corin to see people from all three clans. It was going to be quite tough, but they were almost possessed in their determination to find those responsible for Eliya's kidnapping. Every spare moment Kel possessed was spent with Corin. Kel had spent a lot of time thinking over Tir's words. He never considered there would be such a compulsion to be with his truemate. Not like this. He missed him when he wasn't in the same room. While the rational part of his mind understood this was due to the bonding process, it didn't make it any easier. He was also worried, so deeply worried it drove him to seek out his brother.

"Brother, I need to ask something and I cannot go to father or the clan elders."

"Oh? Sounds interesting." Tir waggled his eyebrows.

Kel snorted. "Yeah, you might not think so in a minute. I need to talk about the bonding process. Now I know what's supposed to happen in a normal situation, but let's face it, my situation is anything but normal."

"Oh, for fuck's sake, please tell me I am not about to have a discussion about sex with my brother," Tir grumbled.

"I'm afraid so."

"Alright, scar me for life, why don't you? Go on." Tir laughed.

"Well, I know in a traditional mating part of the bonding occurs during sex to boost the chances of pregnancy. I know my bumps would pulse, helping to form the bond so my truemate would have increased chances of becoming pregnant compared to not being truemates. I know the ridges are the part of sex which eventually completes the bond. I don't understand all the chemistry, biology and mechanics behind it, but I understand the general principle."

"Yeah, they are the part which completes the bond."

"So my question is, brother, if my truemate is a man and an Offworlder, well, while the ridges may release the bonding compound, is it going to work? While I feel he is my truemate, will we be able to truly become truemates? Will the elders even recognise my mating?"

"Oh, Kel, I wish I knew. I have no idea if the compound will have any effect, but there is one thing I do know, you don't need the compound to activate to be truemates. It's not like you'll be trying to get him pregnant so in some senses whether the compound releases or not won't matter. The part I would be most concerned about if I was you is whether the elders are prepared to accept you as truemates and record it in the register. If they won't, then who would you get to perform the mating ceremony? If you aren't registered and mated officially, then he won't be given recognition as your mate. He's likely to face being treated as a concubine. You know what clan gatherings are like. He's going to have to be strong to deal with the attitude and treatment he gets." Tir sighed.

"I'm not trying to put you off being with him. I think you two are perfect for each other and you deserve every bit of happiness you can get. He's a good man, Kel, and he really is perfect for you. He will challenge you just the right amount, but will never be reckless. He will understand the dangers you face, the pressure of your position, and support you in whatever way he can. In time, once he knows our ways, he will become a key advisor for you. While you focus more on the political and militarial aspects, he will likely focus on the people, the emotions and the softer side of things." Tir held up his hand to stop Kel talking before he even could utter a single word. "No. I'm not saying he's soft at all, but he is a doctor. He will be drawn to that side of our people far more than you will."

"True, and I guess it's what makes him such a perfect match for me. That is why it hurts so much to think of him never being given his rightful status as my truemate."

"Well, you will just have to fight to change it. Know I will be with you every step of the way. We will fight together. We should consider talking to Alix and Kastain about it in the future. If anyone can help, they can." Tir grabbed his brother in a bone-crunching hug, trying in more ways than one to show just how much he supported Kel in this.

"So, back to those three clans. How about we start by introducing him to the Estrivia Clan. You know Niko is a good man. He's progressive like us. His father is a good Chieftain. You know we are making a decent new generation of leaders. I'm hoping it's not them involved. I seriously doubt it, but we have to rule his clan out."

"You're right, it's a good place to start. Oh shit, that means tomorrow night. They are here to confer with our elders on border issues." Kel pinched his nose as he stared into space, reluctance and a feeling of being overwhelmed by everything were fighting for dominance in his mind.

"At least this way you don't have too long to get worked up about it, brother." Tir laughed.

"Yeah, you're not helping things here," Kel raised one eyebrow before tipping his chin up at his brother. "How about we spar? Anything to help me get rid of some of my frustration, and it's about time I kicked your ass again."

"Oh man, fine, but if you mark me, Eliya will have words!" Tir smirked.

"Your daughter is far too protective of you. I swear that girl is a little tyrant in the making." Kel laughed.

"You love her just the way she is and don't try to deny how much you dote on her." Tir knocked his shoulder into Kel.

"Shut it, old man," Kel teased, laughing before running off to the training yard.

"Oh, it's on!" Tir ran after his brother laughing.

Corin and Tate were sat in comfortable chairs opposite each other as they gazed out of the window. It had become their favourite place while Tate was recovering. They smiled as they watched Tir chase after Kel, catching him in a flying tackle. They were having a great time laughing at the antics of the two brothers as they playfully fought, drawing a crowd of guards and soldiers alike. Corin was sure he could see money changing hands as some of the men appeared to be betting on the outcome.

"It's good to see them blowing off steam," Tate commented. "They've been so stressed out over this kidnapping hassle and of course their father."

"Wait, what? What about their father?" Corin wondered.

"Has Kel not spoken to you about it?"

"Uh, no."

"Oh."

Corin narrowed his eyes at his friend. "What, Tate? Tell me."

"I thought maybe Kel had spoken about it to you. Tir was telling me you two must be worried about it all."

"Worried about what? Tate, what the fuck is going on?"

"Kel's father is objecting to him being with you. He doesn't approve of the match." Tate grimaced at Corin. "I'm sorry."

Corin sucked in a breath, a pit forming in his stomach. If Kel's father didn't want them to be together, how likely was it they would survive as a couple? There was enough going against them as it was without any added stress.

"Shit, this is fucked up, Tate. What's the point of carrying on with it then? I might as well just walk away."

Tate shot a look at Corin. "Don't do this. This is probably why Kel never told you about it. I don't think he cares what his father thinks."

"I should walk away, I know I should."

"I'm telling you, Corin, don't do this. Kel loves you."

Corin drew in a sharp breath, his heart starting to hammer painfully in his chest. "What? No, he doesn't. He's never said anything to me. How could you possibly know?" he asked Tate.

"Are you telling me you two haven't said the words to each other yet?" Tate was stunned. It was written all over both their faces. How could they not realise how each other felt? "Damn it, Corin, your man adores you. You need to man up and tell him."

"I can't, Tate."

"You can, buddy, you're just scared. Look, I know you've been burned by men in the past, but Kel isn't like other men."

"Burned? It was worse than burned, Tate. There is some of my past I can't even tell you. But that aside, I found Roccen screwing some hot young twink in our bed when I came back from the hospital having gone to check on his mother! I mean, who the fuck does that?"

"Yeah, exactly, which tells you the guy was a total douche. What happened was not on you, my friend. It was all on him and his need to go for all out prickishness."

Corin burst out laughing. "Is prickishness even a word?"

"Meh, who knows, it just seemed fitting!"

"You, my friend, are one of a kind, you know that, right?"

"Aww, the big softy doctor loves me, is it time for kissy wissies and huggy wuggies?" Tate taunted Corin.

A resigned laugh slipped from Corin's lips. "Fine, you got me out of my pity party here, but don't go thinking this changes anything."

"Corin, all joking aside, please, just talk to him. Tell him how you're feeling. You two work. Looking at you together gives the rest of us hope we can find our own special, epic love. It makes us hope there is someone out there in the universe who is just for us, our soulmate."

"Soulmates? Who mentioned soulmates?" Corin scoffed defensively.

"Stars, Corin, how can you say otherwise? I saw your reaction when you first set eyes on him. Yeah, I might have been in a lot of pain and trying to protect you and Eliya, but I can damn well recognise a look like that. Seriously, Corin, have you ever felt anything even close to the intensity you felt?" Corin shook his head at Tate. "Exactly. I never believed it before now, but you, my friend, fell in love at first sight. What's more, you lucky bastard, he fell in love right back. Trust in those feelings."

Corin sat thinking about the first time he set eyes on Kel. Tate was right. He really had felt such an overwhelming surge of emotions for the man. It almost blindsided him with the intensity. What's more, for every second he spent with the man he found him even more appealing. Sure, he was protective, bossy at times and stubborn, but recognising those flaws and loving him anyway? Wait, shit, did he really just mean the L word? Oh man, he did. He was so screwed.

Tate looked on smiling as it became obvious from the look of stunned comprehension on Corin's face, he finally realised he was totally in love with Kel.

"Now enough of the serious conversation. I want to ogle your man, because, damn, he is mighty fine!" Tate whistled at the brothers still grappling around in the practice yard.

"Hey, get your own!" Corin smacked Tate over the head.

"I wish!" Tate smiled sadly.

They both turned back to the window, happy to while away the morning ogling the men. Those naked torsos on display made some damn fine viewing. *Who wouldn't want to spend the time examining their rippling six packs and those delicious V's of the men's hips?*

Kel and Tir were a pile of sweaty limbs, flat on their backs staring up at the sky as they panted to get their breath back. They were uncaring of the dirt they were lying in, nor how it was clinging to their skin. Sweat was trailing down their faces, and their bodies glistened with the effects of their workout. Stomach muscles rippled and their chests heaved as they fought to get air into their lungs. They simply lay there and listened to the guards around them who were laughing and discussing the sparring match. The general consensus, it seemed, was Kel won the fight, although it was a close call as the brothers were finely matched.

"Hmm," Tir muttered eventually, breaking the silence between the two men.

Kel turned to look at him, raising a questioning brow.

"It would appear we have an audience."

"What? The hulking bodies around us didn't clue you in earlier?" Kel laughed at his brother.

"No, you nut, up in the window. Looks like your man has been watching you." Tir laughed as his brother's head snapped up to the window, a goofy smile appearing on his face when he saw Corin was indeed watching him. "Oh man, you're so far gone, brother. He's got you completely hooked."

"Indeed he has, and I couldn't be happier about it. I would do anything for that man, do anything to protect him and make him happy." He smiled at Tir.

"I'm happy for you, brother, but right now it's time to go and make sure this banquet is going ahead and fill Father in on everything."

"Oh, this will be such fun." Kel rolled his eyes as his lips twisted into a smile. "He's really not going to be happy Corin is my truemate."

"Then don't tell him yet," Tir suggested. Kel's eyes shot to his brother in surprise. "I mean it, Kel, you haven't even discussed it with Corin yet. It's probably sensible to talk with him first. No point getting Father and the elders all riled up if Corin isn't going to agree to be mated to you." Kel growled at his brother. "Yeah, I'm not saying it's likely he's going to refuse you, the exact opposite I imagine, but it's sensible to wait anyway."

"You may have a point," Kel muttered. "Okay, how about we get through this first banquet and I'll talk to Corin in a day or two, once things settle down. I don't want to keep throwing things at him to deal with." Kel sighed. "Right, let's go and get things sorted out." He clambered to his feet, offered his hand to Tir and hauled him upright. Throwing his arm around his brother's shoulders, they walked off together, laughing at the fight and arguing about just which one of them won.

Chapter Ten

The brothers spent the rest of the day running around in preparation for the visit by the Estrivia Clan. Just as they finished up, Laird Nikoben Dastria walked through the door.

"Well, good day to you, my fine friends, and how is everything in the world of the Derin?" Niko smiled as he grabbed them each into a hug.

"Niko, good to see you." Tir smiled at the man. More than ever he was pleased they had a good relationship with the next head of the Estrivian Clan.

"Tir, how is that gorgeous girl of yours? Did she miss her favourite honorary uncle?"

Kel burst out laughing and Niko looked at him questioningly.

"Sorry, Niko, but I think you've lost the top spot in her heart." Kel hugged the man in greeting.

"No chance, it's not possible, say it isn't so!"

"I'm afraid so." Kel smirked.

"So who is this imposter? I'll challenge him to a duel, fight for her honour!" Niko grinned like a fool.

"Why don't you get cleaned up and I'll explain it all tonight," Tir suggested. "Kel, can you make sure our other guests are ready?"

"Will do. It's good to see you, Niko, I look forward to catching up with you." With another quick hug, Kel walked off whistling to himself.

"Wow, he seems happy."

"You have no idea, Niko, no idea. Now go get ready and I'll see you in a bit. We have lots to discuss later."

Niko raised his eyebrows at Tir. "Fine, but you better catch me up on everything. Seems like things have been busy around here."

Leaving Niko at the door to his suite, Tir walked off to get himself and Eliya ready.

Kel was still smiling as he walked into Corin and Tate's suite. He walked straight up to Corin, picked him up and swung him round before kissing him thoroughly.

"Mmm, you miss me, handsome?" A huge grin split Corin's face.

"Yes, and don't think I didn't see you watching me earlier. Like what you saw?" Kel winked at Corin.

"Busted." Tate burst out laughing.

Corin joined in the laughter. "Oh, I don't know, the view could have been better," Corin teased.

Kel growled at him and Corin ran into the bedroom to try to escape him. Corin kept darting around the bed, past the extraordinarily comfortable sofa, nearly knocking over the small side table. He dodged round the chairs at the windows as Kel got closer. He ran back to the bed, jumping and sliding over it. Corin's laughter was echoing off the walls as Kel caught up with him. He felt so small in comparison to Kel. At first he had thought it was going to be an issue, yet now everything about being smaller than Kel made him feel safe, loved and protected. Pinning him to the wall, Kel leaned down and possessed his mouth. It was hot, hard, and carnal in intent. It felt like a flash burn travelling through Corin's body. Every nerve came alive like their sole purpose was to sing for Kel. He submitted to Kel, earning him a growl that his mouth swallowed with a sigh. Kel's hands were everywhere, running over his back, his hips, and his ass. He loved the way Kel's large hands seemed to cover every part of his ass. He was so turned on his hands were shaking as he reached between them and unlaced Kel's trousers, pushing them down his thighs. A tremble went through his body as he realised Kel was commando.

To Kel's surprise, Corin pushed his hands off him. His surprise turned to delight as Corin dropped to his knees and engulfed his cock with his mouth in one smooth move. His mind went into overload.

Never before had someone done this to him. It wasn't something any of his previous lovers wanted to do. They all seemed to be daunted by his size. Corin seemed to have no such reservations.

Kel couldn't stop the sounds he was making. Corin was sucking down his cock with fervour. His tongue kept dipping into his slit as Corin lapped up his precum, and every time he did so, he hummed as though he loved the taste. Those hums were sending waves of pleasure radiating through Kel's body. Kel felt a hand snake down his cock and onto his balls. A gentle tug to them soon saw him groaning and his knees going weak. He threw his arms against the wall in a desperate attempt to brace his body and not collapse onto the floor. The tugging got harder before Corin's mouth pulled off of his cock with a pop. Just as he was about to moan in frustration, Corin took one of his balls into his mouth and sucked. It took everything Kel had in him not to unload there and then. Never had he experienced something so exquisite.

"Corin!" He cried out, panting, his head hanging between his arms, his neck unable to support him, the pleasure was so great. He heard a chuckle and opened his eyes to see Corin looking up at him, eyes shining. Damn, his man really was stunning and he loved everything Corin did to him. He felt a possessive thrill at the way his larger body was caging in Corin's smaller one. His panting was getting faster and he was sure he wouldn't last long. Corin's hand worked his own cock and the sight was beautiful to watch. Moving his gaze to Corin's face had his desire spiralling even higher. The lust and longing etched on Corin's face was driving him crazy. It was calling to the dominant parts of him, making him desperate to claim him, make him his, forever. It was all too much— the sensations, the feelings they were invoking.

"Corin," he pleaded.

"I got you, handsome." Corin smiled as he pulled back before sliding his lips back over his cock.

Kel was so close, he didn't know how much longer he could last against Corin's onslaught. All thought evaporated as Corin took him to the back of his throat and swallowed. That was it, Kel came, screaming Corin's name as stars exploded behind his eyes. His vision started to fade as he struggled to get enough air into his lungs. His knees buckled a second before Corin let his cock slip from his lips and he collapsed to the floor completely spent.

Corin looked on with both pride and amusement at the state of Kel on the floor. His man was lying there in bliss, his eyes constantly blinking and a stunned look on his face. Corin pushed him onto his back before straddling him and raining kisses down over his face. At the same time, he let his fingers trace every ridge of the muscles that covered Kel's abdomen. The soft delicate movements were making Kel shiver and Corin had to suppress a smile at how much he affected this man.

Kel managed to gather the strength to grab the back of Corin's head and bring it down so he could capture Corin's lips. He could taste himself on Corin's tongue and it made him moan. His cock was making a valiant attempt to rise again. Breaking away from the kiss, Kel spoke. "Let me return the favour, babe."

"No need. I came when you did. You looked too hot for me to last." Corin smiled at him as he lay down with him on the floor.

Kel simply tucked him into his side, loving the fact that Corin snuggled in tight. "I'm not complaining, but what brought that on?"

"You looked all hot and sweaty and sexy while you were sparring. It gave me images of what you would look like in bed. I've been semi-hard since. So I decided to jump you." Corin smiled.

Kel burst out laughing at the matter-of-fact way Corin spoke and his heart soared at the simple pleasure of enjoying the moment with his mate.

Chapter Eleven

Corin was getting frustrated. He was supposed to be wearing a pair of leather trousers and they were a bitch to get on and lace up. Kel kept offering to do them up for him. His only response was to let out a frustrated breath. As well as the damned trousers annoying him, Kel was proving to be too distracting for him. The man looked edible in his formal clothes. While he still wore leather, it was a leather kilt. Rather than being bare chested, he instead wore a pale cream tailored linen top. Leather piping ran around the tailored collar of the top. The outfit was completed by leather boots which laced up to the knee. He wore a ceremonial, but still functional, sword in a scabbard at his waist.

"Your help is going to involve taking them back off again." Corin couldn't help but laugh at the lecherous look Kel shot him. Damn, was there a look on Kel he didn't find sexy?

"Well your ass does look mighty fine in those trousers, babe." Kel's appreciation was evident on his face, lust shining in his eyes.

"Behave!"

"Yes, sir!" Kel teased him.

Corin just rolled his eyes in exasperation and finally managed to finish lacing up the accursed trousers. It was still warm, so he chose to only wear his military issue tank top. Besides, it left his wound free, and while it was healing nicely, it still itched like crazy when there was material covering it. He didn't think it would make a good impression on Kel's clan if he spent the entire night rubbing his arm.

Joining Tate in the reception room, he saw Tate must have thought as he did when it came to the clothes. Going for comfort as much as possible and not aggravating his wound.

"Are you sure you feel up to this?" He looked Tate over, checking for any visible signs of pain.

Tate rolled his eyes at him. "Honestly, Doc, I feel alright. Yeah, I'm far from perfect, but it's about time I got up and about. I need to keep fit and on top of things. I can't leave it all up to you after all. Besides, I want to go to the party. You never know, maybe I will find myself a fine specimen of a man just like yours."

"And that's the Tate we know and love." Corin laughed. "I know you're getting better when you start thinking of hot, sweaty man sex."

"You know me, Doc. This place is an untapped source, and you expect me not to want to go? Shame on you, Doc, shame on you."

"Just promise me one thing. If you start to feel tired or sore you will at least tell me, and try to limit any acrobatics, hmm?"

"Yes, mother, I'll be a good little boy." Tate winked at Corin who scowled in return. "Besides, I'm a one man guy now. I'm not looking for a quickie, but it sure doesn't mean I'm not going to enjoy the fine variety on display!" He laughed as Corin returned the favour and rolled his eyes at him.

Kel just stood looking on and laughing at the pair of them. He long ago realised there was never a dull moment around these two; besides, watching the way they were with each other was an interesting insight into the man he was falling deeply in love with.

Just then the door opened and a pink and white tornado whirled into the room, dancing around the three of them. Tir walked in and nodded his head in greeting as he tried to corral his wayward daughter. They were all smiling as she danced about the room, excitement oozing from her at the prospect of a party.

Grabbing Eliya, Kel swung her round in his arms as she squealed in delight. Corin's heart warmed at the sight, before it swiftly plummeted when he realised if he stayed with Kel, he would be preventing him from having his own children. Could he really be responsible for such a future? It was obvious the man as born to be a father.

"I can see the wheels turning there, Doc. What's wrong?" He heard Tate whisper to him.

"What am I doing, Tate? Look at him! How can I deny him any chance of having children? How can I do that to him?"

"Hey, Doc, it's a little early to be thinking about children, don't you think? But if, and when, it's time to consider it, then it's something you will have to discuss together. There are other ways round it as well, you know. Stop panicking and looking for ways out of this. Doc, just for once in your life, give up the control and go with the flow. You need to relax, let Kel take some of the stress, okay?" Tate gave him a quick hug before breaking away, smiling and shaking his head at Kel's questioning look.

"So, Eliya, I have a very serious question to ask my favourite girl." Kel's eyes were crinkling at the corners. "Uncle Niko is downstairs and he was wondering if he was still your favourite not quite real uncle?"

"Unca Niko's here?" Eliya started dancing around in Kel's arms.

"Yes, and he said he must still be your favourite, but I told him he has some competition now."

"He does?" She scrunched up her brow.

"He does, unless you don't think Corin and Tate are also your not quite real uncles?"

"Oh! Oh, ummm, Unca Kel, I donts know, I lubs Unca Niko, but I lubs Uncas Cori and Tatey as well." She looked sad for a moment before she announced, "But it's okay, I'll jus be a lucky girl n habs lots and lots of Uncas, just for me!"

They all laughed as they made their way out of the suite and on down to the party that was being held in the massive banqueting room at the very heart of the keep.

Both Corin and Tate's mouths dropped open at the sight which greeted them. The room was stunning. It reminded Corin of an old rustic lodge. Wooden floors and exposed brickwork formed the shell of the room, but it was the interiors that really made the room amazing. Detailed paintings and tapestries hung around the room. One side of the room was a bank of floor to ceiling windows giving a stunning view of the land surrounding the keep with the mountain off to one side. He could see part of the training yard where guards were still practising. Off to the other side there was a group of children playing games in a field, and a group of women were chatting away whilst keeping an eye on them.

Long tables decorated with crisp white linens ran along the lengths of three of the walls. The middle of the room was left clear. Corin wondered if it was kept that way for dancing. Kel made his way to the far side of the room and walked up to his father, his hand hovering protectively at the back of his smaller mate.

"Sire, you remember the Offworlders, Corin and Tate."

"Yes, I remember." The Chieftain looked down both literally and figuratively at them. He turned to carry on the conversation he was having with one of his advisors, effectively dismissing the group.

Kel's jaw was twitching in annoyance at the behaviour of his father, his hand flexing in a fist at his side. Tir steered the group over to one side where Niko was in an attempt to prevent a scene.

"Alright, babe, remember, if you think you either recognise someone exactly or recognise someone's general appearance, then point them out." Kel's quiet reminder came as he wrapped his hand around Corin's.

"I know, trust me, I want to get the bastards responsible as well."

They were all smiles though as they joined Niko.

"Corin, Tate, I'd like you to meet Laird Nikoben Dastria from Clan Estrivia. Niko, I'd like you to meet Commander Corin Talovich and Lieutenant Commander Tate Riven from the Barin Alliance. They were unfortunate enough to crash onto our planet."

"Ah, but by the looks of things, their loss is most definitely your gain, Kel. Either I am mistaken or you are off the market!" Niko smiled widely at his friend. If it were true, he couldn't be happier for him.

"You bet I am." Kel chuckled while Corin looked embarrassed. He forgot they were still holding hands.

"So are these the gentlemen I have to challenge to a duel for my girl's affection then?"

Corin and Tate looked at each other confused.

"Unca Niko," Eliya whined, "No! They my fwends."

"As long as I am still your favourite," Niko told her.

Her only response was a giggle, earning her a tickle from Niko.

As Niko was distracted, both Kel and Tir leaned in to ask, "Do you recognise him?"

Corin shook his head. "No, it's definitely not him, and looks-wise, he's nothing close to the guy who held Eliya. I would definitely say the guy wasn't from the same clan if Laird Niko is typical looks-wise to his clan members."

This man possessed a completely different build to the man from the caves. Niko was broader than the whip thin man from the caves. His shoulders were wide and tapered down to a narrow waist. He was muscular but not overtly so. His face was defined, but softer than those men from the Derin Clan. His eyes were sea green and he had light brown, curly hair that went to his ears. His face was borderline angelic with full, pouty lips. His eyes sparkled with humour and happiness.

Both Kel and Tir blew out a relieved breath. They really were hoping it wasn't Niko. It would have been a betrayal far greater than either of them could bear. The two clans were extremely close and, as men, they possessed a lifelong friendship with Niko, having spent many a summer staying with Niko or Niko staying with them. They were brought up more as cousins than anything else. Their childhoods were entwined and over the years, it brought the clans closer together. Peace had reigned between the two for the last three decades. It would have had devastating consequences for both clans if it was the Estrivian Clan who had kidnapped Eliya.

"What's going on? And don't tell me it's nothing. You guys are not as subtle as you think, especially when I know you so well." Niko's eyebrows rose in a silent challenge, daring the brothers to deny everything.

Tir tapped his finger against his lips a couple of times, before sighing. "I think it's time we explained a few things, but honestly, it's better we wait until after this dinner. I don't want to risk ears listening in."

"As long as you promise to fill me in, I'll wait. But I want all the other gossip as well." Niko pointedly looked at Corin and Tate.

At the table, the three Lairds were sat with their backs to the wall. Opposite them were Tate, Eliya and Corin, with Eliya sandwiched safely between the two. Tir at first thought it would stop her getting up to too much mischief, but then again with Corin on one side and Tate on the other, he held out little hope of that being the case.

The conversation was light over the course of the meal. They simply told stories of their childhoods. Tir, Kel and Niko were especially interested to hear about life growing up on other worlds, worlds that were vastly different from their own. While they were enjoying the evening, there was still an underlying tension that thrummed throughout the room. Corin was aware of being the focus of attention several times, although he could never be sure which direction those looks came from. At times, it was enough to make him shudder. He certainly wasn't the only one to pick up on the looks directed their way. Tate was feeling the same level of scrutiny. Both of them were incredibly relieved when the banquet ended and Tir and Kel made their excuses for the group. They were beyond glad to leave the oppressive atmosphere and retire to the relative peace of their suite.

Back in the guest suite, the group sat on the comfortable seating dotted about and began drinking one of the clan's best wines.

"So, who is going to fill me in, as it sounds like there is a lot to discuss?" Niko was the first to talk.

"I guess it begins with me." Corin fidgeted and rubbed his eyes. "But you'd better get comfy as this is going to be a long story."

"Does this mean I should take notes?" Niko teased. Kel just rolled his eyes at him, more than used to his way of lightening the mood.

As Corin retold the story of how he managed to end up on the Delphini, the faces of the men around him were a mix of emotions. Even Tate, who had been part of the story, had never heard it all directly from Corin's point of view.

"So let me get this right. You treated the man who was literally dying and this Admiral took offence to the fact you wouldn't treat his little boo-boo?" Niko quipped. It was enough to break some of the tension in the room. "Besides, as an officer, or leader, it's your responsibility to make sure all your men are looked after. You do so before you even consider your own needs. Or is it not the same way with the Barin?"

"Oh, it's the same way all right," Tate spoke, "this admiral is just the biggest arsewipe known to man."

"Arsewipe?" Niko barked out a laugh. "I've never heard that one before!"

"Hey, stick with me and I'll give you quite the education then." Tate winked at Niko.

"Oh, I can tell we are going to have a lot of fun, you and me." Tate and Niko were laughing with each other. The other three men looked on with something akin to horror on their faces at the prospect of having the two of them work in tandem with each other.

Tate suddenly burst out laughing. They all looked on inquisitively. "Sorry, was just thinking about the first time I laid eyes on Corin. Oh man, his face was a picture, but, damn, he can give as good as he gets. I think it's why he fit so well with the squad." He told the men about the impromptu dance they had. "What you guys have to realise is we are kind of badass in our group. We are considered one of the best, if not THE best, of the Avanti squads. We intimidate a lot of people. They tend to avoid us rather than risk upsetting us, but the Doc here? Not him. He walked into a room full of extremely hostile soldiers with his head held high. Then when it came to us? Not only did he not back down, he came right back at us with barbs of his own. He was always going to have our support because he saved one of the Avanti, but that day he earned our respect and our friendship."

"Oh Aladain," Niko swore, taking the moon goddess' name in vain. "I didn't know you were from the Avanti." At Kel and Tir's questioning looks, he continued "Those guys are just about the biggest badasses in the known galaxies. They're the ones who go in when it seems like all hope is lost, and they rarely, if ever, fail in their mission. From what I know, they are both feared and revered in equal measure throughout the Alliance."

"Sounds about right." Corin nodded. "I'm pretty sure the only reason Tate survived all we went through is because he's Avanti."

"Doc, you and I will have to disagree there. Sure, it helped, but damn, man, you're one hell of a surgeon and field medic. You saved me, no two ways about it, my brother." Tate smiled at Corin and threw his arms around him in a brief hug.

Niko leaned towards the two men. "So you guys crashed here and what? Kel rescued you?"

"Nope, instead they rescued Eliya." Tir spoke up.

"Eliya?" Niko tilted his head. "I don't understand. Why would Eliya need rescuing?"

Tate and Corin recounted what had transpired from the moment they crashed to the second they walked into the war room. Tate lifted his tunic top displaying the healing wound on his stomach. "You can see just how extensive my injury was, so you can understand just how great a surgeon Corin is."

"Damn, Tate." Niko whistled. "That's one hell of an injury. I doubt many survive something so serious."

"Nope. I put my survival purely down to the Doc's skill and determination."

"So, by the sounds of it, it was definitely mercs who held Eliya." Niko scowled as the atmosphere in the room suddenly got far more serious. "Now I understand why you had to rule out my clan for the other man. I don't like it, but I do understand it."

"Niko, you're like a brother to us, we never once thought it was you, but we needed to make sure it wasn't another faction in your clan. I am sorry, but I will consider everyone if I have to. I will find who hurt Eliya," Tir vowed.

"Well, for what it's worth you have my full support, you know this," Niko vowed. "Aside from my clan, there are probably only one or two clans who fit the physical description Corin gave us. Now is there anything else you can think of to help us? Any other identifying marks?"

"Oh shit, wait a minute!" Tate suddenly exclaimed. "I'm sorry I didn't think of it sooner, but the guy wore a lot of jewellery for a man, in particular rings. I don't know if it helps at all. Do people here wear a lot of jewellery?"

"Not in general. So while the clothes suggested a nobleman, I'm inclined to think we are talking about someone pretty high up in a clan based on what Tate says," Niko gave voice to what he, Kel and Tir were all thinking. "So you've ruled us out and now what?"

"Martellon has asked for a meeting," Kel stated in a flat tone. Niko picked up on the uneasy look passed between the brothers, wondering what else was going on what they were hiding. "So it looks like I will be joining my sire on a trip to the Farian Clan. We, uh, leave in a week."

Corin's eyes shot to Kel, a look of hurt in them as he hadn't heard this before now.

Niko watched the looks being traded back and forth amongst the men with interest. There was a lot more going on here than he thought. "So if Corin needs to identify the man then I take it he is going with you?" Although for some reason he was sure the answer was no and Chieftain Damron was up to something. Niko had noticed that the man had never been truly happy at Kel's desire for men. The old man would definitely try to change things if Kel had made his intentions towards Corin known.

"Um, no, Corin won't be coming with me." At Kel's words, Niko watched as Corin seemed to withdraw into himself, shutting down his emotions and keeping a neutral expression on his face.

"It's okay, we have to leave as soon as Tate is better. We need to find our teammates," Corin announced. All eyes in the room shot to him. Tate could tell there was something bothering him, but Corin simply shook his head as if to say not now.

"Absolutely not!" Kel roared. "You're not going anywhere."

"And since when do you get to tell me what to do?" Corin shot back.

"I'm not telling you what to do, damn it!" Kel bellowed as his fists were clenching and unclenching at his sides.

"Oh really? So the words 'Absolutely not!' mean it's my decision then?" Corin's voice dripped with sarcasm.

Kel sighed. "Corin, we should at least discuss this. You need to stay here where I know you are and can keep you safe."

"I'm not some pampered little princess you can lock in her tower! I'm a fully trained soldier as well as a medic. I'm hardly some innocent little boy who needs to be looked after, and screw you for implying I am! You say we should have discussed this? What about the way you discussed the fact you're off on some trip, who knows where, doing who knows what? Don't think I can't see the reluctance on your face to even talk about it, let alone go. I can tell you're hiding something from me, yet you have the nerve to have a go at me! At me, for simply wanting to go and find my friends. Well, screw you, Kel, screw you." Corin got up and walked out of the room, slamming the door behind him.

Kel sat there with a stunned look on his face before muttering, "What the ever-loving fuck just happened here?"

Niko laughed, earning him a glare from Kel. "My friend, I would say you just got completely put in your place."

Kel simply scowled.

"Excuse me guys, I'm going to talk to Corin." Tate rose and left the room. He walked into one of the bedrooms to find Corin pacing back and forth. "Hey, Doc, you alright? You seem incredibly pissed off. More so than I thought you would be based on what went on out there." He tipped his head back towards the other room as he spoke.

"Yeah." Corin sighed as he sagged down onto the bed. "I just get the sense there's so much more going on. I feel like they are hiding something from us. It made me realise there's so little we know about them. What's more, I'm feeling guilty, guilty we aren't doing more to find the guys."

"Doc, you know I'm still doing the check-ins at the prearranged time and the guys haven't responded yet, but it doesn't mean they aren't safe. They just might not be able to pick up the signal. I've no idea what sort of interference there could be over long distances, let alone whether anything in the planet's atmosphere is interfering with it. I've been working on the comms to try and boost the signal. Hopefully we can make contact soon."

"We still need to get out there and look for them though, Tate."

"Shit, Doc, I want to find them too, but we have to be sensible. Firstly, we've both been injured. Secondly, we have no idea where they might have landed. We have no idea what sort of terrain and forces we might face if we go hunting for them. As much as I don't want to admit it, it really isn't sensible to go tearing off looking for them. What's more, there's nothing to say they aren't doing exactly what we have done. The last thing I want is them to come here looking for us to find we've left looking for them and no one has any idea where we went."

"Damn it, I know, I just… It pissed me off in there."

"I know it, Doc. Look, if you really want to leave, we can, but honestly? Talk to him, find out what's going on. Don't simply storm off in a bad mood, assuming the worst. You ever hear the old Earth saying Assuming makes an Ass out of you and me? Think on it. Take a breather, then go back and talk, properly."

"Yeah, okay." Corin sighed, capitulation written all over his face. "You're a smart bastard at times, Tate, you know that, right?"

"I'm just awesome!" Tate winked.

In the other room, Kel was cursing up a storm.

"What the hell just happened?" Niko wondered.

"Kel was trying to keep a lot of things from Corin," Tir answered for Kel.

"Okay, looks like you guys are going to have to fully fill me in on what's going on because, damn, this is getting confusing."

Kel started talking. "When I saw Corin for the first time, I felt an instant attraction with an intensity I've never experienced before. I could barely take my eyes off him. Even without knowing if he was responsible for kidnapping Eliya, I was drawn to him. He is the most attractive man I have ever laid eyes on. It's not just physical, there's something about him which calls to my soul and has made me feel complete. It honestly feels like he's a lost part of my soul, one I never knew was missing." Kel sighed. "When I realised he wasn't involved, I felt compelled to spend as much time with him as possible. I simply thought I was falling in love."

"Until we had a talk." Tir smiled.

"Yes, and that was when we realised Corin is in fact my truemate. I never would have thought it was possible otherwise I might have realised sooner. I mean, who knew men could have men as truemates? Never mind the fact he is an Offworlder. So yeah, it was pretty unexpected." Kel sighed.

"But surely all of this is a good thing? We all want to find our truemates," Niko prompted, confused as to why Kel didn't seem happier about it all.

"Oh, it's fantastic and I couldn't be happier. But..." Kel couldn't face saying the words.

"But our sire wants a political match with the Farian Clan. He and Chieftain Martellon have arranged a bonding between Kel and Lady Teriva." Tir took over from the distraught Kel, snorting at the use of the honorific 'Lady.' Teriva was many things, but one thing she wasn't was a lady.

"Oh shit," was all Niko could think to say. "Damn, that woman is truly the devil incarnate."

"Now you see the problem." Tir winced at the horrified look on Niko's face.

"Why not just go ahead with the bonding before they can force this on you?"

"For two reasons. One, Corin doesn't know about truemates yet and Kel is worried he won't agree to it, worried he doesn't feel as deeply as Kel. And two, our sire has got wind of what is going on between them and he has threatened Corin if Kel doesn't comply," Tir explained sadly.

"Even if I can't have a future with him, I will see him safe from my father. I will see him happy and protect him, no matter what I have to do to accomplish it," Kel vowed.

"Surely it's a decision Corin has to be involved in? Look at the argument you just had because he thought you weren't involving him." Niko was trying to be the voice of reason.

"You don't get it!" Kel frowned as a vein throbbed in his neck. "Damn it, if he ends up hating me, so be it. But I will see him safe from my father."

"Have you tried talking to your sire?" Niko appreciated that it was unlikely to make a difference, but surely Kel needed to try.

"He's barely even talking to me. Things have been contentious between us lately." Kel sighed. "I'm going to try again before we get there. There has to be a way around this."

"I would offer to take his place." Tir let out an exasperated sigh before he pressed his lips together. "But we all know Martellon won't accept me as a widower and a father."

"And I thank you for your offer, brother, but you know I would never let you sacrifice yourself for me, even if they were to accept it. There is no way I'm putting Eliya anywhere close to the vicinity of those two." Kel hugged his brother, the two of them sharing a moment at just what Tir was willing to do to give his brother a shot at happiness.

"You should still talk to Corin. He deserves to know. He deserves the chance to fight for you." Niko was adamant it was the right decision.

"No, and I won't change my mind," Kel vowed.

"You're a stubborn bastard, brother," Tir hugged his brother tight, the worry he was feeling evident on his face.

"You love me anyway." Kel managed a smile.

"I do. Why I don't know, but I do," Tir teased.

"Okay, well, there's nothing you can do until you talk to your sire. We just have to hope he can be persuaded, no matter how unlikely it seems. In the meantime, how about I stay here with Tir and keep an eye on your man?" Niko suggested.

"You would do that for me?" Kel choked up.

"I would and you know it. You know I see you as more than friends. You're like family to me and this is what family should be to each other." Niko grabbed Kel into a fierce hug. "I love you, brother."

"I love you too, brother," Kel choked out around the constriction in this throat.

"Now, how about Niko and I go and commandeer Tate and let you go and make it up with your man. We shall keep Tate in one of the extra rooms in my suite for the night. Give you two peace to sort things out." Tir winked at his brother.

"Uh huh, talk, right." Niko burst out laughing. "Is that what it's called these days?" He wiggled his eyebrows suggestively at Kel.

"Idiot." Kel smiled, his voice full of fondness.

Niko knocked on the room door and managed to persuade Corin and Tate to go into the other room. They all watched quietly as Corin walked up to Kel.

"I'm sorry." He spoke quietly, voice laden with an apology. "I understand, Kel, I really do. You like to protect people, keep them safe. What you have to realise though, is I'm my own man. I've lived through shit I wouldn't wish on my worst enemy. I've been the one doing the protecting, been the one making all the decisions. But if this, if we, are going to work you have to talk to me. We have so much against us to start with. If we don't talk, if we keep secrets, then people will use those secrets against us and we won't survive. I'm not saying I want to go either, but they are my team and they are out there somewhere. We have no idea if they are injured, held prisoners, safe or, damn it, dead. You can't expect me not to want to find them." Corin sighed deeply before continuing.

"Tate and I realised you guys were keeping stuff from us. It never bothered us. We are guests here and we have no right to know everything. But, and it really is a big BUT, if I find you are keeping things from us, things that we have a right to know, things about us, or about our missing squad, then you will see the depth of my anger, and what's more, we WILL be over. I do not deal in lies and deceit. Do you understand?"

"No, no, Corin, it's me who's sorry. I am so, so, sorry. I understand, I really do. But you also need to understand I am fiercely protective of what's mine, of those I love. I cannot willingly put them in harm's way. It goes against everything I stand for, everything I am. There is literally nothing I would not do for those I love. But I am sorry. I should have talked to you. I shouldn't have just tried to make decisions for you. It wasn't fair, and while I can't promise I'll never do it again, I will try not to."

"We will talk about what's going on, but how about we leave talking seriously until tomorrow? I just want to spend time with you for the rest of the night." Corin sighed, wanting more than anything to reconnect with Kel properly, to be held in his arms and kissed within an inch of his life, without anyone there to witness such a private moment.

Kel simply pulled Corin into his arms in response, wrapping him up tight, burying his head into the smaller man's neck as he fought back the tears that threatened to overflow from his eyes. They stood embracing each other, reasserting their connection to one another, for the next few minutes, unaware when the three men quietly left them to it.

Eventually the embrace started to turn from comforting to arousing. Kel hauled Corin further up his body, and groaned when Corin wrapped his legs tight around his waist. His hands grasped Corin on the ass, keeping him pressed tight to his body. Corin started to gently kiss his way along Kel's exposed neck. His kisses trailed down and across the top of his chest before working their way back up Kel's neck and across his stubbled jaw, right before dropping a tender kiss on Kel's lips. Kel groaned as he opened his mouth to Corin's onslaught. His leather pants were getting tighter as the blood flow was redirected to his cock. It was rapidly rising and straining against the material, providing a steady rasp of friction, which just increased the level of his arousal.

The feelings coursing through Corin were nothing like he'd ever felt before. They were not going to be simply fucking, they were going to make love. Because he loved Kel, there was no doubt in his mind. The depth and speed of the feelings scared him like crazy, but he wanted them, he embraced them. He would not let what they had go through fear.

Corin ran his hands down Kel's arms, enjoying the feel of Kel's flexing biceps, drifting down over the lightly furred forearms, where all the hairs stood on end and he could feel goosebumps underneath. Finally, he linked his hand through one of Kel's, never once breaking the kiss they were sharing. The other hand was reaching down past his own straining erection, trying to find out how to undo the clothes Kel wore. He was desperate to feel skin on skin, to run his hands over Kel's flesh. His fumbling hands finally found skin. He immediately searched out Kel's nipples, already hard buds. He gently squeezed, eliciting a moan from Kel, causing one of Kel's hands to drift to his hair and tug slightly downwards, the movement tipping his face up to Kel's. Corin smiled to himself. Oh, so his man had sensitive nipples, did he? As he pushed Kel's top off of his shoulders, both of them fumbled about, Kel staggering slightly as he made sure he didn't drop Corin. He wrenched his mouth away from Kel's with difficulty, but he wanted to taste those gorgeous nipples. Trailing hot, wet kisses down Kel's neck and chest, he latched onto a nipple and sucked hard.

"Corin!" A hoarse shout left Kel's lips as one hand tightened in Corin's hair, the other tightened on his ass. "By the moons, your mouth is incredible, please, oh please, don't stop," he begged as Corin's other hand drifted across his chest to tease the other nipple. He alternated between hard tugs, pinches and gentle, soothing circles, all while his lips and tongue were feasting away. Corin let his other hand drift down over Kel's abdomen. His fingers traced each and every hard ridge they discovered. He traced the V of his abdomen muscles, loving how Kel almost flinched at the touch. Light, fluttering movements had Kel's muscles contracting and goosebumps appearing all over his skin. Kel kept shivering, so intense was the pleasure. It was all he could do to keep them both upright as he was assaulted by sensations. He couldn't believe the difference being with his truemate was making. His body was on fire, his cock was rock hard, oozing precum and straining against its confinement. He was at war with himself. The sensations Corin was causing were running rampant through his body, but he needed to feel his mate naked beneath him, needed to touch him, taste him and devour him.

He pulled Corin away from his chest and swung his legs up, carrying him through into the bedroom before standing him by the bed. He tore off Corin's tunic, kneeling in front of him and kissing the skin he exposed. His hands desperately unlaced Corin's trousers before pushing them to the floor. He nearly came on the spot when he realised Corin was naked under them. There was no barrier between him and his prize. He pulled back from Corin's chest and pushed him gently back onto the bed. He tugged Corin's trousers off and watched as he scrambled backwards into the middle, letting his legs fall open in invitation.

Kel stood and stalked forward, too distracted by the beauty on the bed to remember he was still wearing his own trousers. Running his hands up Corin's legs to his hips, he gently grasped them before flipping him over to expose his back and the most delicious ass Kel had ever seen. He gently climbed over him as Corin leaned back to kiss him, mouths locked as both of them rocked their hips into one another with gentle, slow thrusts, back and forth like every moment was theirs to own and control, like they could change every minute and make it an eternity. Soft, slow, deep kisses took over their world as Kel's hand gently grasped Corin's throat holding him in place. Kel placed soft nibbling kisses over Corin's lips before he soothed the sting with his tongue. The scrape of Corin's stubble was incredible against Kel's face, making his nerves buzz.

Corin was more turned on than he should have been by the fact Kel was still partially clothed, yet he was naked.

Kel slowly moved away from those wonderful lips kissing his way down Corin's spine, his tongue tracing each vertebrae as he made his way down. His fingers skirted over Corin's ass before drifting down to his hole. Soaking them with his own saliva he started to gently work one finger into Corin before pouring oil over them all as he pulled his finger out slightly, before thrusting it back in hard.

A long, drawn out "Oh fuck" was all Corin could manage. His breath was getting faster with each passing second as Kel's finger started to open him up. The slow, sensual movements were driving him to distraction— it was as though he was flying, like he was out of control. He reached back and grabbed Kel's head, pulling him up to kiss him, desperate for something to ground him.

All the while they were exploring each other's mouths, Kel kept up a steady rhythm with his finger. The heat scorching him was incredible and he longed to feel Corin's tight heat around his cock. As Corin loosened up, he added a second finger while keeping the slow, steady pace. He gently twisted them, brushing over Corin's prostate.

"Oh God, Kel," Corin cried out as he bucked his hips back onto Kel's fingers, stunned by how amazing those fingers felt inside him.

Kel started to scissor his fingers wide into Corin, opening him up further while his other hand moved beneath to grasp Corin's cock and start a hard, slow pump of that gorgeous cock. His fingers stilled for a moment as he got distracted by the feel of the cock pulsing in his hand. Corin whimpered. It could have been from the feeling on his cock, or the fingers stilling in his ass, neither of them knew and neither of them cared.

Kel slowly pulled his fingers out, ignoring the moan coming from Corin's lips as he flipped him back over. His mouth immediately latched onto Corin's shaft and he swallowed it down. His nose burrowed deep into the hair at the base of Corin's cock. He inhaled the heady scent which was unique to Corin, all musky and man, with a subtle scent that reminded him of the summer rain bouncing off the mountains. His mouth was sliding torturously slow up and down as he hollowed out his cheeks, keeping the suction strong. At the same time, his tongue was dancing in his mouth, swirling and tracing over the cock he couldn't get enough of. Pulling back, he let his tongue dip into the slit that was tempting him, lapping up the precum which steadily oozed from it.

Corin was writhing on the bed completely overwhelmed by the sensations bombarding him. He cried out as Kel's hand tugged on his balls— the blast of pain-pleasure sent his desire skyrocketing to new heights. His hands grasped the sheets below him in a desperate attempt to ground his body after Kel took his lips away. He was continuously moaning. Corin couldn't seem to stop the litany of curses, nor the begging words streaming from his mouth. "Oh stars, Kel, more. I want. I need."

Kel lifted his lips away from Corin briefly. "I've got you, babe, let go and feel. I want to see you, feel you, taste you come apart in my arms."

Instead of returning those lips back to Corin's cock, he again flipped him over. Pushing Corin's knees underneath his hips gave him all the access he wanted to Corin's gorgeous butt. He spread Corin's cheeks and swiped his tongue over his hole in a long, slow sweep.

"Oh fuck!!" was all Corin could manage, aside from the whimpers continuously flowing from his lips.

Kel thrust both thumbs inside Corin, opening him up, allowing space for his tongue. He darted his tongue in and out, first thrusting hard before it gave way to soft swirls. He could feel Corin thrusting his cock against the bedding as though he was desperate to feel the friction. His tongue started to work faster and harder into Corin as he removed one of his thumbs and replaced it with two fingers instead. He immediately aimed for Corin's prostate and mercilessly stroked it.

"Fuck, Kel, I'm close, so close."

Kel was not prepared for this to be over so soon. He withdrew the other thumb and wrapped his finger and thumb around the base of Corin's cock and balls, squeezing hard, stopping him from coming.

"No, please, Kel, I need to come, please, oh please." He was so desperate he didn't even care he was begging like some little slut. The only response he got was what felt like a smirk against his ass.

All of a sudden, a third finger replaced Kel's tongue and Corin's pulse shot through the roof. He was desperately thrusting back onto those fingers as Kel covered his cheeks with kisses. The fingers inside him suddenly disappeared and a sudden slap echoed around the room. His cheek warmed up from the sensation. When Kel moved away from him, he felt the loss acutely.

"Please, I need you to fuck me please."

"It's okay, babe, I'm just getting ready."

Corin turned his head in time to catch Kel stripping, then pouring some of the oil over his incredible cock. The oil highlighted the bumps, making Corin desperate to know what they were going to feel like inside him. They played a major part of his fantasises since he first laid eyes on them.

Kel yet again flipped him over. "I want to see your face as I make love to you. I want to know what I do to you, know the effect I have on you, and more importantly, I want to watch you come apart in my arms."

"Oh stars, Kel, the things you say, the things you do to me. Take me please, I'm begging you. I want to feel you. I want you inside me, owning me, possessing me, making me yours. I want it. I need it."

With a long drawn out groan, Kel lifted Corin's legs up and wrapped them round his waist, waiting until Corin linked his feet together behind him. He lined up his cock and slowly pushed his way into Corin.

"Fuck!! Oh stars, Kel!" The effect on Corin was instantaneous and he cried out.

The sensations were so exquisite he threw back his head, his mouth wide as his scream echoed around the room. The bumps on Kel's cock were rubbing against his inner walls, increasing the pleasure beyond anything he had ever known. There seemed to be extra lubrication and it felt like those bumps were releasing something inside him. He wanted to ask Kel, but he was too far gone at the moment to form the words. There was no doubt in his mind now. He would forever be ruined if they ever went their separate ways. No one else could ever make him feel what Kel was making him feel. As Kel bottomed out, Corin felt those bumps nudge across his prostate, causing shudders to wrack his body.

Kel kept up a slow and sensual pace, not wanting this to ever end. He'd never felt anything so all consuming, never seen anyone look as beautiful as Corin did in the throes of passion. His heart cracked wide open, the man in his arms seeping into every part of it, owning it and making it his.

As his heart was possessed by his mate, he recognized that from now on it would only ever beat for this man. It was no longer his. His truemate owned him, heart, body and soul. Tears leaked from the corner of his eyes at the sensations overwhelming him. The depth of love he felt, the passion, the sense of belonging were all combining to make sure he would be forever changed from this moment on. He took Corin's hand and rested it over his own heart so Corin could feel it beat just for him. Their eyes locked at that moment. Lust and passion shone brightly, but more than lust there was an understanding, an acceptance and, most importantly, love.

No matter how much Kel wanted this moment to last his body took control and he sped up, thrusting in deep and hard. Corin's ankles locked around Kel's waist to keep him from withdrawing too far, keeping them locked together in their passion. Kel couldn't believe just how tight Corin was, his walls contracting and squeezing him with each thrust. Kel's movements sped up, a kind of desperation to them. He wanted this moment to be perfect, wanted this moment to ruin both of them for anyone else in the future. More than anything, he wanted to have this one perfect moment with Corin to carry him through life if his father forced them apart.

Pushing the thought out of his mind and focusing purely on his mate, he realised Corin had reached for his own cock and begun to stroke it. That seemed to shock Kel back into the moment, shutting down his thoughts completely.

"Mine," he growled, knocking Corin's hand away before taking that gorgeous cock and squeezing it in his fist. Every time he bottomed out in Corin, he made sure his fist reached the tip of Corin's cock, giving it a twist and squeeze. He could see Corin's eyes, glazed over with lust, open wide as he did this. Precum was oozing from Corin's slit with every pass he made.

"Kel, Please, I have to come, I can't last."

"Me neither, babe, me neither." Kel groaned.

His pace became wild and erratic and a desperate need took over him. Corin was writhing and screaming out his name. Bracing himself on one arm, he leaned down and sucked on Corin's neck. Hard. That was all it took. Corin erupted beneath him, his cum arching up and out, covering Kel's hand and both their stomachs. The look of absolute ecstasy on Corin's face was stunning, and in combination with Corin's walls clamping down on him, it was all it took to send Kel hurtling off the edge into oblivion.

Pulling his hand away from Corin, he braced himself as wave after wave of cum erupted from him. His vision went white momentarily before going black. His bumps were pulsing, extending his orgasm. Suddenly he heard Corin scream as his walls contracted again. He couldn't believe his bumps triggered a second orgasm for Corin. As both of them finally stopped coming and tried to catch their breath, Kel collapsed on top of Corin, his body unable to support him. He went to withdraw from Corin before he registered Corin talking.

"No. Stay. I want you to stay inside me. Please."

There was no way Kel could deny him anything and so he rolled them both to their sides before he wrapped his arms tight around his man, feeling Corin burrow into him.

It was mere moments later when both men slipped deep into sleep. Neither of them let the other one go.

Chapter Twelve

Corin woke with a feeling of being surrounded. It looked like both of them barely moved all night. He was still wrapped up securely in Kel's arms. His arm was wrapped around Kel's chest with Kel's hand resting over his heart as though Kel needed to know it was still beating. His legs were trapped by Kel's. It was almost as if Kel was holding on tight to him, determined to never let him go.

A soft smile broke over Corin's face as he thought over everything they did the night before. He had never experienced anything so intense. He did not know how to describe it, even to himself, what he experienced then nor what he was feeling now. He was revelling in it as Kel stirred behind him, or more correctly, Kel's cock stirred. It was rubbing deliciously against his ass and he found his cock responding. He felt, more than heard, a sharp intake of breath behind him. The puff of air over his neck sent shivers down his body. Kel's arms tightened around him as his lips were delicately raining kisses over his neck.

"Good morning, babe." Kel's voice was husky and deep. It sent a bolt of lust straight to Corin's cock, which decided to fully rise to the morning's occasion.

"Morning," Corin replied and blushed when he realised just how hoarse his voice sounded. He usually wasn't much of a screamer in bed, but it appeared this was something else Kel brought out in him.

"Mmm, now isn't this a perfect way to wake up," Kel mumbled against his neck.

"Oh, I don't know," Corin teased. "While it's perfect waking up with you, I can't say I appreciate waking up all crusty."

"Waking up this way just means I did my job and made you pass out." Kel chuckled behind him.

"Yeah, yeah, you're just this huge stud, handsome. We should all bow down to your obvious prowess!" Corin teased. Kel's only response was to tickle his sides.

They spent the next few minutes rolling around play fighting on the bed. Slowly the movements turned to passion and kisses replaced the tickles. Corin broke off the kiss, much to Kel's surprise, and pushed him away.

"Stop."

Kel's face took on a wounded look. "Why?"

"I am not doing this while I'm still covered in last night's evidence. Shower time." Corin laughed at the pout on his man's lips before he put him out of his misery. "You going to join me then, handsome?" The smile he got in response made the teasing worthwhile.

Just as they were about to get into the shower, they could hear voices from the room next door. Kel groaned before going to the door to see his brother, Tate and Niko all stood there grinning at him.

"What?" He scowled, grumpily.

"Looks like you guys enjoyed last night." Tate waggled his eyebrows making everyone laugh.

"Huh?" was all Kel could think of to say.

"Your man has marked you, brother! You might want to cover his mark up with a training top in case father sees them. I somehow don't think he would be too impressed." Tir gave Kel a knowing look as he pointed out the love bites littering Kel's neck and chest.

"Yeah." Kel sighed. His good mood evaporated as he was reminded of what he was facing.

"Sorry, brother." Tir grimaced.

Kel's only response was a sad smile and a shake of his head. "I'll go and get ready. We'll be out in a few minutes. His cock was fully deflated now, his passion gone. It was probably a good thing as he didn't want an audience to the gorgeous sounds his man made.

A few minutes later, both men were showered and dressed. Kel was glad his brother thought to bring him clean clothes. He hadn't relished the thought of getting back into his dirty ones.

As soon as Corin entered the room, Tate pulled him to one side. "Everything okay? You get it all sorted out?"

"Yeah." Corin scrubbed his face as he replied. "Well, pretty much. I still don't know what the fuck I'm doing, though."

Tate threw his arm around Corin and gave him a brief hug. "I know, Doc, but sometimes you just have to go with the flow. Enjoy it while you can. What will be will be and all that mumbo jumbo."

A laugh barked out of Corin. "I can always count on you my friend to cheer me up. You have such a way with words."

"I aim to please, good sir," Tate quipped, and accompanied his words with an overly dramatic bow. Both of them laughed, and then laughed even harder when they realised everyone else was looking at them like they had lost their minds.

As they joined the other men, they could feel the tension in the group. Shooting each other questioning looks, they both shrugged, neither of them sure what was going on.

"So does anyone want to explain to me, calmly, what last night was all about?" Corin asked.

"Look, I know my brother went about it the wrong way, but it's really for the best if you stay here. I know we all need you to see if it was someone from the Farian Clan, but they are openly hostile to most clans and hate Offworlders. They tend to attack anyone from the Barin Alliance on sight. It would be difficult if you saw them here, but going there? Such an action would anger them, and truthfully, I'm not sure we would be able to stop them from acting, no matter the consequences to them amongst the clans," Tir explained as they all looked at him wondering how he was going to react.

"Okay," was all he said.

"Okay?" Kel questioned carefully.

"Yeah, Tir explained what was going on and why you didn't want me to go. It made sense, so I don't have a problem with it." Corin shrugged.

Tate laughed as he looked around at the mouths hanging open around them. "What did you expect? You give a reasonable explanation and we're cool with it. Keeping us in the dark and making decisions for us? That's what got the doc so upset. We're smart men remember. I'm Avanti for fuck's sake, and the doc is not only an incredible doctor, he's one of the top ranked trauma surgeons in the Alliance. We understand situations can be volatile and complicated. It was always about keeping him in the dark and treating him like a kid that got the doc upset."

"Yup." Corin echoed Tate's declaration. "Do it to me again and so help me, I'll cut your bloody balls off." Tate and Corin laughed as all three men immediately covered their packages.

"So you want us to stay here while you're gone?" Corin checked and Kel nodded in response, not trusting himself to say anything. The last thing he wanted to do was to fuck this up again. "Alright, but, and it's a big but, if we get information on our guys then we are going to go and get them. I won't stay here if I know where they are." Corin held his hand up as Kel went to protest. "If it happens then we shall bring them back here, if you're in agreement with it?"

Kel breathed out a sigh of relief, glad Corin meant he wasn't going to abandon him. Yes, it was selfish, considering what was likely to occur, but he needed Corin near him no matter what else happened.

"Okay, so in the meantime, can we ask for any help you can spare to boost our comms signals? We know it's working, but we aren't picking anything up. I don't understand it all but Tate's our resident whiz at comms."

"I can help," Niko offered. "I'm not expected back with my clan for weeks, so I can help and not take those two away from anything they are needed for here."

"Thanks, Niko." Tate shot him a grateful smile.

"Oh man," Tir groaned. At the questioning looks sent his way, he grimaced. "Those two working together? I dread to think what they are going to get up to."

As everyone else smiled, Tate sent Tir a death glare, saying, "You little shit, I resent that!" Lunging for him in a playful attack, Tir simply laughed.

The next week sped by. Tate was busy trying to boost the comms. He and Niko were becoming firm friends, which helped ease Corin's guilt over the time he spent with Kel. Although, as each day went past, he was seeing less of Kel and when he did see him, he could tell something was bugging the man. He tried to discuss it, but Kel kept fobbing him off saying he was just tired of all the political wrangling between the clans. Corin wasn't convinced, he was sure there was more to it, but decided not to push matters. He just hoped Kel learned his lesson last time and would share anything important or anything that would affect them.

Corin wanted to spend time looking at their medical facilities and medicines, but he was damned if he was going to spend any time with Doctor Arsehole. Instead, Kel introduced him to a woman who lived in the shadow of the mountain. She had built up quite a following of clan members who went to her rather than the doctor. It seemed he wasn't the only one who wasn't impressed by the prick. Corin had never before felt such an instant dislike for someone. He realised it was probably irrational and he certainly wasn't threatened by the man, so the depth of his feelings unnerved him slightly. It was something he was determined to discover the reasons behind.

As the week went on, despite how tired and grumpy Kel was, they grew closer and Corin fell even more in love with the man. He tried to guard his heart against it as there was still more going on than he comprehended. Yet, no matter what his mind told him, his heart did as it wished. One week turned into two and Kel was still at the keep. As it turned out, no matter what planet you were on politics was still the same. What most people would have worked out in hours, or certainly days, had taken almost the full two weeks. Frustration was evident all around them and Corin did his best to mitigate its effects on Kel.

It was later than he expected, but sooner than he wanted, but Corin knew there was no delaying it any further. It was time for Kel to leave. It was just frustrating him as something still felt off about it all. Yet he hid it all as he sat on the chair in Kel's office and watched him pack away his documents.

"Now promise me you will be careful?" Kel begged.

"I'll be fine, there is nothing to worry about. Tir is staying, as is Niko, and I've got Tate anyway. It's not me you should be worried about, it's you. You're the one who needs to be careful if this clan is as bad as you say they are. People like them are always plotting to further themselves and they don't care who they trample on to do it. So just be careful and watch your six, okay?" Corin asked.

"Your six?" Kel inquired.

"Sorry, it's an Old Earth term. It just means watch your back."

"Ah, I get it. I will, babe, don't worry about me. I'm very used to clan politics, just promise me you will look after everyone here and watch the faces of any visitors. If any of them trigger something, let Niko or Tir know. While I hope there are no threats here, I cannot help but want these enemies out in the open. It's so fucking frustrating not knowing who they are, or where any potential threat is coming from. Damn my father for this. I have no idea what he is thinking or why he isn't taking this threat more seriously." Kel let out a frustrated breath.

"Come on, Kel, you know why. It's us. He doesn't trust us. What's more, it wouldn't surprise me if he still thought Tate and I had something to do with Eliya's kidnapping." Corin's lips morphed into a sad smile.

"Fuck, I'm sorry, babe." Kel strode over to Corin and wrapped him up tight in his arms, relishing in the comfort such a simple action gave him.

"I know you are, handsome, just come back to me, okay?" Corin's voice was laced with all the vulnerability he felt.

"Always," Kel muttered as he tightened his hold. "Are you well? You've looked pale these last few days."

"I'm fine, just tired, stop worrying, I'm a doctor remember." Corin smiled to take the slight sting out of his words. He stood up on tiptoes and brushed his lips across Kel's, letting his lips say what he could not. They stayed locked in their embrace until Tir coughed from the doorway.

"Sorry, guys, but it's time." Tir's tone was apologetic before he left again giving them one last moment together.

Kel framed Corin's face in his hands, looking straight into his eyes. "I love you, Corin. You are my heart, my soul, my breath. You are the very reason my heart continues to beat. Nothing will ever change that. Promise me you'll stay safe." Kel's eyes were brimming with unshed tears as he fought for control.

"I love you too," Corin breathed against his lips. "You are everything I never knew I wanted or needed. You make me whole, make me feel like I can take on the world. You are my one, my only and always will be. But this isn't goodbye, Kel, this is simply an I'll see you soon." With those last words, he closed the distance and kissed Kel long and deep.

Kel shuddered, hoping with every fibre of his being that Corin's words were true. Finally pulling away, they joined the guys in the hall outside the office. He turned to Tate. "Look after him. Keep him smiling if you can."

"I will, I promise." He gave Kel a brief hug before Kel made his way over to Niko.

"Good luck with everything and watch your back. I'll look after everyone here like they were my own." Niko hugged him close to whisper, "Try to get out of the match. You deserve your happiness. If you choose to go against your father, know you have our support no matter what."

"Thank you, Niko, you are a second brother to me. Just promise me one thing."

"Anything."

"No bribing Eliya into making you her favourite uncle!" Kel desperately tried to lighten the mood before Corin and Tate realised there was far more going on than they were aware of.

"Oh, Kel." Niko sighed mockingly. "No chance am I promising such a thing! I fully plan on taking advantage of your absence! All's fair in love and war where Eliya is concerned."

"Bastard!" Niko simply laughed at Kel's words.

"Come here, little brother." Tir grabbed Kel into a crushing hug. "Love you, man, now go out there and fix this. He's perfect for you. You couldn't ask for a better truemate." Tir kissed his brother softly on the cheek before pulling away.

They turned as one and made their way out to the courtyard. The sight greeting them was stunning. Row after row of mounted soldiers filled the space. To Corin, the mounts looked like a cross between the lions and zebras of old Earth. He had heard the animals called Refrinti, but he had never seen one up close. Each one bore a massive mane of long hair, while the hair on their bodies was close against their skin. Their colouring was so reminiscent of zebras it was uncanny. While physically they looked like lions, their height was similar to zebras or horses. They truly appeared to be a hybrid of the two. Kel mounted one standing to the side in a swift and graceful movement just as the Chieftain walked down the steps. They all watched as the Chieftain strode over to his mount and unsurprisingly, because of his level of fitness, he used a mounting block.

With little fanfare, the Chieftain cried out, "We ride!" With a quick contemptuous smirk at Corin, he steered his mount and left.

With one last lingering look at Corin, Kel followed.

Chapter Thirteen

The next week was almost anticlimactic in its peacefulness. There were no father and son fights to contend with, no fights between lovers or friends and, bar the odd lingering twinge, Corin felt his and Tate's injuries were almost fully healed and Eliya was safe and happy. The men simply carried on with what they were doing before Kel left. Then one morning it all changed.

Corin woke up and took halting, painful steps to the bathroom. He was violently sick and his body was aching. He wondered if he was infected by some sort of bug unique to the planet. After all, as a doctor, he made sure to have all the shots preventing all the normal viruses which were prevalent throughout the Alliance. It was one of the perks of being such a high ranking surgeon. The shots were ridiculously expensive, but it was deemed necessary for all medics by the powers-that-be within the Alliance. It was years since he had been even slightly ill. He all but crawled back to his bed. His limbs felt so heavy he couldn't even pull himself up to walk. He was pretty sure even if he managed to, his legs would give out again anyway. Pulling himself back onto the bed sapped him of the last dregs of energy he possessed. He curled into a ball under the covers and let sleep take him.

It was a little while later when Tate entered the room. "Doc, come on, lazy, just because your man isn't here doesn't mean you get to skive." He opened the curtains and the sun made its presence known in the room.

A loud groan echoed throughout the room. "For the love of all things celestial turn off the sun, I beg you," Corin managed to stutter out.

Tate quickly closed them back up and made his way over to Corin. "Doc? What's up?"

"Sick."

"With what?"

"Don't know."

"Hmm, I'd offer to get the doctor for you, but the guy is a prick. What can I do for you?" Tate asked.

"Bag. I'll need a shot of D6."

"D6? Isn't D6 for a virus? I thought you were protected as a doctor?" Tate wondered as he quickly went about getting the shot ready.

"Yeah, I should be, so it's got to be some sort of virus unique to the planet. Damn, I feel like I've been tossed about in a sparring ring with every single member of the Avanti."

Tate gave him the shot before quickly adding another shot to help him rest. If it was a virus, then sleep was going to be the best thing for him. Within moments, Corin was slurring his thanks before passing out. Checking he was settled, Tate ran off to find Niko or Tir. He didn't like the fact Corin fell so ill, so quickly. He spared a thought to wonder if some of it was actually psychological and Corin was in fact missing Kel, but dismissed it just as quickly.

Niko listened as Tate explained what was going on. "That's odd, I've not heard of any new illnesses doing the rounds. Certainly not in my clan in recent weeks and we would have surely seen more evidence of it here."

"Then it's an especially worrying thought. He's pretty ill. I'll have to give him shots, not just to boost his system, but also to put him to sleep. If it's not a virus, what is it?" Tate asked.

Just then Tir joined them, raising an inquisitive brow at their dual looks of concern. "What's going on?"

"It's Corin," Tate said. "He's in pretty rough shape."

They all traipsed back to Corin's bedside and stood watching Corin for a few minutes.

"I haven't seen or heard of anything going around." Tir finally voiced what they were all thinking. "And if Niko hasn't either, then I'm really not sure what's going on." Tir sighed. "I really don't want to get Al'Feram, there is just something about him I don't like. He gives off the appearance of being shifty."

"What about the woman who he was working with?" Tate suggested.

"Which one?" Tir asked.

"I'm not sure of her name, but I'm pretty sure she lived in the shadow of the mountain?" Tate tried to think back to check if Corin had ever mentioned her name.

"Oh, he must mean Herica. A lot of the clan still go to her for herbs and potions. So many prefer the old, natural ways, rather than the new advances," Tir explained.

"Is there any way she would come here? I know a little bit, but nowhere close enough to try to diagnose what this is."

Niko piped up, "I'm more than happy to go and seek her out for you."

"Yeah, good idea. Take my Master at Arms with you. He'll know where to go," Tir suggested.

"I'll sit here and keep an eye on him in the meantime." Tate moved one of the big, comfy seats over to the side of the bed. He took out his datapad and pulled up the schematics for the comms system. He was still determined to find a way to boost the signal and find his missing teammates.

Herica appeared quickly, more than happy to help the man she thought of as a friend. She shooed the other men out the room as soon as she got there. Stern in the face of Tate's resistance, she refused to begin until they all left the room. In the end, Tate acquiesced so Corin could get treatment.

It was a tense time while the men were waiting, but seeing as he had a captive audience, Tate thought he would ask some tough questions.

"So you want to tell me exactly what is going on?"

"What do you mean? Nothing is going on." Tir shot a look at Niko.

"See? The look in your eyes right now? That's what I'm talking about. You've all been hiding something. I picked up on it a while ago. Stars, even Corin has picked up on it. The closer we got to when Kel was leaving the worse it got. And the day he left? Anyone would think the sky was falling from the looks on your faces. You looked like you were sending Kel off to his doom."

"Because basically we did." Tir sighed.

"What?"

"Kel went with our Sire under duress and under orders. He's going to the Farian Clan to mate with Martellon's eldest daughter, Teriva."

"What the actual fuck?" Tate was in shock. "Why the fuck does he not just say no?"

"Because my father threatened Corin. If Kel doesn't do this the consequences to Corin will be severe. I'm not just talking about throwing him off of our land either."

"He'd kill him?"

"Yes, and frankly it's more than likely to be in the most brutal way possible."

"Oh man. So what? Kel plans on coming back with his new wife in tow and shove it in Corin's face?" Tate paced angrily "Because that's not a total bastard of a move at all, is it?"

"You don't understand. My brother is in love with Corin. He's doing this to keep him safe."

"Yeah, right. Sure, I can buy the keeping him safe part. The loving him part? An hour ago, I would have agreed with you. But I'm sorry, not now. No man in love would subject the love of their life to having to watch them with someone else. By insisting Corin stay here, it's exactly what Kel is doing." Tate let out a heavy sigh. "Look, I like your brother, but if he won't or can't be with Corin, then he has to let him go completely."

"He can't."

"He has no fucking choice!" Tate screamed. "I won't stand by and watch Corin go through this. It will kill him. Not straight away, sure, but bit by bit, day by day, he will wither. He will retreat into himself, withdraw from everyone. He'll give up, stop eating, stop living. He just won't care about anything anymore. So as soon as he's better, we're getting the fuck out of here. Thanks for your hospitality and everything, but we're not staying for this."

"You can't leave." Niko finally spoke up.

"You actually agree with all this? I never thought you would agree, Niko. But have absolutely no doubt, we can, and we bloody well will leave."

"No, I mean Kel was going to try to persuade his Sire to let him mate with Corin instead. He was going to try to talk him into a political alliance instead of a matrimonial one with the Farians," Niko explained.

"How likely is it to happen though?" Tate scrubbed his face in frustration. His shoulders felt like they bore the weight of all the stars in the universe on them.

"We just don't know."

"So what? You want us to wait until Kel gets back? And what if he's mated? You'll let us leave whether Kel agrees with it or not?"

"Yes, if he comes back mated I will personally help you both leave and offer you sanctuary with my clan. I will also offer everything and anything we can to help find your friends," Niko vowed.

"You can't do that!" Tir pleaded. "It will destroy Kel to never see Corin again."

"Oh, so instead we have to see Corin destroyed as he can't bear to watch? So what? Kel gets to be mated to a woman, raise a family and keep Corin on the side? Like some dirty little whore? So not going to happen, Tir. If Kel is so under Daddy's thumb he does this, then frankly, he doesn't deserve a moment of Corin's time."

"It's not so fucking simple!" Tir picked up a glass which was sitting on the table and threw it across the room, slightly mollified by the resounding crash that echoed around the walls. It seemed throwing glasses about was becoming a habit of his. "Look, let's calm down and talk about it later. We need to see what's up with Corin first. Will you at least promise not to talk to him about it for the moment? Please?" Tir begged.

"I don't see why I should keep secrets from him. There have been more than enough secrets lately, don't you think?" Tate thought for a moment, his body sagging slightly. "However, I will keep quiet, but only because it won't help him recover. As soon as he's well again, you better damn well believe I'll be telling him about this."

"Thank you for waiting at least." Tir turned to Niko. "Let me know how he is? I would stay, but I need to go and collect Eliya."

"Sure," Niko replied, a weak smile on his lips as Tir left.

"This is so fucked up," was all Tate had left to say on the matter.

"Indeed it is, my friend, indeed it is," Niko replied. They both fell silent, alone with their own troubled thoughts as they waited for Herica.

When Herica finally left Corin alone, both men were deep in thought, but leapt up as soon as they heard the door creak open.

Tate was desperate for news. "How is he?" Both of them stood as she entered the room.

"He is settled and sleeping." Herica scrubbed her face before looking at them.

"So do you know what's wrong with him?" Tate was desperate for some answers.

"Honestly? No." She let out a frustrated breath. "I have done all the tests I can. The one thing I am sure of is, whatever this is, it's not a virus. While it could be something in the atmosphere that is making him react like this, I would imagine you would have come down with it as well." She looked pointedly at Tate.

"Not necessarily, I'm afraid." Tate shook his head. "While we are both from the Alliance, we're from different home worlds. I'm from Therasena and, from what I know, the Doc is a mix. I know he is part Terran, part Barinian, but he also hinted at something else.

Although I got the impression he himself wasn't sure either. All I know is it has something to do with his father and it's a taboo subject for his family."

Herica spoke as she finished packing up all her equipment. "Hmm, then I guess it could indeed be something in the atmosphere, although I still think it's unlikely. I will, however, see what I can research. In the meantime, I have left a tea to be brewed as he needs it, and an oil to be used on his aching muscles. Until I know more we cannot risk doing anything which may make it worse. I shall come back tomorrow, hopefully with more news. If anything changes, then please come and get me straight away."

"Thanks for coming to see him." Tate managed a small smile for the woman.

"You are most welcome, but I consider him a friend so I am glad to lend my services to help in any way I can."

"I'll take Herica back to her cottage if you're happy to stay with him, Tate?" Niko suggested.

"More than."

As Niko and Herica left, Tate yet again took up position beside Corin. He was praying to just about every celestial body anyone believed in to help him.

Chapter Fourteen

The first few days after Corin fell ill were some of the toughest they had ever faced for all three men. Tate used all his limited medical training alongside Herica, but they soon realised all they were probably doing was keeping him hydrated and alive. It certainly hadn't stopped whatever the virus was from rampaging his body. They eventually gave in and brought in Al'Feram, who did nothing more than shrug and say he had no idea. Tate had nearly lost control and attacked the man. It had taken both Niko and Tir to hold him back.

They even discussed the possibility of dispatching someone to go and recall Kel. They knew it wouldn't go down well with the Chieftain, but at the same time, they thought Kel deserved to know Corin was dangerously ill. Simply no one knew what was wrong with him or if he would survive.

Eventually, when they were giving up all hope of Corin pulling through and they were getting ready to retrieve Kel, Corin finally started to respond. To what they weren't sure, but they would take whatever progress they could.

Corin finally became aware of more than the pain that had wracked his body for what felt like an eternity. The pain blessedly lessened to the extent he wasn't living in some tortuous hell. As he prised his eyes open, he became aware of a figure slumped in a chair beside his bed. It was an exhausted looking Tate. His clothes were rumpled, his hair seemed to have taken on a life of its own, and sheer exhaustion seemed to permeate every cell in his body. He was also fast asleep.

Despite wanting to know what the hell had happened to him, Corin didn't have the heart to wake him. Instead, he started to try to catalogue what he could feel within his body. Apart from overwhelming aches all over, whatever was going on seemed to be centred on his abdomen.

Even the slightest movement of those muscles sent pain searing through him. It felt like someone had gathered all his, insides tossed them about together, and thrown them back inside him, letting them settle wherever they landed. He couldn't describe it, but nothing felt right. He was just contemplating whether he could reach the scanner Tate must have left on the table beside him, when he saw Tate's eyes start to flutter, his movements becoming restless. He watched as Tate wearily rubbed his eyes. He sensed a reluctance in the man to even look in his direction.

Was he so badly off? Had he really been that ill? Whatever was going on, he couldn't lay there and watch his friend suffer.

"Tate," he managed to whisper, or at least it's what he meant to say. What actually came out was a combination of a whimper, cough and a murmur. It was, however, enough to gain Tate's attention. His head shot up, eyes wide, before his face broke out into a smile Corin could only describe as being one of pure joy.

"Doc, oh merciful moons, Doc, you're awake." He leaned over the bed, wrapped his arms around Corin and hugged him tight.

He was sure he could feel tears track down Tate's cheeks where they rested against his temple.

Tate simply spent a minute or two feeling Corin in his arms, enjoying the feeling of seeing his friend awake again. Slowly he pulled away, went to the door and turned to one of the guards Tir had posted there in case he needed anything. "Can you go and get Lairds Tir and Niko please. Tell them it's urgent."

"Of course, sir." The guard dipped his head to Tate before leaving.

Tate went straight back to Corin's side, his smile wide. Sitting back in his seat, he took Corin's hand and began to try and explain what had happened. It was pretty tough considering he wasn't exactly sure himself, but he tried his best anyway. When he was just about finished, the door burst open with Niko and Tir entering at a dead run. Skidding to a stop by the bed, their faces registered stunned disbelief and shock.

"By the stars," Niko exclaimed. "I thought he was worse. This is incredible. Welcome back to the living, my friend." He leant over and gave Corin a gentle hug.

"Corin, you had us all so very worried. It's nice to see you back with us," Tir said softly, relief evident in his voice.

"Tate was just explaining what happened. So no one knows exactly what is wrong with me?" Corin asked.

"No. Herica has been by every day and we even got Al'Feram to look in on you. Of course the prick was absolutely no help. He simply shrugged, unconcerned, and maintained he didn't have the faintest idea." Tir growled, "I swear if he wasn't a favourite of my Sire's, I would have kicked him out of the clan long ago."

"Truly, how are you feeling?" Tate was anxious, yet unsure if he actually wanted an honest answer.

"Like death. Whatever this is, it feels far from over, but I'm hoping it's going to continue improving." Corin spoke with a somewhat normal voice but all the men could hear the exhaustion within it.

Niko spoke for all of them. "Look, get some sleep and we can talk more when you wake up. I know you've been out of it, but it probably wasn't that restful. A proper sleep will help. Is there anything we can give you?"

"No, the meds I've been given are enough until we know what it is. It would be great to get some broth at some point," Corin mumbled.

"As soon as you wake next you'll have it," Tir spoke.

They all made their way out of the room and let Corin fall asleep. They would continue to monitor him in shifts as none of them were truly sure he was over the worst, electing to watch him carefully instead. At least now, no one would have to think about bringing Kel back. Bringing him back was something which would have caused far more problems than it would solve.

Over the next week, Corin recovered well. He was still tired more often than not, but at least he wasn't spending his entire time in bed and they were all beyond thankful at his progress. Corin spent his time in the suite resting and working with Herica. They weren't just trying to puzzle out what was wrong with him, but continuing their earlier efforts in comparing their medicines.

Corin was stunned at the effectiveness of some of her treatments. He wished there was a research lab available. He wasn't sure if they would only be effective on the local population or if it would be the same for everyone. Some of her treatments had the potential to be a godsend in the Alliance if they were proven to be effective for all humanoids. There was no doubt they were close to a breakthrough, which gave them double the cause to celebrate. Tate had managed to rig up a booster for their comms with Niko's help. Corin couldn't wait till the next scheduled check-in time to attempt to connect with their friends. He was missing Dax and the guys like crazy. There was not a day when they weren't in both Tate and his minds.

Chapter Fifteen

It was during dinner when they heard loud shouts and happy exclamations echoing throughout the keep. Tate and Corin looked at each other wondering what was going on. Whatever it was, it seemed a happy occasion, rather than an invading or hostile force. They certainly couldn't hear any clanging of blades or shots fired from weapons. They both still found it strange how this clan was an incongruous mix of old and new. They were perfectly happy with technology, but mostly they preferred the old ways. None of the guards carried modern weapons such as guns. Tate had remembered Tir saying that almost all clans were the same. The only place where modern weapons were normal was in the main city.

"The Chieftain and Laird Kelin are back," one of their guards said as he poked his head around the door.

A huge smile broke out on Corin's face, pure joy radiating out from him.

Tate hoped this wasn't going to be as disastrous as he reckoned it would be. He couldn't help but be apprehensive considering everything he discussed with Niko and Tir. He couldn't begin to work out how he would get Corin through this if it was as bad as he expected it to be. As they made their way down to the courtyard, Niko waylaid them to tell them there was a gathering in the Great Hall. Oh, this couldn't be good, thought Tate.

As the three of them took up their positions towards the front of the hall, it was obvious there was going to be some sort of announcement. Niko and Tate exchanged glances.

Tate pulled Niko to one side. "If this goes how I am guessing it will, are you still okay to get us the fuck out of here?"

"Yeah, I'm afraid it's not looking good. I heard a few rumours already as I was coming to get you."

"Fuck! Corin's going to be devastated." Tate grimaced as the Chieftain took the stage with two of the clan elders. Both men re-joined Corin and took up positions on either side of him.

"Doc, do you remember all your training? I mean the ones for political situations?" Tate asked quickly and quietly.

"Yes, of course," Corin answered, puzzled as to why Tate was asking.

"Just promise me, whatever happens, do not let any emotions show on your face. Keep it hidden. Call on your training and maintain a façade."

"Tate, what the fuck? What's going on? Do you know something I don't?"

"Please, Doc, you've got to promise me."

"Okay, okay, I promise. Seriously though, Tate, do you know something I don't?"

"Thank you. As for knowing more, I don't, but I've got a nasty feeling and you know the Chieftain is looking exceedingly smug." Tate simply hoped they could get through the next few minutes without Corin losing it.

"You have a point there." Corin just focused his attention to the front, desperate to see Kel again.

As Corin and Tate were talking, Niko was talking quietly to his second in command, Dariux Valcorn. "I want you to prepare for us to leave, immediately. We'll be taking these two with us. Send someone to start packing up their things. As soon as this nightmare of a meeting is over, we go."

"So the rumours I heard are true then? Laird Kelin has mated with Lady Teriva?" Dariux scowled.

"I don't know if it's happened yet, but if it hasn't, I imagine it will soon."

"I feel for Corin then. It's going to hit him hard. I can't believe Kel would voluntarily give up his truemate like this."

"I still don't fully understand why he's doing this. Far better to risk angering his father then never being with his truemate."

"I'll get everything sorted. I'll get Pacin and Oster to pack their things. They both have medical and tech experience, so they'll be careful of everything. Good luck here." Dariux grimaced as he clasped Niko's shoulder in support.

"I think we're going to need it."

Never had truer words been spoken.

Just as Dariux left, Kel and Tir walked onto the stage accompanied by two other people. Niko recognised them as Lady Teriva and Laird Calahoun, Martellon's daughter and son. His son was still in his teens and Niko wondered how much his age influenced Martellon's decisions and political wrangling. How different would their situation be if Martellon's wife birthed a son first instead of a daughter, Niko wondered? Would they still be in this fucked up situation now?

As they turned back to the front, they watched as the Chieftain beckoned to another man. A harsh indrawn breath escaped from Corin's mouth, his face paling slightly. He shot a frantic look around him, picking out all the guards in the room from both clans before settling on Tate. He was desperately trying to convey something with his eyes. Tate just couldn't work out what it was. Not willing to risk saying anything where it would be so easy to be overheard, Corin had to content himself with using the hand codes the Avanti used to communicate. He repeatedly flashed the danger sign at Tate.

Tate immediately went into full Avanti mode. His gaze immediately shot up, scanning the room, seeking out where this danger was Corin seemed to have found. Nothing looked particularly out of place, but with the new arrivals he couldn't be sure. He certainly didn't see any outward signs of danger, although that didn't mean there weren't any. There must be something to have elicited such a reaction from Corin. Just as he was about to try and ask, the Chieftain spoke.

"My clan, my friends, honoured guests and Offworlders." As he spoke, he shot both Tate and Corin a look which was evil and sadistic to the core. "It is good to be back and I bring joyous news with me. I have worked with Chieftain Martellon and we have brokered a political alliance between the two clans. It's going to bring with it a greater level of peace and security between us all. We will share resources and work together to face our enemies head on when we must. We have some of the greatest minds on the planet between the two clans. The things we will be able to achieve when we combine this intellectual might, with our already substantial military strength, will render us at the top of the clans and let us vie for leadership of the Conclave. No longer will we have to bow down to others who believe themselves to be greater than they are. No longer will we have to face sneering contempt over the size of our military force. We will become more powerful, more wealthy and more influential together. I ask you all to stand with me in cheering this great news for our people."

The three men shot looks at each other as they listened to the Chieftain deliver the speech with all the passion of a newly converted zealot. He seemed driven to become the reigning power on the planet through whatever means necessary. It was certainly something Niko was going to have to inform his father and clan about. If everything was as he feared, then there could be dire consequences for them all.

"While the union is borne out of political will and perseverance it will be sealed with so much more. It was with great joy in our hearts as we watched Laird Kelin and Lady Teriva grow closer as we held the negotiations. It is with an overwhelming sense of happiness and pride that I can announce my son has asked Lady Teriva to be his mate and she has happily accepted."

Tate felt Corin's body stiffen beside him. He watched as a mask of neutrality slid down Corin's face. The mask was in place just in time for the Chieftain to turn towards them and smirk before a look of consternation crossed his face when he got no visible reaction from Corin. Yet Tate knew differently— he could feel the distress pouring off his friend.

"It is a great honour to welcome a daughter into our fold. I am glad my son is settling down and look forward to the many fine sons he will provide this clan. There is nothing more that I could ask for than a new future King or Conclave leader to be born into the family. Tonight we celebrate. Spread the word, the Mating will be performed at moonrise in one week." The Chieftain continued as though he wasn't done subjecting Corin to his own version of hell. "We will come and greet you all personally. We have news of various positions within our alliance which we need to fill and have people in mind from both clans. So I ask everyone to stay until we are done."

"Fuck," Tate whispered under his breath shooting a look at Niko.

Niko moved closer to whisper back to him, "I've got people packing up your things. Don't worry, they'll be careful and get everything put away properly. By the time this nightmare is over, we can leave. I've got everything set up to go immediately, but we can't let on we're going. I wouldn't put it past Chieftain Damron to put you under guard if he finds out you're attempting to leave. We do this quietly and quickly."

"Agreed," Tate replied.

"We're leaving?" questioned Corin, turning away from them briefly as he shut his eyes for a moment. When he turned back, his eyes had taken on a glazed appearance. "Oh fuck, you were prepared for this. Are you telling me you expected this to happen? You knew and didn't tell me? You let me go on believing he loved me?" Corin hissed at them both. His body had gone into fight or flight mode and a surge of adrenaline was coursing through him causing his body to tremble.

Niko shook his head, his brows furrowed as he begged him to understand. "It was only a possibility and we didn't know for sure until it was announced. It's not as the Chieftain says, Corin, Kel loves you, and he's doing this to protect you. Please, I'll explain everything, but not here and not now, it's not safe. Just keep your head held high and don't let them see anything, okay?"

Corin simply nodded, too stunned by everything that was going on to do much else. He was feeling dizzy and disorientated, and he wanted nothing more than to hide from everything and everyone.

Tate moved to stand close to Corin, resting his hand on Corin's back in a gesture of support, hoping it would lend him the strength needed to get through this. They all watched as the group worked their way quickly towards them, until Chieftain Damron stood in front of them, a wicked smirk on his face.

"Ah, here they are, our Offworld visitors." He sneered with a dismissive wave of his hand.

Corin blindly grabbed at Tate's hand hidden behind his back, squeezing for all he was worth. Tate gave him a gentle squeeze back, desperately worried for his friend. It was obvious to him that Corin was going into full blown shock.

They all heard Lady Teriva mutter to her brother, although they had a feeling she deliberately wasn't quiet. "So these are the vermin who have invaded our planet. I can't wait till we get rid of them by any means necessary. They don't deserve a share of what we have here. It's an affront to even have them in front of me."

Well, shit, thought Tate, the woman really was a nasty piece of work. What the fuck was Kel thinking subjecting himself to this?

Tir introduced them. "Chieftain Martellon, this is Captain Corin Talovich and Lieutenant Commander Tate Riven, from the Barin Alliance."

Martellon greeted them somewhat politely, refusing to acknowledge their ranks within the Alliance or even accord them with the politeness of a proper introduction. While he spoke, his eyes shone with an intense hatred that stunned Corin in its intensity, all of which was directed his way.

"Chieftain Martellon." Corin and Tate both dipped their heads, ever so slightly, in the vaguest display of respect for appearance's sake, rather than believing he earned it.

Looking at his face and seeing the ring gracing one of the fingers on his left hand as he brushed his hair away, Corin received the confirmation that his earlier suspicions were indeed correct.

This was the man who had been in the cave the night they rescued Eliya. This was the man who was responsible for everything which happened to the poor little girl. What the hell was going on if someone who was supposed to be supporting you did something so evil? There was definitely more going on than anyone realised. Corin began thinking, his thoughts a jumbled mess. He couldn't wait to discuss this with Kel; then he remembered why he was standing in front of this group. How had he managed to forget so soon? Before his mind could continue its thought process, Lady Teriva was standing in front of him. He called on every ounce of inner strength he had, barely in control of his body any longer. The trembling was increasing and he was barely holding it together.

"My lady." He barely dipped his head this time. This woman oozed manipulation and self-importance from every pore. There was a cold, calculating look on her face when she studied Corin. He refused to crumble and let her see the effect this was having on him. His pride was too great. He was not going to break down in front of the woman who replaced him. With a huff of annoyance, she moved on when she realised she wasn't going to get any sort of reaction from him, let alone the one she obviously wanted.

Then the moment arrived; Kel was standing in front of him. He could see Kel's eyes desperately trying to convey something. There was a beseeching look on his face and his hand was twitching at his side. A look of concern soon overtook the beseeching look as he took in Corin's condition. It was obvious Corin had been ill. He still looked weary and haggard and there was no doubt Kel picked up on it, so attuned was he to the smallest change to his mate.

Corin noticed the look of concern on Kel's face. Well, fuck him, he has no right to know anything about me anymore. He can go fuck off to his bitchy new wife. There was no way Corin was going to acknowledge anything.

"Laird Kelin." Corin dipped his head and watched with a hidden satisfaction at how Kel reared back slightly when Corin used his full name, rather than the more intimate version. "Congratulations. I hope you are both very happy and have the family you both desire and deserve."

"Thank you, Corin." Kel's breathing increased to a shallow, yet rapid, tempo and he rubbed the nape of his neck.

Kel's eyes were unable to look away from Corin, desperately trying to read his features. The knuckles on one hand grew white, so strong was the power in the fist Kel made. Frustration became evident on his face when he could see no trace of any emotion. Corin used every ounce of control he possessed to maintain his mask of disinterest.

As Kel tried to linger, desperate to talk to Corin in any way possible, he was dragged away by Teriva's hand, which he forgot he held. He tried to stop her, but looks from just about everyone except Corin bade him to be sensible and stop.

"Sort it later," Tir hissed at him, "Don't make a scene, you'll just make it worse for him."

With a brief nod, Kel let himself be led off.

"Corin, Tate," Tir simply greeted both of them with an apologetic look on his face before moving swiftly on to the next group of people. After all, nothing he could say right now would help, and having just warned Kel from lingering, he knew it wasn't sensible to focus on them now.

As soon as the group was out of earshot, Niko leaned in to both of them. "Let's get the fuck out of here before this gets any worse. I really don't like this. I don't know what the fuck the Chieftain is thinking."

By mutual consent, the three of them kept silent as they made their way out of the hall and were met by Dariux. Even in his state of shock, Corin felt Tate stiffen beside him. He wondered if they had been caught trying to leave, but when nothing happened, he came to the conclusion he was imagining things. It didn't surprise him considering the turmoil his mind was in.

"This way, quickly. There are increased levels of guards moving about. I have a feeling if we don't go right now it's all over. We need to get you all safe." However, the look of concern on his face wasn't directed at Corin or even Niko, it was instead directed at Tate.

They all moved as fast as they could without arousing suspicion. Thankfully, everyone they did meet were still celebrating the newly formed alliance and were too excited to be focusing on what anyone else was doing. Guards were lax at their posts, women excitedly chattering away to anyone who was near them and the children were all running about laughing. Making it out to the stables was easy and they met with two members of Niko's guard who were standing with their Refrinti mounts ready and waiting.

"Everyone else is waiting a few minutes outside of the walls. We got everything packed up and sent out. It's just us left to go," Oster said.

"Thank you." Niko slapped the man on the back before mounting swiftly. The others followed as fast as they could, although it took Corin a few tries to get mounted. Thankfully, it wasn't long before they trotted straight up to the gate. The guard there stopped them briefly, but Niko managed to charm him into believing they were just out for a brief respite from the hubbub of activity within the keep. Niko was sure it wouldn't have worked if the guard hadn't been so distracted by all the gossip flying about.

When they caught up to his men at arms, Dariux nodded to his sergeant who called out, "We ride!" The entire group broke out into a fast pace, all of them desperate to get away from the Derin and their new alliance with the Farian Clan.

Chapter Sixteen

If you can make one heap of all your winnings
And risk it on one turn of pitch-and-toss,
And lose, and start again at your beginnings
And never breathe a word about your loss;

Tate was concerned for Corin, both physically and mentally. He was still recovering, they both were, and Tate didn't know how much time the Doc had spent riding in the past. It wasn't something everyone in the Alliance was used to. Most planets tended to be more technologically advanced and relied on other forms of transportation. For anyone new to riding, it was going to be arduous, but with the way things stood with Corin, it was not going to be easy, far from it. He wished he knew how Corin was doing mentally. It was obvious he was still in shock. He had yet to drop the façade that he had slammed back in place when this shitstorm started in the great hall.

While Tate was pleased Corin had taken his advice and got through the little fucked up meet and greet without it all going to shit, he was annoyed his advice was now being used against him. He repeatedly tried to engage Corin in conversation. It was useless. At times, he wasn't even sure Corin heard him, at others he was positive he was being ignored. When Corin let his mount drop back slightly so he was behind Tate and Niko, he never spoke a word. He realised there would be time later to see what damage had been done to his friend and now was not it.

Niko was watching all of Tate's failed attempts to engage Corin, not surprised when eventually Tate simply gave up. When Corin dropped back, Niko drew closer to Tate so they could talk. It would certainly help the time go more quickly as they made their way back home. Home— he didn't realise how much he missed his clan. There was nothing he wouldn't do for Kel and Tir, but it didn't mean he enjoyed spending so much time in Damron's orbit. Something had changed in the man since the death of his wife. A new harshness surrounded him. He was more confrontational, aggressive and quick to act without considering the consequences of his actions. He was taking his clan in a bad direction and regressing to the older ways of his forefathers, which were more elitist and purist. Niko hadn't realised how bad it was until he'd seen it with his own eyes. His father was going to be concerned for the friendship they had. He was going to be particularly concerned for Kel, Tir and little Eliya.

They rode hard, pushing both themselves and their Refrinti as much as possible by unspoken agreement. They all knew it was best to get back to their own clan lands. He was glad the border between the two clans was less than a day's ride away. As soon as they were a safe distance over the border, he would make sure they camped for the night. They could take a less punishing pace in the morning.

Corin's mind was all over the place. He kept squeezing his eyes shut in a vain attempt to stop his thoughts and feelings from consuming him. He was feeling cold, breathless and dizzy. His mind was scattered like the petals of a Deris flower on the wind. Tate was trying to talk to him, but he simply couldn't bring himself to talk to the man. He was trying to avoid thinking about what happened, let alone having to talk about it. Not the healthiest course of action, sure, but it seemed the most appropriate at the moment. His mind was still a mess as he tried to process everything. He simply couldn't understand how it all happened.

Did HE— as he now thought of him, not able to even think his name— ever actually have any feelings for him? Had HE simply used Corin for a bit of fun? He wasn't sure he believed Niko when he mentioned HE was doing this to protect him.

What did he need protecting from? Besides, mating with someone seemed a bit of an extreme measure to subject yourself to so that you protected someone. No, he was more inclined to believe HE simply thought of him as a temporary distraction until something better came along. Corin wasn't surprised, it seemed the way his love life went.

For some reason no one ever seemed to think he was worthy, or if they did, outside influences soon put a stop to any relationship. He knew he wasn't anyone special, but he didn't think he was a bad package. He was successful, decent looking, smart and caring. It didn't matter now, it would never matter. He couldn't go through this again, wouldn't go through it again.

Never again was he going to open up his heart and let someone in. It was easier to just go about life without getting involved. Far better to have random encounters in spaceports than this. Of course he wasn't the sort of man who did those things anyway, so it looked like he would spend his life alone. Wanting to switch off this train of thoughts, he tried to focus on the work he had been doing with Herica, although it was no doubt pointless now. He would likely never see her again.

All three men were lost in their own thoughts. The men at arms around them picked up on the tensions emanating from them, and a solemn quietness surrounded the group as they ran. It was these thoughts of Herica that finally seemed to shake some of the numbness from his mind. His eyes went wide and his nostrils flared as the full weight of what had happened clarified in his mind. He brought his Refrinti to an abrupt stop, crying out in a pain filled voice, "No!!"

All around him warriors jerked in their saddles, bringing their mounts to a dead stop as they drew their weapons looking for what had caused Corin to react that way.

"Stars, what is it, Corin? What's wrong?" Tate looked around desperately.

"We need to go back. I need to warn…" Corin was struggling to stay still as his gaze bounced about the place.

"Corin!" Tate roared.

Corin seemed to shake himself free of turmoil. "We need to talk and talk right now."

Niko looked at Tate and caught the man's nod. "We have crossed the border into Estrivian lands already. There's a little clearing just up there. We will break there. Two minutes, okay Corin? Two minutes and we can talk."

Corin nodded, feeling his anger rise at himself for freezing up and not having considered the consequences to his earlier realisations.

Tate didn't realise they had even crossed the border, there was no obvious sign, but he couldn't be more relieved. Corin was obviously extremely distressed about something and Tate had to wonder why he was begging to go back. While he was almost physically recovered from his injuries, he was still feeling sore and twitchy. Used to pushing his body to its limits, he recognised that it was going to take a while to get back to the level of fitness he maintained before the fateful day on board the Delphini.

As Dariux went off to oversee the warriors and make sure the camp was set up around them, Tate and Niko waited for Corin to fill them in on everything.

"I'm so sorry that it's taken me so long to talk. I should have said something as soon as we left, if not sooner, I just… my mind was…" Corin stuttered as emotions started to get the best of him.

Tate laid a hand on his shoulder and squeezed. "It's okay, we know you were in shock, just tell us now. At least we will know and that sounds like the important part."

Corin closed his eyes briefly and took a deep breath before he spoke. "I need to fill you in on what happened back there. And no, I'm not referring to Kel."

"You mean before he walked in? When you tensed up? What else is going on, Doc?" Tate needed answers and he needed them now.

"Shit, you aren't going to like this. I recognised someone in the group."

"What do you mean, recognised?" Niko asked. "How can you have recognised anyone? You aren't from the… Oh shit. You mean…" Niko recoiled from Corin's words as though they had stuck him.

"Yeah, the man from the cave was there."

"Oh, fuck me, you mean he was part of the Farian Clan?" Tate's eyes went wide.

"Oh, I don't just mean part of the clan." Corin barked out a harsh laugh. "I mean the top man himself. I mean Chieftain Martellon is the man I saw that night."

"Oh fuck," Tate exclaimed. His eyes went wide as he realised this was what Corin had been trying to warn him about when he flashed the danger sign. "How sure are you?"

"Very. Even if I hadn't been sure beforehand, when he came over I recognised his ring," Corin explained.

Niko jerked slightly before he drew his lips back and gave a soft growl. "Oh stars, what has Chieftain Damron done. Fuck, this is bad. What the fuck is Martellon up to?"

"I don't know." Corin sighed heavily, feeling weary and ready to just not feel anything at all. "You're going to be the only one who has a hope of answering the question. We don't know enough of the politics, history and relationships between the clans. You must have some idea?"

"Martellon has always been power hungry," Niko mused as he thought. "But I'm not sure what he would gain from kidnapping Eliya considering what's happened with Kel."

Corin grimaced at the mention of the man he loved. He really didn't want to be thinking of him at the moment. He would much rather talk about anything, do anything, other than him. "Look, I need to get some rest. Are you guys okay working out what to do?" When they nodded at him, he breathed a sigh of relief. "I'll see you guys later then." Not bothering to wait for a reply, Corin simply got to his feet and walked away from them.

"He's not taking everything very well," Niko spoke after a moment's silence.

Tate's only response was to snort, then burst out laughing. "Well, what the fuck did you expect? Your buddy there just completely ripped his heart out, treated him like shit, never once thought to explain it all to him, treated him, frankly, like some little woman to be protected. Not once did it even cross Kel's mind to discuss it with him. Damn it, Corin might have had some insight into everything. He might have chosen to walk away before it got too far. He damn well wouldn't have chosen to let himself fall in love when this was going to happen. What the fuck was Kel honestly thinking?"

"I think it's time to fill in the blanks for you, then we can work out what the hell to do about Martellon." Niko rubbed the nape of his neck and a sigh slipped from his lips.

"Oh shit, there's more going on?"

"You have no idea," Niko replied.

Tate sat effectively mute from shock as Niko explained. He found he couldn't utter a single word as his mind attempted to process everything Niko had just told him. Niko himself simply sat there and waited him out.

"So you're telling me people on this planet can literally find their soul mate? As though some celestial being, force or whatever has specifically designed people to be perfect in almost every way for each other?"

"Yes," was Niko's simple response.

"And truemates are normally only members of the opposite sex? Kel and Corin are the first same sex mates on the planet?" Tate clarified.

"As far as we know, yes." Niko thought for a moment. "But it doesn't mean it hasn't happened before. There are some clans we really don't spend much time with. So it's possible it's happened there, and we don't know about it."

"Okay." Tate scrubbed a weary hand over his face. "And normally if truemates are of the opposite sex then a mating virtually guarantees them children?"

"Yes, from what I understand there is an optimal combination of DNA between truemates. Of course, it's not going to be relevant for these two."

"So if finding your truemate is as special as you say it is, then how could Kel possibly go through with this other mating? Surely it goes against everything you say truemates are to each other?"

Niko grimaced. "Well, yes, but Damron has threatened Corin. One of the overriding instincts accompanying any bond, especially a new truemate bond, is a fierce protectiveness. Kel would literally suffer unimaginable horrors, or die, rather than have Corin suffer for even one minute."

"But he is suffering. Sure, not physically, but he damn well is suffering. You can see what it's doing to him."

"But he can recover from that and Kel would rather live in abject misery with Teriva and have Corin hate him then risk anything happening to him," Niko explained.

"So he does in fact love Corin."

"More than you can possibly know. He's devastated, he tried so hard to find another way, but in the end accepted this as his fate."

"Part of me can't help thinking he really is a stupid bastard for doing this, but I do understand. I'm just not sure Corin will. I'm not sure even telling him is a good idea either. If, and it's a big if, but if he does believe all this, he'll insist on going back and being with Kel anyway and screw the consequences. It's liable to make matters worse, certainly in the short term. But, and this is another big but, if I don't tell him, then he may never trust me again. He's already pissed off at us for not telling him of the mating between Kel and Teriva sooner."

"Frankly, this whole thing is fucked up and makes me wonder..." Niko's voice trailed off and a look passed over his face. It looked like horror combined with a sudden comprehension. "Oh shit. I think I know what's going on."

"Why do I get the distinct impression things are going to get even more complicated?" Tate snorted.

"So we've been trying to work out what Martellon would get out of kidnapping Eliya? How about this for a theory?" Niko wrinkled his brow. "Now, it has been known for a long time Martellon is power hungry. The Derin Clan is big and one of the most respected clans on the planet, a fact Martellon has always been jealous of. He's never gone after it. I think even he knows he would lose in a direct assault. His military forces are nowhere near good enough to succeed in a normal battle. So what if the devious bastard thought of another way?"

"Another way?" Tate queried.

"Well, what if he planned for Kel to marry Teriva and for them to have children. It would give him an opening within the clan. Any child born from the mating would be a future clan leader to influence."

"Not with Eliya about." Tate was positive about that.

"Exactly, but by kidnapping her and say, getting rid of her, it would leave the way open for his grandchild. We already know the Chieftain's getting more unstable, and if Tir and Kel were both disposed of, then he would gain the clan leadership by the backdoor, taking over until the child came of age," Niko explained his theory.

"Well, fuck me." Tate rubbed his brow as thought about it. "That's horrifying, devious and sadly makes sense. No one would suspect him until it's too late, especially as there is now a full political alliance in place. "

"Indeed, it would be assumed he would be happy with the power he gets by association."

"Damn, he's a sneaky little fucker." As Tate mulled over Niko's suggestion, he realised just how much it made sense.

"And with Damron as unbalanced as he is right now, it is unlikely he would believe any accusations, no matter who they came from." Niko sighed as more pieces of the puzzle fell into place.

"I'm guessing as well that we won't be able to go back and try and warn Kel and Tir either."

"It's unlikely, and frankly, incredibly dangerous. I imagine Martellon has already made sure to integrate himself and those he trusts within both the clan and with its members as much as possible, to try and prevent just such a thing happening."

"So what do we do now?" Tate wondered.

"We do the only thing we can. We go back to my clan and try to find evidence and a way to get to Kel or Tir without tipping off Martellon," Niko suggested. "As soon as we get home, I will speak to my father and see what he suggests. It's more sensible to go home first and bring him in on this then risk going back to the Derin and starting a fight we are ill prepared for. What I will do is send a rider back to the Derin carrying a message for Tir and Kel. It's a start at least, and right now? It's the only thing we can do."

"I think we have to bring Corin in on this." Tate carried on even as Niko shook his head. "Look, firstly he has a right to know as he's in the middle of all this, just as the rest of us are. Secondly, he has more right to know than me, considering who he is to Kel. I know him, and he will probably choose to ignore the whole truemate aspect of it, but whatever his personal feelings to do with Kel, he will not sit to one side while Martellon attempts this. It's not in his nature to not do anything. He will want to do whatever he can to protect Eliya. He adores her, we both do. Trust me, I'm not looking forward to the conversation with him, but if I'm honest, I really don't see another way."

Suddenly a voice broke into the conversation. "Tate's right, you know, Niko," Dariux said as he joined them. "I was watching over you and I overheard everything."

"You shouldn't be listening in on private conversations, Dari." Tate's angry glare was directed at Dariux. "This has nothing to do with you!"

"It has everything to do with me!" Dariux insisted. "This is my planet, our clans and, most importantly, my friends. I cannot and will not sit by and watch this happening and do nothing. And my name is Dariux, use it." He let out an exasperated sigh. He rolled his eyes when Tate just smirked back at him.

Tate muttered to himself before sighing and saying, "Fine, join in the discussion. You're right to get involved. You might be able to help more from a military aspect if needed. I can do a lot, but I don't know the nuances of this planet well enough. I'm sorry for snapping. It's all just getting crazy now."

"Well, well, an apology and a comment from you that isn't a complete insult, I might almost say it was a compliment. I feel privileged." Dariux winked at Tate as he spoke.

"Oh, bite me, D." Tate glared at the man.

Niko looked on as the two men bickered back and forth. He was getting suspicious there was more going on between them. He would definitely have to keep an eye on them both. It would certainly be a pleasant distraction to everything else going on around them. "So, Dariux, you think Tate is right? We should tell Corin?"

"Honestly? You don't really have a choice. We're going to need allies wherever we can get them. The more minds on this problem the better. As long as Tate think's it's the right thing to do, then I agree with him," Dariux spoke, ignoring the look of shock on Tate's face.

"Really, X? You agree with me?"

Dariux simply winked at Tate.

"Okay, look, it's getting late, so it's probably best if we talk to him tomorrow. For now let's all go and get some sleep. There's nothing that can be done right now," Niko ordered them.

The three men stood and started going back to their sleep rolls, lost in their own thoughts. Not one of the men slept easy. All of them were plagued by nightmares. Death and destruction were a common theme, and as much as the effects on the whole population was disturbing, it was the deaths of their friends that were the hardest to bear. These images would plague them for many a moon to come.

Corin's dreams were just as troubling, but in a different way. He dreamt of a future. A future which involved him and Kel, happy, but the most surprising thing was in his dream he saw children, their children. The fact the children resembled them both? Heart-breaking.

As the men at arms went about dismantling the camp, Tate realised it was almost time to do the comms check.

Checking with Niko it was safe to go ahead, he retrieved his gear from one of the guards and went through the process of setting it all up. Niko joined him, offering to speed up the process. It wasn't long before the new adapted system was up and running. He went through the process of trying to contact any of his teammates. At this point he was merely going through the motions, more sure than ever it wasn't going to work. Too much time had passed and he wasn't sure, even if they were able, his teammates would still even attempt to make contact. They had probably drawn the conclusion he and the Doc were dead.

"Alpha Dawn, calling for a Sunrise." A crackled, slightly distorted voice broke through his internal musings.

"Shit!" He exclaimed, scrambling for the mic. "Alpha Dawn, this is Sunrise! We can hear you!"

"Holy heavens! Tate, is that really you?" Dax's voice came through the line.

"Dax? Yeah, it's Tate! Stars, it's good to hear your voice. Who's with you? Are you safe? What's your status?" He threw out the questions in quick succession.

"Damn, Tate, it's good to hear your voice. Are you and Corin okay? I'm still with Bell, we're both alright. We've been holed up in a little village. Bell was injured, but we managed to get him patched up. We've been scouting the area trying to work out which way to start moving. We're safe, though, so it's all good. I'm not sure how far from you we are but it can't be too far. We saw your pod go down hard so we've been pretty worried. I've been trying to raise you on every check-in," Dax spoke, relief saturated his voice.

"Thank the stars!" Corin exclaimed.

Tate hadn't been aware Corin was with them, but he was more than happy for him to share in good news for once. "We've been trying to contact you. I've boosted the comms system. I'm not sure if it's helping or if it's a proximity thing. We're doing okay." Tate hesitated as he spoke, not sure of how much to relay over the comms, but Dax immediately picked up on his hesitation.

"Tate? What's happened? Talk to me," Dax ordered.

"It's long and pretty bloody complicated, but we are alright. Both of us suffered some injuries, Doc managed to save my life a few times. We got taken in by one of the clans on this world."

"That's great news. We should start trying to make our way to you." Tate could hear the relief in Dax's voice.

"Well, we, uh, needed to leave and I wouldn't suggest going there," Tate hedged.

"Oh?" That one word from Dax held a wealth of questions.

"It's a long story, and one better explained in person. We are on our way to another clan. You are going to be welcome there though." Tate shot a look at Niko as he realised he should have checked before suggesting it. Niko simply smiled at him and nodded.

"Okay, but you *will* fill me in on everything when we get together. Bell and I have been getting pretty antsy staying here, but we weren't sure which way to even head out. It's fantastic we will be made welcome. Can you get a bearing for us?"

He conferred quickly with Niko before speaking again. "To the north of where we crashed there is a mountain. You need to go west of it. You will come across a lake. We will be on the western side of the lake. It will be close in size to a town so you won't be able to miss it."

"Perfect, I have no idea how long it will take to get there, but we will get there, I can guarantee that. Nothing will stop us getting to our friends," Dax vowed, conviction ringing through his voice like a bell.

"Shit, it's going to be good to see you guys. Any news on Hunter and Bray?" Tate asked.

"No, and I'm guessing then you haven't heard from them either. But on the basis we are all still here and okay, we have to believe we will find them." Dax was going to do everything in his power to ensure it happened.

"Yeah, we've been hoping you all made it, and after talking to you, our hopes are renewed. Listen, we're just packing our camp away, we rode hard yesterday and we'll be riding hard again all day, can we reconnect this evening?" Tate hoped Dax would agree. He was pretty sure they were all desperate to get to the Estrivian Clan.

"Sure, you guys get where you need to be, we can catch up again later. It's going to be good to see you." Dax sighed. "Alpha Dawn out."

"Acknowledged, Sunrise out."

Tate let his head drop as they broke comms. His body sagged as relief radiated out from him. A burst of pure happiness soared through him, lifting his spirits. It was such a release of stress to know at least some of their friends had made it.

"Damn, some good news for once." He smiled.

"I'm so pleased for you guys." Niko said with a grin.

Even Corin managed to smile at them. His own relief was written all over his face. "Thank fuck we've got good news for once. I was beginning to think we were cursed! It will be good to see those two again and I have a feeling we are going to need them in the coming weeks." Corin couldn't be more relieved that more of the Avanti would be around to keep them all safe.

Chapter Seventeen

Time was of the essence as they hastily finished packing up the camp. The quicker they were settled in Niko's keep, the quicker they could plan. The main thing troubling Tate was yet again being the bearer of bad news to Corin. This was getting to be a habit that he was distinctly unimpressed with. The steady paced they maintained kept conversations to a minimum. Even Niko's men at arms were quietly intent on getting home, no doubt happy at the prospect of returning to loved ones.

By early afternoon, even as exhausted as they were, the excitement began to build. Tate wasn't sure why until Dariux leaned over from his left and said, "They know we are nearly home."

"Was I asking you, D-man?"

"Seriously, the name is Dariux, that's D.A.R.I.U.X. There I've spelled it out for you in case you have problems." He laughed when Tate's eyes were sending daggers his way. Oh, how he loved to rile this man.

Dariux's grey eyes were glinting with a variety of emotions, flickering across his face too fast for Tate to determine exactly what they were. His body stiffened at the close proximity of the man. He should have been able to keep his reaction in check better. He was a fucking Avanti, and they were trained to show a neutral front in all situations.

So why was he unable to control himself around this man? Just what was it about Dariux that drove him crazy in more ways than one? What's more, why did the infuriating man have to know he affected him? The smirk Dariux had thrown him said it all, he knew. The question was what did he know? Tate wasn't even sure he knew. Damn, his brain was confusing even himself. He quickly forced himself into warrior mode and ignored the man, choosing instead to focus back on Corin.

Corin watched the group as they approached what must be the Estrivian Clan keep. There seemed such a genuine level of happiness spreading throughout the men. It was enough to make his lips quirk up ever so slightly at the side. He was glad even if he couldn't be happy, other people could. He overheard the two guards in front of him chattering excitedly. The youngest, who can't have been much older than twenty, was desperate to get home to his mate. It soon became apparent she was heavily pregnant and due to give birth in the next two weeks.

He drew in a short, sharp breath when he heard about how worried the guard was for them, as it appeared there was no midwife in the clan at present. Leaning forward, he gently tapped the man on the shoulder to get his attention. "Sorry, I couldn't help but overhear you talking. I know I'm not a midwife, but I am a damn good doctor and a surgeon. It's been a few years since I've seen a birth, but I will happily be by your mate's side when it's time. I will do everything in my power to keep them safe and healthy. You can be sure of it."

The young man wore a stunned look on his face as his friend turned to Corin. "Thank you, doctor. He has been so worried. He was going to have to rely on the women in both families to help, and poor Lexin has been stressed about it."

"I am glad I can help and there is nothing better than seeing new life come into this world." Corin raised his first genuine smile in days as he spoke. Despite not having much interaction with children over the years, he had always had a soft spot for them. There was something about their innocence that melted his heart.

The young man finally found his voice. "Doctor, do you mean that?" When Corin nodded, Lexin let loose with a loud, joyous shout to the stars startling the men who turned to watch him almost dancing in his saddle. "Doctor, I really, really can't thank you enough. Whatever I need to pay, tell me, whatever you need, whenever you need then let me know. We will find it done."

"There is no need for any of that. I will not charge. I would be honoured to assist you."

Niko joined in the conversation. "Thank you, Corin. It is something which has been troubling him deeply."

"You have no midwife as a clan? Surely you must have a doctor who is capable of assisting women through childbirth?" Corin was stunned. How could there be no help?

"Not really. For some reason there seems to be an absence of decent doctors on this planet. The one we have simply isn't used to dealing with childbirth." Corin noticed that Niko's face bore traces of the long-term worry he must be feeling at such limited resources within his clan.

"Well, I'm here for now, so I will do what I can." Corin smiled at those listening around him.

"Thank you, my friend, there are a lot of people in the clan who will be greatly relieved and appreciative of your help."

"So how far away are we?" Tate joined in on the conversation, glad Corin was still talking and hadn't withdrawn back into himself.

"About an hour away." Niko's lips started to spread into a small smile and his shoulders sagged. "I am relieved we are nearly home. We will have a lot to discuss with my father. I hope you'll both join me. He will no doubt want to talk to you both anyway. He's one of the clan leaders who supported joining the Barin Alliance. He could see the benefits of such a move would far outweigh the negatives. Besides, we need to work out what to do about Martellon and warning Kel and Tir. "

"Then we shall be happy to talk with him," Tate answered for them both.

They continued chatting about Niko's lands, what they could expect from various clan members and how different it was from Tir's clan. Tate was glad Niko used Tir's name, not wanting anything to happen that might prompt Corin to retreat into his shell. The convoy broke into a run as they approached the gates of the keep. Their arrival had been noted by the sentries, and so they were greeted by a welcoming party. As soon as Niko dismounted, he was enveloped in a massive hug from his mother, his face peppered with kisses even as she scolded him for being away for so long.

Corin turned to Tate. "So, it really doesn't matter where you are in the seven universes, it's a mother's mission in life to always embarrass her children!"

A bark of laughter broke out from Tate, who tried to school his features, but ultimately he failed. He was far too pleased to see some of the old Corin leaking through and it gave him every reason in the world to laugh.

"Oh, son, you have no idea!" A man turned to them smiling. "That's positively mild for my wife, but, shhh, don't let her hear me or I'll be in bad books for days!" The man was chuckling as he spoke, the love he obviously felt for his wife shining bright in his eyes, enhancing the laughter lines that bracketed them.

Corin and Tate grinned at each other, already feeling the happier and more welcoming atmosphere in this clan. They hoped it was the start of good things to come.

It felt so good to Niko to be home. He had missed his parents and his clan more than he realised, and with the level of drama going on in Tir's clan, he was glad for the peace and happiness that always surrounded his home. The last few months were incredibly gruelling for him. He had undertaken a tour of four of the clans, Tir's being the last. While physically it wasn't too big a strain, although he hated all of the travel, it was the strain on him emotionally and mentally that had been so gruelling.

He pulled his father to one side. "We need to talk, urgently. There is something very wrong at the Derin Clan."

Alix closed his eyes briefly and let out a deep breath. "Will waiting one night change anything? Are people likely to lose their lives if we wait? You are just home and your mother wants to spend just one evening with you without any problems. Can we give her that, son? She's missed you more than she can say, we both have."

Niko looked into the eyes of his father and saw the silent plea in them. He nodded. "It's urgent, but there won't be much more we can do before morning anyway. I've already done what I can."

"You are sure?" Alix checked. He would stop everything if he needed to, but he wanted to see just one night of his family happily together. He realised looking around him that the men needed to let the stress go, even if it was just temporarily. When Niko nodded, he smiled. "Good. Now let's go inside and let your Mami smother you." He laughed at his son's good natured grimace.

After speaking to his father, Niko realised that his parents' choice to hold a celebration upon his return was a blessing in disguise. He was glad Tate and Corin could at least have one night of happiness and relaxation before they all returned to the issues which plagued them. He knew that when he told his father everything he was going to get pretty worked up over the latest actions of Martellon. Martellon's latest actions were certainly not going to help their rocky relationship when next they met at the Clan Conclave.

At the party later, Niko spent most of his time smiling, albeit it with a sadness lurking deep within his eyes. Watching Tate and Corin interact with his clan members was enough to make him laugh at times, smile at others. His cousin accosted Tate straight away and they were currently dancing around the ballroom, giggling away as Tate told her all sorts of stories and jokes. Tate's strength, even while injured, was obvious as he held six year old Alyndra off the floor as they danced. They were laughing away and smiling at everyone as they danced past the guests seated along the walls. Many of his clan were watching in open appreciation. Desire was evident in a lot of eyes, and Niko could see many of the young, unattached women hatching plots to gain his attention.

The elders of the clan were looking on with an indulgent smile and a healthy dose of respect for the stranger in their midst who would take the time to make a young girl happy. Of all of the watchers, Niko paid close attention to the reactions of his best friend and the head of his guard, Dariux. Dariux's entire being was focused solely on Tate. Frustration, approval, happiness, joy and lust shone in his eyes. Niko realised he would have to keep a closer eye on those two. He wasn't sure what was going on between them, although it was obvious something was, and he was certainly determined to find out.

Corin was waylaid as soon as he entered the party by Lixiss, Lexin's mate. She all but sobbed in Corin's arms when she saw him, constantly muttering her thanks. It was obvious that word was already spreading amongst the clan as there were currently five pregnant women in various stages, with what looked to be like their mothers and sisters, holding court around him. He hoped such a happy situation would be enough to keep Corin from withdrawing too far into himself. Although he had suspicions that once Corin managed to recover from the shock of everything, he would be fine. Niko was sure Corin was the type of man who wouldn't let anything stop him from all the good he could do. Every so often he saw Corin look off into the distance with a sad smile, other times his face bore a quiet anger. He knew on both occasions his mind, and heart, were back on the Derin Clan.

He wasn't sure Kel would be fine though. Based on his appearance upon his return from the Farian Clan, it was already painfully obvious Kel was suffering deeply. Niko truly hoped there was some way to bring the two men back together. He had never seen another mating with two people quite so in tune with each other as quickly as these two. The love radiating from them both had been there for all to see. His attention was called away from his two new friends by his father. He reluctantly turned knowing he was going to have to stall him without worrying him. He would not ruin what could turn out to be the last happy clan gathering for a while.

Chapter Eighteen

If you can talk with crowds and keep your virtue,
Or walk with Kings - nor lose the common touch,

The morning brought a return to reality for the men, but the night off had been enough to recharge their batteries, to have a night where they were able to at least partially relax. They had managed to suppress the constant worry niggling at the front of their minds, at least a little bit for one night. It gave them all a chance to step back a little and to examine everything with fresh eyes, something which was going to be sorely needed when they met with Alix. Entering his father's suite of offices with Corin and Tate in tow, he gave his father a quick but solid hug before introducing the men.

"Father, although you met briefly yesterday, as a formal introduction, this is Captain Corin Talovich and Lieutenant Commander Tate Riven of the Barin Alliance." Niko indicated each man in turn as he spoke. "Guys, this is my father, Chieftain Alixandr Dastria." As the men bowed to the Chieftain in greeting, he gestured for them to sit with him as Niko poured them all a sweet tea that was a speciality of their clan.

"So judging by the looks on your face, son, I'm not going to like what you have to report." Alix had a wry smile on his face.

"No father, I doubt you are." Niko's voice was laden with the stress of everything going on. "First, let me fill you in on my visits to some of the clans as the early part of my trip went well. Afterwards, we'll get to the tough stuff." Niko began a rundown of all the clan news before finally starting on Tate and Corin's story. The men looked on as Alix's face was shifting between a range of emotions, from incredulity, to horror, happiness to anger, heartbreak to apprehension. When he finished, they all took a shaky breath, an attempt to release the tension building in the room, although both

Tate and Corin maintained a wary and apprehensive air about them. While they got on great with Niko, they really didn't want a repeat of what happened with the Derin Clan.

"What an absolute fucking bastard," Alix spat out, stunning both of them.

Niko smirked at them. "I told you my father was different!"

"Who the fuck does he think he is playing with people's lives like this? Gentlemen, I hope you learn you will always be welcome here. Even if you hadn't become friends with my son, I would have offered you sanctuary from Damron." Turning to Corin, he continued, "More than anything, young man, I am sorry your introduction to our planet has been so painful, both emotionally and physically. We would never think to make light of a mating bond. We consider it the greatest gift you could ever receive and to see it treated with such disdain and contempt is truly horrifying. Now, that's not to say there is anything wrong with political matches, but if someone were to find their truemate it would override a political match no matter the consequences to the clan. It is simply the way we are."

Corin smiled at him. He liked the man. This was the sort of man you would want as your clan leader. Hopefully life would be easier while they stayed here.

"Now fill me in on exactly what you think Martellon is up to. I think I'm beginning to understand from what you have just been saying." In reality though, Alix was truly worried about just what his son was going to tell him.

Niko went through everything they had discussed at the camp the previous night. Their worries and thoughts about just what Martellon was up to.

"So we were discussing what Martellon would get out of kidnapping Eliya. With as power hungry as he is, we worked out that he is attempting to take over the Derin Clan, from the inside. He has always been jealous of the power Damron wields. Over the last couple of years, Damron and Martellon have been getting closer, I just never realised how close. But I thought about it and Martellon would know that he would never win a battle between the clans. If he engineered it so that Kel mated Teriva and they had children, then it would give him an opening within the clan. Any child born from the mating would be a future clan leader to influence. With the kidnapping of Eliya, it brought him one step closer to his goals. If that had succeeded, I imagine he would have gone after Tir and Kel next." Niko grimaced. "We worry he still might."

"Stars, we need to warn them." Alix started to pace the room. "We aren't strong enough to go up against both clans. We don't have enough warriors."

"No, we don't." Niko was sure about that. "When we worked out what was going on, I dispatched a rider to take a message to Kel and Tir. I'm hoping that Martellon won't have completely taken over things in the short space of time we've been gone."

"Smart idea, son. The quicker we can warn them the better. I can't risk sending you back, I won't risk sending you back, you mean too much to me. The only thing we can do right now is to wait for them to send a message back. Until then we just have to hope those two boys are smarter than they've been over Corin." He sent a sympathetic gaze Corin's way.

Tate laughed. "Well, that can't be hard because the pair of them have been bloody idiots."

Even Corin had to laugh at that one. "I do love you, Tate. You can always make me laugh, no matter what."

"I aim to please, good sir." Tate performed a flowery bow, before taking Corin's hand in his and running kisses up and down his arm. Corin scowled but couldn't hold back the laughter.

Alix smiled at the two of them. He turned to Niko. "I like them." He laughed.

"Yeah, they are good men, and great friends to each other. With everything they have been through, it's amazing they can still smile."

"What do we do if the warning doesn't work?" Corin asked.

"It has too." Alix furrowed his brow as he thought. "We just have to wait and see what message the rider comes back with. If we need to do more then, we can. Until then we will just have to focus on other things. Worry over it when we can't change anything will do little good."

Just as Tate was about to speak, the Chieftain interrupted him. "Now as for your friends, they are always welcome here and I will have our sentries and scouts keep an eye out for them. If they find them, they will arrange a guide here. As for the ones you have not heard from, I shall send riders around the other clans and see if there is any news for you."

Tate smiled as he thanked the Chieftain. "We would really appreciate it, Sir. It's been hard not knowing anything about them."

"It's the least I can do, and please call me Alix. Enough of that Sir carry on, makes me feel old and boring! Now, Corin, I understand you will be helping out our mothers-to-be when the time comes." He called out for one of his advisors. "Please let them know what you need and I shall make sure you have it. It is a relief for us all to know there will be someone who can help the next generation of our clan into the world."

"Then, if you wouldn't mind, I will let Tate fill you in from our end, and I'll go with your advisors to get everything set up. While Lixiss has two weeks to go, we all know babies have a way of deciding when it is time to come into the world. I would rather be ready if the little one becomes impatient to see his parents." More than anything, Corin didn't want to be around when they went into greater detail about everything that happened with Kel.

"Of course. Once again, you have the thanks of the entire clan for this."

"No thanks are needed." Corin smiled. "What's more, I am more than happy to help out with any other medical situations if it's needed. I'm sure Tate can fill you in on all my credentials if you require them."

"We don't, but thank you and yet again we will be severely in your debt for this."

Corin simply shook his head and smiled as he made his way out the door with the advisor in tow.

As soon as Alix was sure Corin was out of earshot, he turned to his son. "Now tell me why Kelin has decided to be a stupid bloody idiot and do what his father wants and so denying his truemate? Corin seems to be a good man, and from what little I have seen, he would have been perfect for Kel."

"I like him." Tate smiled at Niko as he nodded towards Alix.

"I like you too, son." Alix smiled.

Niko smiled at the pair of them, glad that Tate seemed to be settling into the clan already. "So, Kel thinks he's protecting him. He said he would rather never have Corin in his life, and be hated by him, then have his father go after him," Niko explained to his father.

"And Kel doesn't believe he has the strength to protect his own mate? He thinks so little of his own skill? Or does he think so much of his father's ruthlessness? Either of which, it matters little. He will be subjecting himself to a living nightmare if he continues down this path. The ramifications for them both will be horrid." Alix was horrified at the prospect of what they would both suffer.

"Ramifications?" Tate asked with a wary tone.

"Yes. It is not commonly known, but there are consequences to refusing your truemate. Most people don't know because I cannot think of it ever happening before. Certainly not in my lifetime. Now, ultimately it is Kel who has denied his mate so normally he would suffer first. However, as Corin is an Offworlder we have no way of knowing if his physiology will either accelerate or decelerate the process. I am assuming he has been in good health apart from his crash injuries?" Alix asked.

"Oh shit!" Tate exchanged a look of horror with Niko, as exactly what Alix said sunk in. "No, no he hasn't been in perfect health. In fact, he became seriously ill about a week after Kel left."

"Explain how he was ill. We have to hope it was merely a coincidence." But Alix didn't believe his own words and he certainly didn't expect Niko or Tate to either.

As they both explained what transpired with Corin it became painfully aware to Alix that Corin was suffering from was indeed Matesickness. He had no doubt, within days, Kel would start to feel the effects as well. "Okay, I'm sorry but from what I know of Matesickness, it does appear as though it's what Corin is suffering from. As far as he is concerned, well, it is normally, far, far, worse for the mate who has denied the bond. Usually the denied party suffers very little. As I said, it is likely Corin's unique physiology that has made him more susceptible than usual. Hopefully the effects won't last too long for him."

"Is there any cure for it?" Tate hoped there was. If not, he would make sure Corin worked on developing one.

"Not as far as I am aware, but there is a lot of information in the Mystic Archives. I will have our historian find any relevant information and have it passed on to Corin."

"Thank you, Alix, at least there is something that can provide a small measure of reassurance to us." Tate was more pleased than ever they made the journey with Niko. It would have been so much worse if they stayed with the Derin. Yes, Corin was still sick, but now at least there was hope for a cure. What's more, since they'd left they'd made contact with two of their squad, only two to go.

"Father, how bad is it likely to get for Kel?" Sure, Kel was being an idiot, but he was still a good friend.

"Bad I'm afraid. Really bad. It is likely he will slowly deteriorate, become completely bedridden, before finally slipping into a coma." Alix gave them an incredibly sad smile. "It is more than likely he will die from the effects."

"Fuck," Niko whispered, his eyes wide, fear and shock fighting for equal dominance on his face. He had never even considered it could be so bad. "All because he denied his truemate? Surely there are sometimes good reasons for such actions?"

"Yes, there are situations where you could deny your truemate and it doesn't result in the sickness, but they would need to be exceptional circumstances. Which is not the case here. Besides which, it's not just Kel denying his truemate, it's the fact he's taking another mate in his place, and it's such an action which makes the sickness so severe."

"Can it be stopped? Or reversed?" Tate asked.

"I am unsure. The only way it would even be possible is if Kel accepted Corin as his truemate after denying him. Even then I don't know if it will be enough."

"I honestly don't know if Corin could bring himself to accept Kel after everything he did. I don't know if he has it in his heart to forgive him. Sure, intellectually he could do it to save Kel, but emotionally? I simply don't know." Tate was weary, weary of everything going wrong. Weary of the two of them having to face crisis after crisis.

"It's kind of a useless point though really, isn't it? Kel believes he's doing this for the right reasons. He believes he's doing this to save Corin. He certainly knows Corin is his truemate and he would die to protect him. Convincing him of another course of action will be all but impossible," Niko explained to his father.

"There is much more to consider as well. If Kel backs out of his mating agreement with Teriva then Martellon will not take it lightly. The alliance will no doubt crumble and Martellon will aim to take over the clan by force. He already manipulated situations so he could benefit either way with the kidnapping of Eliya or this mating. He is power hungry to the extreme. He's devious, manipulative and frankly, crazy. The disintegration of this agreement will have a devastating effect on the whole Conclave of clans, not just those two."

"So just how bad is Corin?" Alix asked.

"He was totally out of it for days, violently ill. He has recovered a little, but he's lost weight, he seems lethargic, pale and weak. We called in a woman called Herica who he was working with. Working on what med supplies were in our packs and what Herica had, he's been drinking a tea compound twice a day, which seems to be helping ease the symptoms, but we haven't been able to do much else. Honestly, I'm very worried about him. He's a good man, always happy to help people and do the right thing, no matter the cost, but he was ignoring everything until we found out Lixiss needed help with her baby. He seems to be withdrawing into himself more and more. Whether it's the effect of the Matesickness or just his feelings about Kel, I don't know," Tate explained.

"Well, most importantly, we shall have to make sure we have plenty of his tea in stock for him." Alix then turned to Niko. "Son, I will need to speak to the elder council first and see what they say, but we are going to need to come up with a plan. I won't sit idly by and be unprepared from the fallout on this, no matter which way it goes. Once I'm done, I will come and find you. Why don't you catch up with whatever you need to do and have Dariux show Tate around our military complex? I'm sure as he is Avanti, he would appreciate looking over our facilities. And Tate? I know you are still recovering, but please feel free to make use of anything you need. If there is anything else we can provide, just let us know. Treat our clan as your own, our home as your own. Both of you are very welcome here."

"Thank you, Alix. We really do appreciate everything you are doing for us. I wish we crashed closer to you at times. Yet I cannot be upset, we were able to rescue Eliya. I'm sure you understand my meaning though." Tate smiled.

"Indeed I do, Tate, indeed I do." Alix stood and dipped his head at Tate as he left.

"Come on, Dee Dee, show me around. Let me see what you've got." He smirked at the pursed lips on Dariux. *Oh, it's such fun to rile this man.*

Alix turned to Niko once they were alone. "Now is that everything, or is there something else you are keeping from me that you didn't want to discuss in front of them?"

"Surprisingly, no, Father. They are good, honest men and will go out of their way to do the right thing. Even as injured as they were, they still rescued a stranger and risked their lives to return her to her family. Honestly? If they were members of our clan, I would have been proud and I am honoured to call them my friends."

"Good, then they are truly welcome here. Make sure they are treated as the honoured guests they are." Alix reached for a hug from his son. "Now give your old man a hug before I go suffer those old windbags from the council."

Niko huffed out a laugh at the same time he soaked up his father's embrace. It really was good to be home.

Chapter Nineteen

Corin was in his element. He was given free rein in a suite of rooms in the medical complex. They arranged for one room to be an office, two were exam rooms, a third a surgical theatre and then a stock room. He went through what they already carried in stock and was staggered at the level of medicines and equipment they had access to. He guessed this was part of the reason Alix was in support of the Barin Alliance. There really were so many benefits to joining, but he would never try and persuade anyone one way of another. It actually took very little time for everything to be arranged just the way he wanted. Thanking all the men who had gone out of their way to help, he went off in search of Tate.

Corin found Tate in a sparring session with Dariux in one of the gyms at the training complex. He was sure it was supposed to have been a simple workout, but from the look of it, it was anything but. For whatever reason, Tate was trying to exercise his demons on Dariux. Dariux was certainly giving as good as he got, if anything he was being deliberately provocative, taunting Tate, teasing him. There was a lot of tension in the air and unless Corin was very much mistaken it was definitely sexual in nature. Maybe something happened between the two men that he didn't know about? He didn't even know if Dariux was gay. Whatever was going on between the two, there was certainly quite the crowd building as their showdown continued. Niko plopped down on the bench beside him.

"Hmm, makes you wonder, those two fighting like that." Niko nodded his head at the sparring duo as soon as he sat down. "Did something happen between the two of them?"

"I was just about to ask you the same thing." Corin laughed. "It would certainly seem as if something is going on. Tate deserves to find someone special. He's an amazing man who too many people overlook as he tends to be a bit of a joker. He's so much more. He cares deeply, is fiercely loyal and protective to those who deserve it.

He goes to places you and I could never imagine. The horrors he sees would have you and me crying, and begging to have our memories altered. Through it all, he keeps on going, all the Avanti do. I know they have this totally badass rep throughout all the known universes, but really they simply do what has to be done. They don't enjoy it, they don't revel in it. They witness the worst the universe has to offer and still they come back and face it all over again. No matter how much they might want to give up, they keep going, knowing most times they are the only ones who can keep people safe. Each and every one of them deserves to have someone who can help them through the nightmares, who can support them when they grow weary, who can love them enough to break through the tough exterior to get through to the man beneath."

"You know," Niko mused, "I never once considered the effect it must have on them to do what they do. I have gone to war many times, seen things I wish I could unsee, but, never, could I ever, contemplate going through one day of what they endure. They have my respect and no doubt the respect of just about every military man out there, no matter what planet they are from. It has been an absolute privilege to know Tate, and you, of course. I am looking forward to meeting the others. Is there any more news of how close they may be?"

"Tate checked in again this morning and the signal was much clearer so I am guessing it's been a proximity thing. At least I hope it was why we suddenly got the signal back. I just wish we knew what happened to the other two."

"Honestly? Most of the clans would take them in if they came across them. There are only one or two who would be openly hostile. The only other problem would be if they came across the mercs instead. I imagine, though, bar being gravely injured, they would wipe the floor with them. You have to realise, the average military man on this planet will be absolutely no match for those men. Try not to worry. My father will do everything in his power to find them all for you," Niko reassured him.

"Thank you, Niko. You have been there for us from the first moment we met. Don't think I don't know how helpful you were in getting us out of there. I may not have been in the best frame of mind mentally, but I do know the risks you took to help us, particularly me. I will never be able to repay you for your kindness."

"Corin, I would do it all over again, any and every time. There was no way I could leave a friend to suffer like you did. Please, please understand, we are all here for you no matter what. We will support you through this problem with Kel. I know you don't really want to talk about him, but there are a couple of things I would like you to listen to if it is okay?" Corin simply nodded his response.

"Kel is a good man. He does love you, of that I am sure. He is truly, deeply, madly in love with you and it broke his heart to do what he did. He didn't do it for power or alliances or even because he was ordered to by his father. He did it to save your life, pure and simple. I'm not saying it was the only option open to him, but it was the option he decided was best to keep you safe. Now, I know you can handle yourself just fine and have Tate to back you up, but it's in our genetic imprint to do anything we can to protect those we love. The need to protect goes to a whole new level when it comes to our truemates. Kel appreciated that doing what he did would have you hate him, but he maintained he could live with such hate if you got to lead a long and happy life without him."

Niko watched as a single tear escaped from the corner of Corin's eye. Neither of them acknowledged it, but it was there none the less. "I don't want you to give up on him just yet. I want you to wait and see if there is a solution that can be reached before you let the hate you feel harden in your heart. I know it hasn't yet, or you wouldn't be hurting as much as you do. Please, don't give up yet, my friend. I want you both to have the happiness you deserve, and if there is anything I can do to get you both there, then I will."

Corin's breath was stuttering slightly as Niko's words seemed to burrow into his mind like a Valinian worm. He looked at his friend with raw, red eyes. "I'll try, yet at the same time, I cannot be expected to stay this way, forever in limbo. One way or another I will need to resolve this."

Niko released the breath he had been holding. He really was pleased to hear Corin's words. "And I will do everything in my power to help you through this. Now why don't we lighten the mood and ogle these damn fine bodies on display?" Niko sent a leer in the direction of all the men who were stripped to the waist in preparation for their own sparring sessions. It looked like the fight between Tate and Dariux was coming to an end. Corin hoped there wasn't too much patching up for him to do. While he waited, he turned his eyes to the feast of flesh Niko was ogling. Whatever was going on with Kel, it didn't hurt to look and those bodies were definitely worth looking at.

"Have we heard anything back from the rider yet?" Corin asked. It had been playing on his mind constantly.

"Not yet, but that's not surprising. I wouldn't expect him for at least another day. He will probably stay at the Derin overnight if he can, just to get some proper rest." Niko smiled softly at Corin, trying to ease his worry.

"Will he be safe there? I don't want anyone else getting injured."

Niko had to smile. The doctor in Corin never went away. "He had better be. All riders have a banner attached to their mount. It's green with a white X on it. It shows that they are official messengers and not to be attacked or the full weight of the Conclave will be brought to bear."

Corin sighed with relief. "Thank the stars for that. You will let me know when you hear something?"

"I will do." Niko gently squeezed Corin's hand as they both turned back to see just how much damage had been done between Tate and Dariux.

"Well, Cupcake, I have to say, don't give up your day job. It's going to be a while before you can beat me." Tate suddenly found himself pinned on his back, face to face with a scowling Dariux.

"My. Name. Is. Dariux. Use it!"

"Aww, my little teddy is all angwy wib me. Does he want a cuddle?" Tate asked in a childish voice.

"Urgh." Dariux climbed off Tate and stormed away without another word. Yet, if he dared admit it to himself, he actually quite liked Tate finding nicknames for him, and didn't that just annoy him?

Chapter Twenty

$\rightarrow$O$\leftarrow$

If you can dream - and not make dreams your master;

Corin yet again woke with a start from confusing dreams. He had been standing in front of his friends, old and new, holding Kel's hand as they spoke the words of the mating ceremony. The joy he felt was all consuming. It felt like his soul was singing to the stars, coupled with a sense of completeness, of being exactly where he was supposed to be, which was right by Kel's side. The mating aspect alone was confusing to him when he woke, but the worst of the dream was the fact he had been heavily pregnant.

His dreams were really starting to disturb him. They were breaking his heart. It was something which was never going to happen. Not only had Kel sent him packing, choosing to mate with a woman, but he was also a man for crying out loud! How could he ever end up pregnant? It just made no sense whatsoever.

The dreams were distracting him. They were keeping everything fresh in his mind and it was painful to have to keep thinking of Kel when all he wanted to do was forget. He wanted it all to go away, wanted everyone to stop asking him if he was okay. No, he wasn't, and he didn't see it changing any time soon. What he really wanted to do was to curl up into a ball and give up, crying his eyes out, but he was stronger than that. He knew he was. It wasn't in his nature to give up. It never had been and it never would be.

No matter how much it hurt, he was going to get up and carry on. He wasn't the first to have his heart broken and he wouldn't be the last. What made the difference was how he dealt with it and worrying his friends was not the way to go about things. Besides, he was going to need to be on top form if he was going to be delivering babies. He would need to ask someone about the dreams if they kept appearing, but for now he was going to get on with his life.

Corin met Tate for breakfast and had to suppress the smile on his face and the laughter in his chest when he saw the pain Tate was in. The parts of Tate's body he could see were covered in bruises and scrapes. He had a considerable black eye and a swollen, split lip which was currently curled into a grimace to complement the huge scowl gracing his face.

"Well, if you will choose to fight, it's what you get." Corin smirked at his friend.

"Shut it, you, he was asking for a beating. He's just so, so annoying and frustrating and distracting and arrogant and, and..." Tate was rambling on.

"And distractingly sexy?" queried Corin. His comment earned him an even bigger scowl. Corin watched on in amusement as Tate's eyes were suddenly shooting bullets across the room. Following his gaze, Corin saw Dariux walking into the room. "Well, at least you gave as good as you got." Dariux looked as bad as Tate did. He also seemed to be favouring one side of his body as he walked. "Look stop by my med rooms at some point this morning. Let me check nothing's changed since I gave you the brief look over yesterday after your bout." When Tate went to complain, Corin simply gave him what he called his stern doctor look.

"Fine." Tate caved at the look directed his way. "Anyway, what made you happy this morning? I'm not complaining, mind, it's just good to see you smile."

"I decided I just have to get on with life. What's the point in wallowing in sadness? It won't change anything. It's not helping me and I know it's worrying you, so I decided to try to work past everything. It's not going to be easy, but it's what I need to do."

"I'm proud of you, Doc, and you know I'm here for you no matter what. Whatever you need, just say the word." Tate drew Corin into a massive bear hug, holding on tight before letting him go. When he caught Dariux watching him, he simply raised an eyebrow in question and had to smile at the scowl he got in return.

As Corin walked past Dariux on his way out, he ordered him, "My med room for a check-up when you finish." He stopped Dariux's complaint with a look before he even voiced it. "It's not voluntary. You will be there."

Sighing, Dariux simply replied, "Yes, Doc."

Corin was glad to see neither Tate nor Dariux's injuries were too severe. He gave both a couple of booster shots to aid the healing process and wrapped Dariux's bruised ribs. He sent them both on their way with an admonishment to take things easy for the next few days. He didn't really believe they would, but hey, at least he tried.

Just after he saw Dariux out, a wave of sickness engulfed him. He didn't know if he wanted to collapse to the floor in a heap or run for the bathroom. His insides were churning and rebelling, so the hasty retreat to the bathroom won out. A few minutes later, he sat slumped and exhausted on the floor. He felt worn out from being so violently sick. He wondered if this was the virus returning. If so, he really hoped they could stop it getting worse. He wasn't relishing the prospect of enduring this every day. Staggering back to his office, he made himself a sweet tea and took some vitamins, seeing as he hadn't been able to keep his breakfast down. When he finally felt on a more even keel, he opened his door to the first of many pregnant women waiting for his attention. Lixiss was the one he chose to see first as she was by far the closest to delivery. He was exceptionally relieved to give her a clean bill of health and he hoped the rest of the day went as easily as her appointment.

⟩O⟨

Corin was starting to panic. He had seen three women in their first trimesters of pregnancy and their symptoms were all startlingly familiar. Morning sickness, dizziness, feeling more emotional. Coupled with his tender stomach, he wondered if his dream was trying to tell him something. There was no way he could be pregnant. Could there?

Having finally said goodbye to the last woman and the last of walking wounded who needed help, Corin decided it was time to seek out some help of his own. He realised the only one who would be able to offer him any suggestions or advice was likely to be Alix, and sighing, he went to find him. Sitting and explaining his dreams was embarrassing, but it needed to happen. He was worried it was something to do with either this truemate stuff they kept talking about, or he was indeed somehow, someway, pregnant. He really wanted to know one way or the other what he was facing and if he was likely to get worse. He was sure it was the doctor in him, but he would always rather know than not know, no matter whether it was good news or bad.

Alix listened intently as Corin explained all the dreams he was experiencing. He paid attention to everything. Some things he was sure Corin didn't realise could be important, but some of his descriptions of the mating ceremony were surprising. Surprising because of just how accurate they were. For someone who had never seen one, it would be impossible to know. It made Alix realise this could very well have something to do with the mate bond Corin was experiencing. As for the pregnancy part of it? He struggled to know what to say. If the other parts were somewhat accurate, could this be? When coupled with the symptoms Corin was describing, it seemed like it was just entirely possible he was indeed pregnant.

"So it's stupid, right?" Corin's voice begged Alix to agree with him. "I mean, no way could I be pregnant, and as for the mating part, well, I won't be mating with Kel seeing as he has already mated with someone else."

"I hate to ask this of you, Corin, but there are species throughout the galaxies where the males can get pregnant. You must know of such species."

"Of course I do, but I'm not part of... Oh shit." Corin's eyes went wide and his hand flew to his mouth as he stuttered to a stop.

"What is it?" Alix gently probed. He had a feeling he could guess at the answer though.

"My mother has never spoken about my father. I was never really sure why. I simply thought he was a complete arsehole and I was probably better off not knowing him. But what if the reason she didn't tell me was because of something else? I can't believe she wouldn't tell me something as important as being able to carry children. So it leaves the question as, what if she didn't know? Maybe it was a one night thing, maybe she never told him she was pregnant? Maybe she simply didn't know he was a member of a race which could have male pregnancies? Shit, all of these are possible as options." One of Corin's hands gripped the table beside him, the other went to his forehead. He ran the palm up and over his hair as he tried to digest this new information. He was starting to stress at all the possible options and the ramifications of them when Alix interrupted him.

"Slow down, son, just calm down. Firstly, we don't even know if you're pregnant. If, and it's still a mighty big if, but if, you are indeed pregnant, then I am guessing what your ancestry is might very well be the least of your problems. How about we focus on one problem at a time?"

Corin knew Alix was right intellectually speaking, but it wasn't helping him accept the possibility he might indeed be about to become a father. What would happen if he was? It wasn't like his life was stable right now. Even before the crash, his life had been filled with chaos after his run in with the Admiral. What's more, if he was indeed pregnant, then he was going to be a single father. After all, Kel was mating Teriva. Damn, this was one incredibly fucked up situation.

"Look the only way to move on from this is to make sure one way or another. I am presuming you have the means here to test yourself?" Alix prompted.

"Yes and no," Corin explained. "If I was a woman then yes, we could easily test hormone levels, but, seeing as I would automatically have different hormones at different levels I don't think the test would give an accurate result one way or the other. The only way for us to tell would be to try and scan my abdomen and try to pick up either a baby or evidence of a pregnancy. The only problem is I don't have that sort of scanning equipment. It's not exactly something which gets carried in a battle pack. The scanner I did have was left of the Delphini in our hurry to leave."

"Well, seeing as you have a new med suite set up, partly for pregnant women, I'm sure they added one in for you. If not, I presume one is on the way. We can check it out, and as soon as we have it, you can go for a scan. In the meantime, I want you to stay calm and carry on as normal. Either you are or you aren't, and there is nothing you can do to change the results. I will do some research into these dreams and see if it is the mate bond or if it's just your mind playing tricks on you."

Corin let out a harsh breath that turned into a bitter laugh. "I kinda don't know which option I prefer if I'm honest."

"I don't blame you, son. I'm not sure I would know either in your position. Now, what are you going to say to Tate? I understand if you want to keep this from everyone else, but are you considering keeping it from him?"

"No. I won't keep this from him, but who knows how the hell I tell him. It's not like I can just walk up and say hey, Tate, guess what, I'm having a baby! Fuck it. I think I need a little bit of time to get my head around all of this. I certainly never expected this when I woke up this morning!" His hand rubbed the back of his neck as he spoke, as if he was unconsciously trying to ease the tension in his body.

"If you are pregnant, what will you do?" Alix wondered if Corin even had an answer.

"The only thing I can do. Have and raise the baby, as a single father, I'm presuming. I certainly won't get rid of the baby and I won't give it up. I will raise it myself if I am indeed pregnant. Whether it be here on this planet, or whether I make it back to the Alliance, I don't honestly know."

"Will you let Kel know?" Alix wondered, although there was one thing he was sure of— it was going to be very hard on Corin either way.

"Fuck, I don't know. I would say yes, but at the same time no, considering the circumstances. Martellon will spit blood if he finds out and it will just put the baby and this clan in danger. Yet I just don't see how I can deny him his rights to be a father no matter what has gone on between us. Fuck! I swear that man has done nothing but cause me problem after bloody problem since the moment I met him. There is going to come a day when I am going to seriously kick his fucking behind, no matter how damn fine it is."

Much to Corin's horror and embarrassment, he promptly burst into tears, great gut-wrenching sobs that echoed around the room. It was the last straw, and the wall he had built up to protect himself disintegrated. *Oh crap,* was all he could think, *please, don't let this be more of those emotional mumbo jumbo moments I've been feeling all day.* If so, this flipping sucked and he was never even going to so much as roll his eyes at anything pregnant women did ever again. Suddenly, he was enveloped in strong, comforting arms that he clung to like they were the only thing keeping him from spinning out into oblivion. When he was finally calm, he looked up to say thank you to Alix only to discover it was in fact Tate who held him.

Seeing the confusion on Corin's face, Alix explained, "They came in just as you broke down. I haven't said anything to them about what's happened, but they are both intensely worried about you, son. Maybe it's for the best you do talk to them, tell them what's going on. The more support you have around you the better." Alix's eyes were full of sympathy yet imploring him to talk.

"Doc, whatever is going on, you know you can trust us." Tate spoke softly into Corin's hair as he held him tight. "There is nothing you can tell me that will change what I think of you. You are my best friend and I love you dearly. Please, let us help you."

"Damn it, I don't really have an option, do I? It's not exactly as if you aren't going to find out anyway under the circumstances."

"Find out what?" Niko asked "What in the stars is going on?"

"Okay, you guys better sit down and make yourselves comfy, this is going to be one hell of a shock." Corin watched as Niko warily sat on the seat closest to him. Tate on the other hand, made no attempt to move from his position holding Corin as they sat on the floor.

By the time Corin finished talking, both Tate and Niko were in stunned disbelief. "By the moons! You think you're pregnant?" Tate shouted. "What the fuck?"

"Are you disgusted by me? Do you hate me now?" Corin avoided looking at his friends, a huge blush staining his cheeks.

"Why would we hate you, Doc?" Tate tilted his head to look at Corin. "I've already told you there is nothing you could tell me that would change what I think of you. You are my best friend, I love you dearly, and if you are pregnant? Then you have my full support. I can't replace Kel in the daddy role, but I will be an uncle and dote on the little one. I'll be there every step of the way with you." Tate smiled gently at Corin as he spoke. "What the hell do you do now, though?"

"First, I do the scans and if it's confirmed, then I start preparing I guess. Oh, and decide what to do about Kel. It's kind of poetic though, if you think about it."

"How so?" Niko asked.

"Well, I was going to suggest training at least one of the women to act as a midwife. That way if I leave there is someone here who has the skills to help every woman through childbirth. I guess now it's going to be more important than ever. I'm guessing if I am pregnant the only option is going to be a surgical removal of the baby, but I'm going to have to do some research. Not least of which is going to be checking my genetics. I think it's about time I knew exactly who I am, don't you?" Corin got up and started walking towards the door. Turning back, he looked at the three men still sat at the table and cocked his head to one side. "Well, aren't you coming?"

They all took one look at each other before jumping up and jogging after him. There was no way they were going to miss this.

Once they reached Corin's medical suite they all split up looking for anything that could be a scanner.

"Found it!" Tate yelled from the second examination room which Corin hadn't even looked into. There was no need as it was only him working here. He approached the room with a high level of trepidation, but also a growing amount of excitement. It was as though as each minute passed by he grew more and more in love with the idea of having a child. It was something he had never thought could happen seeing as he was a gay military doctor. Now things were changing, he realised this was something that might just have been a hidden desire within him. Now he was just as worried about how he would feel if he wasn't pregnant, in comparison to how he would feel if he was.

"Okay, who wants the honours?" Corin removed his tunic before laying on the exam table.

"The honours?" Niko asked.

"Yes, scanning me. It's going to be difficult to scan myself, so I need one of you to do it." Corin waved the scanning wand at them.

They all looked at each other, none of them really wanting the responsibility of being the one to tell Corin the results. In the end, Tate stepped forward. "Of course I'll do it, Doc. I wouldn't be anywhere else than helping you. Just tell me what to do."

As Corin talked Tate through the procedure, the tension in the room was slowly increasing, yet it was coupled with an undercurrent of excitement. Taking a deep breath, he lay back and let Tate smear his stomach with a conductive gel. Taking a deep breath, Corin centred himself and watched the screen.

Tate's hands shook slightly, nervous energy flowing through him. This was by far the weirdest, most surreal and yet emotional situation he had ever been in. He gingerly pressed the wand to Corin's belly and moved it around trying to see if it picked anything up. He had no idea if he was even doing it properly when suddenly a faint whooshing sound could be heard from the machine. All eyes in the room shot to Corin before looking back at the screen. While there was nothing to see yet, the whooshing noise they could hear was definitely fast and regular.

"Holy heavens." Corin stuttered out a breath. All eyes shot to him as a radiant smile started to break like a new dawn over his face. His eyes lit up with an incandescence of pure joy.

"Doc?" Tate prompted.

"It's a heartbeat. That's a baby's heartbeat you can hear. I'm... I'm really pregnant," stuttered Corin.

"Wow, just wow, Doc, congratulations." Tate dropped the wand, embracing Corin in a massive yet gentle hug. Alix and Niko quickly followed suit before they all stepped back. "How about we see if we can get a little look at the baby rather than just sound?" Tate ran the wand over Corin's stomach in a slow, methodical manner. Eventually something flickered on the screen. Moving the wand slowly back, they all watched as what looked nothing like a baby and everything like a giant bean filled the screen. They all watched as the middle of the bean was pulsing in time to the whooshing heartbeat. It was obvious they were all looking at the baby's heart.

There was no screaming and jumping for joy, no mad dances around the room as he had seen other people react. There was simply an overwhelming feeling of love cascading through Corin. It seemed to start from the top of his head before travelling down to his toes. There was absolutely no doubt in his mind as to the path his future was going to take. It didn't matter where he lived in the future, this baby would be his whole life. Even if Kel wanted nothing to do with him, he would let him know. Kel deserved to hear it from him, and the baby deserved the chance at a second father. He held no hope it would change things between him and Kel, but damn it, he missed the man and hoped it would.

All three of the men watched as Corin processed the fact he was indeed pregnant. They watched as the happiness spread through him, radiating out to them. Pleased for him, smiles were soon gracing all their faces. It was very obvious Corin was taking it as good news.

There was one main thought on his mind though and that was Kel. He turned to Alix. "Is the rider back yet?"

Alix sighed. "No."

Niko drew in a sharp breath. "He should have been."

"I know."

"So what do we do now?" Corin heart stuttered with worry over the friends he had left behind at the Derin clan, for Eliya, for Tir, but mostly for Kel. No matter how much he tried to tell himself not to, he still cared too much, loved too much, to ever stop worrying about his man. Even if that were no longer the case, his heart would always belong to Kel.

"Now we send another rider and see what happens." Alix sighed as Niko went to complain. "Son, we don't really have much of a choice anymore. I don't want to risk another rider, but the first one could be lying injured somewhere. He might never have made it. The only way we can be sure is if we send another one. I will step up patrols around the route to the Derin to make sure he's not lying injured somewhere."

"You're right, I don't like it, but you're right."

"I know." Alix winked at his son, trying to break the solemnness of the moment.

"Now enough of that for a few minutes. It's a time of celebration. Let me hear that heartbeat again. You can't get a more glorious sound than that."

Niko and Tate shared a quick look with each other, well aware of what Alix was trying to achieve. They both threw themselves back into celebrating with Corin.

Chapter Twenty One

It was a week later that Corin was sat watching the men train with Tate and Niko. They were enjoying a leisurely afternoon in the sun. Tate and Niko had taken to spending as much time as possible with Corin to keep his mind off the Derin. A shout suddenly rent the air. "A Rider approaches! Summon the Chieftain! Summon the Laird!"

All three men scrambled up and went to meet the rider.

"You bring word from the Derin Clan, Rider?" Niko demanded.

"I do."

"Where is the letter then?" Niko demanded as Alix and Dariux joined them.

"There isn't one," the Rider replied, nervously.

"Why not?" demanded Alix.

"Things are complicated at the Derin Clan, Chieftain, but I was able to speak with Laird Tir briefly. It's why it took me so long." The Rider was fidgeting as he spoke. "He asked me to convey a message to you."

"Well, come on then!" demanded Alix. "Tell me!"

"He said 'Tell Chieftain Alix his message has been received and understood. Tell him it's being dealt with.' That's all I have, sir. I came back as soon as I could."

A collective sigh ran through their group. Corin sagged in relief. Tate stood behind him and wrapped his arms around his friend. "I've got you. Just relax. They are safe."

Corin turned around to Tate with tears in his eyes. "Even though he is with Teriva now, I haven't stopped loving him. I was so worried about them all."

"We all were. But we can stop now."

"We can." Corin smiled, the first genuine smile Tate had seen in a while.

"You are sure that is the message he gave you?" Alix demanded.

"Yes, sir." The Rider nodded.

"Then thank you. Did you see any sign of the other Rider?"

"No, sir, but I was told he had been sent back with a message from Laird Tir."

"Okay, thank you." Alix turned to one of the officers near him. "Oster, will you see to the Rider for me?"

"Of course, Chieftain." Oster dipped his head and motioned for the Rider to follow him.

Alix pulled Corin into a hug, gently stroking his back, feeling the tremble in the smaller man.

Corin looked up with teary eyes. "Thank you for doing that Alix. It's such a relief."

"It is for all of us."

"What of the other Rider then?" Corin asked.

Alix frowned. "I do not know, but I will send a scouting party out to look for him. All we can do is check Estrivian lands though."

"It is something at least." Alix squeezed Corin gently before turning him back to face Tate. "Now why don't you three go back to ogling the men?"

Corin and Tate laughed at Niko who was spluttering, red faced at being caught by his father.

Alix just laughed. "It could have been worse, your Mami could have seen you." Alix just laughed even harder at the look of absolute terror on Niko's face. He was still laughing as he walked back into the keep.

Tate and Corin sniggered as they sat back down. No matter how embarrassed Niko was, he still joined them. The three of them smiled and joked, feeling lighter than they had in a while.

––––––––––––––– >O< –––––––––––––––

The next few weeks were a blur of activity for Corin. He was helping Alix research the Matesickness, although thankfully, apart from the dreams which were now occurring several nights a week, the other symptoms were lessening as time went by. He was also lucky; while his hormones were all over the place and he had a tendency to burst into tears at any moment, he only suffered from morning sickness occasionally. His body was changing and the pregnancy was starting to become obvious.

He reckoned he was probably somewhere around the two month mark, but both he and the baby appeared to be bigger than he would have expected at this point. It was a conversation with Alix that shed some light on the confusion. Apparently on their planet pregnancies tended to last around seven months, rather than the usual nine of Terrans and eight of Barinians. He was just waiting on the final genetics test to see if he could isolate the other part of his ancestry. He thought if it was proving dominant enough to get him pregnant, then it was likely the pregnancy would follow the rules of that race rather than his other ancestry.

Lixiss had given birth to a beautiful baby girl and they elected to call her Grace in honour of him; it had been his mother's name. He was deeply touched and like most of the clan, doted on the little girl. He spent lots of his spare time with mother and daughter, realising it would be good practice; he took the time to get used to changing nappies, feeding and bathing.

The more time he spent with the young family, the more he became content with what he was facing. His heart still hurt for Kel and not a day went by where the man didn't consume his thoughts, but he was learning to live with the pain and hoped the arrival of his little one would help to heal the scars on his heart.

Tate and a young clan woman were working with him to learn about aiding in a birth. Alasandra was gifted and he was pleased the clan would be able to call on her should he have to leave. Tate was determined to support him every step of the way and, should it be necessary, it would be him who bore the responsibility of cutting open Corin when the time came.

At times, Tate seemed not so much distracted as preoccupied, and Corin had a sneaking suspicion it had something to do with Dariux. The two men were either constantly in each other's orbit or avoiding each other like the plague. The sexual tension radiating off the two of them whenever they were together was apparent to everyone in the room, well, apart from them it seemed. Corin smiled to himself. When they eventually gave in to what was going on between them, he reckoned it would be a love story to rival those from the histories. Smiling to himself, he looked up as a series of beeps echoed throughout the room. With a sudden start, he realised it was his genetics results. Not wanting to do this alone, he called for Tate to be there with him.

"So we find out what you are then, huh?" Tate said, more to fill the silence than looking for an answer to his question.

"Yeah." Corin seemed worried to Tate.

"Hey, you know it makes no difference to me what you are. You'll always be our Doc and there is nothing in all the known universes that will change my feelings. You're family, Doc. Sure, not by blood, but by choice and choice is far more important than any blood connection. Besides, there is no chance you would ever get rid of me. I'm looking forward to being an uncle!"

Corin smiled, but then his face fell as he finally worked up the courage to ask Tate a question which had been plaguing him since the day he found out about the baby. "Do you think the guys will react badly? Think I'm weird? You're right, you know, you guys are a family to me and I would be devastated if they weren't accepting of this. I don't want to lose them over this."

"You won't, Doc, in your heart of hearts you know you won't. The guys will support you as much as I am. Your baby will be the youngest ever Avanti and we will befriend him, protect him and support him the same as any other member."

"And if it's a girl?" Corin wondered.

"Then not only will she be like a Valkyrie of Old Earth, but she will be treated like a princess by all the guys. I will just have to both laugh and feel sorry for her when it comes to her dating in the future! A concerned dad is one thing, concerned uncles another, but a squad of Avanti backing her up? Man, anyone she dates is going to have to have balls of steel to face us!" Both of them burst out laughing at the prospect. "Now let's find out those results, hey?"

It took Corin a few minutes to interpret the results, but when they came through, it confirmed he was part Terran, part Barinian and the other part was Zinari. The Zinarians were indeed a race where both sexes could carry their young and this was also known to be a very dominant trait. They were all humanoid in appearances and in truth, they looked very similar to Terrans. The only startling difference was Zinarians were often born with natural tattoos on their bodies, a way of marking their clans, something which Corin hadn't inherited. The most pressing point for Corin at the moment was their pregnancies tended to only last around six months; so he was guessing he had no more than four months to go.

"So, Doc, is it good news?" Tate was anxiously waiting for Corin to finish reading.

"Shit, sorry, Tate, yeah, it's good enough. I'm part Zinarian."

"Cool, Doc, they're not too bad, a pretty decent race and their warriors are kinda kick ass. I have to say though, I always wondered where you got your gorgeousness from!" Tate waggled his eyebrows and blew him kisses. Both of them laughed.

Just then the door burst open, Niko entering at a dead run. "We just got word your friends are a few hours out." He was panting as he spoke. Corin realised he must have ran all the way to give them the news.

Corin and Tate both broke out into huge grins, Corin's eyes full of tears once again. At least this time it was happy tears.

Tate and Corin greeted Dax and Bell as they rode into the courtyard with happiness in their hearts and smiles on their faces. Both men raced over to them and the second they dismounted, there were hugs and backslaps all round. Corin's ever present emotional mumbo jumbo meant his eyes were wet with tears yet again.

"Fuck, it's good to see you guys," Dax said.

"Indeed, it is good to find you both in good health." Bell smiled as he spoke.

"Hmm, well for the most part we are, and it's Doc you need to thank for it. He saved my life so many times, I think I'm losing count!"

Dax spoke above the general chatter of the courtyard, "Well, it looks like we have a lot to catch up on. First, though, who do we have to thank for this sanctuary?"

Both Alix and Niko stepped forward at his words. Tate gestured to each one in turn as he made the introductions. "This is Laird Alixandr Dastria and his son Nikoben of the Estrivia Clan. Alix, Niko, these are my squad members and friends Commander Daxin "Dax" Rydoc, and Lieutenant Bellan "Bell" Nimeri." Both men dipped their heads in greeting.

"Thank you for allowing us entry to your clan and for giving Tate and Corin safe haven. When we found out, it was a weight off our minds not to have to worry about them. We are in your debt." Dax bowed formally.

"Nonsense, young man, it is an honour to have these two here. Now, why don't you come inside, freshen up, and meet with your friends. We can talk properly at the evening meal," Alix said.

"Thank you, sir, it would be much appreciated."

"It's no problem at all, and drop the sir. As friends of these two, you can call me Alix, and my son, Niko. Niko, help show them to the guest suites and I shall see you all later."

"Yes, father." Niko gestured for them to follow him and he led the way into the keep.

Once they were all settled in the guest suite, clean and with food in front of them, Dax filled them in on what happened with the two of them.

"We only just made it into the pod in time. There were explosions all around us. The cruiser was breaking apart at the most incredible rate. Although I can't say I'm surprised, given how big a heap of junk that thing was. Anyway, as we were last to get to our pod, we watched the two of you ahead of us. Bray and Hunter's pod seemed to make a controlled descent, although we couldn't track where they landed. Your pod got hit by some of the debris from the Delphini. Our best guess is it took out one of your stabilizers as you started to spiral down towards the surface of the planet. As if losing a stabilizer wasn't bad enough, we could tell your pod was speeding up at the same time. I swear you were surrounded by a flaming shield as you breached the atmosphere. I have absolutely no idea how you survived as we lost track of you from then on. Honestly? We didn't expect you to make it. Your pod must have been in one hell of a state when you crashed."

"Yeah, it was pretty fucked up from what I remember." Corin laughed.

Dax continued with his story. "So our landing was actually okay. It was about as controlled a pod landing as you could manage and I have to thank Bell for his skill in flying. Bell has some serious skills when it comes to piloting." He smiled at Bell who dipped his head in acknowledgement. "We spent the first few days desperately trying to raise both pods on comms. At times we were sure we heard something, but I'm not sure."

"Well, if you did, it wasn't ours," Tate explained. "Our pod was shot to hell and I'm pretty sure just about every system was broken. Hell, there was more wiring than hull left by the end of it."

"So if we did hear something, then it must have been Hunter and Bray. It gives me hope, maybe, just maybe, they survived. It is something we will need to work on more. I'll look over the comms with you, Tate, see what mods you've done and see if we can't boost it further." Dax smiled at his friend and fellow teammate. "Anyway, so Bell was injured in the landing. He had a puncture wound to his chest and some broken ribs. I managed to get him patched up as best as I could before we were found by some people from a little village. They took us in and helped nurse Bell back to full health. I spent my time trying to raise either of you with no success. Eventually we realised we were going to have to leave the village and start looking. It must have been a couple of weeks after we left when we made our first radio contact with you. Then, it was simply a matter of time till we got here. We've been lucky, it's been relatively uneventful for us since we landed. What about you guys?" Dax was anxious to hear what happened to them both. Corin and Tate seemed to have a heavy burden on their shoulders. He was guessing things really hadn't gone well for his two friends.

"It's probably best if Corin explains what we've been through for the most part. I seemed to spend more time unconscious and in pain than anything else," Tate told them. Dax and Bell exchanged worried glances at his words, but looked to Corin and waited for him to tell them what they were sure was going to be one hell of a story.

"Fucking hell, Corin. You really are one hell of a doctor." Bell said after Corin explained up to the point where Tate was fully recovered, without really mentioning what was going on with Kel.

"I certainly would not be here if it wasn't for the skills Doc has. I owe him more than I can ever possibly repay, although I will spend my life trying to do so," Tate vowed.

"No, you won't, you stupid idiot! You know I don't expect anything. How could I possibly not save one of my friends? Besides, you have saved me as well. So it's probably best we simply call it quits." Corin raised his eyebrow at Tate in a silent challenge.

"Hmm, well, I do beg to differ, Doc, but hey, if it's what you want."

"So how did you two get from the other clan to here? I would have thought you would have tried to stay in one place to make it easier for us to find you," Dax queried.

"Well, we originally planned to stay, but it all went to hell in a handbasket. We were left with no choice but to leave. Niko and his father were kind enough to offer us sanctuary here, which has been fantastic. They truly are good people." Tate smiled at Niko as he spoke.

"Okay, so you better fill us in on the rest of it then," Dax commanded.

Corin couldn't bear to give voice to what happened with Kel so he simply got up to go and sit by the window leaving Tate to fill Dax and Bell in.

Dax raised his eyebrows in surprise at Corin's behaviour, but looked puzzled when Tate simply shook his head and mouthed, "Leave him be."

By the time Tate finished their story, Dax and Bell had spent more time with their mouths open in shock than Tate believed was actually possible. He was convinced their jaws would suffer for days. Disbelief, incredulity, surprise, sadness, empathy, concern and many more emotions were flickering across their faces.

Rather than try to give voice to the racing thoughts in his head, Dax simply stood and walked over to Corin. Wrapping his arms around the man from behind, he held him tight, trying to reassure him nothing had changed in their friendship, nor the support all the Avanti would give him. He felt Corin sag against him in obvious relief.

Bell joined them, gracing Corin's temple with a gentle kiss before saying, "Doc, we will be here for you every step of the way. Nothing will ever change that. What's more," Bell smiled as he gently laid a hand on Corin's belly, "I can't wait to be an uncle."

"Your baby will want for nothing, Doc. We are all here for you and the baby, every step of the way. Never fear you will lose us or our support," Dax added.

It was enough for Corin's crazy hormones to have him in tears yet again. The two men simply held him tight as he cried with relief and happiness at the acceptance of his friends. Tate and Niko simply watched, smiling at Corin and the deep acceptance of their friends.

Chapter Twenty Two

Over the next two months, Dax and Bell soon grew to love the way of life in the Estrivian Clan. They were such naturally friendly people who made them welcome at every turn. From the Chieftain right down to the youngest child, they all greeted them warmly. Both Dax and Bell were soon in as high a demand as Tate for sparring sessions. Not only did the men at arms find the practice somewhat fun, it was helping to hone their skills as a fighting force. What started out as a simple bit of fun soon grew into them training the men for real. They all knew what the situation was with the Derin and the Farian Clans. It could escalate at any moment and they needed to be ready.

While the three Avanti worked with Niko and his men, Corin continued to work in his medical suite. He finished his research into his heritage and finally created a plan which could be enacted when it came to him giving birth. He hoped he followed his Zinarian genetics and developed an opening in his abdomen, allowing them easy access to the baby, especially as it was designed to be naturally self-healing and would slowly close after the birth. If not, Tate was going to have to cut him open, something neither of them relished the prospect of. Although having a plan brought a great sense of relief to all as he was now a good four months along. There was only between two and three months left to go.

His dreams were still there and were now more frequent than not. He never admitted it to anyone, but he was becoming increasingly concerned for Kel. In his dreams, Kel was deteriorating fast with the Matesickness. He was becoming increasingly convinced the dreams were trying to tell him something. Part of his soul was screaming at him to go and help Kel. It was an impossible task, because even if Dax, Niko and the others let him go, there was no way of knowing what welcome they would be given.

There was no way he could put his friends or baby at risk, no matter how much he still loved its father. It mattered little whether he and Alix believed they had found a way to reduce the effects of Matesickness. He didn't need it and there was no way he could get the help to Kel, something that was definitely becoming an increasing source of frustration to him.

He needed to have hope. Hope Herica was able to develop their combined research without him. If she couldn't, then their discovery was likely to be Kel's only hope, a hope that was pointless under the circumstances. Thoughts of Kel were still the only dark spot in his life, still the one area where he wasn't happy. He needed to accept it though, he needed to move on with his life, let Kel go in his heart and mind and focus all his love and energy on their child. Thoughts of his baby always brought a smile to his face and a burst of happiness to his heart, providing a little sunshine on even the gloomiest of days.

Corin may have been happy everything appeared to be going right for once, but for others, life was painful and heartbreaking.

>O<

Tir was going out of his mind trying to find someone, anyone to help Kel. His brother was ill. There was no doubt he was battling a virus of some sort. Herica was doing all she could, seeing as the clan doctor, Al'Feram, had gone missing. Life was quickly becoming intolerable in the Derin Clan. Tir was juggling Kel's health, keeping Eliya safe, as well as trying to avoid her temper which had escalated when Niko, Corin and Tate left. She was definitely missing them.

On top of it all, Teriva was becoming a screaming she-devil. She was not a woman who enjoyed being denied what she wanted. More than a little put out Kel had continuously put off their mating, she was now furious it was no longer possible with Kel bedridden. Her attitude to the clan members was disgusting and there were many who refused to deal with her. More than once he caught her striking one of them for failing in some impossible task she set.

The hardest thing he was dealing with was, by far and large, the death of his father. Al'Feram had sworn there was nothing he could do after the riding accident, but Tir was more than a little dubious. The accident seemed so contrived; his father was an excellent rider. Stars, in his younger days he led a battalion of Refrinti in battle. His ability was second to none. There was absolutely no way in Tir's mind something so simple as a fallen log could have killed him and his mount. Those massive feline beasts were known to be incredibly agile and steady on their massive paws.

What's more, his injuries hadn't seemed so severe to start with. Al'Feram should not have had any problems getting his father back to full health and fitness, so how, and why, did he die? There were too many things happening around Tir for him not to be suspicious. The question was what could he do about it, and what's more, who could he trust? With his father gone, Kel seriously ill, and some of the elders refusing to see him, the only man he could turn to was Carn, his best friend, confidant, and his and Kel's Master at Arms.

"Tir, we have to do something, anything. The clan is in trouble. Your father was murdered, of that I have no doubt, and Kel is dangerously ill. If something happens to you, the only one left is Eliya and someone has already tried to kidnap her. This all seems so remarkably coincidental." He grimaced at Tir who sighed in reply. "Yeah, we both know it isn't. The only logical conclusion is Martellon is trying to take over the clan, one way or another. It's the only circumstance that fits."

"See, I thought about it, but surely Corin would have said something when he saw their clan enter?" Tir was at war with himself. While he knew things were in a precarious state for his clan, he almost didn't want to acknowledge just how deep the mire was they were engulfed in.

"Fuck, Tir, when did you expect him to say something? Just announce it to all and sundry the second they all walked in? Or how about when it was announced the love of his life was mating someone else? No? What about when he was forced to play nice to the woman who stole his man? There was never a single point he could have mentioned anything without the room descending into full blown chaos and probably a bloody battle. If you think about it all, this is the most logical explanation. Besides, I was watching Corin when the group entered. I knew he was likely to react badly when the announcement was made, but until the announcement, there was no reason for him to believe there was anything odd going on."

"I'm not sure I understand what you're suggesting, Carn." Tir's confused gaze was fixed on the young Master at Arms.

"Tir, Corin reacted, badly, when Martellon entered. Not at first when the rest of the clan entered, although he did seem to focus on them a little more. No, when Martellon entered, he visibly stiffened and schooled his features. His military training must have kicked in. His face was a total blank slate. I could see him whispering and gesturing something to Tate, and honestly, I'm betting it was because he recognised Martellon, or at least someone in the clan, but Martellon seems the most likely fit."

"I guess it makes sense." Despite all the evidence in front of him, Tir almost didn't want to believe any of this. If he did, it meant the clan was in far deeper trouble than he already believed they were. "But here is something I don't understand…"

"What?"

"If Corin did recognise him, and I'm still not sure by the way, but if he did, then why the stars didn't he say anything?"

"Tir." Carn sighed. "When those introductions were forced on him, which was a total bastard move by your father by the way, but when he was introduced to Martellon, his eyes widened ever so slightly in recognition as he took his hand. Think about it, Tir. Martellon wears some pretty distinctive jewellery and Corin did talk about a ring he had seen."

"Oh fuck. You're right." Tir started to think, and think hard about what options were open to them. "How long…"

"How long have I been wondering this?" Carn asked.

"Yes."

"Since last night, kind of, but really for all of about ten minutes." Carn laughed bitterly. "There were a couple of things niggling at my mind, but I just couldn't put all the pieces together. And now I almost wished I hadn't. I wish I was wrong, but I don't think I am. It was your father dying that really made me puzzle over the whole thing. I don't get it, he was far too good a rider."

"Yeah, I don't either."

Carn ran a frustrated hand through his hair. "Okay, but even if we consider the fact that Corin couldn't have said anything before he left, which I get your point on that, but even thinking that, then why hasn't anyone said anything sooner? Corin must have said something to someone. Even if it was only to Tate, then surely Tate would have said something to Niko?"

Tir pinched the bridge of his nose as he considered everything that Carn was saying. "That is the part I don't understand in all of this. Neither Corin or Tate are malicious in any way, and no matter how they felt about Kel, they would have said something to Niko. And Niko would have sent a Rider."

Carn blew out a frustrated breath. "Stars, even if they had waited till they saw Alix, then he would have sent a Rider."

"So why haven't we heard anything? There hasn't been a single Rider come into the clan since they left. It all just makes no sense." Tir was getting more and more frustrated as they tried to work out what was going on.

"I don't know, I really don't fucking know." Carn pinched the bridge of his nose, before taking a deep breath, trying to clear his mind.

"Fuck!" Tir picked up a book lying on the table next to him and hurled it across the room.

"Do you think we got it all wrong? That it wasn't Martellon?" Part of Carn almost wished that were true. He knew in his heart of hearts it wasn't though. "Do you think something could have happened to Corin? I mean he was ill before he left. It would explain everything. And we know Kel is ill. Could they have the same illness, is that it do you think?"

"Stars, it could be. It's one of the only things that would make any sense. Yet I don't think so. Even if Corin was ill, it doesn't explain why nothing was said straight away. Stars, this is one fucked up mess." Tir growled low in his throat.

"You're not wrong there." Carn let out a bitter laugh.

"So what the fuck do we do now?"

"Well, honestly? Someone is going to have to go and see if they can persuade Corin to come back here."

"What?" Tir said, surprise evident in his tone.

"Whatever Kel is suffering from seems similar to what Corin went through, although Kel is much worse. Herica is doing everything she can, but it's not enough. Even if Al'Feram were here, I wouldn't trust the bastard as far as I could throw the little traitor. Which leaves Corin as our only hope of saving Kel."

"Then Kel's dead," was all Tir could choke out, grief and despair overwhelming him at the prospect of his brother dying on top of everything else.

"See, I don't think so. Corin loved him, probably still loves him. I can't see his feelings changing any time soon. He was devastated when the mating was announced."

"Exactly. Why would he help when he was betrayed in such a way?"

"Because deep down he loves Kel, and no matter what, he won't want him to die, even if he can't be with him."

"You want me to gamble my brother's life on the hope Corin still loves him? On the hopes that Corin himself isn't ill?"

"Fuck, Tir, what other option do we have? Kel will die if we don't, so honestly, I don't see what harm it can do. We owe it to Kel to at least try."

"Fuck. Fuck, fuck, fuck, you're right. I just, I'm struggling here, Carn. I'm losing everyone and I don't know what to do." Tir sat down heavily onto the nearest chair. His head and arms hung limply between his legs.

Carn crouched in front of Tir, lifting his face up so he could look him in the eyes. "Then let me help, Tir. You know me, know I wouldn't suggest this if I didn't think it was going to work. One of us has to ride out there and ask Corin to come back. Who knows the reception we will get, but we have to try. At least Chieftain Alixandr won't want to push clan relations so we should at least get through the door."

"I'll go," Tir vowed.

"You can't, Tir," Carn said softly, "they need you here."

"No, I need to be the one to ask him."

"No. I have to be the one to go and you know it. You are needed here." Carn put his hand up to stop Tir talking. "Think about it. If you leave, it leaves the clan wide open for Martellon to take control over. You'd be lucky to have a clan to come back to. What's more, you would be devastated if something happened to either Kel or Eliya and you weren't here. No. I have to be the one to go. I'll take a squad with me. Anything larger and it will slow us down. I'll leave Antorn here to act in my stead. He's a good man and I wouldn't have him as my second if I didn't think he was in a position to take over from me if need be."

"Yeah, he's a good man. Okay. I don't like this at all, but okay. You've made your point and as much as I hate to admit it, it's valid and you're right. But you have to promise me you'll do everything you can to persuade Corin to come back. I can't lose my brother as well."

"I will, Tir. I promise I will. Besides, I think we need to get answers as to why they didn't warn us about Martellon."

"When will you leave?"

"I'll arrange everything so we ride out at first light."

"Good. I don't think we can wait much longer." Both men realised just how true that statement was. They really were working against the clock now and they needed to hope Corin would come through for them. The alternative really wasn't worth thinking about.

Chapter Twenty Three

An accident at one of the new cottages being built for members of the clan meant Corin was busier than he had been in years. The clan doctor was old and struggled to keep pace with things and so it was down to Corin to save as many lives as he could. Tate, Dax and Bell all helped along with any medics they had amongst their men at arms.

There were four men seriously wounded, two with life threatening injuries, and about half a dozen walking wounded. Corin was racing around as much as his pregnant belly would allow. He was shouting out instructions to everyone as he worked as fast as he could. Tate stood beside him as Corin talked him through operating on the man who had a greater chance of survival and whose injuries would be easier for Tate to fix.

All the while, Corin was in a race against time to save the man on the table in front of him. He worked fast to do a temporary fix on the young man, which he knew would hold long enough and keep him stable enough to go and help Tate. As he moved across to Tate, Bell took over monitoring his patient for him. Working quickly and in tandem with Tate and the clan's doctor, they managed to save the man. He was going to have a long road to recovery, but he would survive and surviving was the important thing.

"I'll go see if I can help Dax and Niko with the less injured. Shout if you need any more help and take it easy, you're looking really tired. You aren't going to do anyone any good if you collapse." Tate cast a wary eye over Corin's appearance as he spoke.

"I will be as careful as I can," Corin replied as he was fully focused on his task.

In the great hall, Alix was trying to keep the relatives of those injured calm, a thankless, but necessary, task. The elders were doing what they could, but they were keeping pretty much to the older members of the clan. He was thankful he had help, but it was a difficult task and it left him to deal with the more emotional younger members. Mind you, it was probably for the best the elders weren't known for being particularly sympathetic and empathetic at times. Suddenly the great doors opened and Dariux strode in. He walked straight up to him with a man striding beside him. He was vaguely recognisable, but Alix couldn't place him.

"Chieftain, this is Carn from the Derin Clan. He is Laird Tir's Master at Arms. He has been sent by order of the Laird and new Chieftain. He is requesting to talk to Corin. He has implied it was of utmost urgency and extremely important."

"Carn, welcome to the clan, but I'm afraid it really isn't a good time right now." Alix's attention was split between the envoy and his clan members. It barely even registered this was someone from the Derin Clan and he could ask how things were going.

"Chieftain Alix, I am sorry, I can see you are very much needed by your clan at the moment, but it really is a matter of life and death, Laird Kel's to be exact. I really must insist on a chance to speak with Corin."

"Okay, it's just not possible at the moment." Alix raised a hand, forestalling any complaints Carn was about to voice. "He's in the middle of performing surgery and I will not interrupt him. Once he has finished, I will get word to him, but right now he is focused on saving lives." Alix gestured to a seat at a table near him. "Why don't you sit, rest and eat while you wait."

"Thank you, Chieftain, I would appreciate it. What about my men?"

"Dariux will get one of his men to see them settled. They will be taken care of." Alix then pulled Dariux to one side. "Go and see how things are going. It might be best to try and talk to Tate before Corin. This probably isn't going to be an easy encounter for him. I'm already worried about him being on his feet for so long. Not that we really have a choice. He is the only man who can save those men and I really don't see him sitting aside while he can do something."

Dariux snorted. "Yeah, there is no way Corin would ever sit down if someone needed his skills. Don't worry, Sir, I'll go and see how things are progressing. It would be good to have some news for the clan members."

As Dariux walked away, Alix had the ominous feeling the day was just going to get worse. He turned to Carn. "I don't have much time with everything going on, but I will need you to fill me in on everything. I think we have a lot to talk about."

Carn was confused. It sounded like the Chieftain knew what was going on. But if he did and Corin wasn't ill then why did no one send a Rider? Why did no one warn them? "Yes, Sir. I think we do."

Alix took a long, measured look at the man, nodded and returned to looking after his clan.

Dariux really didn't want to have to relay this message. Tate was not going to be happy. He and the Avanti were becoming even more protective over Corin as the months went by. They were all eagerly anticipating becoming uncles. As he walked into the med centre, he sought Tate out. When Tate's gaze landed on him, he motioned him out into the corridor. When it looked like Tate was going to refuse, he mouthed, "please, it's serious," to him, hoping it was enough to convey to the man he wasn't angling for one of their normal verbal sparring matches.

Tate walked out with an expression on his face, which implied he was ready to kick Dariux's butt and damned if he didn't find that sexy. Mind you, he found everything about the man sexy, he just wished Tate felt the same way. As soon as Tate was in earshot, he simply said, "It's about Corin."

Tate's whole demeanour changed in a split second. Concern etched on his face. "What's up, Ree? I'm watching out for him. He's pushing it a little, but I won't let him wear himself out."

"It's not about the way he pushes himself even though it's a concern. There's a visitor upstairs who is demanding to see him." Dariux ignored the nickname, especially as he quite liked that one, and spoke carefully as Tate narrowed his eyes. "It's Carn from the Derin. He says it's a matter of life and death about Kel. The

Chieftain wanted me to come down and talk to you about it first, as well as checking on how everything is going down here."

"So Alix isn't sending Corin out to talk to him right now?"

"Fuck no, he's fiercely protective of him. He wanted me to talk to you about the best way to approach this. Honestly, he sees Corin as a second son. There is nothing he wouldn't do for him."

"Yeah, I know, this is just the last thing he needs. He's bloody exhausted, but he won't back down, not while he can save someone. Fuck, I'm so tired of all this bullshit. He just needs to catch a break. If I'm feeling like this, you can only begin to imagine how Corin's feeling. The last thing he needs is more bad news from the bloody Derin. Have they not sorted everything out about Martellon? Surely we would have heard something by now if they needed more help?"

Damn, Dariux wanted to hug the man. He was looking a little fed up. Chances were though he would get a punch in the face for the privilege, so yeah, that wasn't something he was going to try anytime soon. "Honestly? I have no idea why this is the first time we are hearing from them since the Rider came back. All I know is Carn is here and asking for Corin's help."

"I want an honest opinion, Dariux. Do you think we should talk to Corin about this?"

Dariux's mouth dropped open. "You're asking me?" It wasn't just the fact he was asking. Tate had used his full name and he couldn't believe how much he hated it.

"Look, I know we butt heads all the time, but it doesn't mean I don't like you and it doesn't mean I don't respect you or your opinion. Corin is your friend too. So yeah, I want your opinion."

Well, shit, thought Dariux, this man really was a bundle of layers and confusing ones to boot. "Well, the way I see things, I don't think we really have a choice but to talk to Corin. From what I've heard about everything which has happened, people keep hiding things from him. There are so many secrets and half-truths around him it's a wonder he trusts anyone anymore."

"Fuck, you're right." Tate rubbed the back of his neck, trying to relieve at least some of the tension that was rapidly building up there.

"Look, Corin is far, far, stronger than anyone seems to be giving him credit for. He's coped with more since he's been here than anyone deserves to endure. Through it all, he has not lost who he is. I think if you keep this from him, he will be pissed beyond belief. I hate to say this as well, but he still loves Kel. I see it whenever Kel's name is mentioned. Yeah, Kel hurt him. Whether his actions were right or not is immaterial. Kel really hurt him, but you can't just switch off a love so strong."

"I know, and if I'm honest, I don't think Corin actually wants to stop loving Kel, despite everything the man has done to him. Corin still holds out hope they could be together." Tate sighed before mumbling to himself, "And don't we all wish there was someone who could love us like that, like we were someone's world."

"So we're going to talk to him then?" Dariux prompted, wanting the conversation back on safer ground.

"Yeah, he's nearly finished. Just do me a favour, okay?"

"Anything."

"Help me keep an eye on him?"

"You can count on me, Tate," Dariux vowed.

"Yeah, I can, I really can." Tate looked at Dariux, a look that had Dariux confused, but now was not the time to try to interpret what it meant. Instead, the men made their way back inside to wait.

Corin was the last to finish and exhaustion was seeping into his bones. All he wanted was a hot bath, a hot tea and a nap. One look at the men around him and he knew it was just a dream. Something else was going on. "What is it?" he demanded as soon as he joined them.

Dariux took the lead and spoke. "Carn from the Derin is upstairs, insistent to speak to you."

"Well, he can wait. I'm tired, I'm cranky and junior is waging war on my insides." At the inquisitive looks from everyone, he carried on, "Junior is currently dancing on my stomach and bladder. I swear

I feel like a training bag going through a sparring session with you guys."

The men all snickered at his description. "Oh, you can laugh, yeah, sure, it's funny, don't mind me suffering away here. Nuh-uh, don't skimp on the sympathy, will you," Corin snarked at them all, making them laugh loudly. "Ooh, just you wait till you're suffering, remember who controls the drugs around here!" He let out a mock evil laugh.

"Um, Doc, you wouldn't, would you?" Dax raised his eyebrow, but Corin just smiled sweetly in return.

"Corin, I know you don't want to see him, but he says it's important. It's a matter of life or death." Dariux watched as Corin sucked in a breath before continuing. "It's Kel."

"Oh shit."

"Fuck," came a chorus of swearing from everyone.

Corin simply closed his eyes, sighed, drew in a deep breath and walked out the door, not even bothering to remove his blood-soaked surgical gear. His friends raced to catch up to him.

Just before Corin burst into the great hall, Bell put one of his large blue hands in front of Corin and stopped him. "Hold on a moment."

"What?" Corin asked, confused.

"Doc, look at yourself. If you go in there dressed as you are, you're going to scare the relatives and clan members. Let someone go in and get him. We can go wait in another room," Bell suggested.

"I'll go." Dariux jogged past them into the hall.

Corin looked down at himself and realised Bell was right. He let them lead him into another room and, realising the state he was in, he simply stood rubbing his back which was aching badly now. He looked at the chair longingly, but there was no way he was going to ruin a chair.

As Carn walked in, Corin took a good look at his face. Exhaustion was etched over every inch of it, his eyes were pools of sorrow, his hair a mess, as though he had spent days running his hands through it. One look at the man and Corin realised it would indeed be very bad news. Steeling himself, he waited for Carn to speak.

"Corin, I'm sorry. It's Kel. He's dying." Carn managed to get out past the restriction in his throat.

Time seemed to slow for Corin. He could see everyone turn to look at him. He saw lips move, but could not work out what words were being spoken. Hands reached out to him as he stumbled backwards, but his vision was blurring. What little he could see was covered in spots. A ringing was taking up residence in his ears. His heart was starting to stutter and his mind was closing down. He thought he had been prepared for whatever news Carn brought.

But he wasn't.

Chapter Twenty Four

$$\longrightarrow\!\!O\!\!\longleftarrow$$

All of the men reached for Corin at the same time as soon as it became obvious he was going to collapse. He was paler than anyone ever should be. They could all see the tremble wracking his body and the wild eyes darting back and forth. They watched as his hands grasped for purchase on nothing but thin air.

Dax was closest to him and managed to reach him just as his legs buckled and his body shut down. The muscles on Dax's heavily tattooed arms rippled as Dax caught Corin and swung him up into his arms. Taking one look at him, Dariux left the room at a sprint to get a med kit. Bell was opening windows. Tate was getting a blanket to wrap him in as Dax cradled him in his arms.

"What the fuck?" was all Carn managed to say.

Tate rounded on him. "You asshole, you couldn't have broken the news any easier?"

"I didn't know that was going to happen! You can't blame me."

"Shit, you could have made an educated guess! Look at the state of him, I mean really look, you bloody idiot. He's just been in surgery for fifteen hours straight, no breaks and rather than take even five minutes to clean himself up, he came straight here. And you wonder why blurting it out like you did had an effect on him? Fuck!" Tate turned his back on Carn and bent to focus on Corin.

His head snapped round, the snarl of his lips dying when he saw an out of breath Dariux holding a med kit out to him. His expression softened and he smiled his thanks even as he opened the kit. He thought about giving Corin a Battleboost shot, but stopped at the last second.

"Why aren't you giving him the shot?" Dax voice was betraying his agitation.

"Because I don't know if I can give it to him in his condition. Shit, we never discussed a situation like this. Damn it!" Tate swore. Instead of using the boost, he dug out a pod of salts. Snapping them open, he wafted them under Corin's nose. Damn, the smell was nasty, but it seemed to do the trick. Corin was starting to stir.

As Corin came to and made to sit up, he felt gentle hands restraining him. "Take it easy, Doc. You're okay."

"Shit," was all he managed to say.

"Sounds about right, Doc." Dax quietly laughed, and Corin felt the rumbles in the body holding him.

"Shit, you didn't give me the boost, did you?" Corin asked.

"No, I was going to, but I didn't know if it was safe. So I just used the salts," Tate said.

"Good, the boost isn't a good idea unless it's really needed, not in my condition."

"What condition?" They all heard Carn ask. Tate found himself wondering how Carn had failed to notice Corin's larger than normal belly.

Everyone looked at each other, then at Corin.

"He's going to find out shortly anyway, and honestly I can't believe he hasn't noticed. It's not like I've been hiding it. Oh, and can someone get me a top. I really want to get this tunic off." Corin looked down at the bloody surgical gown that was swamping him from his neck to mid thigh.

Looking around to see if there was anything they could use and realising there was nothing, Dariux whipped off his own tunic and passed it to Corin. "Here change into this. It might be a bit big in places, but it's better than nothing." He smiled as Corin thanked him before realising he could feel eyes raking over his body. As he turned round, he saw no one looking, but a small smile lingered on the Tate's lips. Hmm, maybe the man wasn't as immune as he thought.

Once Corin was more presentable, Dax helped him to a chair. Turning to face Carn, he watched as his condition finally dawned on the man.

"Sweet moons! You, you're…" Carn stuttered. "It can't be, it's not possible!"

"Oh, I can assure you it's very much possible," Corin quipped, "you can hardly deny it with the proof right in front of you!"

"Is it Kel's?" Carn's gaze snapped up from Corin's belly when he heard growling and muttering around him. Putting his hands up in supplication, he said, "I'm just asking."

"Yes, it's Kel's. What? You think he's some kind of whore?" Bell advanced on Carn, his pale blue body seeming to stalk forward with all the gracefulness of the Refrinti cats. "Who the fuck are you to accuse him of such a thing?"

Carn gulped as the anger radiating from the man enveloped him. He was thankful when Corin reached up an arm touching the man. "Back off, Bell. It's okay. It's got to be a surprise to him. Carn's a good man, alright? Please? He helped Tate and I as much as he could when we were with the Derin."

"Fine." Bell sat back down. "But I'm keeping an eye on him."

"Look, Carn, we can discuss everything else later, just, just tell me about Kel, what's happened?" Corin all but begged.

"That's just it, we don't know for sure." Carn sighed. "Within a couple of days of you leaving, he collapsed. We all thought he was just tired, especially as he seemed to bounce back a little at first. Then after the Chieftain died he…"

Corin interrupted him. "Wait a minute? The Chieftain is dead? Damron is dead?" At Carn's nod, Corin asked, "What happened?"

"It was a riding accident. Or it was made to look like one anyway. He should have recovered, but Al'Feram, the clan doctor, was adamant there was nothing to be done. Honestly, after Al'Feram saw him, he deteriorated rapidly before dying. Al'Feram has disappeared, so you can imagine what our suspicions are. So as Tir and Kel were both trying to deal with their father's death, Kel got worse again and rapidly this time. This time when he collapsed, we couldn't help him. He spent the next few weeks barely able to get out of bed, fighting whatever illness he had. Then last week he slipped into a coma. He hasn't woken since. Herica has been dealing with him. We hoped she might have some luck as it seemed like he suffered from the same thing you did, but there was no improvement whatsoever. Tir and I agreed I needed to come here and ask you to go and see him. You're his only hope of living now."

No one seemed to notice Alix had slipped into the room at some point, but he certainly made his presence known now. "So let me get this straight, you've got suspected murders, someone attempting to overthrow your clan, vipers in the midst of you and you want us to let Corin go back there? Not a chance. Did you not take heed of our warnings? We told you what was going on with Martellon. If Tir chose to ignore them…"

"What warnings? We've heard nothing from you! Not a word. We finally came to the conclusion this is all about Martellon and now I find out you knew all along and did nothing! How the fuck could you just leave us to our fate without so much as a warning?"

"Now wait a bloody minute there, son," Alix barked out, his nostrils flaring as he tried to rein in his temper. "We sent a Rider and when he didn't return we sent a second. He came back with a message from Tir. The message was 'Tell Chieftain Alix his message has been received and understood. Tell him it's being dealt with.'"

"Let me see this message," Carn demanded. "We never saw a single Rider."

"The Rider said Tir couldn't write one, he implied it wasn't possible and that it was just a verbal response." Alix closed his eyes and grimaced. "By the moons. I think we have been played. I think that first Rider is probably dead somewhere and the second one is in leagues with, I'm guessing, Martellon. Fuck!"

Niko looked at his father, taking in just how angry he was. He turned to Bell beside him. "I have never, not once, ever seen him this angry."

"I can't say I blame him." Bell shook his head. *This planet really is a twisted mess of political intrigue.*

"If we can find proof, then we can go to the Conclave. You know Riders use a banner." When he received puzzled looks from Dax and Bell, he explained. "The Banner shows that they are official messengers and not to be attacked or the full weight of the Conclave will be brought to bear. They are supposed to be allowed free passage amongst any clan, in any place, without fear of attack or harassment. They are supposed to be accorded with respect, treated well and offered shelter at all times. If, as it's looking likely, someone got to a Rider, then we need to find proof. Riders are under the jurisdiction of the Conclave. They will take whatever action they deem necessary to deal with those responsible for interfering with one."

"Finding the proof is the problem." Alix sighed. "Right now though that is the least of our worries. Martellon and just what he is up to is my main concern."

"Our biggest concern right now is Kel," Carn reiterated. "We need Corin's help. Corin is our only chance of Kel pulling through this."

Alix walked over to Carn. "Son, I know what you're asking but it doesn't change the facts and you want us to let Corin go back there? I can't agree to that, I won't."

"Alix." Corin voice was gentle and when Alix turned to face him, he continued, "I know you care, I know you and everyone else here wants to protect me, but I have to consider it."

"You can't, Corin. It's too much of a risk. If Martellon or Teriva realise what's going on with you…" Alix looked at his belly pointedly. "They will try to kill you. You and the baby are going to end up standing in the way of them taking over the Derin."

"What choice do I really have though, Alix? Damn it, I try not to, but I still love the man. I can't just sit back and let him die. He's the father of my baby, for stars' sake. He may never want me, may have never really wanted me in the first place, but my child still deserves to know both its fathers. I'm going. I have to."

Corin let the chorus of raised voices wash over him as he mentally prepared for what he needed to take on this trip. He knew he was incredibly close to finding something that would keep the symptoms at bay, but there was still some distance to go before he created a cure. There was only going to be so much he could do. No matter what skill he possessed, it was more than likely Kel was going to die anyway. And thinking about the possibility was shredding his heart into pieces.

Tate watched as it appeared as though Corin simply shut down while they all argued around and over him. It wasn't helping Corin, and the stubborn bastard looked to have made up his mind anyway. Tate wasn't really surprised. He knew Corin still loved the man. Stars, he'd have been more surprised if Corin hadn't wanted to go.

He walked over to Corin, pulled him into a bear hug, and announced to the room, "I will go with you. I don't like you doing this. I understand it, but I don't like it. You will, however, go with us to back you up. There can be absolutely no compromise on this. You will never be alone at any point in time, no matter what. I don't care what sort of emergency happens, or who it happens to. You come and get one of us first. Do I make myself clear?"

"I promise, Tate, and thank you. It means everything to me that you're with me on this." He tightened the hug between them. One by one, Dax, Niko and Bell joined them in the hug and pledged to go with him.

"I don't like the thought of you going, I hate it, but it is your choice and I support that. You need to get some rest first though, I insist." Alix pulled Corin away from his friends and into a hug of his own. "You will look after yourself and the baby and you will be careful, do you hear me? You may not be my child biologically, but I see you as a second son."

Tears were in Corin's eyes at Alix's words. They had grown close over the last couple of months, talking about his hopes and fears, of the past and future. Alix was becoming the father figure he never had and always wanted.

As Corin was finally getting a chance to clean up and get some rest, the group all met in the reception room of his suite.

Carn was the first to speak. "I promise we will keep him safe. I will guard him with my life. We wouldn't have asked under the circumstances, but the clan is struggling enough as it is with Damron's death. If something happens to one of the sons, it's going to be catastrophic. Tir was going to come himself. I forced him to stay. If he came in my place, then I doubt there would have been a Derin Clan as we know it to return to. Oh, don't get me wrong, Martellon isn't doing anything overtly, but slowly and surely he's getting people he has influence over into places of import."

"How by the grace of the moons did they manage to do this so quickly?" Alix asked.

"We think they were planning this for a long time. It's been too neat and far too perfect in its execution," Carn replied.

"It makes sense considering everything we know." Tate had put all the pieces together, the last bits falling into place with the information Carn provided.

"I'm not following?" Carn stated, his face a mask of incomprehension.

Tate explained what happened on that fateful day when Kel returned from the Farian Clan, how Corin recognised Martellon as Eliya's abductor and what they discussed afterwards. He told Carn of Corin's shock at the news and how as soon as they all realised what was happening they had dispatched the Rider, in a desperate attempt to warn them, as they knew it was too risky to return.

"Fuck." Carn's shoulders slumped and he sighed dejectedly. "So many opportunities wasted to stop this. Lives lost or torn apart, a clan in chaos and you're telling me if Kel had just said no to his father and stood his ground these things might not have happened?"

Dax joined in the conversation. "From everything I've heard, I'm sure it wouldn't have been so simple and the blame can't be put on Kel. If the Chieftain was how everyone described, I have a feeling if it hadn't been this incident, then it would have been something else which was the tipping point. If Kel refused and with the little girl safe, they might just have gone for a direct assault as an alternative. Such a move would have been devastating for both clans— there is no doubt the death toll would have been huge. So sure, while this has been hell on Corin, and these two Lairds of your clan, it's probably been the least nightmarish situation for the clan itself."

Alix rubbed his temples for a moment. "The simple fact is Martellon has been power hungry for many years. No matter what the individual Chieftains, Lairds or even King Kastain have said, no matter the warnings, the Conclave of Clans have ignored what he's been up to. He has too many supporters on the council. I'll be sending an envoy to the King shortly. I won't risk sending a Rider again. This will be a full envoy with a protection squad. They simply cannot ignore this any longer. If both sides have to call in for support and alliances, we are going to be in all-out war. There are too many rivalries sitting on a blade's edge of action."

Corin's horrified voice from the doorway startled the men. They hadn't heard him open the door. "Are you telling me the stability of this world rests on my ability to heal Kel?" Corin's face blanched at the thought and he started to unconsciously rub his arms, as though trying to warm himself up.

"Corin, so many events, plots and machinations are in motion now that no one single thing is going to bring us back from the brink of this. Whether you save Kel or not, there is one thing you need to be totally sure of. This is *not* on you. Do you understand me?" Alix held Corin's gaze until Corin gave a small nod. "Good, I refuse to have you accept any sort of blame for this. The blame lies fully at the feet of both Martellon and Damron, rest his soul."

Bell laid a hand on Corin's shoulder and squeezed gently. "You can't think like that, Corin. You need to focus. The only thing resting on your ability to heal Kel is Kel's life. The other things should not factor into this. One man, he's all you think about here, he's all you focus on. One man only, no more, no less, just him." Bell argued, everyone else nodding their heads in agreement.

"One man. Kel. I can do that." Corin looked up at him with a sad smile. "Thank you, Bell, I was starting to panic there."

"I know." Bell gave Corin a brief hug, leaving his arm around Corin's waist as a silent show of support, and as a way to lend him strength.

"Okay, so we leave in the morning. Corin, are you going to be able to make the journey?" Carn was worried about his friend.

"Yeah, it's going to be bloody uncomfortable, there's no doubt about it, and we're probably going to need to stop regularly. The little one just loves to fight with my insides. Girl or boy, I have a feeling this one is going to be a warrior!" Corin's comments brought smiles and laughter to the group. "Oh sure, laugh all you want." Shooting them all the evil eye, he continued, "I will have my revenge. Just think, you all want to be uncles, yes?" At their eager nods, he gave a wicked laugh. "Being an uncle means you get to deal with his stinky butt." He burst out laughing at the groans echoing around the room. "Revenge, my dear friends, sweet, sweet revenge."

"Okay, so apart from nature breaks, can I suggest you take the pace a little slower." When Corin went to object, Alix stopped him with a wave of his hand, his rich brown eyes filled with sorrow and worry. "You won't be any good to Kel if you're exhausted or bedridden yourself because you pushed yourself too far physically. I know you don't want to be treated differently, but the fact remains you are pregnant. You do need to take things easier. It's not being weak, it's being sensible."

"He's right, you know," Dax added, "the last thing we need is you being too exhausted to treat Kel."

"Fine, but if I say I'm good to carry on, then you have to trust me both as a doctor and a man who knows his own body. I won't push myself, but I won't have you treat me like a child who needs coddling."

"Agreed. Now is there anything you need to prepare for our journey?" Niko asked.

"A couple of herbs from the forest for the elixir Alix and I have been working on. I need to talk to Alasandra and make sure she's ready to take over the care of the pregnant women. Check she has no questions. Afterwards, I can pack up my gear."

"Good then we should be okay to leave at first light," Niko said. "Rest now though, I can collect the herbs. Tate can pack your gear. You just need to look over the women."

"Thank you." Corin rose from his seat and left them chatting while he went to get some rest.

Whilst Corin slept, the men made plans to protect Corin at all costs. It wasn't just because he was a friend, honorary Avanti, honorary son, father of a Derin child, love of Kel's life, it was more. Corin was simply a good man. Loved, respected and cherished by all. Each and every man there would give their lives for Corin, they just hoped it wouldn't be necessary.

Chapter Twenty Five

By the time morning light had broken over the balustrade of the keep, the men had assembled everyone and everything they needed. As Corin was saying his goodbyes to Alix, he looked around wondering where Tate was. Shrugging it off, he continued saying goodbye to Alasandra.

Tate was in deep thought as he was walking through the keep when suddenly he found himself pinned to the wall. Looking up in surprise, he found Dariux in front of him. He had both of Tate's hands pinned above his head with one large hand. For reason's unknown to Tate, he didn't even attempt to struggle. He simply blinked and waited for Dariux's next move. He could feel Dariux's body pressing into him. It made every nerve in his body come alive, sparks snaked through every connection. He felt himself getting hard and squirmed slightly hoping Dariux didn't feel it. The man confused him, enthralled him and scared him all at once.

Dariux gently lifted his other hand, cupping Tate's face before leaning in to say, "You will be careful. You will keep safe and you will not be injured. Do you hear me?" When Tate didn't respond, he continued, "I said do you hear me, Tate?" Tate gave a short nod, his eyes never leaving Dariux's. "You will look after yourself and when this is over we will talk. I'm not ignoring this any longer."

Tate's body was on fire from the combination of Dariux's words and actions. Every feeling he had tried to ignore, every feeling he had tried to bury deep, came roaring to the front of his mind. They overwhelmed him, consumed him and narrowed his focus down to Dariux and nothing else. His heart beat wildly, a small tremor wracked his body and yet his voice was steady when he simply replied, "Yes, Ree."

At Tate's words, Dariux's eyes flared with desire and his head dipped while his hand reached into Tate's hair and tugged, slightly tipping Tate's head back. Tate's breath stuttered in anticipation, his mouth parting in both invitation and as a means to breathe through his body's reaction. It was all the invite Dariux needed. His mouth possessed Tate's, dominating him, branding him. mapping every part of his mouth, consuming Tate's breath and giving his own in its place.

Tate whimpered as the kiss grew carnal. He couldn't believe he, a grown man, fucking whimpered. The sound excited them both and their hips started to thrust into each other. The feel of their hard cocks brushing against each other caused Tate to groan, a groan that was greedily swallowed by Dariux. Just as Tate thought his body was going to combust, Dariux slowed the kiss down. Gentle sweeps replaced the thrusting pace of his tongue. Feather light brushes of lips against his replaced the harsh, punishing assault of moments before. The kiss became even softer until their lips were simply resting against each other, breaths mingling as they fought for control.

Dariux slowly lowered Tate's arms, brushed one last soft kiss over Tate's lips, and let his hand slip from Tate's head onto his cheek in a gentle caress as he backed away. "See you outside, handsome," was all he said as he strode away from Tate, whose eyes were firmly fixed on the globes of Dariux's butt as he turned the corner.

"Holy shit!" Tate whispered to no one in particular as he slumped against the wall struggling to get back his equilibrium. His gaze darted back down the corridor to where Dariux had been moments before, as though he needed reassurance it was real. His mind was a whirlpool of conflicting emotions all battering away at his self-control. Forcing himself to push against the tide, he pushed his feelings to the back of his mind. Straightening up and drawing on his years of training, he took an unsteady step towards the courtyard. With each step, his body responded as it should, his mask slipping into place, his mind back in control. By the time he made it out to the group, the only evidence of what happened were his lips, which were raw and swollen. It was enough to get a questioning look from Corin when he noticed, but Tate simply shook his head. Now was not the time. Instead, he quickly mounted and turned to face Niko.

"We do this for our friends, old and new. Keep it together, watch each other and, above all, protect Corin and the babe. Let's ride!" With that, he kicked his mount into action, the men falling in place around him. Corin was at the heart of their group, an echo as to how he was at the heart of them all.

$$\longrightarrow\!\!\bigcirc\!\!\longleftarrow$$

The journey took twice as long as the trip to the Estrivian Clan did, even though it was just as urgent. Corin was deeply uncomfortable, but kept quiet over the depth of his suffering. He was slightly frustrated over the treatment his friends were giving him. He knew it was done out of concern, but it didn't make it any easier to cope with. He didn't think they even knew just how protective they were being, which was one of the main reasons he never brought up the issue. What's more, he didn't want to appear ungrateful.

The first night they broke for camp brought a blessed relief to Corin's aching bones, or rather he was sure it would if he could actually climb down off his mount. Huffing out a frustrated breath, he looked around for who would help him without making the biggest issue over it. Spotting Bell, he motioned him over.

"Uh, Bell?" he asked, squirming in his saddle.

"Is something up, Doc?" Bell queried.

"I, uh, cantgetoffmymount," Corin mumbled the words together as his face flushed red.

"What?" Bell asked. Oh, he knew what Corin said, he was just teasing him a little.

"I can't get off my mount," Corin huffed out before they both looked at each other and started laughing.

"Oh, fair damsel, let me come to thy aid. Never fear your gallant knight is here." Bell followed his words with a dramatic bow, his golden plait swinging back and forth with the movement.

"Why thank you, kind Sir." Corin did his best impression of a curtsy while still atop his mount. They were still laughing as Bell carried him, bridal style, over to the fire Dax was already working on. Dax was looking up at them snorting with laughter, trying to hide it by hiding his face.

When he was finally standing on his own two feet, Corin started to gently stretch his back, trying to work out the kinks. He groaned in relief when the aching muscles started to ease from their cramped position.

Dax stood up walking over to Corin, patting him on the belly. "How did the little one hold up?" Just as he finished asking, the little one in question promptly kicked the hand resting on Corin's stomach. Both of them looked down, then back up at each other with broad smiles gracing their faces.

"Well hello there little one, it's nice to meet you!" Dax teased as he rubbed Corin's belly in response. Another gentle tap under his hand seemed to say hello back. Laughing Dax gave Corin's belly one final rub before he returned to setting up the fire. "Sit it won't be long before we have hot water for your tea and then I'll get started on some food." He brushed his light brown hair off his forehead, unused to his new longer hair. He'd left the sides shaved in but was growing out the top.

"It suits you, you know." Corin smiled.

"Hmm?" Dax asked, distracted by preparing Corin's tea.

"Your hair. I like it like that."

Dax smiled widely. "Thanks. Seeing as we aren't in Alliance territory, I thought I would grow it out, see how I liked it."

"It looks good. Handsome." Corin winked.

Dax smiled and passed over the tea. "Now drink up while I get started on some food."

"Thank you, Dax, I can help though."

"It's fine. I think one of Carn's men needs a little bit of treatment though. He got kicked by his mount when it got spooked by a rodent as he was dismounting."

"Where is he?"

"Carn's going to bring him over. Bell, would you get his med kit please?"

"Sure thing, boss." When Bell returned with the kit, he turned to Corin. "I'll sort your mount out. Just see to the man, then take it easy."

"Thank you, Bell. I appreciate it."

Both the tea and the food went a long way to helping Corin feel better, but he really was not looking forward to another day's full ride. He was just contemplating another tea when one appeared in front of him. Looking up, he saw Tate on the other end of the arm holding it out to him. "So you want to talk about what happened earlier?" he asked Tate as he motioned to his lips.

"Nope," was Tate's succinct response, his vivid blue eyes flashing with emotion.

"Aww, come on, Tate, you kept bugging me about Kel. Make a pregnant man happy and keep him distracted?" Corin practiced his doe eyes and pout on Tate.

"Jeez, Doc, that's so wrong!" He burst out laughing. "Bah, it's working though!" He scowled at Corin as he spoke. "I don't know what happened, one minute I was walking down the corridor the next, bam, I was pinned up against the wall and being devoured in just about the best damn kiss I have ever had in my life. It was hot as hell. Completely surprising, but still hot as hell."

"Dariux I take it?"

"Yes, and the man is so infuriating, so annoying, so frustrating."

"And hot as hell?"

"Yeah, that too, Doc, that too."

"Well, just do what you want, Tate, it's your decision to make, yours and his, but damn you two together would be hot as hell!"

Tate laughed. "I know, right?" He winked. "I mean, he's all chiselled and he's got these eyes that seem to burn their way through to my soul."

"Don't forget those cheekbones, because, wow, are they gorgeous." Corin whistled.

"Yup, they are a work of art, those cheekbones." Tate smiled softly, causing Corin to hide his grin behind his mug of tea.

Corin sighed with relief as the tea soothed his bones and helped him relax. It was enough to ease him into a deep, dreamless sleep, right there in front of the fire. Rather than wake him, Bell walked up and scooped him up again, before laying him gently on his sleep roll, covering him and walking away.

The second day was the same as the first, the only difference being the slight change in scenery as they crossed from Estrivian lands into Derin lands. Getting as close as they could before making camp for the night left Corin sore and irritated, but glad the journey was nearly over. It was mere minutes after he had managed to eat that he was once again in a deep sleep. It wasn't much later Corin woke from a nightmare screaming. His breath was coming in fast pants, eyes cloudy from a combination of fear and shock, his body trembling as it struggled to overcome the nightmare's effects.

Niko, as the closest man to him, was by Corin's side in seconds. He simply wrapped Corin in his arms and held him tight as he ran his hand up and down Corin's back in an attempt to soothe the man. He could feel tears pooling on his shoulder from where Corin's head rested. He didn't attempt to discuss it with Corin. He knew it must have been bad and if Corin wanted to talk, he would.

A few minutes of the strength Niko provided saw Corin calm enough to mutter a few words for Niko to hear. "I dreamt he died." Those words had Niko holding Corin tighter, offering as much support as he could without having to say anything. What could he say? There was no reassurance in the world he could give. They all knew just how dire this situation was and just how prophetic Corin's dreams were turning out to be. Niko sent out a silent plea to the universe, a plea they would come out of this with both his friends alive, even if they couldn't be together. Niko simply continued to hold Corin tight until he finally dropped back to sleep, this time, thankfully, into a deep, dreamless sleep.

Chapter Twenty Six

Dawn saw excitement and apprehension building in equal measure amongst the group. Corin didn't know what he was feeling, other than a single, simple desire to see Kel, to help Kel, to heal Kel. It wasn't long before they had made their way to the keep gates.

Carn's own men were posted on the way into the keep. They soon fell in around their leader, forming a barrier between the group and any of Martellon's men they might encounter. The added bonus was they were also kept hidden from prying eyes. If they were lucky, it would buy them more time with Kel before anyone other than Tir realised what was going on.

They made it to Kel's suite without anyone noticing they were there, not even clan members. It appeared as though many were staying inside, out of the way of Martellon and his men. Carn went in first to make sure the coast was clear. He soon ducked his head back out and motioned them in. Once the door was shut behind them, they all took a breath, relieved to have made it this far. Just as Corin started towards the bedroom, Tir walked out of it.

"Oh heavens, Corin!" he exclaimed, rushing over and embracing him in a massive hug. "I truly hoped, but I wasn't sure if you would come."

"How could I not? I still love him, Tir, no matter what has happened."

Tir's eyes were beseeching Corin to understand. "I truly am sorry for everything, Corin. I really wish things had happened differently."

"Me too, Tir, me too." As Corin pulled back from the hug, he felt the moment his physical state registered on Tir.

Tir's arms stiffened as his eyes dropped to Corin's belly. "What the fuck?"

"Um, yeah, surprise! You're going to be an uncle!" Corin had to bite back a laugh at the look on Tir's face. It was a hybrid of confusion, fascination, joy, sadness and simple incredulity.

"How, What, Why?" Tir stuttered.

"I will explain, Tir, but now is not the time. I need to see him. Fill me in on everything, then you can go and see Tate and Niko who can explain it all." Corin gently prodded Tir in the direction of his brother's room.

When Corin walked into the room, he gasped in shock at just how weak and small Kel looked in the bed. His gorgeous giant of a man looked so small it was making Corin freak out slightly. His skin was chalk white and covered in a sheen of sweat, his hair was a mess and plastered to his head. He lay on his back, propped up slightly by pillows behind him. He looked to have lost weight. Corin rushed to the side of the bed and immediately checked for a pulse. He breathed slightly easier when he felt it, slow, but steady. He felt Tate beside him and mumbled a thank you as Tate started passing equipment to him. He immediately passed out one of his tea mixes to Tir and asked him to get some made up. As soon as the monitor was set up and Corin had taken a baseline of all his stats, he opened up the vial of elixir he made before he left. He added a dose to the booster and injected it directly into Kel's bloodstream.

"What did you give him?" Tir asked as he returned with the tea.

"I've been working on an elixir which will hopefully help with this."

"You know what it is then?" Tir asked, although it wouldn't change anything, he was desperate to know what was wrong with his brother.

Corin was too distracted working on Kel to answer Tir's question. He left answering up to the other men in the room.

Niko pulled Tir to one side. "It's Matesickness, Tir."

"What?" Tir all but shouted. "I didn't know Matesickness was real. I thought it was just one of those stories told around the fire at clan gatherings?"

"It is, it's extremely rare, but then again how many people do you know who voluntarily walk away from their truemate?"

"Oh sweet moons. Will he die?"

"We hope not. Corin has been researching it and working with my father to develop this elixir. It has lessened the effects to a manageable level in Corin, but as he has a different physiology than Kel, we don't know for sure if it will work. We just have to hold on to hope."

"Hope is all I have left, Niko. Everything else has fallen to shit."

"We heard, and we plan on helping with everything else as best we can. Now there is a *lot* to fill you in on. We finally put all the pieces together when Carn came for Corin. Leave Corin to work on Kel and come next door while we fill you in." Niko led a subdued Tir out of the room, and the others followed until it was only Corin and Tate left.

Corin kept checking Kel's pulse, his breathing. He needed to reassure himself, even if the monitor was already displaying the information. "Right now there is not much we can do but sit and wait. The tea is ready and being kept warm, so the minute he wakes we can give him some. As always the waiting is the hardest part of things at times like this." Corin's head bowed, his shoulders sagged and a shudder wracked his body as he spoke.

"We just have to have hope. Do you have any idea how long the elixir will take?" Tate wished, just once, something would go perfectly for them.

"I don't even know if it will work, Tate, let alone how long it will take." Corin sighed. They both sat in the chairs beside Kel's bed and settled in to wait.

Niko finished bringing Tir up to date on everything they had been through, making sure he explained exactly what had happened with the Riders, or as much as they had been able to piece together with Carn's help, a small smile on his face as he took in the shock on his friend's face. "So, now you know everything."

"I'll fucking kill him. I will tear him apart with my bare bloody hands."

"Corin?" Niko caught movement out of the corner of his eye as all the Avanti stood as one and made to walk towards Tir.

"No, you idiot, Martellon." Tir cracked his knuckles, trying to relieve some tension, some aggression.

Niko sighed as the men sat back down again.

"Thank fuck the mating never went ahead." Tir sighed.

"It didn't?" Niko asked incredulously.

"No, Kel was putting it off as much as he could. Then Teriva decided she wanted a big celebration and insisted on waiting till it was arranged. The only thing was Kel fell ill before it could happen. She threw a fit when she realised it couldn't go ahead. She's been taking it out on the staff ever since. It's more than I need though. The clan is in mourning. I'm in mourning, and Eliya is distraught. She's too young to cope with losing her grandfather and her uncle being ill." Pure grief was shining in his eyes as he spoke.

"I've just not been able to throw Teriva and Martellon off our lands. I've had no proof they have been involved in any of this. If what you say is true, then I have to notify the King as well as kick them out."

"My father has already sent an envoy. Besides, we have to notify them of the situation with the Riders."

"Thank you, Niko, to you, your father and your clan for stepping in where we failed." Tir drew Niko into an embrace.

"You know I would do anything for you guys anyway, but Corin deserves nothing less than total support. He is a good man. He works tirelessly to help others and despite everything, he wanted to leave as soon as he heard about Kel. We had to force him to wait till the morning." Niko smiled at the memory.

"Everyone involved has my heartfelt thanks. After the way this clan has treated Corin, I'm amazed anyone even considered trying to warn us." Tir smiled sadly.

"Stars, Tir, Corin feels guilty because he didn't say anything right away. But he was so deep in shock over Kel I don't think anything registered. He was on complete autopilot. As soon as he remembered and told us, we broke for camp and sent a Rider. Knowing what I knew, I couldn't risk us returning. It was too dangerous. I'm sorry."

"Nothing to be sorry for, my friend. Sending a Rider should have been enough. I take it we don't know what happened to the first Rider?"

"No. Nothing, no trace of him anywhere." Dariux answered.

"What about the one who lied?" Tir wondered.

"As soon as we get to him, we will hold him. He left to take a message to the northern clans and hasn't been back since. Mind you, it wouldn't surprise me if he went into hiding," Dariux mused.

Tir rubbed at his temples. "What do you think happened with him?"

Dax answered this time. "My best guess is that he was compromised one way or another."

Tir looked at Dax then at Niko inquiringly.

"Sorry, I forgot to introduce you. Tir, this is Commander Daxin 'Dax' Rydoc and Lieutenant Bellan 'Bell' Nimeri. Friends and teammates of Corin and Tate. Guys, this is Laird Tirathon, 'Tir' Tharn, brother to Kel. Or I guess it's actually Chieftain Tir now?"

"Sadly, yes, it is." Tir turned to Dax and Bell. "Welcome to you both. It's good that Corin and Tate were able to connect with you. I know they were deeply worried."

"Thank you." Bell dipped his head towards Tir. Dax just watched the man, more wary than Bell.

Just then, the door burst open and in stormed both Martellon and Teriva, with a squad of their guard behind them. Dariux, Niko's men, Carn and his men at arms immediately stood and flanked both Niko and Tir. Bell and Dax took up positions beside them and protected the door at their back.

"Yes, Martellon? Is there a problem?" Tir went on the offensive in what was likely to be a battle of words. His only hope was the words didn't turn into wounds. If he could keep this peaceful, it would be better. If not, he was going to take every last one of these bastards down. No one fucked with his family and Martellon had been fucking with them for months.

"We were informed by my guard a hostile force had breached the keep."

"Well, as you can see there is no hostile force. Just my men and some friends." Tir was calm in the face of Martellon's obvious excitement at being able to progress with his plans.

"Why are your men at arms here if you are being visited by friends? Surely you don't need a guard about when friends are visiting?" Martellon grin was cocky.

Niko snorted to himself, muttering under his breath, "Well, if it's friends like you, then anyone would need a bloody army!" The only one to catch his words was Dariux who struggled to suppress the bark of laughter that threatened. Instead, he shot Niko a wry smile.

Tir smiled, "My men at arms are here because they escorted MY friends through MY lands to MY keep and to MY rooms. As such it's none of your business."

"Of course it is. Teriva is the Lady of this clan." Martellon's expression radiated cockiness.

"No, she isn't. She is as yet unmated. Remember the ceremony with Kel had yet to go ahead, so she is nothing to this clan yet. The lady of the keep? The honour of such a position falls to my daughter." Tir calmly batted away Martellon's verbal attempts to rile him and gain further control of the clan through the back door.

"Ah yes, tell me, where is the lovely Eliya today?" Martellon asked, hoping to goad Tir, to force him to get aggressive and react.

"Oh, she is safe and cared for, have no worries about her." Tir knew the implied threats to his daughter were going to start soon, and now they had, more than ever he was glad he had surrounded his daughter in a virtual ring of steel, having split both his and Kel's guard. Half were sharing the duty of looking after them, half the duty of looking after his daughter.

The Chieftain's guards were keeping an eye on some of the elders, the ones he knew still supported them, and the overall keep. This was on top of all the normal guards the clan was guarded by. Tir had been very careful to make sure he surrounded his family only by people he was sure would protect them with everything they had; those who wanted their clan back and stood with him against Martellon.

Martellon's face was a scowl. His first salvo in this battle of words had not hit the mark as he hoped. "It still doesn't explain what so many are doing here. Why would you need three sets of men at arms in this room? My men are more than capable of protecting you. You know, since the alliance began, we made sure to have them stationed throughout the keep."

"Oh, I am well aware of what you have been doing since the alliance began. Make no mistake Martellon, this is MY clan, not yours. It is NOT your place to question what I do or where I send my men. However, since you asked so.... Nicely," —Tir quirked an eyebrow at his own choice of words— "I will tell you. They literally only arrived mere moments ago. We were simply catching up and arranging where we were going to house them all. I mean, your men have taken up what little space was left in the barracks. So it looks like I will have to house them all in the suites, which are free here on the family wing." Tir knew his words would piss off Martellon greatly. The last thing Martellon wanted was Tir's guard and supporters close. He was desperately trying to isolate him. "I am sure they won't mind roughing it in the royal wing for a bit." Tir laughed. "Besides, did you really expect the heir to another clan to be travelling without his men-at-arms?"

"Ah, yes, Laird Nikoben Dastria, tell me, just why are you here?" Martellon demanded.

"Well, it's really none of your business, Chieftain Martellon, but I'm here to see a sick friend and to pay my condolences on the death of the Chieftain Damron. Yes, I heard about his death." Niko watched as Martellon's gaze snapped his way, breaking the glaring match he had been having with Tir. "Yes, it's a travesty a man such as Chieftain Damron should lose his life in such a simple manner. What's more, it's tragic Al'Feram couldn't save him. I wonder? Where is Al'Feram now? I ask purely in case we have need of a doctor, of course."

"He has gone missing. I expect he was worried about how Tir would react." In fact, Martellon ordered his Master at Arms to personally kill the man. There was no way he was going to let some old fool babble his secrets, disrupt his plans, and live.

"Oh, he was right to be fucking worried," Tir muttered under his breath. As Niko and Martellon were talking, Tir took the opportunity to look around. The men on his side of the room were alert, hands resting gently on weapons. He knew they were ready to engage Martellon's men at a moment's notice. On the other side, Martellon's men looked wary. Some of them were shooting concerned glances at each other when they thought there was no one watching them. Tir couldn't fault the men. They were doing what their Chieftain ordered them to do, but he could tell some of them were not happy with the way things were going. Maybe there was hope for the clan yet.

Dax turned to whisper to Bell, "We better hope Corin and Tate stay next door. This guy has no idea who we are, but you can damn well bet if he catches sight of those two, things are going to get dicey fast. If he realises Corin is pregnant, it's probably going to push him over the edge. Getting rid of this family was always going to look suspicious, but if Corin and the baby disappear or die, then it's going to be a nightmare scenario. Alix will step in. I truly have no doubt he will step in all swords at the ready. It would bring another clan into the mix and all of a sudden we are going to be thigh deep in a full on war."

"Then we better hope the stars are with us and he stays next door. But I'm afraid to say, knowing Corin, if he has heard any of this I can't imagine him sitting still in there, can you?" Bell quirked his brow at Dax, both of them thinking of Corin when he was all riled up.

"No, and that's what worries me." Dax sighed and refocused his attention back to the men in front of him.

"Look, Martellon, Kel is still ill. There is no chance of any mating going ahead now, no matter how much you and your daughter want it. What's more, if and when Kel wakes up I don't think he'll be prepared to go through with the mating anymore, considering the circumstances. It's best if you just leave the keep, leave our lands and forget about the alliance." Tir knew what Martellon's reaction was likely to be, but he needed to at least try and prevent the bloodshed which was becoming increasing likely.

Tir's statement finally prompted Teriva to join the conversation.

"No! Daddy, no! You promised me I could mate with Kel. You said he was mine. I want him and we aren't going to leave here until I get him." Her voice was almost a screech it was so shrill.

The men around her were hard pressed not to laugh at the picture she was presenting. Oh, she was beautiful, there was no doubt about it, but her soul was as black as tar, right to the core. She may have been acting like a spoilt brat at this moment, but Tir knew Teriva rivalled her father for her cruelty, hatred and self-serving ways.

"Tir, this mating is going ahead, it was agreed as part of our alliance, you cannot change that. You cannot back out on the deal. We will take the clan if you do," Martellon announced to smug smiles from his daughter, her expression screaming victory.

"Oh, you can try, but know this, if you attempt to, it will be bloody, it will be harsh and it will be long. We have the superior military might and we will be victorious. I will not, EVER, consider surrendering or allowing my clan to fall into your hands. You may have been able to fool my father, but you do not fool me. You have already done enough damage to us, but no more. I am giving you the chance to walk away, against my better judgement, because of my respect for your clan, not you. I don't want to cause them hardships. I don't want innocent families to lose their husbands, sons and fathers over a war they cannot win, for a man who doesn't care about them." Tir knew his words would mean nothing to Martellon, or Teriva, but his hope was that the words would resonate with those guarding him.

"Pretty words from a pretty man. But make no mistake, I am not leaving and Kel will mate with Teriva. I will own this clan, one way or another." Spittle flung in all directions from Martellon's mouth as he spoke, such was his anger. His hawk like face was twisted into a vicious snarl.

"And, as I have said before, It's. Not. Going. To. Happen." Tir spat out each word.

"I give you forty eight hours to cede Kel and this clan to me, or we will take it by force." He continued as his voice dripped with sarcasm. "And I'm going to be so sad to have to announce the tragic accident which cost the lives of Tir and Eliya to the clan. They will look to Teriva and I to help them rebuild. Look to Teriva to provide Kel with children, a task I'm sure she will thoroughly enjoy!" Martellon's eyes shone with a combination of depravity and anticipation.

Tir snapped. He lunged for Martellon. Threatening his daughter yet again finally tipped him over the edge of his pent up anger. Carn and Dariux yanked him back before he could touch the man. A growl tore from his throat as he realised he couldn't reach Martellon.

Martellon just stood there and laughed. "Two days, Tir. You have two days, then all this" —he gestured around them— "is mine." He spun on his heel, his men flanking them as he stormed out the door.

Tir slumped in Carn and Dariux's arms. The fight was draining out of him. He was tired, so devastatingly tired, and battling a war he didn't know if he could win. His family and clan were dropping like little flying Jinties around him. He wasn't sure he had anything left to give.

Noticing the look on Tir's face, Niko stormed over to him and yanked him to his feet. Grabbing him gently by the jaw, he forced Tir to look at him. "Don't you bloody dare quit on me now, you idiot. Fight, you stupid bastard, fight. Fight with every breath you have, fight with every last strand of mental ability you possess, fight with every bone, muscle and sinew, just bloody fight! You come at Martellon from every direction, with every weapon in your arsenal be they physical or mental. By the stars, fight!"

"I can't." Tir's head bowed and his body sagged.

"You can and you will. You have us now and we won't abandon you," Niko promised.

"I know my father started all this, him and his bloody alliance, him and his bloody desire to gain greater importance in the Clan Conclave, but I still miss the bloody bastard. I'm not ready to take over this clan. I don't want to be responsible for all these lives, I can't be! What if I fail? What if I lead them wrong? Niko, I'm not ready!" Tir's eyes were imploring Niko for something, anything, he just wasn't sure what.

"You are ready, and in your heart you know this. Look, when was the last time you slept? Ate? Spent some quality time with Eliya? Do you even remember?"

"No," was all Tir could manage to say.

Dariux spoke up. "I'll sort it all out, get him fed, some sleep and to see his daughter. It might be worth bringing her up here now anyway. It will be better if everyone is closer together rather than split our forces. Maybe Corin can give him something to sleep."

"Good idea. Arrange the food and the move. I'll get Corin in here. The rest of you start comparing notes so we can work out how to get the clan out of this goddamn mess." With a heavy heart at everything his friends were enduring, Niko turned to the door to Kel's room and sent up a plea to the fates for at least one thing to start going their way.

Corin looked up as Niko walked through the door. "I've already got a sleeping aid ready for Tir," he said with a sad smile.

"You heard it all then?" Niko asked.

"We did, and realised it was going to be much safer for everyone involved if we stayed in here. The longer we can keep Martellon and Teriva from knowing Corin is both back here and pregnant, the better. If they are acting like this now, then they will literally go all out crazy when they find out." Tate nodded to Corin as he spoke. "Getting him to sit still through all that was a challenge though!" Corin simply scowled at Tate as he laughed. "I had to threaten to dish all his secrets up when Kel woke up to get him to stay here!

They are juicy little secrets as well." Tate winked at Corin as he spoke.

"Seriously. You. Me." Corin pointed to each of them in turn as he spoke. "We're going to come to blows soon." He scowled at both men as they laughed. "One word. Nappies!" It was his turn to laugh at the men's faces this time.

"Aww, c'mon, Doc, Sweetie, Honeybunch, Babycakes, my little Sugarplum. You wouldn't do that to gorgeous old me. Would you?" Tate fluttered his eyelashes at his friend.

"Damn, Tate, that is so wrong!" Even as Corin spoke, he couldn't stop laughing.

Smiling, Niko turned to Corin. "So any changes? I realise it's probably far too soon, but it would do Tir the world of good to know there was some improvement with his brother. Anything at all would be helpful."

"Actually, yes." Corin smiled at the look of shock on Niko's face. "His vitals are improving already and we're sure we saw eye movement under his lids. It's a bit early to be sure, but I think the elixir might just be working. Mind you, from what Alix was talking about, it's possible it's because I'm close. I simply don't know."

"Thank the moons!" Niko whispered. "I tried not to put too much hope on this working. I didn't want to be disappointed, yet at the same time, I never really expected it to work." He grimaced slightly at his own words. "It's not that I don't think you're a brilliant doctor, Corin, you are, it's just nothing seems to go right anymore. I couldn't believe this was what was going to change it all."

"It's okay, I wasn't really hopeful myself. If anything, I'm amazed it seems to be having an effect. The doctor in me is cautiously optimistic about Kel's chances of, if not beating this totally, then getting to the point where we can manage his symptoms. Now why don't we go and sort out Tir. Tate, are you alright here until I come back? I really don't want to leave him alone just in case there are any side effects."

"Of course." Tate smiled at Corin, glad to see some of the weight on his shoulders lifting. Corin still amazed him on a daily basis. His capacity to keep going when everything around him was crumbling, to stay strong when everyone else was buckling, truly amazed him. Corin really was one of the finest men he had ever met and he was very glad to call the man his friend. Who knew one tenuous connection back on the Delphini would lead them here? To be as close as they were? Tate let his thoughts drift as his eyes continuously flicked between the monitor and Kel's face.

When Corin walked into the reception room, he was stunned at the sheer anguish present on Tir's face. It was obvious the man was close to his breaking point, if he hadn't in fact already reached it. He gingerly squatted in front of the chair Tir was slumped in. Cupping his face, he smiled softly, while his other hand was checking the strength of his pulse. All the physical signs were pointing to exhaustion.

"Can you manage to eat?" When Tir just shook his head, Corin responded with a simple, "Okay, it's okay, Tir. I've got it from here, I'll keep everyone safe, you don't have to worry now. I'm here." As Tir simply looked at him Corin gave him a compound of vitamins, minerals and natural endorphins to help his mood. The second shot he gave was to put Tir into a deep sleep. It would hopefully keep the man out for at least ten hours. Struggling to stand, he grasped the hand that was extended out to him, not caring who it was. He huffed out, "Thanks, damn, it's hard to move carting this one around." The comment earned him a snigger from Niko, who had helped him. "Can we get him moved to the second bedroom? He'll pass out in a matter of minutes."

"Sure." Niko bent and hefted Tir into his arms. *Damn, the man was strong,* thought Corin. Once Niko settled Tir on the bed, he asked, "Is there anything else we can do for him?"

"No, just let him be, I'll keep checking on him." As Corin went to return to the other room, he swayed slightly. Niko grabbed his arm quickly.

"Whoa there, Doc, take it easy. You alright?"

"Yeah, I just need to sit and eat something. I should really rest, but with these two needing attending too, I don't have the time." At

Niko's frown, he went on, "I promise I won't push myself too far. I won't risk the baby. You know I won't, but realistically, I'm the one who needs to monitor them."

"Hmm, okay, but here's the deal. You sit, eat and then stay beside Kel's bed. I don't want you running back and forth. We will keep an eye on Tir and get you if we need you. Promise me though, if you feel worse, you will let one of us know."

"I promise, Niko, and trust me, I'm not running anywhere!" He snorted as he gestured to his belly. Niko swung his arm around Corin's shoulders, giving him a one armed hug as he led him back to the table and food.

They found everyone discussing what they were going to do about the threat from Martellon. There was no doubt they were all taking it very seriously. The man was borderline insane and it made a very dangerous enemy to deal with. He simply sat, listening as he ate, acutely aware of just how much he and the baby needed the nutrients.

"Look, Chieftain Alix sent the envoy to King Kastain. We can only hope for a swift response, preferably in the form of men," Dariux said.

"How likely are we to get such a response?" Dax asked. "I mean, I presume it's the same here as on pretty much every planet and in every alliance. Politics and political wrangling will always influence what happens in these situations. Just how much support does this guy have?"

"We are lucky. The King's father was a childhood friend of Alix and Kastain sees him as an honorary uncle, so I imagine he will trust his judgement on this. Besides, Martellon's behaviour is being noticed amongst some of the Conclave, so there is hope both the King and Conclave will respond."

"Did we actually send someone to the Conclave though?" asked Carn. "I thought because of all Martellon's supporters, we were waiting to see what support the King gave first?"

"We are," Niko answered. "But if we gain the King's support we will be in a better position with the Conclave and he can summon them immediately. It will be faster this way."

"The only question is how likely is it the King, or the King's guard, will make it here within the forty eight hour window Martellon gave us?" Dax wondered.

"That, my friend, is the big question. One where I simply don't know the answer. He could be here in as little as twenty four or as much as seventy two hours. So, it begs the question, can we hold out till he gets here, if he's coming at all, with the forces we have?"

"Well, you guys are well trained anyway, plus we've been teaching your men at arms some new tricks Martellon's forces won't be expecting and that's going to be a big boost. Best of all though? You have us. The Avanti aren't the most feared group across the seven systems for nothing. The four of us can do more damage than four legions given the right equipment."

It was that statement which made them all realise just how lucky they were that the random nature of the universe had seen the men crash on to their planet. Many of them sat back to contemplate the all-out war, which would have occurred if they hadn't been there, or the alternative of the complete and utter decimation of the Derin Clan. No doubt, the other clans would have soon followed. For those who believed in some ultimate force in the universe, they sent up a heartfelt thanks. The others? They simply thanked the universe for its interference.

Eventually, Dax spoke once again. "How about Dariux, Carn and I get together and see what we can come up with? Unless there are others amongst you who you trust to come up with battle plans?"

"No, I think the three of you would be best at it," Niko spoke for them all.

"I can go with someone and see to any equipment?" Bell offered.

"Perfect." Carn beckoned to one of his officers. "This is Vrastin, he can help with whatever you need. Vrastin, stay out of Martellon's way and spread what word you can about what plans we are making. Set up some sort of runner system so we can keep our men updated."

"Will do, boss." Vrastin saluted Carn as he and Bell made their way out of the suite.

"I'll go and watch Kel and send Tate in. Come get me if you need me." Corin spoke as he hauled his weary body to standing.

"Take it easy, Doc." Dax's voice was full of concern.

"I will."

As the men worked on plans, Corin was glad to sit down and rest a little. There was no change in Kel beyond the initial ones and Corin was trying to calculate when he could next give him another dose of the elixir. Damn, he wished he had more research behind him. He was doing this blind and it worried him. He had to come down on the side of caution rather than risking doing more damage than good, he just wished he knew where the line was.

They needed more time for everything. More time to plan, more time to help Kel, more time to help Tir. They always needed more fucking time. He huffed out a frustrated breath. He was so tired, physically and mentally. This pregnancy was taking a harder toll on him than he let anyone know. Although it wasn't just the pregnancy, it was everything else as well. More than anything, he missed Kel. If he was honest with himself, it was the situation with Kel which was causing him the most problems. His heart was constantly hurting. He was tired of faking it until he made it. He missed him. He missed being kissed by him, being held by him, talking to him. Shit, he just missed him period.

"Fuck, Kel, I feel so lost." Corin felt tears trace down his cheeks in a silent plea. "I feel so, so lost. I have so much going on and it's too much to take in and process. I miss being held by you. I miss your support. I miss your laugh, your voice, your smile. Fuck, I miss everything about you. I thought I could do all this. I thought I could watch you be with someone else. I thought I could handle it. I thought I could raise our baby by myself, only seeing you occasionally when you came to see the little one. But I can't, it hurts too much. And now, from what Tir said, you haven't mated her. I don't know what to think about that. I don't know how to feel. I hope it means you still feel for me. I hope it means we have a chance. I just miss you. I felt so safe in your arms, so loved. When you held me tight and told me you loved me, well, it made me forget everything going on around us. I felt only you, I saw only you, I heard only you. Damn it, Kel, I love you."

With those words, Corin gave up and climbed onto the bed beside Kel, sobbing quietly. He held Kel's hand tight in his own and tried to just enjoy the few minutes' peace, enjoy simply existing beside the man who held his heart. The comfort he drew from the simple touch, the simple connection, had the stress start to fade, the tears stop, the tight muscles start to loosen and his breath start to slow. Slowly, his eyes started to flutter, and for the first time in months, Corin slipped into a restful sleep.

Chapter Twenty Seven

Tate had to smile. He opened the door quietly and found his friend fast asleep beside the man he loved, hands clasped together. Taking a quick peek at the vitals monitor, he saw Kel's vitals were stable, so he closed the door and went back to planning. Corin needed his rest and he couldn't think of a better way for him to get it.

The next time Tate peeked into the room to check on them both, he stood there with eyes wide, as he mouthed, "holy shit" into the air. He forced himself to blink several times to make sure he wasn't hallucinating. Corin still lay on the bed, but was turned onto his side. It wasn't Corin, who surprised him, though.

It was Kel. Kel had turned onto his own side and lay behind Corin. His face was buried in Corin's hair with one arm tight across his man's chest, keeping him pinned to him. Corin's hand rested atop Kel's. Both of them were breathing slow and deep, at peace. Tate didn't know what caused him to smile the most, the fact the elixir was obviously working, or Kel's instinctive need to have Corin in his arms. Tate slowly backed out of the room before turning to everyone else. "Um, guys, I think you'd better come here. Just be bloody quiet, alright?"

They all slowly got to their feet, wondering why Tate was acting so funny. Not a sound was made as they all stood in the doorway, staring at the scene on the bed. Slowly, smiles replaced shock. Happiness radiated from one man to the next in a chain reaction. A whispered "Fuck yes!" had them all quietly sniggering as they backed out of the room, shutting the door and leaving the two men to their rest.

"So I guess we can presume the elixir is working then?" Niko's eyes were alight with joy as he spoke. "You reckon we should try to wake Tir or let him sleep?"

"I would suggest sleep," Dax spoke after a minute. "If we wake him now the chances are he will want to go in and talk to Kel and its best if all three of them get the rest they need. As it is, we are all going to have to call on every little bit of resolve we have to get through the next two days. If they get rest now, it will help us all in the long run."

The men all went back to their previous tasks, but the mood was considerably lighter. The peace which descended on the room as the men worked was soon shattered as the little dynamo called Eliya danced into the room with her guard.

"Tatey!" She launched herself across the room and up into his arms. Her arms around his neck squeezed as tight as she could. All the while she was smothering his face with kisses. "I missed you, Tatey."

"I missed you too, Honeybunch."

"Where's my Cori?"

"He's resting. He'll be up soon and I bet he's going to be so excited to see you."

"Where's Papi?"

"He's resting as well."

"Good. He been tiwed, coz of the bad man and lady," Eliya said solemnly.

Oh, out of the mouths of young ones, Tate thought. "That's right. So why don't you sit with us and eat something. You can tell me everything you've been up to since I last saw you."

Eliya graced Tate with a beaming smile and promptly launched into a retelling of her life over the last few months. Tate couldn't help but smile at how exuberant she was. He was smiling because no matter how much darkness was surrounding her, she still found joy in some of the simplest things. It made all of them realise just how much they were fighting for. Who they were fighting for. Their resolve to win against Martellon grew with each moment in her presence.

All the planning was done. There was now nothing they could do until Martellon made his move. Vrastin and Bell had been able to find an extraordinary stockpile of munitions and weapons. They were also able to gather the ingredients to make a decent pile of explosives. They brought those ingredients back to the suite, leaving the rest in the hands of their supporters to divide out amongst themselves and hide until the moment they were needed. It had the double bonus of not just arming them, but preventing Martellon from getting his hands on it. Bell and Dax were now working solidly on assembling their explosives. They were keeping them small in the hopes they could limit the damage to the keep and clan buildings, as well as keeping innocents out of harm's way.

Corin was the first to wake up. He simply lay there for a few minutes. He was revelling in the feeling of warmth and comfort that surrounded him. He hadn't felt this good in months. He wasn't questioning the change. He just accepted it. He slowly started to fully wake up. It was then he noticed the reason behind his warmth and comfort. He was being held, the question was by who?

The only person in the room with him was Kel. Stars, Kel! He looked down at the arm wrapped around him. How was it even possible? Had the elixir actually worked? Oh sure, he had hoped, but if he was honest with himself, he never really believed it would have any effect. It wasn't as if their luck was particularly good at the moment.

With a great deal of trepidation, he slowly turned his head, scared out of his mind. He was either imagining it or his mind was playing tricks on him. His eyes slowly raised and zeroed in on Kel's face. Oh, by the stars, Kel really did move, it really was Kel holding him tight. His heart took up a staccato rhythm. Joy and a little bit of fear were battling for supremacy in his mind. If Kel was indeed out of his coma, then Corin was ecstatic. He truly thought his man was going to die.

But even the happiness consuming him couldn't prevent the fear of Kel once again rejecting him. Oh, he now understood the reasons behind it, but the clan was still in grave danger. Would Kel yet again give him up to save the clan? He wasn't selfish enough to believe his happiness carried more weight than the safety of so many people, but he couldn't help but want someone to see him as the most important thing in all the universes. Would the baby make a difference? Then again, did he want Kel to be with him just because of the baby? The answer to that question was no, he didn't. It wouldn't work out for any of them in the long term if that was the case. Oh, but how he wanted a life with Kel. He wanted them to be a family, wanted the epic love others experienced. He'd already decided if Kel wanted him to, then he would stay on this planet. There wasn't really anything for him to go back to the Alliance for. He just hoped things would work out for him, Kel and the baby.

"Mm, now there's no better way to wake up. Please tell me I'm not dreaming? I've been living in a world of nightmares, not able to talk, to let anyone know I could hear them. It was like I was trapped in my own personal hell. Physically, my body was not under my control, but mentally, I was here. Please tell me it really is you, Corin? Please, please, tell me I'm not dreaming? I never thought I would get a chance to hold you again, to tell you how much I'm sorry, to tell you how much I made a mistake, to simply tell you I love you. You saved my life. I'm sorry, so, so sorry, Corin. I'm so bloody sorry, it's destroying me. I fucked up so badly. I thought I was doing what was for the best. I thought I could live without you. I thought it wouldn't hurt you. I thought you could go on and live your life in peace without the drama I bring. But I can't do it. I can't live without you. I don't want to. I need you in my life. I want you in my life. I'm so bloody sorry. Can you ever forgive me? Could you ever find it in your heart to give me another chance?"

Corin's mind was blown. Shock was coursing through his body. It was everything he dreamed of. Everything he wanted. Everything he needed. There for the taking. So why couldn't he speak? Why couldn't his lips form the words? Fear. Yet again, fear was consuming him. He knew he needed to battle his demons and he needed to start now. Forcing his mouth to work, he coughed, clearing his throat. "I, I forgive you, Kel. You must know I would always forgive you. I love you. I think I have from the very first moment I set eyes on you."

"So why can you not even look at me then, babe?" Kel was worried. Corin's words were saying one thing, but he was holding himself apart from him. He was keeping his distance and it was breaking his heart.

Corin sighed. "There's something I need to tell you."

Oh, sweet stars, thought Kel. *Had Corin found someone else? Someone who treated him right? Treated him as an equal?* If Corin still wanted him, there was nothing he wouldn't forgive. "Babe, nothing you can say will make a difference as to how much I love you. There is nothing more I want in this life than to spend it with you. You truly are my life. I would do anything for you. I know it's not an excuse, but I did what I did to protect you. I'm sorry, so bloody sorry." Kel broke down, tears streaming down his face, anguish permeating his soul.

"No, no, Kel. Stars, no. I forgive you for everything. I truly understand why you did it. Do I wish you spoke to me about it first? Yes. Do I wish you hadn't done it? Yes. Do I understand why you put the clan first? Yes, of course I do."

"Corin, you don't understand." Kel sighed, it was time to be truly honest with his mate. "I did it to keep you safe, for no other reason. If I'm honest, with both of us, the clan didn't even enter into my mind, all I thought about was you. I couldn't bear the thought of anyone hurting you. I couldn't bear the thought of you suffering. I did what was in my power to protect you, even if you hated me for it. I know I should have done it for the clan, but it was you, all for you. You consume me. Every thought, every breath, every moment I exist, I do so for you. You are my world, my heart, my very breath. You my dear, sweet, sweet, man are everything to me. This life means nothing if you are not in it. It felt like someone was severing part of my soul when I gave you up to save you, but your safety meant everything to me. I would suffer anything to know you live, suffer anything to know you are happy and safe. It was you, Corin, all about you, all for you." Tears were now flowing freely down both their faces. Both of them felt as if their hearts were breaking at the thought of never spending any time with each other, at the thought of living their lives without each other. "Don't give up on us, I beg you."

"I'm not," sobbed Corin.

Kel drew in a deep breath at those words. *Was it possible? Might he be able to have his mate in his life?*

"I want to be with you, Kel, more than anything. But we have to be honest with each other and I have to tell you something. I want you to promise me if it's too much, you will walk away. I will understand. I don't want to even consider my life without you in it, my heart is breaking at just the thought of it, but I want you to know if that's what you choose, I will accept it."

"Babe, there is nothing, nothing, you can say that will make me leave you again. Please, please, look at me. I need to see your face."

"I can't, Kel. I can't say this while looking at you and watch the love you feel for me fade. I can't see you look at me with disgust." Corin was trembling he was so scared.

"I would never, could never, look at you in disgust, babe. But if you can't look at me, I understand. But please, Corin, please tell me. You're scaring me."

Corin drew in a sharp breath. It was time to find out, one way or another, just which direction his life was going to go in. "I'm pregnant," he whispered.

Silence reigned for a few minutes. With each passing second, Corin's heart was freefalling. This was it, goodbye.

"I am still dreaming?" Kel whispered.

"Dreaming?" Corin managed to choke out through the constriction in his throat.

"Yes, dreaming. It's the only explanation I can come up with. The only way I am given my heart's every desire. It has to be a dream."

"What do you mean?" Corin was nervous. Kel didn't seem to hate the idea. Was it just possible? Might it all work out?

"I love you so very much, Corin, and the one thing, the only thing that ever brought even a hint of sadness to my heart, was the thought

I would never be able to have a family with you. Never be able to hold our child in our arms. Never be able to see that side of you, to watch you nurture our children, to allow some part of you to continue in the universes forever. Yet now you tell me it's actually happening? I have no idea how it is even possible, but I know I must be dreaming to have everything I've ever wanted right here in front of me!"

"You, you're happy about it?" Corin's wide-eyed gaze flew to Kel's face.

"If you can promise me it's real and you want to be with me, then yes, yes, I'm happy, happier than I ever thought it would be possible for a man to be. Please, babe, please, I beg you, tell me this is real."

"I can do more than tell you," Corin whispered, as he took Kel's large hand which he still held against his chest, and gently drew it down to his belly, letting it rest on the swell of their child.

There were no words Kel could give voice to which could even begin to explain the depth of feeling and overwhelming love consuming him. His body started shaking. Deep, bone-wrenching sobs trembled through his body.

Corin was confused. Based on Kel's words he thought he would have been happy. "You're not pleased." He said it as a statement, not a question.

"I'm overjoyed, babe. I'm so bloody happy I think my heart might burst," Kel managed to choke out.

"Then why the tears?" Corin really was confused.

"Because, I just realised how much I nearly gave up. How much I nearly lost. Oh stars, Corin, I love you." He moved his arm and forced Corin to turn around, desperate to look into his mate's eyes, to let his mate see the truth behind his words. He tipped Corin's chin up, forcing him to look. "Hey, beautiful," he spoke softly, as his eyes hungrily devoured his mate's face. "I love you so, so, much and I couldn't be happier we're going to be fathers. You have given me everything I have ever dreamed of. You are everything I ever wanted. My heart, my soul, stay with me, be my mate, let me keep you and our family safe, protected, but most of all let me love you."

"Yes," was all Corin managed to choke out before Kel's lips met his in a soft, gentle and all-consuming kiss.

On the other side of the door, a crowd was unashamedly eavesdropping on the two men. Each and every one of them surreptitiously wiped their eyes dry. Not one of them remained unaffected by the love pouring out of the room. There was no doubt in any of their minds; it was a love of the ages, a love for those stories told late at night by mothers to their children. The happily ever after kind of love. Those listening just hoped they could keep it that way.

With a soft knock on the door, Tate hoped they didn't mind the interruption, but they all needed to see it with their own eyes. Kel had been so close to death, it was almost beyond comprehension he managed to turn the tide. The elixir Corin and Alix created truly was magnificent.

"Come in." The smile in Corin's voice was obvious.

Tate's face transformed into a wide smile as soon as he caught sight of the two men on the bed. Kel was sitting up against the headboard and Corin was lying in front of him, with his back resting on Kel's chest. Kel's arms were wrapped tight around Corin, keeping him close. Both their hands were linked together and rested on the swell of the baby. Kel's face was buried in the crook of his mate's neck. They seemed perfectly content in each other's arms. Neither of them made any attempt to move when all their friends trooped into the room.

The first one to the bed was Carn who simply said, "My friend, it is so good to see you back with us. I'm going to go and get someone who is going to be desperate to know you're awake." He immediately strode out of the door to get Tir, glad for once he could give the man some good news.

"Tir, you need to rise." He gently shook the lump in the bed.

"Go 'way, don' wanna know anything,'" Tir mumbled, still half asleep.

"You'll want to see this, Tir," Carn singsonged at his friend.

"No."

"Get your ass out of bed, Tir, this is bloody important." Carn couldn't face a petulant Tir. Eliya was bad enough at it, but her dad? Too much.

"Damn, I hate you, Carn." Tir was definitely still pouting.

"Uh huh, boss, let's see if you still feel that way in a few minutes."

Grumbling, Tir stumbled out of bed, wiping the sleep from his eyes, and wearily followed Carn. Sure, the sleep might have rejuvenated his body, but he really didn't want to have to face the same problems all over again. He wanted to go back to sleep and hide, but no, Carn was dragging him through the suite. He couldn't even bring himself to care where they were going. When he registered they were stood in Kel's room and everyone was looking at him expectantly, he was confused. What the fuck was going on? His eyes were blinking, trying to wake up. It was a cough from the bed area which finally jolted him awake. His head snapped to the bed. His eyes processed what he saw far faster than his mind.

"Oh sweet stars!" He ran to the bed, dropping to kneel at the side by Kel. He gently reached out and touched Kel's face. Tears were streaming down his cheeks, silently. "Brother, oh stars, you're awake."

"Tir," —Kel's own voice was croaking it was so full of emotion— "Tir, I'm going to be a father."

"I know, brother, I know. I'm so happy for you." Tir gently cupped Kel's face as if he needed the constant contact to reassure himself Kel really was awake.

"I thought I'd lost Corin and now, not only do I have him back in my life, but he's gifted me with a child. Oh stars, Tir, I never knew such joy could exist."

Tir leant up and wrapped both men in his arms. A simple embrace between them that held so much love and joy. "I can't believe the elixir worked. Oh, Corin, you gave me back my brother. There is nothing I can do to ever repay you. You haven't just given him back to us, you make my brother happy, you fill him with joy. I, I can't find the words."

Corin gave Tir a gentle kiss on the forehead. "There's no need to try."

"How're his vitals? Are there any lingering effects? Should we be worried? Will it happen again? Is he cured? He won't relapse, will he?" Tir sent question after question at Corin at a rapid rate. It was as though he needed the reassurance.

Corin smiled as he addressed Tir's questions, explaining to everyone what little he both knew and could be sure of. He knew everyone needed to be reassured, not just Tir. "As far as I know, the elixir worked. If he feels any more effects, then we might need to give him another dose. As for will he be cured? Not from this elixir. There is, however, a permanent cure, but it is totally up to Kel on whether he wants to do it. I cannot and will not force it on him, and no one else in this room will either or you really will meet my wrath. It must be his decision and his alone. I will accept whatever he decides."

"Stars, it sounds bad," the men all said at once.

"I guess it would depend on how you look at things really," Corin hedged.

"Babe, whatever it is, if it keeps me with you and the baby, I will do it, no matter what." Kel was trying to reassure Corin.

"The only cure, from what we know, is to complete the truemate ritual. I won't force you to choose such an option, Kel. I want to spend the rest of my life with you, make no mistake about it, but I won't force you into it. If you don't want to make me your truemate, I will find another way. I will make it my mission to cure you, I promise."

"Babe, how could you possibly think I would want anything else but to go through the truemate ritual? I love you. The ritual is what I want even if it didn't have any effect on my life, even if it wasn't going to help save my life. I want you. I want our baby. I want us to be a family. I don't just want to live together, pledged to one another, I want it all. Please, Corin, go through the ritual with me. Not to save my life, but because you love me, because you want to make your life here with me, forever." Kel's eyes were beseeching Corin.

"Kel, you already know my answer. Yes, of course my answer is yes!"

Kel tightened his hold on Corin. "Babe, I think you've just made me the happiest man in the seven universes." Happy tears glistened in his eyes, joy and relief palpable in the air around them.

"Welcome to the family, Corin." Tir was beyond happy at the way his brother's life was finally coming together. Life had looked so bleak for all of them less than twelve hours ago. Now? Now they had hope, they had love, they had friends and, most importantly, they had family.

Chapter Twenty Eight

"Unca Kel? Unca Kel, you're awake?" Eliya wore the widest grin on her face. "Uncle Cori, you're here!" Eliya performed her trademark happy dance before she went to jump onto the bed. Both Tir and Niko grabbed her before she could land.

"Careful, sweetie, Uncle Kel has only just woken up and Uncle Cori has news for you. Now if you want to cuddle them, climb up and hug them, carefully, remember?" Tir stressed.

Eliya climbed as gently as a three year old could and nestled in close to both men. Suddenly, she noticed Corin's belly.

"Why you belly so big, Unca Cori?"

"Well, sweetie, you know how Uncle Kel and I love each other?" As he spoke, Corin was stroking her hair from her face.

"Uh huh."

"Well, we're going to have a baby."

"Huh, so I gets a sister? Or a bwother?"

"Well, it would be a cousin, but yes."

"So I gets a fwiend to play with?"

"Yes, sweetie. When they're a bit older, you will."

"I likes that, I does, Unca Cori. But I still be big girl and you still lub me, won' you?" Eliya's voice was slightly fearful and Corin's heart broke a little at all she had suffered over the last six months. It was more than most adults could cope with let alone most little ones.

"Oh, sweetie, of course. There will never be a day when I don't love you. Uncle Kel and I will always love you and be there for you. So how about you come snuggle in tight with us and say hello to your new friend?" Corin took her hand as she snuggled into them tightly and placed it on his belly. The next few minutes were filled with joy and laughter as the baby started to kick out at her hand. Her laughter rang around the room. Eventually, she started to tire and was scooped up by her father who took her into the other room to put her to bed for the night.

"So there has obviously been much going on while I have been ill. Who wants to fill me in?" Kel looked around at all the suddenly very serious faces. Oh, this so wasn't going to be good news. He knew he wasn't going to like what he was going to hear, but it didn't make it any less necessary. His rage at the actions of Martellon and his bitch of a daughter knew no bounds and was soon whipped into a frenzy as more and more details emerged about their actions. Fury at himself started to consume him. His part in this fiasco was very apparent to him. He wondered how anyone could find it to forgive him.

"Stop right there, Kel," Niko admonished him. "Don't think I can't see those connections you are making in your mind. Yes, you did as your father wanted. Yes, you agreed to a mating with Teriva, but agreeing does not make you accountable for their actions. I know you, Kel. You would have taken any alternative offered, rather than put your clan at risk. You would have sent Corin away and refused a mating if it was what you thought was the best move. THIS is not on you. Do you hear me? You are not responsible for it, and not one of us here lays any blame on you. I repeat, this is not on you."

The other men who were sitting around Kel all leant their agreement to Niko's words. Still, nothing would change how much responsibility Kel felt, but he vowed for all their sakes he would try to move past it. Letting anger and resentment at himself burn itself deep into his heart would only hurt them all in the end.

Kel was annoyed at Corin. Oh, he loved the man, with everything in him, but right now he hated the doctor side of his mate. He was having to endure the wonderful scents and aromas of the food his friends and family were eating. The rich spiciness of the Arcon root combined wonderfully well with the heady, earthy, yet incredibly rich scent of the Dashan, one of the types of cattle they bred on their higher lands. They were both some of his favourite foods and his mate was not allowing him to eat any of it. Instead, he had been ordered to only sip at a broth holding the barest amount of food in it, yet was packed with nutrients. Oh, Kel knew it was the only thing his stomach was likely to tolerate, but he didn't have to like it.

"Oh, stop already with the pout, you big baby! It's only for twenty four hours, just to make sure you're okay. Afterwards you can start eating normal food, slowly." His mate was laughing at him and didn't that just make him pout all the more while shooting out evil looks to anyone who dared to find the exchange funny.

"I'm sorry for laughing, brother, but it's just so good to see you getting back to normal, and yeah, if you can be a big moany baby like this, then you're getting back to normal." Tir was sniggering even as he spoke.

"Oh, brother, those are fighting words. When I'm better you, me—" he pointed at Tir. "Sparring match. You're going down."

"Bring it, brother!"

"Okay, who is going to open the betting pool on this one then?" Niko was smirking at the two of them. Nothing changed with his two friends. They always loved to antagonise each other and it was nice to enjoy the simple, normal moment between them.

"I'll start the book on this one. I think there might be a fair few takers who want to bet on this rematch! The last one ended up having a near legendary status amongst them men." Carn turned and looked at the three Avanti members with a great amount of speculation in his eyes. "What about you guys? Any takers? I'm sure our men would love to watch you spar. There have been enough stories circulating around from Dariux's men."

The Avanti grinned at each other. "Sure, why not," Dax answered for them all. "You have to know the smart bet's on us though, right?"

"Hmm, we shall see," was all Carn said. "I reckon we can give you a good show."

"Bring it!" Dax winked at Carn.

Tate found himself thinking of sparring with Dariux and didn't the thought have him as hard as a rock in seconds. His mind was swirling with thoughts of having him, wrestled to the ground, with Dariux grinding on top of him. He knew his face was flushed when Dax spoke.

"You alright there, Tate, you look hot?"

"I'm fine, Rux." Tate choked out, ignoring Dariux's knowing smirk. Damn the man— he was the most infuriating, obnoxious, irritating, gorgeous, sexy, man he had ever met.

Later in the evening when it was finally just Kel and Corin in the room, they were on the bed relaxing. Fed up of talking and reliving the last few months, Corin simply lay in Kel's arms, soaking up the peace of being back with him and the happiness surrounding them like a gentle breeze on a spring day. Neither of them could stop touching the other. Soft, gentle caresses that simply reaffirmed they once again held each other. Gentle traces of arms and hands, soft sweeping motions across Corin's belly, all of them were slowly arousing. Corin turned his head to the side, giving Kel access to his neck. Gentle kisses trailed up and down, and soft nips to the skin were followed by a gentle tongue to lap away the sting. Corin's body arched at the sensations Kel was causing. When a hand started to tease his nipple, Corin cried out.

"Stars, they're more sensitive now."

"Damn, I've missed feeling your body in my arms, babe. I've missed caressing you, tasting you, touching you, being inside you. I want you, Corin, so bloody much. I always have, never doubt it, not for even one minute, one second. There is no feeling greater in this world than the feeling of being balls deep inside you. Fuck, I want your ass, baby. I want you so bad. Every time I have you in my arms, it drives me insane. The power you have over my body, my heart, is incredible."

"Then take me, Kel, I'm yours, you know I am. I want you, I want you to possess me, to own me, to make me yours. Claim me, Kel. Claim me now."

"Oh fuck, baby, you drive me insane." Kel shuddered as his cock became rock hard. Lifting Corin's arms up, he stripped his tunic off before pushing his linen sleep pants down and off his legs. Pushing

Corin up slightly, he stripped himself before gently laying them both down on their sides on the bed.

"I think this way will be best, babe. I don't want to hurt you or the little one. I need you to tell me if I hurt you. I would never, ever, forgive myself, babe, if something happened. Promise me."

"I promise, Kel." Corin wore a soft smile on his face. Even when they were both horny enough to burst, his man was still taking care of him.

Kel lay behind Corin, his chest pressed in tight to Corin's back, his cock trapped between them. The friction of them moving against one another was a delicious type of agony. Nowhere close enough to satisfy him, but oh-so-deliciously arousing. Kel's hand grasped Corin's cock, gently stroking it, keeping his focus purely on his shaft, ignoring the head. Corin all but growled in frustration at the teasing. At the same time, Kel's other hand moved down to play with his balls. Just like his nipples, Corin couldn't believe how much more sensitive they were.

"Fuck, Kel, more. Stars, it's not enough. I need. I, fuck!" Corin gasped the moment Kel's hand touched the head of his cock. He hadn't known being pregnant would make his body so sensitive. It was incredible; the sensations were magnified beyond belief. When Kel dipped his fingernail into his slit, Corin nearly came from sensation overload. If it felt this good now, he was sure it was going to kill him when Kel was finally deep inside him, but, stars, what a way to go. Corin didn't want this to be over so soon. He had to force himself not to come. Using every mental trick he knew, combined with his fingers wrapped tight around his own shaft to restrict the blood flow, he just managed to pull himself back from the edge.

Kel gently lifted Corin's leg and rested it over his own. The position kept the pressure off of Corin's belly and opened up Corin for Kel to play with. Bending his knee and planting his foot on the bed gave Kel all the access he wanted. It left all of Corin on display, like a feast awaiting a king. Grabbing the oil from the bedside, which someone had conveniently left there, Kel soaked his fingers before gently tracing small circles around Corin's hole and over his taint. Corin was already writhing about in Kel's arms. Damn, his man needed to come so badly and wasn't it the biggest turn on ever that it was him who was having this effect on him, thought Kel. Slowly, but surely, Kel slipped one finger inside of Corin. He teased his prostate, brushing by it with a soft touch then tapping it for a sudden jolt.

The dual sensations were driving Corin crazy, but when Kel snaked his other hand down to fondle his balls, his world exploded into a riot of feelings and sensations. His whole focus narrowed down to that one area. Nothing else existed but Kel, his touch, his caress. He snaked one hand back to grab onto Kel's butt, forcing him to thrust up against him. Grabbing Kel's ass hard, Corin forced himself to rock back against it.

"Fuck, babe, how horny are you?" Kel gasped at the need pouring off of his mate.

"Please," Corin whimpered. "Oh stars, Kel, please."

No matter how much his mate begged and moaned, Kel was determined to take his time. He was enjoying taking his mate to new heights. One finger slowly became two. Twisting and scissoring inside him, the gentleness was driving Corin crazy, yet at the same time he wouldn't have it any other way. There was no doubt in his mind Kel was making love to him in the tenderest way possible. Two fingers finally became three. The finger rubbing on his prostate was sending him into another orbit. His eyes were rolling in his head, such was the intensity of what he was feeling.

Kel was being driven crazy by the sounds his man was making. He couldn't hold back any longer. He needed to be inside of Corin, feeling his warmth, his tightness. It felt like he was coming home. He was home. It no longer mattered where he was, it just mattered he was with Corin and their child. As Kel slid his cock deep into Corin, he simply held himself still for a moment, soaking up the feelings. Soon enough the desire to move became too much. He felt an all-consuming need burn through him, a need to fill his mate again with his seed, to brand him. As he started to move, the bumps drove them both insane. They were far more sensitive than any other part of his cock, and the slightest touch was driving him wild. He was barely holding it together, both physically and emotionally.

Somehow it felt as though his bumps were getting bigger and with the change in size came an increased level of pleasure. He paused for a brief moment to wonder if it was something to do with them being truemates who had finally accepted each other, before the sensations blocked out all thoughts.

It was too much for Corin. Somehow, someway, Kel's cock felt bigger this time around. The minute the bumps rubbed his prostate that was it. He came, hard, everywhere. Rope after rope of cum crisscrossed his stomach and chest. The force even had him painting his own neck. His hands grasped for purchase on anything they came into contact with. The fingers of one hand were digging in hard to Kel's hips, hard enough that no doubt finger-shaped bruises would be visible for days. His other hand fisted the covers tight as his body arched away from Kel, driving his ass even harder onto Kel's shaft until he couldn't tell where Kel ended and he began. White light filled his vision. If asked, he couldn't be sure he hadn't blacked out. When he became aware again, Kel was gently stroking his belly, his face, in fact, all of him. Kel held still, he was still buried deep, waiting for Corin to come down from the pleasure overload. Corin blinked open his eyes to see a beautiful smile.

"Hey, baby. You okay?"

"Uh huh," was just about the only words Corin could manage. When his eyes were a little more focused, Kel once again took up a slow and tender pace. He leant up as best he could and kissed his man tenderly, letting the arm underneath him support his weight. Lips never leaving each other, he swallowed Kel's moan a split second before he felt his insides seared by the heat of Kel's cum. Corin rocked slightly, both prolonging the orgasm for his man as much as possible, and bringing him down slowly.

They both relaxed onto the bed, breath heavy in their chests despite the slow and tender pace. Corin positioned himself so his belly was comfortable. Reaching back, he grasped Kel's hand and rested it on the swell of their baby, the three of them connected, the two of them safe in Kel's arms. The bliss radiating between them made their eyes shut as they slipped gently into a dreamless sleep.

The morning found them all well rested. The stress of Kel being ill was starting to fade into a distant memory. The worry now was whether they could hide Kel's recovery and Corin's pregnancy from both Martellon and Teriva. If they found out, their plans to get rid of them would not go well. Martellon would be livid at his plans being thwarted, Teriva no doubt livid at the loss of Kel. It would be obvious to all that now that Corin carried his baby, there was no way he would mate with anyone else, no matter what the consequences. She had planned on having Kel as a mate for a decade and to lose him now would see her react. It was simply going to be a question of exactly what she was going to do, and when she was going to do it.

"Look, I understand the reasons as to why you think I should hide and not let them know I'm awake, but is it really the best option?" Kel was going crazy not being able to confront them. He wanted to have it out with them. He wanted to vent his anger, his frustration. He was so pissed at his father, but his father was dead and his resentment left burning a hole in his soul. He needed to be able to confront them. He didn't want his resentment to fester like an open wound and leak into his life with Corin. Besides, it wasn't in his nature to hide. Surely they all understood that? "I need to do this. I need to have it out with them. Have we considered how it changes things?"

"Honestly, I don't know. They will certainly want you back, now more than ever." Tir understood his brother's frustration. Was it the right move? He wished he knew.

"It will definitely provoke them," Bell, ever the strategist, summarized. "The question is will they decide to retaliate straight away? It's the risk we have to face and if they do, are we ready? Honestly? It would be better if we could wait until the original deadline. If we can hold off till then, hide you until then, it might work in our favour."

"How so?" Carn wasn't sure he followed Bell's reasoning.

"Look at it this way. If we wait and then reveal Kel at the last minute of the deadline, it might be enough to unnerve them. It might be enough to make them reckless and make mistakes. Which, in turn, could be enough to tip the balance in our favour. Besides, we are waiting for the king and his forces. Are we sure we want to provoke them early and risk not receiving reinforcements in time?"

"Stars, Kel, he has a point. I know you won't like it, but it's probably for the best to wait." A sympathetic smile was playing across Niko's face.

"Fuck!!" Kel went to punch something, but Corin's hand wrapped around his fist instead.

"Babe, come on, twenty four more hours. Is that really so bad? If it gives us an edge, then it has the potential to save a lot of lives in the clan. Is that not worth it?" Corin implored.

"Aww, babe, you don't fight fair, you know that?" Kel scowled.

"Never said I did, handsome. I never said I did." Corin leaned up and gave Kel a brief kiss in apology.

"Urgh, fine, you win. I'll stay hidden. Oh, but, babe? Just you wait. I'll get my revenge on you for not backing me up." The scowl Kel sent Corin was ruined by the smile hiding behind it.

"Bring it, handsome." Corin simply winked at his man, a small smile playing across his face.

Now they were all back on board with the original plan, they discussed any changes they needed to make. There was one big question on all their lips. Could they count on Martellon being able to rein in his daughter? They knew in reality she was the wild card in this. She was evil and manipulative to the core. The devious bitch had a way of always coming out of a situation like she was an innocent party. It was her they really needed to be careful of, that was for sure. They truly had no idea how she would respond when all her plans lay in tatters.

"Whatever happens, Corin, you must stay safe and protected. I want you to stay with the guard and Eliya. You will be protected there."

"Absolutely not, Kel. You know you might need me to help any wounded. Seconds can count, let alone the minutes it would take you to get any wounded to me. I cannot, and will not, risk anyone's life to protect myself. I simply don't work that way, Kel, you know I don't."

"Don't you know I can't lose you all over again, babe? It would destroy me. I would not survive it a second time. You can't put the little one at risk, please. I'm not telling you to stay safe, I'm asking you, I'm begging you, for my sake, please, babe?"

"How about if we find an area closer to the battle? It means you can get any injured to me quickly, but it's also not as far away as Eliya will be. At least it would also give an extra layer of defence for her. Please, just think about it? I don't want to risk the baby, but I would never forgive myself either if you or one of our friends died because I couldn't get to them quick enough. Please, can we find a way? A compromise?"

"It's not a bad plan, Kel," Dax added his opinion.

"It would be great for us to have a failsafe to protect Eliya, and if anyone did get injured, we could get them to Corin and then back to the battle quickly. It's a good plan. If you look at it sensibly, you know it is."

"Fuck." Kel was pacing as he cursed. "Damn it, I know it's a good plan, but it doesn't mean I have to like it. I don't, I really, really, don't, but as long as we have protection in place for both Eliya and Corin, then I will agree to it."

Corin stepped up to Kel and wrapped his arms around the man. "I'm sorry, handsome. I wish I could stay hidden the way you want me to, but I wouldn't be me if I did. I wouldn't be the man you love if I kept myself safe at the risk of everyone else. I do not want to lose our baby, I won't risk losing our baby. Please trust me. I need to do this." He finished off with a gentle kiss to Kel's lips.

Kel's arms held Corin tight, his head resting on top of Corin's, simply breathing in the unique smell of his man, all summer rain and wild flowers. It was a smell that brought peace to Kel with each breath in.

Dariux watched the two with a hint of envy. He was incredibly jealous of them both— more what they experienced with each other, rather than him wanting one of them. He wanted a love as deep as they did, he wanted to have a man to love and hold, protect and cherish. He just wished the man he wanted for the role felt the same way. Why was it he never seemed to be the one who got it all? He would just have to accept it may never happen. It didn't mean he wasn't going to work damn hard to get his man though. He just needed the right plan of action. When this whole sorry business was over he was going for it and Tate had better look out, he had him in his sights.

Dax looked on and smiled. Corin deserved to be cherished the way he was. The man had been through so much, had given up so much for so many people, he deserved to be the centre of someone's universe the way he was now. The level of love pouring off Kel was incredible and Dax knew whatever happened to him and his Avanti teammates in the future, he could be secure in the knowledge Corin was safe, loved and happy. They just needed to get the clan sorted first.

The more Dax thought about it the more he liked this world. People here were prepared to step up and fight for what they believed in, even when there was no benefit to themselves. These were the sort of people he could surround himself with. Life in the Alliance was becoming its own brand of hell. They were increasingly being sent on missions of a dubious nature. He wasn't even sure how many of them were truly legitimate hits anymore. Watching Corin be treated like garbage by everyone was especially difficult. As a neutral world, the Alliance possessed no reach here. They couldn't come after him. It was definitely something to think about, although there was no chance any of them were leaving until they found out what happened to Hunter and Bray.

Chapter Twenty Nine

They were fine-tuning the plans to keep Eliya and Corin safe when there was a subtle knock on the door from one of their guards stationed outside. It was a warning they were about to have company and not the sort of company they would want either.

Kel and Corin raced back into the bedroom, Corin shooting everyone a death glare when there was quiet laughter at the way he was starting to waddle. Oh, he was going to make them suffer for those laughs. He would just have to be creative in his revenge.

Martellon and Teriva strutted into the room like it was theirs. They were behaving as if the clan already belonged to them. Their arrogance was truly astounding.

"So we are twenty four hours in. You still have made no move to cede either the clan or Kel to me. You are pushing it, Tir. Do you want your clan bathed in bloodshed? I will not back down. I want this clan. Teriva wants Kel. Those are the only things capable of stopping the bloodshed. Do you not care? Would you rather I kill your clan members? Is that it? Do you really not care about them?"

"Of course we bloody care, you prick," Tir spat out with venom. "But it doesn't mean I'm just going to hand over my brother to you. Besides, what the fuck do you plan to do with him? He's unconscious, for star's sake. It's not like he could go through a mating ceremony with her." Tir really was confused as to why they were so desperate to get hold of him.

"Well, of course he can." Martellon smirked.

"How? It's not like he can actually say the words of the ceremony to bind them. Seriously, why are you so desperate to get a hold of him?"

"We have our ways— I certainly don't need to explain it to you. Suffice it to say, if you hand over Kel, he will be mated and a father within the year. We will control the heir to this clan, one way or the other."

In the other room, it took everything Kel possessed to keep Corin in the room. The anger radiating off his mate was almost physical in its intensity. His face was twisted into a vicious snarl. "I will kill the fucking bitch. They are dead. I will kill them with my bare fucking hands."

"Babe…" Kel tried to get Corin to calm down. "Babe, I'm here, I'm safe, she doesn't have me, she won't ever have me. You need to calm down, babe. Please?"

"Let me out there, Kel," Corin demanded.

"I'm sorry, babe, but I can't. You know I can't. We already agreed they can't find out about me. What do you think will happen if they see you? There is no way in all the known bloody universes I am putting you, or the little one, at risk." Kel wrapped his mate tight in his arms, simply holding him, trying to reassure himself his mate was safe and wasn't going anywhere. Eventually, he felt the tension ease from the body in his arms, but then the shaking began.

"I can't lose you again. We need you."

"And you're not going to lose me. Now give me a kiss, calm down, and let's listen to what else is going on, okay?" Kel settled Corin snug in his arms while they both turned their attention back to the conversation in the other room.

"Fuck, you are one sick, twisted bastard. You would rape Kel? You really think the Conclave is going to stand for such actions? You think I am going to stand for it? Or this clan? Do you honestly think we would all stand by and let it happen?"

"You think the Conclave will find out? How? When there will be no one left to tell them it was anything other than consensual? It was common knowledge Kel agreed to the mating. We will just make it known he was not well and returned to his loving mate's clan to recuperate. There will be no one left from this clan to dispute our version of events."

"And just how are you going to explain away all of our deaths? That kind of thing gets noticed by the Conclave."

"You will die in a tragic training ground accident, I'm afraid, and if your clan doesn't want bloodshed, they will keep quiet."

"You really are one nasty piece of work!" Tir really was disgusted by Martellon's plans. He didn't think he could be any more relieved Kel had already woken up, but he was. He would never have forgiven himself if Kel had been left to such a fate.

"I won't be dying anytime soon, Martellon, and it will be over my dead body that you take Kel or anyone else in this clan as hostage. Now get the fuck out of my suite, and the fuck out of my clan. This is your last warning. If you persist down this road, I will see you destroyed and your clan broken up or given away. You will bear the full might of the Conclave if you don't cease."

"I don't see the Conclave here, Tir. Your threats mean nothing. They never have. You are weak. Why do you think your father turned to me for an alliance in the first place? He didn't think you were strong enough to lead the clan after him. Turns out, he was right. You'll go down in the histories as the man who destroyed one of the greatest clans to exist. The man who gave away his family's birthright. How does it feel, Tir? How does it feel to be such a failure?"

Before Tir even got a chance to respond, Dax, Bell, Tate and Carn all stepped forward and crowded both Martellon and Teriva. It was Dax who spoke. "Get the fuck out of here right now or you WILL know the wrath of the Avanti. This is your only warning. Do not cross me, you will not like the consequences. There is not a man among your forces who could stop me from reaching you."

Even Martellon, as delusional as he was, was not someone who would willingly cross the Avanti. He turned, dragging his daughter by her arm as he left the room. "Twenty four hours, Tir. Twenty four hours and this clan is mine. One way or another."

When the coast was clear, an irate Corin stormed out of the room, Kel following, trying to calm him down.

"I, uh, take it you heard all of it then?" Tate cautiously asked.

"What do you think?" snarled Corin. "I will fucking kill the bitch. Doctor's creed or not, she deserves everything that's coming to her."

Tate smiled at the looks of shock on some of the faces around them. This was a side of Corin not many people got to see. The mild mannered doctor had a core of steel. If you fucked with those he loved, you had better watch your back. "She will get what she deserves, they both will. But you need to calm down a little."

"That's what I've been telling him." Kel smiled at Dax, glad someone else agreed with him.

"How the fuck do you expect me to calm down?"

"I don't know, but you need to try, for the baby's sake." Tate tried to get Corin to see reason, but even as he spoke he started to look around for the med bag in case he needed it.

Corin huffed out a sigh. "Shit! Why do you always have to be right? Both of you?" He shot evil looks at both Tate and Kel.

"You think it's just us, babe? Look around you." Kel motioned to the other men in the room. Each and every one wore varying degrees of concerned looks on their faces.

"Don't think those looks of concern will stop me from remembering all the looks you gave me when I left." Corin snapped at them, his expression conveying just how annoyed he still was.

Those concerned looks immediately swapped to fake innocence.

"Oh trust me, I saw it all. So I waddle. I'm pregnant, you bunch of bastards." It was enough to lighten the mood in the room. Even Corin himself was reduced to sniggering away. He was well aware of how he must have looked. Kel, bless him, tried valiantly not to laugh, but even he succumbed eventually.

"I'm sorry, babe. Would it help if I told you that you looked cute?"

"Cute? Cute! Grown men don't look cute. Grown men are sexy, they're gorgeous, they're handsome, dashing, chiselled and rugged." Corin almost, almost, stomped his foot, but then at the last second he realised it would just make him look even more cute in Kel's eyes. "Bah." He plopped down onto the sofa and ignored them all.

"Aw, babe, you're all that to me and so much more. You're gorgeous, you're sexy, charming, and handsome. Yes, you're cute as well at the moment, but it doesn't make you less of a man. You're still the most amazing and gorgeous man I have ever known. I love you. Please don't ever forget that." Kel sat next to Corin and hugged him to him tight. The other men all settled around them as they went back to discussing what they had heard.

"Okay, so I've calmed down, a little. Mission accomplished. It doesn't change the horrifying things which were said though. Aside from their plans, how they were planning to go about everything is what concerns me most. I dread to think how they planned on getting Kel to perform. We need to stamp out whatever it is, as soon as possible."

"It is something I will be bringing up with both the King and Conclave. It's probably better if I do it, as a more neutral party. I don't want it dismissed on the basis of the dispute between your two clans," Niko explained, a sentiment they could all agree upon. "I guess, as Kel is safe, it's not a major concern for the moment. Let's get through the next few days and we can discuss it further."

"Agreed." Tir's voice was laden with sorrow.

"Brother, please tell me you are not taking anything they said as fact?" Kel asked.

"Why shouldn't I? Why did father make the alliance if what Martellon said wasn't true?"

"Because, if you think about it and accept it, our father was losing his mind. He was like that from the moment our mother died. We should have seen him deteriorating long ago, but we failed him."

"You didn't fail him." Carn was adamant about that. "Not one of us really understood just how bad he was getting. The guard never noticed either, not until the very last few weeks when it was too late anyway. Remember most of the guards were around him day in and day out. You cannot accept the blame for this. You have always been who the clan wanted to lead them. You are kind and compassionate where needed, strong and righteous at others. You guide with a firm and steady hand without dragging us into needless battles. The clan stands with you and behind you. You are our Chieftain now, in name, deed and our hearts. Do not let Martellon's words get to you. It is what he wants. He wants you to second guess yourself. He wants you to adjust whatever plans you have. He wants you to fail. Don't let him succeed."

"Thank you, my friend. Those words mean more to me than you will ever know." Tir rose and embraced his friend and Master at Arms.

Sighing, Tir went back to discussing what was left to do to enact their plan. "How are things going with the men and equipment?"

"Everything is in place. Tate, Dax and Bell have been incredible in planning the right level of defence, which, hopefully, should take out some hostile forces while minimizing any civilian casualties. The men have been handpicked carefully. Our officers are making sure none of Martellon's spies are learning about our plans. We still don't know who all the spies are, but we have already apprehended four and have them locked away where Martellon's forces can't find them." Carn was pleased at the great job his officers had been able to do. "Our officers have weapons stockpiled in strategic places and are ready to go on our signal."

"What about the civilians?" Corin asked, the caregiver in him always concerned for innocent lives.

"We asked two of the elders, who we trust, to arrange to have meetings in buildings well away from any potential fighting. Word has been spread, so hopefully it keeps people out of the firing line. We will have a heavy guard around both places just in case Martellon's forces decide to play dirty."

"Good."

"Eliya will be in one of the secret rooms here in the keep. The only people who know about the room are myself, Kel and Carn. Carn will lead a group of men he implicitly trusts there, and protect her with everything they have. His second, Alcorn, will stay with her. As much as I wish he, or I, could stay there, we are best used on the field. The clan need to see us front and centre defending them."

"I will be by Tir's side," Kel added. "We are hoping the shock value will be enough to make Martellon and his forces back off. If not, then hopefully, showing everyone I am alive and well will be enough to spur our forces on."

"Just be careful, all of you," Corin pleaded.

"I will lead our men in once the battle has started," Niko promised. "We want Martellon to believe we have turned tail and ran. It should allow us to come from behind and take him in a two front attack."

"Where will the Avanti be?" Kel wondered exactly who was going to be where.

"To start with, we will man the explosives. If we can use them as intended, we should take out a lot of their forces. We're hoping to block off parts of their forces from the others. If we do, then those stuck could be apprehended and secured. It would reduce the amount we have to fight in the end," Dax explained. "Afterwards, we will join Kel and Tir at the front of the battle."

"Where are we putting Corin?" Kel hoped it was somewhere extremely safe and well fortified.

"We thought the guard house on the edge of the keep itself would be a good idea. It's easily defensible and has the space to treat any wounded. What's more, it will be close enough that they can retreat back to Eliya if needed."

"Who will be guarding him?"

"I will," Dariux said. "Kel, I will guard him with my life. He will not come to any harm, I promise you. Carn has shown me an escape tunnel which is linked to the guard house. If we become overwhelmed, we will put him and a couple of men in there to go and meet up with Eliya. I will then guard the door, with my life, and blow it if I have to once I know Corin is far enough away."

Kel sighed with relief. While it wasn't the ideal situation for his mate to be in, it would be as safe a place as they could get without him being secured beside Eliya. "Thank you, my friend. That you would protect him when I cannot means everything to me."

"It's what friends do. What's more, Chieftain Alix would have my hide if anything happened to him. Alix sees him as another son. You are the two people I would not want angry with me. Trust me on this, he will be safe."

"Happy now, handsome?" Corin asked.

"As much as I can be. Just promise me…"

Corin cut Kel off before he could finish his sentence. "I will. You know I'll be okay. Trust me, trust in our men, in our friends."

"What happens when we get to Martellon?" Bell asked.

"We want him disabled, not killed. I want him to face the Conclave for his actions," Tir vowed.

"We have split our weapons equally, so the squads have both firearms and swords, although the men are not all trained in the use of firearms. That's something to work on in the future. I would suggest only giving weapons to the few men who know how to use them. The last thing we need is people dying by our own hands. What of Martellon's forces?" Dax wondered. "I have heard you all say his clan follows the old ways. Does this mean he won't be using anything other than swords?"

"His men are more than likely only to have swords. Himself? I imagine he will have some other form of protection. He will definitely be armed with firearms, no matter what he says his views are," Tir explained.

"Okay, so our plans are in place and we meet him in the courtyard at the deadline. Before then, we have to simply wait." Kel hated waiting, all soldiers did. It was the calm before the storm and many a battle had started early when people became impatient and volatile.

"Uh, guys." Corin looked at them all. He couldn't believe they were forgetting something so big. "Are you not forgetting something? Or should I say someone?" They all looked at him in confusion.

"No, we have gone over the plan repeatedly. Everything, and everyone, is covered. We have looked at all the angles. Nothing has been missed." Dax and Tir were sure, both nodding as Tir spoke.

"It's fine, babe, we've gone over everything. Try not to worry too much. I know you're worried about us, but it will be okay. We've got every angle covered." Kel assured Corin.

Corin looked at all of them and couldn't believe they had forgotten the bitch. How was it even possible they hadn't factored her into everything? He raised an eyebrow at them all in query as he simply spat out one word. All his feelings were conveyed in his accent as he spat, "Teriva."

"Oh fuck."

"Shit."

"Damn it."

Curses rained down on them from everyone present.

"How the fuck did we forget about her?" Dariux asked the question they were all thinking.

"You ignored her because she's a woman. You forget women can be just as devious, manipulative, cold-hearted and vicious as men. Do not ever let her appearance fool you. Part of me thinks we have only just taken the sheen off her behaviour— corner her and I dread to think how she will react. We need to deal with her. She cannot be allowed to try and play the 'poor me, I was just doing what my father wanted' card."

"So what do we do about her?" Dariux wondered out loud.

"We hope she is with her father. If not, I will break off, find her and subdue her. She will not escape to harm anyone else. I will not underestimate her. We have seen many a woman like her on our missions with the Avanti. I am well aware of how women can be," Bell assured them.

Kel and Corin both sighed in relief, trusting in Bell.

"Corin, I will not let her go. She has caused my friends too much pain and heartache. Have no fear she will face the consequences of her actions."

"Thank you, Bell, I really, really, need her to face the Conclave and face punishment for her crimes."

"She will."

Deep worry was still written all over Kel's face. He really didn't like the idea of Corin being anywhere close to the danger. They could all see it. Not one of them could think of a way to reassure him. Then again, he wasn't looking forward to seeing even one member of his clan in danger.

It was Dariux who finally came up with a solution to Kel worrying about Corin. "Do your comms still work?"

"Yes, we still do our daily check-in. We still hope we can raise Hunter and Bray. Why?"

"Can you not keep one with Corin and the other with Kel? Or someone close to Kel? That way, if anything happens, he can turn back and go to Corin. It might help Kel keep focused on the battle."

"Good idea." Corin smiled.

"Thank you." Kel smiled at Dariux. "It would be helpful. I don't want to be distracted while fighting."

"Okay, so have we covered everything this time?" Tir hoped so. Things were starting to get very complicated. Everyone was getting antsy and the quicker this confrontation was over the better. "I will settle Eliya first thing in the morning. I don't want to leave it to the last minute. Then, I will meet you all here. I would suggest you spend tonight with those you love and care for. While I live in hope we don't lose anyone, tomorrow we have to realise it is possible."

Tate couldn't understand why his heart started to beat faster at those words, nor why his eyes shot to Dariux who was staring at him intently. Thoughts and feelings were swirling through his mind, such was the maelstrom, he found he couldn't pin even one emotion down in the hopes of working out exactly what he was feeling. And why was it he felt like his heart was breaking when Dariux smiled at him sadly before getting up and walking away.

Corin's heart broke for the two men as he watched the interplay between them. He wished there was some way he could push them along. It was so obvious to everyone else how they felt for each other.

"There is nothing you can do, babe, but hope it works out," Kel whispered in his ear.

"But Dariux is so in love with him and Tate just can't see it. Instead he just looks so lost and confused."

"I know, babe, and I promise you, when we get out of this we will do everything we can to help them get together."

"Thank you." Corin smiled at his man as he kissed him gently just below his ear.

"I could never refuse you anything, babe, you know that, but your love and concern for your friends is part of what I love about you."

Corin relaxed into Kel's embrace, finally happy and reassured of the depth of Kel's feelings for him. How he wished for his friends, old and new, to find such passion and joy in their lives.

They spent the evening telling stories, funny ones, embarrassing ones and even sad ones, all of them choosing to spend their time together rather than split off. The events of the last few months had brought them all closer together. They were like a brotherhood now and not one of them could think of a better way to spend the night before battle than with each other. Even Dariux returned, as though he could not bear to be away from Tate, no matter how much pain it caused him. It was sad to watch Tate's mood improve and yet he didn't seem to see it, nor understand the reason behind it.

For Corin and the Avanti, it was a chance to learn more about the men they had come to regard as family, and the planet they were beginning to call home. As the conversation flowed, Dax became more convinced this was somewhere he believed they could all be happy living. Besides, he didn't like the prospect of losing Corin. The man had become such an integral part of their lives so quickly, it would seem wrong not to be near him. He also knew, as Corin and Kel had already seen, that there was something between Dariux and Tate. No, he was going to have a serious discussion with them all about relocating here.

As it always does, time marched on and it was time for sleep. Corin and Kel retired to their bedroom. Their movements were unhurried as they slowly undressed each other, taking the time to simply appreciate one another. Simply enjoying the moment of being together. Before long, the excitement between them was building.

This time, it was Corin who took the lead. He pushed Kel back onto the bed, smiling, when Kel simply raised his brow at him. "It's my turn, handsome. I want to drive you wild, make you desperate for me, begging for my touch."

"You already do, babe. You already do."

"Strip, now," Corin demanded.

"Fuck," Kel cried out, rock hard at both the words and the dominance his mate was displaying. He'd never seen this side of Corin, but damn, if it didn't turn him on. He loved the fact his mate was strong at times. He needed someone to challenge him and he certainly wanted an active partner in bed. Life would be boring if they didn't mix it up. Corin really was the ideal mate for him. That was the last conscious thought he had before Corin once again pushed him back onto the bed, this time fully naked. Lust seemed to explode outwards from Corin's eyes, blazing its way to sear across Kel's skin, igniting him. He was already writhing on the bed from anticipation and his mate hadn't even touched him. Stars help him when he did.

Making sure to work around his belly, Corin crawled on his hands and knees over Kel, running his tongue up the inside of Kel's leg in slow, sensuous circles. His breath drew out goosebumps on the damp skin. His tongue traced up and over Kel's taut abs, tracing each indentation on the way, before he gently sucked on Kel's Adam's apple, eliciting a deep groan from his man. Brushing his fingers down Kel's chest, he made no attempt to go slow as he leaned down and swallowed Kel to the root in one go. The sensations were different from anything else he had ever felt before. Kel's bumps were caressing the inside of his mouth, pulsing against his tongue as he lapped around it. When he swallowed deep, he could feel the bumps flexing against his throat, forcing his throat to work on Kel's cock.

"Oh stars, Corin!" Kel cried out.

Corin smiled around the cock in his mouth and hummed, happy he was driving his man insane. Every time he let Kel's gorgeous cock slip out of his mouth slightly, he ran his tongue around the head, dipping it into the slit and lapping up the precum pooling there as a present for him. He flicked his tongue against the sensitive spot just below the head, before tracing over every bump with his tongue. Each one was treated to a swirl before being flicked hard.

"Oh, sweet moons!" Kel was moaning and writhing beneath him.

Corin could tell his man was trying to hold back, but he didn't want him to. He wanted him to lose control, to give it up and embrace the moment. He took Kel's hands and placed them on his head, guiding Kel into controlling his movements, controlling the speed. He opened his mouth, angling his neck to allow Kel to fuck his throat. While it started off with slow movements, Kel as cautious as ever, it soon became so much more. It was driving Kel so insane he lost himself, and some of the tenderness from his touch faded, replaced by a scorching desire. Soon Kel found himself fucking deep into his mate's mouth. Corin's hand was tugging on his balls, squeezing them tight, the bite of pain exquisite in counterpoint to the softness of Corin's throat.

As Corin let go of Kel's balls, he reached up and slipped a finger into his mouth, soaking it in a mixture of his saliva and Kel's precum. He let his finger drift down, down past Kel's balls, rubbing over his taint before drawing lazy circles over the hole which was already pulsing for him. He dipped one finger in as he looked up and watched Kel's eyes fly open in surprise. "Want me to stop, handsome?"

"Oh fuck no, it feels, it's… Oh fuck!" Kel managed to hiss, as Corin's finger slipped all the way inside him. "Oh fuck, baby, I want you to fuck me. I want to feel you inside me. I want you to be my first."

It was Corin's turn to have his eyes fly open in surprise. "You've never?"

"No, it wasn't something I ever thought I wanted. But I find myself wanting to try everything with you. I feel this compulsion to have you inside me. To have you brand me the way I brand you. For you to claim me, mark me as yours."

"Oh fuck, Kel, now I've got to have you." Corin growled.

Kel shivered at those words. Oh fuck, his mate was sexy when he went into full dominant mode. He wondered why he had ever been concerned about bedding his smaller mate.

Grabbing the oil Kel passed him, Corin slowly stretched Kel out. It felt different from what he was used to. Although, admittedly, he'd only ever topped one man. In fact, he'd only ever been with three men in total. But something about Kel's butt was both different and incredible. It was hot, tight and rippling. With two fingers stretching and scissoring, he finally worked out the difference. There were bumps inside Kel's passage, similar to those on his cock. Precum leaked from him at the thought of how they would feel on his cock. He was getting desperate now, desperate to feel Kel wrapped around him, but he refused to slide inside Kel before his man was ready.

"Fuck, babe. I want you, now, no more playing, give me your cock. Now!" Kel almost cried in frustration, he was so desperate.

Corin let his lips slip from Kel's cock, leaning back to strip quickly. Kel helped him by all but yanking his trousers down and off his legs before lying back on the bed. "Take me however you need to, babe, whatever position works for you. As long as I have you in me, I'm happy."

Corin kneeled on the bed and dragged Kel towards him. He rested Kel's butt on his thighs, spreading Kel's legs wide on either side of him to accommodate his belly. Tilting his hips up, he gently thrust inside Kel in one long, slow movement before bottoming out. He waited for Kel to adjust to the feeling of being filled by him. When Kel started trying to move on his cock, he figured it was a sign for him to take his man. He started a slow draw, in and out. Those bumps were incredible, dragging along his shaft— the intensity was mind-blowing. He was being massaged every time he fucked in deep. Every stroke made his eyes roll further back into his head. When he knew Kel was comfortable, he couldn't hold back any longer. He started to hammer into Kel, the pace as fast as he could go considering his larger state.

"Oh sweet moons, babe. More. Damn it, more, take me, I want to feel it for days. I need to feel it, need to feel you. I want to feel you. Now fuck me, damn it. Hard."

"Oh fuck, Kel. You feel amazing. You want to feel me?"

"Yes!"

"For days?"

"Yes, damn it!"

"Then take all of me." With those words, Corin thrust into Kel. Hard, fast, and almost brutal in its intensity. There was nothing tender about it. The head of his cock was ramming against Kel's prostate, spike after spike of pain-pleasure rippling through Kel. Those bumps were constricting against Corin, milking him on every thrust. Both of them were panting hard. Pleasure was spiralling them higher and higher.

Kel was fucking himself onto Corin, meeting every thrust with a downwards slam of his body, doubling the speed, force, and pleasure of their passion. Kel couldn't contain the pleasure, it was too much, too intense. His spine was tingling, his cock throbbing, his balls aching. Electric shocks were sparking all over his body, and without even a touch to his cock, he exploded. Cum tore out of his slit, painting both of them. Stream after stream landed on them both, providing visual evidence of just how much he enjoyed being possessed by his mate. His vision was fading as he felt Corin tense a split second before a burst of heat filled him.

"Kel!!" Corin's hoarse shout echoed around the room, even as he never stopped moving, forcing every drop he released deep inside his man before he collapsed forward slightly, bracing his arms on the bed to keep his belly safe, breath harsh and fast, chest heaving.

As his vision returned, Kel eased Corin out of him before scooping up his man and laying him gently on the bed. Getting a wash rag from the bathroom, he gently washed Corin down before washing the cum off his own body. Both clean, he lay down next to

Corin and scooped him into his arms, pulling the cover over both of them. "Damn, babe, that was mind-blowing."

"I didn't hurt you, did I?" Corin asked tentatively.

"Only in the best possible way, babe. You gave me exactly what I needed and wanted. It was amazing. You were amazing. I loved it. I love you."

"Good." Corin sighed quietly.

"Go to sleep, babe, you're exhausted. Relax, I have you, safe in my arms. You and the little one are here in my arms and I couldn't be happier. Now sleep, babe, and dream of me."

Corin simply smiled as his eyes drifted closed. Exhausted and satisfied, it was a dreamless sleep which took him that night.

Kel spent hours simply holding the two most precious things in the world. He took the time to memorize every part of the man, tracing every curve of his face, every crevice of his body, committing it all to memory. As his mind was drifting, he felt a thump under his hands. His eyes jolted open in surprise and he stared at Corin's belly. There it was again, a distinct thump against his hands. Their baby was saying hello.

"Ah, little one, hello, beautiful. This is your Papi. I can't wait to meet you, but right now you need to stay with your daddy and get bigger for us." The smile on his face as he stroked his baby through Corin's belly was radiant. He felt another gentle thump against his hand and then his little one settled, letting his daddy sleep. The feeling of his child moving beneath his hand had joy encircling his heart. This perfect night was one he wanted to hold dear and cherish, both as he went into battle the next day and forever after.

Chapter Thirty

$\rightarrow$O$\leftarrow$

As dawn crested over the horizon, the men were already up and about. Breakfast was served buffet style on the massive table in the reception room. Conversation was both subdued and full of anticipation. Not one of them was looking forward to a battle if it came down to it, but they were more than prepared to meet any challenge they were presented with. They would meet it head on with both force and resolve in their hearts. Their battle leathers were all laid out, the leather supple from repeated wear and marked by the odd scratch from close calls with blades and bows. Swords were polished and sharpened, harnesses ready.

The Avanti's equipment was all laid out and checked, guns cleaned, ammo prepared and comms ready. Dax and Bell tried to check in with Hunter and Bray, but nothing. At one point, Bell was convinced he heard a crackle, but when they heard nothing further they left it for the next check-in. They knew now was not the time to focus on it, they just hoped waiting another day was not going to mean they missed their friends.

Corin and Kel walked out of the room wrapped around each other, laughing and smiling. As they broke apart, Tir raised his eyebrows at his brother. There was something different about him, that Tir couldn't put his finger on. When Kel just smiled at him, he narrowed his eyes. Kel's hand was caressing Corin's belly, a tender smile on his face. Tir had to smile at the love and joy radiating from his brother. Whatever happened today, it was worth it, just to see his brother so content. There was one point recently where he was sure he was going to lose his brother, another where he thought the man his brother used to be was gone forever. Corin coming back had changed all that.

"I felt the little one move last night," Kel told his brother. "It just felt like such a special moment. To finally have some interaction with the little one, last night of all nights, was magical."

Corin was smiling at Kel as he spoke. "It's not so magical when your bladder is their dance floor."

Kel just kissed him gently on the temple, saying, "Worth it in the long run though, babe."

"I know."

Kel was deliciously sore this morning and could still feel Corin from last night, which was exactly what he had wanted. It was a constant reminder of what he would be fighting for today.

"Where's Eliya?" Corin asked.

A small giggle came from beneath the table. Corin looked down to see a set of eyes peeking out at him.

"What are you doing down there?"

"I'm playing with Talisel."

"Who is Talisel?"

"Talisel is her little Faronine pet."

"Faronine?" Corin mouthed at Kel. Kel merely pointed at the floor where Eliya was.

Corin watched as a small purple and white striped furry blob gently nipped at Eliya's fingers. It was small, with a short, yet bushy tail, and big, floppy ears. Vivid green eyes peeked out at him from a feline face. Tiny paws playfully batted at the hand which was tickling its tummy. Corin was the first to admit it was a cute looking thing and it was obvious the two had a great friendship.

With a smile, Corin left her playing with her pet, glad there would be something to distract her today as well as company for when she was hiding.

"So what time does everything happen?" Corin was anxious to get the day over, but at the same time, never wanted it to happen. He could only hope they made it through the day without losing anyone. He really hoped his pregnancy wasn't going to affect his ability to perform trauma care at the rate he knew he was going to need to. Panicking was not going to help him. He needed to keep a cool head and hope everything would go okay.

"We will go down and wait in the courtyard in about an hour. I'm hoping it will unnerve him slightly. We are going to need to hide Kel somewhere close until the time is right for him to reveal himself."

"So it's just waiting now? Damn, I hate waiting." Corin scrunched up his face, eliciting a gentle laugh from Kel.

Tate snorted. "Is there anyone who doesn't?"

"Tate? Can I talk to you for a moment, in private please?" Corin ignored the questioning glance Kel was sending his way.

"Sure." Tate was up and walking to the bedroom within moments. "What's wrong?" He prompted as soon as the doors were shut behind them.

"I know you guys will do your best to keep yourselves safe, so I'm not going to ask you to do anything along those lines. I do, however, want to ask you to hold onto something for me." He passed a small wrapped package over to Tate. "Inside, there is both an audio and video recording of the baby's scan and heartbeat. There's also a letter to Kel in there. If something happens to me, I need you to pass it on to Kel."

"Nothing is going to happen to you, Corin. You have to know we'll keep you safe." Tate was positive of that.

"I know you will, but you know if they catch sight of me and realise I'm pregnant, all bets are off. They will come at me with everything they have. Kel being alive and me carrying his baby keeps him out of Teriva's reach. It's going to piss her off beyond belief. Couple it with the fact this baby will stop them gaining control of the clan if, suns forbid, Kel, Tir and Eliya are injured or die, then they won't stop hunting me."

"Fuck, Corin, you have to stay with Eliya. It's just not worth the risk."

"It is, and you damn well know it! You guys need me out there, I'm the only one who has the skill to save lives. I have to be there. I won't concede on the point."

"Fuck." Tate grabbed Corin and hugged him tight. "Don't you dare go dying on me, Doc. Who is going to keep patching me up?

Who's going to help me figure out what's going on with Dariux? Don't you dare leave me, Doc. I need you, Dax and Bell need you, Tir, Eliya, Alix, we all need you. But most of all? Kel needs you, you are everything to him, so you better keep yourself safe, or you will destroy him. You hear me?"

"I don't plan on dying, Tate, I really don't. Just promise me one other thing?"

"Shit, there's more?"

"Just promise me, if it comes down to it and there is a choice, then save the baby over me. For Kel's sake?"

"Fuck, Doc, I can't promise that. Kel needs to be the one to decide."

"Then, just promise me to tell him it's what I want if it comes to it, alright?"

Tate sighed. This was not a conversation, nor a responsibility, he wanted, but he agreed anyway. How could he do anything else? Squeezing Corin tight, he slapped him on the butt. "Now, go out there and reassure your man before he panics and storms in here thinking I've accosted you!"

It was enough to lighten the mood and they both walked out of the room smiling. It was enough to have Kel relax, no longer worried about what they had been talking about. That was exactly what Tate hoped for.

It was a little later when Tir left with Eliya and her guard. It was the unspoken sign for them all to get ready. Nerves faded as all the men slipped into battle mode, their focus settling on the plan for the day. Even Corin slipped into doctor mode. Faces impassive, they were ready and waiting by the time Tir returned. Kel swooped Corin into his arms, holding him close as he gave him a tender kiss, full of love. Gently bending down, he kissed Corin's belly before standing once again to take his place alongside his brother.

Wrapping a cloak around both Kel and Corin, they walked out of the suite and were immediately flanked by faithful men at arms. The two men were kept hidden in the middle of them all. With one last squeeze of Corin's hand and a whispered "I love you," Kel slipped off into a side room to wait. Closing the gap around Corin, they took him to the guard house where Dariux and his men broke off from the group to stand watch over Corin.

In the courtyard, Niko and Tir put on a big display of saying goodbye, knowing there were eyes watching their every move from the second they took their first step into the courtyard. Knowing Martellon's spies and sentries were quickly passing on the word of their appearance, Tir simply stood and waited, his men at arms by his side as Niko rode out. He was calm, his men at arms strong and still, all well trained, not one of them let their nerves show. They were just as eager to get this over with, but more importantly, just as eager to get rid of Martellon.

Subtle hand signals were being exchanged between Tir, Dax, Carn and their loyal forces. Everything was ready, the men in place. The only question left was if this would descend into a battle or would Martellon actually choose to walk away? No matter how unlikely it was, a hope still clung to some of them.

"Are the civilians safe?" Tir whispered to Dax.

"Yes, I just got the signal there. We are good to go. Any casualties should hopefully be at a minimum."

"Good, I want as few men as possible to be hurt today. I want no more damage and heartache brought upon this clan by Martellon. I want this to end. Today. One way or another." The friends simply stood and waited, no more words needed.

No one moved. It was as though every soldier in the keep held their collective breath. The tension was a palpable, breathing entity. It swirled amongst them, reaching out, touching each and every one of them. A gentle caress as if to remind them all, I am here. The more experienced soldiers shrugged off its toxic touch, focusing their minds, steadying their hearts, and simply waited. Martellon's men struggled. They were shifting from foot to foot, anxious and restless, the touch working its magic on them. Anticipation was a dangerous thing. It made men reckless, quick to react. The slightest shift would see a flurry of movement and the battle would begin no matter what the leaders wanted.

Martellon sauntered out from one of the barracks, a squad of no doubt hand-picked men surrounded him. His arrogance knew no bounds. So sure was he of Tir's surrender, he was still dressed in his court finery. No concessions were made to the possibility of battle.

"So you have assembled your men to surrender to me then?" He sneered at Tir, secure in his attempts to have driven Tir into an emotional state of loss, grief, self-doubt, recrimination and submission.

Tir simply quirked his brow, choosing to reply succinctly, "No."

"No?"

"No." Tir smiled a dangerous smile. "No, I will not be surrendering to you."

"Ah, so you have chosen to hand your brother over in the hopes I will spare you then?"

"Again, no."

Martellon was puzzled. Never before had his mind games failed to work on a conquest, be they the women he took to his bed, the political opponents he ridiculed, or the clans he destroyed.

"You can't mean to fight? You, with no father to lead, no brother to lean on? You can't possibly hope to succeed against me!"

"I can, and I will." Tir was keeping calm, no matter how Martellon reacted, he was not going to trigger the verbal traps which were being laid down before him. "Listen and listen carefully. There will be no surrender by us, we will not hand over my brother, we will not hand over our keep. We will not hand over even one tiny speck of land to you. You cannot come here, try to wheedle your way into our lives, attempt to subjugate us, mock us and enslave us. We will not stand idly by and watch as you attempt to destroy us.

"We. Will. Fight. We will stand up for those around us, we will harbour every man, woman, and child, safely, if they wish to be here. We will drive you from our lands. We will send you running back to your own keep like the coward you are. Walk away,

Martellon, walk away, or be prepared to battle. To battle a clan that, you have tried, and failed to take away, a clan which remains strong and true to those around them. A clan that is prepared to fight to their dying breath to defend their way of life.

"We. Will. Fight. We will fight for our very freedom, we will fight for our loved ones and we will fight for our lives. Once again, I say no. No, to handing over my brother. No, to handing over MY clan, and no, to any other deal you attempt to make. Make your choice, now, Martellon. Stand and fight us, or turn tail and run like the coward you are."

The Derin were stunned, proud and amazed. Never before had they heard Tir speak with such passion, such conviction and such honour. As one, they stood straighter. As one, the pride of the clan suffused them. As one, they stood prepared to die for everything Tir spoke about. As one, they would die for their clan, their friends, their lands, but most importantly, as one, they would die to keep their loved ones safe. Backs ramrod straight, weapons held with a gentle grip at the ready, they simply waited.

"How dare you!" screamed Martellon. "How dare YOU talk to ME that way? I WILL have this clan, I WILL have your brother and most of all, I WILL have your head!" Spittle was flying everywhere as Martellon ranted at Tir. He was pacing back and forth across the courtyard, his steps uneven, his pace agitated.

Tir knew then that the day was not going to end any other way but with a battle. Looking around at the men standing strong beside him, he was proud. Proud of all that his clan was, proud of the men they were, proud of his friends who stood beside him, who risked their lives for them. His heart swelled with love and gratitude. Whatever happened today, if he lived or died, he would hold his head high, knowing he said no to Martellon, knowing he did everything in his power to protect the clan and Eliya. His only hope was she would be happy and safe. In his heart, he knew Alix would take her in and for that he would be forever grateful.

Tir simply waited out Martellon as he paced. A calmness swirled about his men. Martellon's forces were suffering. He could see even they were affected by his words. They knew this would be a battle to the death. They knew the Derin would fight with a righteous wrath. Many didn't want to be there. Many wondered how they could walk away, if they could walk away, yet not one of them risked it. Tir could see it in their eyes, hope dying for an easy end to this confrontation.

"Surrender!" Martellon suddenly screamed, angered beyond belief. "I demand you surrender."

"No." Tir shook his head. "How many times, Martellon? How many times do you need to hear me say the word no? Make your choice."

"Give me Kel and we will leave, give me Kel and I'll let you all live." Yet again, Martellon tried to weasel his way to success.

"How many times does my brother have to deny you, Martellon? How many times before you hear the words?" Kel almost laughed at the look of shock on Martellon's face as he stepped out of the shadows. "I will not be going with you, and I most certainly will not be mating with Teriva. I have a mate, a truemate, and there is nothing and no one in this world that would cause me to deny him."

Joy spread rapidly throughout the Derin. Not one of them thought Kel would pull through, not one of them believed it possible to recover from such an illness. Hope sprang up amongst them. Truemates were so rare, they were considered a true blessing, to the couple, the families and the clan. This was a portent of good things to come for all. They just needed to stand fast this day. As one, they were overjoyed, pleased to see someone they cared for well and happy.

Martellon staggered like he had been physically struck. "You!"

"Me." Kel smiled a dangerous smile. "Not quite what you planned for today, is it, Martellon?"

Martellon was both livid and slow to recover. His feelings were written all over his face, his shock too great, his control on his emotions slipping. He really hadn't been expecting Kel to make an appearance. In fact, he had been counting on Kel staying in a coma. He knew it would be the only way he could get him back to his own keep. After the death of his father and the influence he wielded over his sons, there was no way they would gain control of Kel by any other means. How did he lose control of the situation so quickly? He knew he had backed himself into a corner. If he backed down now he would be ridiculed at the next Conclave, ridiculed by every other clan leader. No, it was all or nothing now and he knew it.

"Damn the fucking Derin," he muttered, more to himself than anyone within range. "Damn them all to every exploding star and black hole possible. Damn them to the very deepest pits of hell. Louder, he asked, "How?" Martellon wanted to know what, or rather, who had thwarted his plans— he would make them suffer for their actions.

"What does it matter?" There was no way Kel would ever let slip how he had recovered. He would rather die than put his mate in Martellon's sights.

"It matters to me!" Martellon's face contorted as he spoke.

Even Martellon's own men were looking at him as if he was crazy. The man was almost foaming at the mouth, such was his anger. Some of Martellon's men were fidgeting, their bodies restless, as though it was sheer force of will that kept them in place. It was common knowledge that anyone betraying Martellon was dealt with swiftly and thoroughly, their families dying alongside them in a show of Martellon's dominance.

"Well, seeing as I don't care what matters to you, then you'll never know. Now, you have two options here. One, run, and run fast. Take your clan and get the fuck off our lands, or two, stay and fight. A warning, if you stay and fight, you will die, your men will die, you will not be victorious."

"Fuck you!" was the only verbal response Martellon sent their way. Instead he drew his sword and shouted the attack order.

Within seconds, the Derin had taken up defensive postures and met the charge head on. A loud piercing whistle rent the air. Dax was signalling to Bell to let loose on the explosives. As the first swords struck, so too did the first explosive volley. A rumbling sound rent the air as the wall of the unused south-eastern most barracks crumbled in on itself, cutting off the supply of Martellon's men. No help would come from the forces he had hidden there, sure that no one had detected them.

Bell could hear curses streaming from the ruins. There was a scrambling noise as the men pinned down tried to free themselves. Bell wasn't worried. The blast was perfectly executed. There would be no moving the rubble without a large amount of help and time. He swiftly moved off, skirting through the shadows, avoiding the pockets of fighting he came across. He only stopped briefly when it was evident a Derin man needed help. Then, he was swift in his defence of the men he aided, dispatching foe after foe with lightening quick strikes of his blade. His legacy as a swordsman for the rulers of his world made itself known. For many years, he had been the Collective's chosen champion for the Five Moons Championship, winning the competition eight years in a row. He was considered the Master Swordsman of the Kingdom. Taking off before the enemy were even down on the ground, he ran on.

Dodging through the fighting men at the keep entrance, he sprinted across to his second site, the normally empty barracks on the west of the keep. Again, the explosives were set off with precision, trapping the reinforcements inside. Hopefully the casualties were at a minimum. It was not their intention to wipe out the Farian Clan, just to disable them while they dealt with Martellon.

Skirting around the stables, he made his way to the explosives at the training centre. Cursing, he saw there was a battle raging in the blast zone. There was no way he would risk all those lives. Instead, he drew his sword and ran, hurling himself straight into the action.

Sliding under the outstretched arm of one of the Derin men, he swept his blade out in an arc, taking out the two men who were about to attack the officer from behind. A grunted thanks was thrown his way, but his focus was on the three men who were advancing on him. Eyeing up their skill with a practiced ease, he discounted the man of the left. He looked to be nothing more than a trainee, barely out of his childhood.

The battleground was no place for him. Turning his blade, he brought the softer foible end of the blade down on top of the trainee's head with just enough force to knock him out. Quickly swinging his blade back round, he parried the lunging attack directed his way, dropping his centre of gravity as he did so, which allowed him to use the momentum of his swing to turn his opponent's blade away. He brought the hilt of his sword around to drive it into the solar plexus of his enemy, taking him out of the battle, yet letting him live. As he engaged the last of the trio, he heard the distinctive sounds of battle all around him. He hoped his friends were faring well. It was a fleeting thought, his training too ingrained to let his mind wander for more than a second.

Kel was frustrated. Martellon was immediately surrounded by the squad he kept close at all times. The self-serving prick was using his men as a human shield. These men were well trained, his personal guard. They would not be easy to dispatch. He could sense Tir battling on his left, Tate on his right. He could feel weakness in his limbs from his time spent bedridden, and could only hope his muscles held out, yet he would keep fighting until he dropped. His pride demanded nothing less. Every parry and riposte he made were sending shocks travelling through his arm. He tried to keep it relaxed, knowing to tighten the muscles too much would increase the damage and strain they were under. He could already hear the screams of the injured and dying from all corners of the battle. Shouts rang out, echoing off the walls. He was waiting for the third blast to come, anxious to know what was keeping Bell. He managed to ground out a question to Tate. "Where the hell is the next blast? We need to take more of these men out!"

"I don't know, Bell should have set it off before now. Something must have happened." Tate's focus remained on the man he was fighting.

"You think Bell is...?" Kel found he couldn't complete the sentence. He had a deep respect for the quiet man and hoped nothing untoward happened to him.

"No, I don't." Tate was adamant. "He's too good to be taken down by these idiots. There's probably a reason why he can't detonate." He let out a series of whistles, a combination of shrill and deep, slow and long. A moment later, a whistled reply came. "He's fine, but can't detonate, just as I thought. He's covering the training centre instead."

"Shit, that means we have more to take on than we hoped." Tir joined in with a grunt as he quickly sliced through the sword arm that was poised to strike out at him.

"We will be fine. We just need everyone to hold their ground." Tate had complete confidence in their plans.

"At least our men have taken up the arms we left hidden for them." Tir was pleased another part of their plan was coming together. He just wasn't sure if they had enough warriors to be victorious with his forces so split. He would not take men from their protective details unless he had no other choice. The civilians, elders, Corin and Eliya needed to be protected at all costs. If they pulled back from those places now, it was likely all would be lost.

Dax was fighting by the blacksmith. A sneaky bastard from Martellon's forces had attempted to use the forge to start a fire. With the way the battle was raging, the fire would have been uncontrollable within minutes, the consequences devastating. It looked like Martellon had issued orders for the Derin to be destroyed at all costs if he couldn't take them. Having dispatched the fire-wielder, he kept up guard, sending a couple of men off to protect the stores. He wished he could spare more, but the simple truth was they were already spread too thin. Hearing the whistled code between Bell and Tate, he understood why. During a brief lull where he was only fighting one man, he hit his comms unit. "Corin, Dariux, report."

"We are fine, Dax. We have injured, but so far there is nothing life-threatening. As yet, no enemy has ventured our way. What of the battle?" Dariux asked.

"It goes. Be watchful, they have fire-starters amongst their numbers. Already tried to take the blacksmith."

"We need to send someone to the stores, they would go up fast."

"Already done. Do you have eyes on the meeting hall?"

"I do, it's covered, no need for more men. They could probably spare a couple if needed." Dariux offered.

"No," Dax grunted as he threw himself out of the way from a diving attack that came from the roof of the blacksmith. Why they thought it would take him off guard, he didn't know. It barely even broke his concentration.

Rolling back up, he drove his sword through the heart of his attacker, sparing no remorse for dispatching someone who behaved so cowardly. "I don't want to risk leaving them vulnerable." He continued talking to Dariux once he was back on his feet. "Let me know if you see anything suspicious or somewhere that needs help fast. The Avanti are used to moving quickly. We will act as a quick strike force where needed."

"Will do."

"Can Corin hear me?" He didn't want what he was about to say to be overheard.

"No." Dariux's voice was filled with worry. His body immediately went into a defensive position, he was on high alert. There must be a reason Dax wanted to keep something from Corin.

"I'm slightly worried about Kel. He's not even close to the level of fitness he needs to be here fighting. He's still suffering the effects of being ill, but the stubborn bastard won't take a back seat. Can you keep an eye on him from there? If you see him falter, even the smallest amount, contact me and I'll make him pull back. Just keep it from Corin. He doesn't need to be any more worried than he already is."

"You've got it. I'll keep a close watch on things," Dariux promised.

"Hopefully it won't come to that." Dax knew, however, that by the end of this battle, every single man would count.

Chapter Thirty One

———————— ❯O❮ ————————

If you can meet with Triumph and Disaster
And treat those two impostors just the same;

Corin worked hard and fast. He was glad there were no major injuries so far, but there were an increasing number of smaller ones. He was thankful two of the clan women and one of the men at arms possessed some medical training, even if it was in small amounts. At least they were able to deal with the least injured. The women had insisted on joining him against their mates' wishes. He would be forever thankful for their help, but he vowed to himself, he would send them to safety at the first sign of trouble coming their way.

Niko was just about at the point where he felt he had waited long enough, when he spotted movement off to the right of the keep. "Fuck. Fuck. Fuck. Get ready men, we ride in five." Those close to him finally picked up on what he had already seen. A large, very hostile force was racing towards the keep, Martellon's flag at the front. "As soon as they are through the gate, we ride and ride hard. Take them from behind as quickly as possible." Looking at the group, he took in the size. There was no way all these warriors were from Martellon's clan, which meant Martellon had extra allies involved in all this.

A piercing war cry rent the air. All movement ceased for a moment, the entire battlefield seemed to turn as one and look towards the keep gate and the force riding through.

"Fuck!" screamed Tir. "Be on guard, incoming!"

Kel wondered if all hope was lost. He could see Martellon's smug grin through the men guarding him.

Niko and his men tore through the valley in pursuit of Martellon's extra forces. The massive pounding of Refrinti paws echoed around the valley, sounding like the rolling thunder on the plains of Haril. Every man pushed their mounts flat out. The earth was almost shaking with the intense impact of so many paws. The well trained beasts ran in formation, a perfectly formed squad. They didn't even break stride as they closed in on the gates. "Rolling dismount, men!" Niko ordered. "It's too busy in there."

Each man let go of the reins, swinging a leg over the battle harness, perching on the stirrup, while keeping one hand resting on the pommel. As each man came upon the gate, they gave a quick pat to their mount, before pushing up and off from their foothold. The power of the jump pushed them up and out of the way of the mounts behind them. The second their feet hit the ground the men sprinted to one side, the mounts continuing on to clear the way for those behind them. The manoeuvre was as seamless as ever, the hours of practise well worth it. Soon Niko's entire squad was running as one living, breathing mass into the battle. The trainees at the back of the squad immediately looked after the Refrinti war beasts who were gathered off to one side, more than used to the manoeuvre.

It was Kel's tiredness that caused him to forget the plan, so it was a surprised grin that found his face when the next war cry rent the air a few minutes later. This one he knew well. "Thought you had the upper hand, did you, Martellon?" He shouted with joy evident in his voice. "Did you really think our friends would abandon us so easily? So readily? They have more honour than you, more integrity."

"Fuck you, Kel. I will have this clan, or burn you to the ground. I shall not leave even one of you alive. Every man, woman and child of this clan will succumb to my wrath. You and your brother will be last, forced to witness the complete and utter destruction of the Derin."

Kel didn't bother to respond, it simply wasn't worth engaging the man. Besides, he didn't need the distraction. Individual battles were raging all around him and he knew he was beginning to lose what little strength he started out with.

Niko's forces were helping to turn the tide, but as good as all the men were, the numbers they faced were simply close to overwhelming. Niko was stunned at the sheer number Martellon had been able to marshal. There was definitely no way all these men came from his clan. There were simply too many. He could see where the pockets of fighting were intense, as well as several places where the Avanti had made good use of explosions. Whatever happened, he would stand beside his friends to the end, even if it meant his death. He would die with honour, protecting the innocent members of the Derin, protecting those he cared for.

Bell and the men at the training centre finally managed to push the onslaught back far enough that he was able to call for a quick retreat. The men who had quickly fallen under his command obeyed him without question. The Farian forces, however, looked stunned, they simply stood there in confusion, unable to work out why the Derin were pulling back when they had the upper hand.

Their confusion soon led to surprise, and horror, when Bell activated the explosives near him. The ground around the training centre blew up and out, raining mud, rocks and debris down between the two forces. Looking around in shock, Martellon's men saw they were pinned in place with no escape. A frustrated roar seemed to grow as each man became aware of his predicament. Leaving five men there to watch in case they managed to escape, Bell led the rest into the heart of battle.

Bell made it to Dax without breaking too much of a stride, simply swinging his blade to the side to knock men out of his way. "It's not looking great."

"There were reinforcements from somewhere. We might have to pull our forces back a little. The only problem will be maintaining a guard around both the guard house and the meeting hall if we do it, plus, it will make the other structures much more vulnerable." Dax kept swinging, thrusting and parrying even as he spoke.

"Definitely last resort measure then." Bell whirled around to spear through a man who was intent on creeping up on them. "Can you hold here? I've managed to block a couple of squads off at the training centre. I need to go and find that bitch Teriva. I'm hoping if I can capture her, it might force Martellon to back off for a bit."

"Go, we will hold this. I think it's time for the guns to come out to play though." Dax slipped away from Bell and the other men, racing to take up a position on the roof of the blacksmith. Their ammunition was limited, so they agreed to mostly restrict it to the Avanti who would use it to turn the battle when they could. The few warriors who were trained in firearms had a small supply each to be used at their discretion. He had been pleased during the course of the battle to see they had not mindlessly wasted the ammunition, instead using it sparingly and only when truly needed. Lying on the roof, Dax quickly took up a prone form, adjusting his scope with practised ease. Soon, shots were ringing out as man after man dropped from his precision strikes.

Bell raced into the keep, sure Teriva was hiding in there somewhere. She had to be. He noticed a couple of civilians hiding in one of the first rooms he came across. "Have you seen Teriva?" he asked the shaking duo.

Scared out of their minds, they simply pointed down the corridor, the eldest woman mouthing, "Kitchens" to him.

Nodding in thanks, he raced on. Despite how desperate he was to find her, he wasn't reckless. He took the time to check out each room as he passed. His Avanti training wouldn't let him do anything else. Peering into the war room, he found a couple of Martellon's forces trying to rip apart the Derin Clan seal, the room almost completely destroyed.

Taking a pair of throwing knives from his tactical vest, he threw each one in quick succession, both hit their targets in the hearts with practiced ease. As he kept searching for Teriva, Bell added another tally to his mental hit list. He hated each kill, no matter how necessary they were. It was weighing heavier and heavier on his heart. He was going to have to reconsider his future with the Avanti for the sake of his own sanity, but now was not the time to dwell on such thoughts.

Reaching the door to the kitchens, he cautiously used one of his tactical devices to peer around the door without being seen. Huddled in the far corner, on the floor, was Teriva. Four guards stood at attention in front of her. It was the opposite of what he expected, and he wondered where the devious bitch they met earlier had gone. Was this all an act to elicit sympathy? It didn't matter, her actions to this point had set her destiny in stone, no matter how repentant she was going to appear to be. Bell sauntered into the room, his hands clasped behind his head in the universal surrender position. "It's okay, boys, I surrender, you can take me in as a hostage."

The guards looked at each other smirking and motioned him to step forward. "Reckons we be getting a pay raise for this 'un Vinty," one of them said.

"More whoring and drinking for us then!" The other men let out great grunts of laughter as the first man motioned Bell forward.

Too busy laughing, they failed to notice Bell's hands shift behind his head. So intent were they on their perceived good fortune, two of them died with smiles on their faces, never having seen the twin throwing blades Bell let loose from behind his head. The third man went down with a thrusting lunge of Kel's sword a second later, a combination of laughter and dawning comprehension on his face.

As Bell whirled round to the fourth, he could see the man was struggling to draw his sword from his scabbard, screaming "shit, shit, shit," as he did so.

Those words were the last he ever spoke as he tripped over one of the other guards in his frantic attempts to draw his blade. The lunge propelled him straight onto Bell's outstretched sword. His death was instantaneous.

Teriva's whole demeanour changed when she saw there were no guards left to protect her. Rather than playing the weak and pathetic woman, a role she knew wasn't working on this man, she swapped into full on seductress mode.

"Come now, handsome." She trailed a hand down his face, her nails scraping lightly against the skin. "You don't want to take me too, do you, hmm?" Brushing her finger over his lips, she carried on, "Don't you want to play with me?"

As she leaned in close, Bell grabbed her hand, spinning her around into an arm lock. "Never, not once would I ever play with you, even if my very life depended on it." Yanking her other arm round to join the first, he bound them with some thin rope from his Tac vest. Pulling her after him, he dragged her through the keep and out of the front door.

Descending the keep steps, they were met by chaos. Individual fights were raging all over the keep grounds. There was no decisive attack plan from Martellon's forces. The Derin and Estrivian Clans were attempting to drive them into one area, but were struggling. It was costing too many men to keep so many small fights going. They just didn't seem to have enough forces to give a final push to sway the battle their way.

Bell's gaze flicked to the guard house to see a battle raging just outside its doors. He let loose with a shrill series of whistles, directing Dax's attention that way. Hearing the acknowledged whistle in return, he continued dragging a screaming Teriva towards Tir.

Dariux was in trouble. Suddenly, a group of soldiers swarmed them. Perhaps they were looking for escape, perhaps they knew who was hiding in the guard house. In reality, it mattered not. He and his men simply attempted to stand their ground, protecting everyone inside at all costs. Dariux ordered Corin, "Retreat Cor, retreat, I don't know how long we can hold them."

"I can't, if I leave this man now, he will die. I've got my hand plugging his heart, for fuck's sake!" Corin screamed right back.

"Shit, this is going to be a close one then. Just get out of here as soon as you can or Kel will have my hide."

When all he heard back was an affirmative grunt, he flicked the comms button to get Dax's attention. "Dax, we're in trouble over here. We're being overrun and Corin's in the middle of surgery and can't leave. I don't know how long my men and I can hold out. The numbers outside are increasing rapidly." In fact, they were outnumbered five to one and even with all the skill they possessed it was never going to be good enough.

"I've already seen it. We're on our way to you. Hold fast for as long as you can." Dax, Tate and Kel were running as best they could through the fighting all around the keep. They left Bell with Tir and some of the men who had been with both in charge of Teriva. They were trying to gain Martellon's attention. To see if they could stop the bloodshed with her as a hostage.

Corin was trying hard to finish the surgery. He knew if they stood any chance of surviving they needed to leave soon, but he couldn't just abandon his patient. He heard more than saw part of the guard house wall collapse inwards, men pouring in after it at the same moment he was sewing the last stitch to the man's skin. Grabbing the weapon beside him, he turned to face the onslaught. The men were circling as best they could around the room, trying to flank them on all sides.

"Get the fuck out of here, Corin," Dariux yelled at him.

"I can't, the way is blocked." Corin was panting with exertion. Partly from the constant surgery, partly from the pregnancy, but mostly, from the sheer physical strain of trying to wield a sword on top of all the other stresses on his body. He was starting to wish he had agreed to carry a gun, but he had let the others have them as supplies were short. While he was a hopeful man, he knew hope was not a boundless entity and they were coming close to the point of no return. Suddenly they heard fighting on the other side of the door.

"We're here," Dax bellowed from the other side. "Hold on."

"Hold on, babe, just hold on for me." Kel's voice quickly followed Dax's.

Corin's relief turned to horror a moment later as one of the soldiers slipped on the bloody floor, his swing arcing wide. As Corin was already pinned in place fighting, there was nowhere for him to go to avoid the impact. In that split second, he tried to steel himself for the impact, turning his body as best he could to protect the child he carried. But the hit never landed. Suddenly the men fighting him were yanked away and he got a good look at what had happened. "Oh, Stars, no." He dropped to the floor in front of Dariux.

"I tried, Corin, I tried as best as I could to protect you. I'm sorry I failed." Dariux rasped out, blood mingling with his words on each exhale.

"No, Dar, no, you did good. You saved me. Now let me save you, okay? Just hold on for me, please." As Corin spoke, he was ripping apart packages of equipment. Slamming an injector gun against Dariux's skin, he shot him with both Battleboost and a pure shot of adrenaline. A voice screaming near him finally registered on his consciousness.

"Corin, babe, please tell me you are okay!" Kel sounded distraught.

"I'm fine, I'm uninjured, but Dariux is bad, I need help and fast."

Suddenly Tate was beside him. His face was a white mask of fear and horror. "Fuck, Doc, save him, please. Don't let him die."

"I won't, but I need help. Strip his tunic off him and start cleaning the wound. I need to see what the fuck is going on."

Doing as he was told, Tate worked as fast as possible, talking to Dariux with every breath, uncaring of who was around to hear. "Don't you dare bloody die on me, Ree. You made me swear to make it out so I expect you to do the same for me. You just fucking hold on while Corin fixes you. You hear me?"

Dariux sent a weak smile Tate's way. He really did love the nickname Ree. "I'm sorry, Tate. Sorry I got hurt, sorry I'm too late," Dariux rasped out, his eyes barely focused on Tate's face as tears rolled down both their cheeks.

"Too late for what?" Tate was sniffing back his tears as he worked. His throat hurt with the pressure constricting it.

"Too late to tell you just how much I love you, just how much I wanted to be your mate. I was too scared you would refuse me. I wasn't honest with myself and I wasn't honest with you. I'm sorry, so bloody sorry. Just know, I loved you then, I love you now and I will love you for an eternity." Those were the last words to fall from Dariux's lips before the vitals monitor he was hooked up to went wild.

"Fuck, he's in cardiac arrest." Corin leaned over Dariux, working as best he could around his belly to resuscitate him. "Tate, get it together! I need you, damn it. Help me!" But one glance at Tate and he saw the utter devastation on his face. Suddenly another set of hands replaced his.

"Doc, carry on doing what you need to do to help him. I've got this." Dax spoke even as he took up Corin's efforts to keep Dariux's heart pumping, hands clasped onto Dariux's chest taking over the work for his heart.

It was a race against time to repair the damage the sword had done to Dariux's abdomen. It had sliced through his skin in a long gash, and blood was pooling everywhere. Yet at the same time, by some miracle, all the organs seemed to be intact, bar a small slice to his liver.

Corin thanked the stars that Dariux's momentum as he flung himself in front of Corin deflected the blade enough to stop him being killed outright. Just as Corin was about to start work on fixing the internal damage, he noticed Dariux's lung was collapsing. Grabbing more of the equipment which was scattered around him, he worked to inflate the lung. Reaching for one of the machines, he picked up the probe and pierced through the skin and muscles. On the side of Dariux's body, there was a sudden rush of air as the lung started to fill.

He was thankful the machine was monitoring the air levels in the lungs. It meant he could focus on other things. One problem down, a couple more to go. Performing one of the fastest stitching's in his career, he repaired the damage to the liver as one of the women who was helping began mopping up the blood. Grabbing the injector, he swapped out the pods and shot Dariux with a full vial of plasma booster in the hopes it would negate the effects of his massive blood loss.

Suddenly, a tiny blip was heard from the monitor, its welcome sound loud even over the battle that still raged near them. The blip became two, then three. Slowly, but surely, a rhythm started to appear on the screen. It was still very irregular, but it was there.

Kel leant down next to Corin. "Are you sure you and the little one are both okay, baby?"

"I'm sure. I'm tired and weary, but we're alright. You're not injured?" His eyes were visually inspecting his mate, making sure he was telling the truth, even as he carried on working on Dariux. Kel looked tired but okay.

"We've pushed them back from here. I'm going to leave Tate here, he's no use to anyone at the moment. Dax will look out for you all. I need to go back to Tir. Be safe, my love. Be safe." With a quick, harsh kiss, Kel stood up and dove back outside, straight into fighting mode, battling his way to his brother with one last look back to where his man was being protected.

Kel may have won his mini battle to protect Corin, but they were losing the war with Martellon. His brother and Bell had secured Teriva to a post which was attached to the blacksmith, so they could concentrate on fighting. As soon as he reached them, he raised his sword for what felt like the thousandth time that day and swung at an approaching enemy.

"Are Corin and the babe alright?" Concern laced Tir's voice.

"Yes, but Dariux took the blow meant for Corin. They are working on him now, but his heart is barely beating. It's not looking good." Kel was devastated at the thought of losing Dariux.

"Shit!" Tir was cursing up a storm as he fought, his strikes becoming more vicious in his anger.

It was then that Niko finally reached them. "What's happened? Who is down?" He knew from their faces it was bad, but he felt his heart break at the news his closest friend was dying. Every swing of his blade became more aggressive, every thrust more decisive. He would take out as many as he could for his friend, for all his friends. "I think Martellon may have snuck out, leaving his forces to fight. I can't see him or his Master at Arms anywhere." He managed to bite out the words even as his jaw was clenched in anger.

"Fucking bastard, although I'm not surprised." Kel motioned to Teriva at the post. "At least we have someone to take before the Conclave if we survive this."

"That's a bloody big if though, Kel. We need the bloody universes to align just right to have even a hope of making it through this day, let alone winning this fight. We may have the skill, but sheer bloody numbers are overwhelming us." Niko smiled sadly at his friends.

"Well, if we are going down, at least we are going down fighting. I can't think of a better way to go than protecting our clan, our friends and those we love." Kel was sure about it. He just hoped his two greatest treasures survived, even if he didn't.

Chapter Thirty Two

From the faces all around them, it became obvious the Derin were all coming to the same conclusion they were, yet, suddenly, a shout of pure joy rang out above them all. Confused, they all hunted for the source, but then another sound grabbed their attention. A rhythmic thumping once again echoed through the valley, as the sound got louder, more shouts of joy joined the first. Hope was beginning to unfurl in the chests of the Derin. Suddenly a voice boomed out over the heads of everyone present. Friend and foe stopped to listen.

"By order of King Kastain, hostilities will cease. Anyone caught disobeying your King will be met with lethal force. Lower your weapons and stand down."

Shouts of delight echoed from every corner of the keep and its grounds. It seemed Alix's envoy had made it to the King and brought him here just in the nick of time. An exhausted Kel could stand no more. His legs gave way as he crumbled to the ground, simply too tired to even address his King properly as the toll of the last few months finally caught up with him.

The men sagged as one, sword arms drooping, barely able to keep their weapons from scraping on the ground. Leaning against one another, they were beyond weary, blood-soaked, bruised and battered. Yet with the aches and pains came relief at surviving the day. The aid of the Avanti had been game changing. Tir had no idea what would have happened if they hadn't been there. The clan would no doubt either be under Martellon's control or no more than a pile of ashes.

Tir wearily dropped to his knees beside his brother, checking his vitals, making sure he wasn't injured. Thankful all was well, he figured his brother was simply exhausted and his body had finally said enough and shut down. If he was honest, he didn't know how

Kel had remained standing for so long, let alone found the strength to fight. All around them the enemy were lowering their blades and surrendering to the King's forces. Within minutes, the King himself was striding towards them. He had a moment to wonder what exactly was going on, when he heard a sharp intake of breath from beside him. Suddenly Bell was running across the courtyard with a whoop of joy.

At the same moment, two of the men riding alongside the King looked across at Bell before jumping down and meeting him in the middle of the battlefield. Slamming into each other, the three men were all shouting at once, hugging each other like crazy.

"Stars, Bell, is it really you?" the shorter of the two asked.

"Fuck, Hunter, we thought we'd never see you again." Bell pulled both men in tight again as though if he let go for even a second they would disappear forever.

"We? Does that mean Dax survived okay and is with you?" Bray was anxious to know if their team leader and friend had survived.

"More than that, my friends, more than that! We met up with Tate and Corin as well. They are here with us."

"Stars! Really?" Smiles were wide on all their faces.

"Come on, I'll take you to them, although it's a bit chaotic with them at the moment. Corin was working his doctor magic last I heard." Bell was all but dragging them behind him as he strode to the guard house. He was desperate to bring light back into their lives and what could make them happier than finally being reunited with their friends?

Corin was battling hard to save the life of the man who had saved his. There weren't enough ways in the universe for him to repay the ultimate act of sacrifice and kindness Dariux had displayed with that one move, but at least if he saved the man's life, it would be a start.

"His vitals are getting stronger." Dax bit his lip as he stood over them, watching.

"I think we might just have turned the corner. He's stabilizing and I can't find any more bleeds. If we can somehow give him a blood transfusion, things should improve a lot more. I'm type 7, it looks like Dariux is type 13 so I'm out. What about you?" Corin prompted Dax.

"Type 9, so it rules me out as well, but I think Tate might be 13." As he spoke, Dax was trying to get Tate to respond. "Tate, Tate, come on, buddy, I need you to wake up."

When Tate continued to be unresponsive, Corin gave him a small shot of adrenaline. "Tate, damn it, you need to snap out of it. I think you can help Dariux."

"Dariux is dead, my Ree is dead!" Once again tears filled Tate's eyes. They burst over the rims and flowed down his cheeks.

"No, he's not, look. I said look, Tate!" Corin forced Tate's face round to look at Dariux lying on the floor. The monitor slowly beeping away with a slightly steadier heartbeat.

"He's still alive?" Tate was shocked. He was convinced Dariux was dead.

"Yes! Now I need to know what blood type you are. I've given him plasma, but he needs a transfusion and fast. It's not like I have tons of stockpiles here, so I'm hoping someone is a match."

"I'm type 13. Can I help?"

"Yes." Corin smiled. Dariux might just live to see another day.

"Then take whatever you need, Doc."

Corin set up an emergency battle transfusion— it was fast, messy and far from ideal, but it should be enough. He had tubing running directly from Tate's vein, into Dariux, transferring the life-giving blood. As he worked, he kept looking at Tate. He was suffering badly. His eyes were red-rimmed, streaks showed in the blood and mud caking his face. The tears had left a bizarre network of criss-crosses on his skin, giving him an almost tribal appearance. Almost immediately, the colour in Dariux's body was returning. Corin took as much as he felt he could before stopping the transfusion.

"Take more if you need it, Doc." Tate was adamant he would give whatever was needed for Dariux to survive. He wished there was something special about his blood that would suddenly fix Dariux, and wasn't that just a stupid thought?

"I've taken enough. I won't leave you short. Besides between your blood and the plasma, it should be enough."

"When will we know if he's going to make it?" Tate asked, a small quiver evident in his voice.

Corin knew Tate was barely holding it together. He didn't think Tate even knew just how deep his feelings for Dariux ran. "If he makes it through the night, he will make it. But it's going to be a long, slow road to recovery and there probably won't be any improvement for a while."

"As long as he makes it. It's the only thing that matters."

Just then, the door burst open and all three men swung around to see what was going on. Dax had leapt to his feet the instant he heard the noise, sword in hand, ready to strike.

At the sight that met their gaze, all three of them showed varying degrees of shock across their faces. Dax was stuttering, "How, what, where, how?" Before he even finished, he had been scooped into a bear hug by Hunter, Bray grabbing Tate in a similar manner. Behind them, Bell was looking on, smiling like crazy at the sight of all his friends back together in one place.

Corin knelt back down, his focus back on Dariux, not wanting to risk missing even the slightest change in his condition.

"Doc, you made it." Bray was grinning down at Corin, his soft emerald eyes sparkling with happiness. "Now get your butt up here and give us a hug."

Corin grasped the hand Bray held out to him, thankful for the offer as getting up these days was starting to be more difficult. He almost dropped back on his butt when Bray let go suddenly. Looking up to see what was going on, he almost laughed at the look on Bray's face. His eyes were wider than any he had ever seen. Mouth hanging open, Bray's eyes were focused intently on his belly.

"How, what, am I imagining… Are you… how's it even possible? Fuck, that's just, fuck!" Bray was stuttering as he took in the changes to Corin. His face paled slightly, bringing the subtle ridges running down the side of his neck into even sharper contrast than normal.

Corin smiled at both Hunter and Bray. "Yes, I am pregnant. I'm mate to a man from this clan and, due to some quirk in my genetics, I am indeed pregnant. Baby is due in about four weeks from what we can gather."

"Holy shit, Doc, that's awesome! Congratulations!" Hunter's purple hued eyes swirled even faster than normal as he took in the changes in Corin.

Both men hugged Corin as tight as they could without squeezing the baby.

"How in the hell are you here, now?" Corin suddenly thought to ask.

"I was wondering how myself, Doc," Dax chimed in.

"Can you leave him?" Hunter indicated the man Corin was tending to.

"Go, Doc, I will keep an eye on him. I'll come and get you if anything changes." One of the women helping him touched his arm softly. "He'll be alright with us, I promise."

"Thank you. Just come get me the minute anything changes, okay?"

"I will do, Doc."

The men walked out together, smiles on all their faces at finally being back together.

In the courtyard, controlled chaos reigned as the King's forces worked to restrain all of Martellon's forces. The King stood to one side talking to Niko and Tir as one of his men tended to Kel on the ground. Sudden movement caught all their attention as Corin broke free from his group and ran, as best he could, to Kel's side. Dropping to his knees beside him, tears were in his eyes as he feared the worst. His hands started to frantically map his mate's body, desperate to find the source of his injury.

"Corin, Corin!" Niko shouted at him. "It's okay, he just collapsed from exhaustion, he's not hurt. I promise, Corin. He's alright."

A massive shudder went through Corin's body. His heart was racing, sweat was beading on his skin and he was shaking. He struggled to get his reactions back under control. He really thought he was once again losing the man he loved. "Sweet moons, don't bloody scare me like that! A little warning next time would be appreciated, I thought he was dead!"

"Oh stars, Corin, no, I'm sorry I didn't think." Niko knelt beside his friend, throwing an arm around his shoulders in a small embrace. "He's okay, I promise. The King's medic has been looking after him."

Corin looked to the man who was indeed monitoring Kel. A smile on the man's face exuded warmth. His eyes were heavily crinkled at the sides and his mouth was bracketed by lines as though he spent many hours laughing and smiling. He exuded a homey warmth. "He is doing well, his vitals are stable and I don't see anything more than exhaustion wrong with him. I'm Taynor, by the way."

Corin smiled at the man. "Corin, and he's been ill with Matesickness. He shouldn't really have been up and about as much as he was, but the situation with his clan demanded it."

"Matesickness?" Both the King and Taynor drew in a sharp breath. "Just what the fuck is going on here, Tir?" The King bellowed.

"I think it's best if we move to one of the suites and fill you in, Kastain. We need to move both Kel and Dariux anyway. One of our suites is already set up as a meeting place," Tir suggested.

"Lead on then, my friend." Turning to his Master at Arms, Kastain nodded.

Antares, the King's Master at Arms, turned to his men. "Make sure Teriva is secured somewhere and put a heavy guard on her. I will deal with her later. Watch out for Martellon returning and if anything changes, come and get us."

Corin and Taynor went to get both men settled onto beds in the suite. Taynor had been able to get a hold of some more blood and a proper transfusion was set up for Dariux. They hoped it would be enough, but they made sure there was a medic with him at all times. It was going to be a very long process to get him even close to being fully fit again. Thoughts of the future were premature though, they needed to keep him stable enough to make it, both through the night and the next week or so first. Corin wasn't convinced he hadn't missed something in his tired state earlier, especially considering how fraught the situation had been. Seeing as Dariux was stable, it was something he put to the back of his mind.

Kel was easier to settle. There was no doubt he would need weeks to recover properly and, while it would be a slow process, he would get there. Corin would make sure his man recovered just fine, and was planning on pampering him as much as he could, nursing him back to full health before their baby was born.

Chapter Thirty Three

Once both patients were settled, food had been dished up and minor wounds attended to by the two doctors, they were all finally ready to discuss everything which transpired to get them to this point. Corin was exhausted and not sure if either he, or Tate, were truly up to recounting everything yet again. Each time he told his story, he felt drained. He looked at Tir hopeful, his eyes begging for what he found his mouth could not.

Tir nodded. "Let me explain for Corin and Tate as well as myself and Kel. It's been a crazy couple of months and I want Corin to save his strength. He, more than most of us, needs to take it easier."

"Very well, on you go," Kastain agreed.

By the time Tir got to the point of Corin and Tate leaving for Niko's clan, Corin had fallen asleep, curled up on one of the deep, cushioned benches dotted around the fireplace. Taynor had draped him with a cover after quickly checking his vitals, deciding it was best to just let him sleep.

The new arrivals were stunned at everything that had happened here.

"Fuck!" whispered Hunter, "How the fuck did Corin manage to get through all of that? The strength of resolve he must have found to keep going each and every time he was knocked down must have been astounding."

"He truly is one of the most remarkable men I have ever met." Tir glanced at Corin with respect.

"So how did you get from Corin leaving, your father's new alliance, and Kel mating Teriva, to where we are now?" Kastain probed, his fingers fiddling with the black scruff on his chin.

Tir continued talking. About how much his clan had suffered, his father's death, Kel's illness, Martellon's threats— everything was laid bare for the King. He left nothing out, not the hopes, or fears and certainly not the soul deep horror he felt at everything they had been through. He broke down as he described his worries over his daughter and her future.

"Talking of Eliya, where is my gorgeous girl?" Kastain smiled.

"She's in the suite next door. Carn is watching over her. He has kept her safe through all of this, sacrificing his place in the battle to watch over her. I think she's asleep now, but I know she would love to see you again." Tir smiled at the King. "You know she adores you."

The King returned the smile. "And I adore her." The King knew deep down that the story wasn't over and he wondered if the men were going to be able to get through it all without either collapsing through tiredness or a serious emotional outburst from at least one of them. He was doing his best to be patient and wait out the whole story, but it was hard to just sit there when you knew someone else had all the answers you needed.

"I'll take over the story from here if you want?" Niko indicated a drink sitting at Tir's side. "Take a breather." He smiled at the look of thanks his friend sent his way.

Niko continued where Tir left off, leaving nothing out. When Niko explained everything that had happened with the Riders, Kastain was livid. His hands continuously flexed as he struggled to control his temper, a testament to just how angry he was. He had been taught as a young child how to school his features to hide his emotions, but that ability was failing him now.

"I will be informing the Conclave of this. Have you been able to find any proof?" When everyone shook their heads, he closed his eyes briefly and took a deep breath, trying to school his features. "We will have to see what we can find out." He turned to Antares.

"I will put some of our officers on it." Antares waved over one of his guards and whispered into his ear.

"Okay, carry on, you better fill us in on the rest. There is nothing else we can do about the Riders for the moment." Kastain grimaced.

As Niko finished filling them in, Taynor seemed particularly interested in the research his father and Corin had done on both the Matesickness and Corin's pregnancy. Finally, they were discussing the battle and the run up to it. Every nuance of Martellon's actions were considered and discussed.

"Well, we have a lot of questions for Teriva. That young lady, and I use the term very loosely, has a lot to answer for. Once I have gained information from her, I will take this to the Conclave. We will meet some opposition there, I have no doubt about it. All said and done though, Martellon still has a lot of allies, however, the fact he turned so violently on another ally might work in our favour. If any of his alliances are rocky, we may be able to sway them to our side. We really need to deal with this one way or the other. For too long, he has been left to his own devices. Yes, my Father was guilty of simply standing back and watching, but I am not the same as him. I won't stand idly by while this planet suffers from the actions of one madman."

A yawn from across the room distracted them all, and they all watched on in amusement as Corin stretched, exposing his belly. They could all see the baby moving away underneath the taut skin.

Laughter bubbled around them as Corin admonished his baby, poking his belly. "Sure, wake your daddy up, why don't you? Just because you're bored! You think it's fun for me when you play fight with my insides, huh?" With every poke he gave his belly, the baby seemed to kick right back. "Bah!" Corin threw his arms up in frustration. "You win, I'm awake, now settle down, I don't want a backache again!" He turned towards the men sat around the room and blushed deeply as they all watched him, smiling.

"That truly is an amazing sight." Hunter grinned from his position near the King. "And I have to be honest, Doc, it kinda suits you!"

"What? The fact I waddle? Or the fact I'm as big as a sun?"

"Ha-ha, Doc, no, I meant impending fatherhood."

"Yeah, all joking aside, I really can't wait to meet the little one, even if I'm so not looking forward to the birth!" Corin grimaced at the thought.

"Have you worked out how it's going to happen yet?" Taynor was intrigued about the whole thing.

Corin joined him and started discussing the various options. The other men soon tuned the pair out when the discussion got down to blood and body parts. There were some things men just didn't want to contemplate.

"So, do we know just how much Teriva was involved in all this?" Kastain asked. "We need to make sure we have everything right before we take it to Conclave. What's more, I wished we had some sort of proof about Eliya's kidnapping. It's going to be hard to get the Conclave to believe it. Going after children has always been a big no-no. Not many will believe it. Add in the fact, conveniently, Corin is now mated to Kel and a lot of the Chieftains and Lairds will be very suspicious of the accusations."

Tate sighed. "We have no proof, bar our descriptions. Although, we can lead people to the caves where it happened. I have no idea if there would be any evidence left which would prove our version one way or another."

"We will just have to see what we can get out of her, I guess." Niko was beyond frustrated. Even with the support of the King, this was going to be an impossible few months. "You know, to change the subject for a little break, what I would most like to know is how Hunter and Bray came to be with you."

The King burst out laughing, even as both Hunter and Bray flushed bright red. Now didn't their blushes pique the interests of everyone else in the room? "Oh, this is going to be so much fun!" The King couldn't stop laughing. "Do you guys want to explain this or shall I?"

"Stars, I'll do it," Hunter groaned. "So, yeah, we went off in the pod, much like you guys. We left just after you, Tate. We saw your pod crash spectacularly. We were pretty fucking worried about it, but there wasn't much we could do. The other pod seemed to be faring much better, but we didn't get a good look as by then we were hurtling towards a forest ourselves. We thought at first we were going to smash into the trees, but we bounced on something and went up and over the forest.

"We landed in, well, shit, I don't know what to call it, but man, was it the most disgusting thing you have ever seen or smelled. Damn, it was worse than the Delta sector. Anyway, we landed in this sticky goo." Hunter gagged as he recounted their tale. "It really was nasty shit, it stuck to anything and everything, seeped through clothes, the works. We could feel it sliding down our skin. So once we had everything we could carry from the pod, we hauled arse through this stuff and climbed out. The only problem? We chose to climb out into this field covered in flowers. All I can say is the flowers at least looked nice, but man, they were full of prickly shit, and they smelled just as bad as the bloody goo. The combination was the stuff of nightmares. I swear I will never get the smell of that shit out of my mind." They both shuddered as they recalled it.

"So, this idiot here," —Bray was pointing to Hunter— "Decides before we can get into fresh clothes, jumping into the lake we came across would be a good idea. I guess, it could have been a good idea," Bray amended at the look Hunter shot him. "So yeah, there we are, bare-assed naked and we jump into the lake, all our stuff piled up just on the edge, happily washing that shit off. Then I swear to the seven universes I felt something brush by my leg, something big.

"I was trying to decide if I really did feel something, when suddenly, these two big ass eyes peek out of the water at me. Stars, I jumped so bloody far! This roar reverberates around us and the water is going crazy, you know? So, the pair of us leg it out of the water as fast as we can, hopping around on the hot soil beneath us, trying to dig out our weapons, when suddenly all we hear is laughter. Turning around, there are like five big assed burly men stood there, doubled over laughing their bloody butts off at us. There we are, still butt naked, tackle swinging in the breeze, yelling about this creature out to get us, when out of the water climbs the sweetest, although giant, animal you have ever seen. I swear this thing behaved like some overgrown cub."

Everyone in the room, including Hunter and Bray, were doubled over in laughter. Corin begged, "Oh stars, stop, please, stop, I can't take anymore! Shit, the baby's awake now!" To emphasise the point, the baby kicked out against the glass Corin was holding resting against his stomach. The damn thing went flying across the room, setting the men off all over again.

"So, we were the men standing around watching." Kastain was smiling away. "The so called 'monster' in the lake really is the sweetest, loving, most gentle creature anywhere. The little ones all play with it, so it really was quite funny to watch. So, that was our introduction to the Avanti. Not exactly the bad-asses we expected from the rumours that fly around! Once we knew what was going on, I offered them shelter until they could meet up with you. When they heard about this clan having problems, they offered to come with us in case there was anything they could do to help. None of us knew their friends would be here, so it looks like it all worked out for the best." Kastain looked at all the Offworlders around the room. "Please know that if you decide to stay on this planet, you are all welcome to stay with my clan as a whole or individually."

Murmurs of thanks echoed from all the Avanti. Despite all the problems they had faced since crashing onto this planet, they had never been made to feel more welcome anywhere. More than ever, each one of them was thinking about putting roots down here.

Quiet conversations took the place of the raucous laughter from moments before as the men slowly relaxed after the long, hard day. The peace they were all beginning to enjoy was suddenly shattered by a shout of "Doctors!" Alarms blared from the bedroom.

Both Corin and Taynor raced into the room and quickly joined the medic at Dariux's bedside. Corin took in the erratic rhythm coming from the vitals monitor before catching sight of the wrappings around Dariux's abdomen. Blood was seeping slowly and steadily through. "Shit!" He grabbed a knife and immediately sliced the wrappings off. Blood was oozing freely from the wound and with one quick look at each other, Corin and Taynor started to prep Dariux for more surgery.

The group of friends watched from the door as the stitches were cut open and Dariux's wound widened back up. The blood was running more freely now. As Taynor was trying to soak up the blood to see what was going on, Corin gave Dariux shots of Battleboost, plasma and adrenaline. Even with the second transfusion, they would have to be very careful. He was losing far too much blood. Turning up the painkillers they were pumping into Dariux, Corin immediately got to work. Sliding his hands directing into the stomach cavity, he started to lift the liver up to allow Taynor access to the stomach. Corin gently checked out Dariux's liver wound as Taynor checked the stomach for any lacerations. The repair he had done to the liver was intact and no further damage was present. Taynor gave the stomach the all clear.

"Where the seven moons is the blood coming from then?" Taynor cursed. "Let me hold the liver, see if you can slip under the stomach and check out his spleen."

Corin wasted no time is sliding his hand further under the stomach. His fingers met something hard and sharp. "Shit, there's something here. How the fuck did I miss this?" He was fuming with himself. How could he not have noticed? Trying to push the thought to one side, he drew his focus back to saving Dariux. Feeling around the shard, he calculated that it must have been a very small sliver of the sword that struck him.

It can't have been more than half a finger in length and thin. It was digging into the side of his spleen. The sharp point must have dragged across it. Small lacerations were all over the spleen. Gently, he removed the sliver, dropping it into the bowl one of the medics was holding out for him. The medic waited while he cleaned the area, making sure there was no more metal present. Taking the mesh held out to him, he worked as fast as he could at repairing the damage. Like the mesh had repaired Tate, he hoped it would be just as successful for Dariux. He stitched the silicon mesh gently to the spleen before taking one of the activating agents the medic handed him. Changing his mind, he looked back and said, "Pass me agent B. I'm not sure we need a permanent mould here. Agent B will hold the mesh in place as the spleen heals before it dissolves slowly into the body." The medic quickly passed over the agent as Taynor continued to hold the organs out of the way.

"The bleeding has stopped." Taynor observed, "It looks like it's working. Vitals are stabilizing again. They are slow, but getting steadier."

"Good. Okay, I've repaired the spleen. Let's give it all a quick wash out, and check a final time there is no more damage." The two men checked everything as they carefully placed the organs back in place. Once everything was done, they worked in tandem. Corin was sewing Dariux's wound back up as Taynor started to check blood levels, measure infection control doses and pain killers. Finally, everything was done and Dariux was once again gaining more colour, both his vitals and breathing evening out. Sitting back on his heels, Corin simply watched for a few minutes. He took solace in the fact he had been able to fix what he had missed.

"Amazing job, Corin." Taynor turned to him. "I would be honoured if you would teach me some of what you know. Your skill in trauma care is outstanding. It's something I haven't been able to study as much as I wanted. It's hard to gain entry to the schools when you aren't part of the Alliance."

"I'd be more than happy to help another doctor, but don't knock your skills. You did great." Corin sent a smile Taynor's way.

The two men went about cleaning up. All the while they monitored Dariux, their friends looked on from the doorway. "Damn, he is incredibly talented." Kastain's voice was full of awe.

"I know. He was one of the highest ranked trauma surgeons in the Alliance before the Admiral took offence," Dax explained.

"Well, the Alliance's loss is truly our gain." Kastain's focus was still fixed on Corin, his jaw still slack from everything he had witnessed.

"Uh, guys?" Corin shot a pleading look at everyone in the doorway. He was too weary to even be embarrassed over what he was about to ask. "I, uh, can't get up. Any chance of a hand here?"

Dax took one look at how tired and pale Corin was and bent down, scooping him up into his arms before carrying him into the bathroom. He went about helping Corin wash the remnants of surgery off before opening the door and shouting for clean sleepwear as Corin dried himself. Once Corin was dressed, he once again scooped him up and took him back to the reception room, propping him up on one of the comfy seats.

Tate passed a mug of tea over, smiling at Corin. "I figured it was my turn to make sure you drank your tea." They shared a laugh at the reference to all their earlier escapades.

Kastain watched the interaction between the friends with interest. Dax had been so tender to his friend. There was something about Dax that kept drawing his attention— the man was absolutely gorgeous, there was no doubt about it, and that thought alone was disturbing him. He had never been attracted to a man before, so why now? Was he even attracted or was he just in awe of the man and everything he was about? Stars, he was too tired to work this out. It was a puzzle he would have to leave for another time. There was far too much to be done before he even considered something for himself. Then again, wasn't that the story of his life?

Soon Corin's colour was pretty much back to normal and his joints were not aching quite as much as they had been. He looked around at the slightly concerned faces he kept seeing looking his way. "I'm fine guys, really. It's just been a long ass day. Coupled with it being difficult to sleep at times, it's nothing major, or worth worrying about, okay?"

The men were nodding their agreement at him, yet he somehow doubted his comments were going to stop them worrying, not that there was anything he could do about it. "Look, I'm going to go and watch over our patients for a bit, then climb in next to Kel and sleep. I think the proximity might help him some— the Matesickness still clings to him a little."

As everyone bade him good night, Tate asked if he could join him for a few minutes. With a nod, the two of them slipped into the bedroom and got settled in the chairs by the beds to watch over both patients.

Chapter Thirty Four

"How are you doing, Tate? Really, not some standard 'I'm fine' response either. I truly want to know. I was a bit worried about you earlier." Corin was the first to speak once the door was shut.

Tate sighed, running his hands over his arms as if trying to warm himself. "Honestly? I don't know. I, I know I lost it earlier. Damn it, Corin, I don't understand what's going on with him. He frustrates the hell out of me. We clash one minute, yet the next all I want to do is kiss him. We fight so hard, yet I crave him. I long for him. I need him in my life, but I can't have him. I can't do it. I think I love him, yet I can't have him in my life. It would hurt too much to lose him. I would never survive such a loss, not for one minute. It's destroying me to see him like this." Tears were streaming down his face as he finally gave voice to some of what he was feeling.

Corin sighed and moved closer to Tate. He grabbed Tate's hand and squeezed it tight, trying in that one grip to convey love, warmth, friendship and strength. "Oh, Tate, I understand what you are trying to say, but you need to think about things before you make any rash decisions."

"I have thought about things."

"Truly thought them through? Have you considered how you could have to watch him fall in love with someone else if you walk away? Have you considered how those feelings you have now, well, they won't go away anytime soon. You'll still crave him. You'll still need him, still want him, still love him. Pushing him from you won't change it. It will simply make you both miserable."

"I can't risk it. I lose everyone, Corin. Everyone I have ever loved has left me in one way or another. Through death, through fights, distance, through just about everything. How can I possibly love him and then lose him as well? It would truly be the end of me, Doc. I can't. I just can't." Tate sobbed.

"Tate, let me tell you a story." Corin knew this was going to be one of the hardest stories and talks he had ever done, but it would be worth it if it could help his friend. "I fell in love. I fell in love with Aaron, hard. I was twenty when we met and twenty four when he died. He was a wonderful, wonderful, man. He was a cop. He went out of his way to help anyone who needed it. We were going to get married and look at adopting kids." Tears were tracking down his cheeks unchecked now. "Everything was booked, everything organised. It was a week before the ceremony and his last night on duty before his leave started. It was supposed to be a routine call out. A small disturbance at a bar on a spaceport. From what I know, it started out routine. He and his partner stopped the argument before it got really out of hand. It was nothing more than a simple misunderstanding between two alien races.

They had the situation under control, everything was calm. Officially, they still don't know what started it up again. Unofficially, I've been told it was an off-duty cadet. He decided he was a big man and wanted to prove how good he was to the other cadets." Shudders were now wracking his body as he fought for control over his emotions.

It was Tate's turn to squeeze Corin's hand, his turn to offer strength to his friend, his turn to provide comfort and support. They really were both a mess and if Corin wasn't pregnant, he might have chosen to have this conversation while drinking.

Taking a deep, shuddering breath, Corin continued with his story. "The cadet started to mouth off to one of the aliens. As it turns out, this guy, well, this guy was on one of the Barin Alliance Founders security detail, and frankly one of the best warriors the Alliance has ever seen. He took exception to being berated by a cadet. He went for the boy. Aaron and his partner stepped into the fight to try to protect the kid. The other alien? He took advantage of the chaos going on and went to knife the warrior. Only Aaron took a step sideways at the last second to avoid a punch. Instead of being punched he moved right into the path of the knife. It pierced his heart and he died, instantly." Both men were sobbing quietly now, the look of anguish on Corin's face was heart-breaking to see.

"I'm so, so sorry, Corin. Those words are meaningless, I know, but it doesn't change the fact I am." Tate drew Corin into his arms for a brief hug before Corin continued.

"So the day I was supposed to marry the man I wanted to spend the rest of my life with? Well, it was the day I had to bury him instead. It came close, very close, to destroying me. I lost a year of my life to grief. I drank. I ignored friends and family. I lost my job, nearly lost our house. I pretty much lost everything. Then, one day, I was sitting in this little park near the house we had shared and this old man sat next to me. He said he could see the sadness pouring off me. We ended up chatting for hours. Day after day, I went back to that park and every day he was sitting there, almost as if he was waiting for me. It was his willingness to just listen to me rant, to cry, to shout, to let all the emotions out that saved me. I finally let go of everything I had been feeling. Two months later, he came to the bench with his son. It turned out his son was a medic in the Corps and offered to support my application if I signed up. I knew then it was the right thing for me. So we walked off to the recruitment office the same day and I joined up. And now? Here I am."

Corin stood up and went to check on Dariux, adjusting his medication in the pump slightly as he struggled to get his emotions under control. Walking back to Tate, he sat back down, a sad smile on his face. "I still miss him, you know? I miss the innocence we had back then. But there is one thing I am very sure of. I wouldn't change anything about the time we spent together. I have no regrets. Yes, it hurt, more than you can possibly fathom, to lose him, yet, I got to love him for four glorious years. I got to live, and I mean really live my life with him and no one can take those memories away."

"And now you have Kel." Tate smiled at Corin.

"I do. But you know being with Kel hasn't been easy either. I nearly lost him as well. Because of what happened with Aaron, I backed off from Kel. I kept a little bit of me apart from Kel at the beginning. I didn't ever want to hurt that way again. You know how conflicted I was about everything. I let him walk away from me and you know what? It didn't hurt any less. It wasn't easier because I chose to let him go. If anything, it hurt more. It hurt because I knew I had let him go without ever really having had him in the first place. I nearly lost him because I wasn't prepared to fight for him, I wasn't prepared to fight for us. Damn, it's been hard, so bloody hard getting here, getting to the point where we are happy. It's hurt like hell, but we are stronger now than we ever could have been. Honestly? Loving them and letting them go is worse. It's so much worse, Tate. It will destroy you." That was one thing Corin was very sure of.

"But how can I live if I lose him?" Tate just didn't understand how he would survive it.

"Let me ask you something. How will you live if you don't? Isn't love always a risk? Everything carries risks, Tate. Every action we complete can change things. Look, nothing is going to change for a while. His recovery is going to be slow. Take your time, get to know him, and if you still think walking away is for the best after that, then do it. But don't close yourself off to the chance at love. You show more courage than any man could when you are with the Avanti. Take courage and bring it into all areas of your life. You are an amazing man, Tate. Give him the chance to love you and heal you the way you deserve."

"Oh, Doc." Tate broke down, sobbing in Corin's arms. Corin knew it would be the first stage of Tate healing from whatever it was in his past that had made him so scared to love.

Corin decided to try something. He knew he drew comfort from Kel's physical touch, so he took Tate's hand and wrapped it around Dariux's. Almost immediately, the shudders slowed down, the gut-wrenching sobs eased and his breathing slowed. It made Corin think, what if they were truemates? More than ever, he vowed to help Tate heal and become the man he needed to be to accept the love freely offered to him.

Eventually Tate managed to calm down. He still looked emotionally raw but they were both beyond tired, running on sheer adrenaline. Corin said softly, "We need to talk more about all this, Tate."

Sniffing, Tate stuttered. "I know, it's time I faced my past, but not now, okay, Doc? I can't do it now. Just, soon, I promise. Right now, we have so much going on and I can't afford to be out of it. So please give me time?"

"Oh, Tate, of course I will. We will talk at your pace and no one else's. Just promise you will come to me any time you need me."

"I will, Doc, I promise. You know, you really are an exceptional man. Kel is one lucky man."

Corin smiled sweetly. "I think we're both lucky."

"You need some sleep, Doc. Climb in properly with your man. I'll keep an eye on Dariux. I'll wake you if I need to."

"Remember, Tate, you are loved. There are a lot of us here who love you. Don't ever forget that." Corin climbed into bed beside Kel and was surprised when, on apparent instinct, Kel immediately pulled him close and wrapped his arms tight around him. With a deep sigh, Corin let the stress of the day go and slipped into a deep, dreamless sleep.

Chapter Thirty Five

————————>O<————————

Over the next few days, Corin battled hard to keep Dariux with them. There were a couple more close calls, but they got him through it. Throughout every emergency, Tate was at Dariux's bedside holding his hand, trying to infuse his strength through their link. While Corin spent his time with his patients, the Avanti were working alongside Kastain, Tir and Niko. Teriva was being difficult and refusing to give up the details on her father's plans. For such a self-serving woman, she showed a remarkable amount of loyalty. They had expected her to turn almost immediately. Dax was guessing her fear was keeping her quiet. They left her to it, hoping by ignoring her and not giving her the attention she craved, she would give up and start talking about Martellon's plans.

A week later, they were all sat around eating breakfast. They were all fed up, exhausted and struggling. Teriva was playing on all their minds, a constant thrum of awareness in the back of their consciousness. No matter what they were doing, she was there. They couldn't move on without sorting this out. Martellon was still out there plotting and they were no closer to finding him or working out what his ultimate plan was. Even as they were locked in this battle of wills with Teriva, they were working hard to get the keep back into working order. It was hard, physical work, and at the end of every day, the men were truly exhausted. There was no time for romance, no time for enjoying each other's company or revelling in the fact the Avanti were all together again. It was constant from the moment they woke to the moment they fell into bed exhausted at the end of every day.

Corin was pleased with Kel's progress. He was starting to wake more often and for longer periods of time. His body was slowly but surely repairing itself. Corin just wished there was more he could do. More for Kel, more for Dariux, more to help rebuild the clan, more to force Teriva to talk.

"Well, the building will be finished today." Tir broke the silence that had descended over them all.

"Thank fuck!" Hunter murmured. "Hey, I don't mind doing it." He returned Dax's glare. "It's just my damn muscles ache and I'm sick of bloody splinters in my hands."

"Aww, you big baby, you want me to fix your little boo-boo?" Corin was sniggering away.

Hunter was scowling. "Bastard." His face soon burst into a wide grin though. Corin's giggle was too infectious not to.

"Now that's a sound I love waking up to," Kel said from the doorway.

"Kel!" Corin was on his feet and running to his mate before Kel had even finished speaking. He gently hugged Kel, but Kel was having none of it and wrapped him up in his arms, holding him tight. They simply stood for a few minutes holding each other, revelling in the contact and closeness. The sounds of the others talking washed over them. The only thoughts in their minds were of each other. Eventually, they were content enough to walk over and join everyone at the table.

Kel dragged Corin onto his lap, ignoring his mate's protests that he wasn't well enough. He wanted his mate and their precious cargo safe in his arms. There was nothing anyone could say, or do, that would stop it from happening. His hands rested on the swell of their child and he gently caressed a hello through Corin's skin.

"So, you guys better fill me in. What have I missed while I've been out, again, and what can I do to help?"

"Oh, hell no, handsome." Corin turned, scowling at his man. "You may be up and about, but as your doctor, I'm not letting you go running about getting into all sorts of trouble. It will just put you straight back into bed. I'm sure you don't want that."

"Okay, okay, I'll be a good boy. But you're wrong about the bed. I wouldn't mind being back in bed if you're with me and we were having a whole lot of fun." Kel peppered his words with giant kisses up and down Corin's neck.

"Yeah, please, no talking about your sex life. I so don't want to be imagining my baby brother having sex." Tir's face was crumpled in disgust. The others were laughing along at the banter between the two.

"Why? You could probably do with some tips. I mean, it's been a while, hasn't it, old man?"

"Oh, them's fighting words, brother dearest. You better watch out. The minute Corin gives you the all clear, you're booked for a sparring session. We'll see who the old man is then."

"Oh, you're on." Kel smiled at his brother. "So just what has been happening while I've been out of it? I see Dariux is still pretty rough. How's he doing?" Kel hoped Dariux would be okay. He owed the man so much for protecting Corin and the little one. There was nothing he would not do for the man. All he had to do was ask, and if it was in Kel's power, he would grant it.

"He's getting better," Corin reassured everyone. "I'm pleased with his progress, although, it was pretty touch and go there for a while. But he's a fighter. I don't know what he's holding on for, but whatever it is, it's pretty powerful stuff. He's fighting with everything he has."

Kel looked at Corin, a question in his eye. At the subtle nod he got in response, Kel had to struggle to hide his smile. Well, it seemed as though all the tempestuous behaviour between Dariux and Tate was coming to a head in passion. He was glad for them. They really looked like they would be perfect as a couple. He would have to quiz Corin later, though, as there was such an air of sadness and vulnerability around Tate. "So where are we?"

"Well, Martellon escaped, but we do have Teriva in custody, although she's not talking. We were just trying to think of ways to make her talk. None of us are much for the idea of certain interrogation tactics," Kastain informed Kel.

"Oh, if it needs doing, I'll volunteer. The bitch needs taking down a couple of steps off her 'I'm better than you' perch." It was something Kel would actually relish. Of course, he wasn't going to tell everyone he would. He wasn't bloodthirsty, but she had caused him and his family so much pain and heartbreak, he wanted her out of their lives for good. The look on everyone's faces said they knew exactly why he would be so happy to do it.

"Please don't for one minute think we haven't done it because we don't approve of doing it. She needs to face the consequences of her actions. It's just ingrained in us not to treat women so badly, but damn, the bitch really does need to pay for everything she has been a part of. The only problem is, we don't know for sure just how much of it she was involved in." Niko really wished he had better news for Kel.

"How many people did we lose?" Kel was not looking forward to the answer. The loss of any of his clan was going to weigh heavy on his heart and he would hold the guilt of each and every one for a long time to come.

"Actually, thanks to the two amazing doctors here, we only lost three. What's more, there was nothing that could have been done to save them. Their injuries were just so severe, there was simply no way to recover. Apart from those three, we have about fifteen who are still recovering, but it could have been so much worse." Tir was full of praise for both Corin and Taynor. They truly had worked miracles on the injured. The clan would have been decimated if it hadn't been for both of them and the Avanti. "About forty or so have already recovered from their wounds. Of those, at least half would have been lost if it weren't for these two."

Kel turned to Taynor. "Thank you. The words aren't enough, but thank you for everything you have done."

"You are most welcome, but even I am in awe of the skill your mate displays. The Alliance are mad to have let an admiral behave so unjustly, but their loss truly is this world's gain." Taynor was thrilled at the prospect of being able to learn from Corin. The man had a natural level of skill Taynor was sure hadn't existed in a very long time.

"Babe, I always seem to find myself thanking you." Kel squeezed Corin tight. "You have brought so much to my clan, to me. There will never be enough words to explain what it means to me, or enough ways to show you just how thankful we are. You are a true gift to my clan, but most of all, you are my greatest treasure."

Corin may have smiled at Kel's words, but it still didn't stop him smacking the man on the arm. Even as everyone around them laughed, Kel looked indignant.

"Hey! Why are you hitting me?"

"Don't you ever refer to it as your clan again. It's our clan. You hear me, Kelin Tharn?"

Kel shuddered. "Damn, babe, you're sexy when you're mad."

Corin's lips quirked up into a smile even as he puffed out a frustrated breath. How could he stay mad at the man when it looked like he was about to be devoured? Because the look on Kel's face right now? Damn, it was doing delicious things to his nerves. His anticipation was climbing.

Kel waggled his eyebrows at Corin, picking up on his reaction. "Later, babe. I'll live up to the promise later." He planted a kiss on Corin's lips as a down payment, although, much to Corin's annoyance, it was a very chaste kiss.

Corin gathered together a plate of food and one of his teas, passing them to Kel. "Aww, babe, are you taking care of me? You're really sweet." Kel was grinning away, knowing his remarks would rile his mate.

"Oh, bite me!" Corin growled.

"Any time, babe." Kel was waggling his brows at Corin.

"Oh, for fuck's sake, you two, knock it off. It's too early for this shit!" Tir groaned. The rest of them simply burst out laughing.

"So, all joking aside, how bad is the damage to our clan then? I mean buildings as well as the people?"

"Well, it was better than we expected it to be. I have to say, Bell's skills with explosives has a lot to do with the lack of damage. How there wasn't more still amazes me. We've spent every day since then repairing everything. Everyone's pitched in from the Avanti, to Niko's men, to Kastain's men. We owe a lot of people for all the help they have given us." Tir was beyond thankful he had all these amazing people who he was lucky enough to call friends.

"My heartfelt thanks to you all." Kel was overwhelmed at all the support they had been given through the last few months.

"Pfft," Kastain rasped. "I am quite sure you would do the same for us if we needed you."

"Of course, my liege." Kel performed what could only be described as a flowery half bow, which was an interesting manoeuvre considering Corin was still perched on his lap.

Kastain's only response was to throw a dumpling at him.

"You know, you guys amaze me at times." Dax smiled at them all.

"How so?" Niko cocked his head.

"Just the way you interact with each other. It's like you're all brothers. There is nothing you wouldn't do for each other. You have such an amazing friendship, the teasing is fantastic. It reminds me of Avanti squads, same as the completely irreverent way you treat each other. Mind you, I bet you lot were a handful when growing up together."

"Oh, the stories we could tell." Kastain winked.

"Oh, I have got to hear these." Corin was going to get all the dirt he could on Kel. He couldn't wait to find out what his man had been like as a child.

"Nope, our esteemed leader is not going to utter a word if he wants to keep his hide. Besides, I have far more dirt on him than him on me." Kel so didn't want Corin hearing stories. No, he much preferred to hide his wild and reckless youth.

"Hmm, you're threatening your King?" Oh, Kastain knew he was going to have fun with this. "I could devise some cruel and unusual punishments for you."

"What about if I beg sweetly?" Kel sent a look that was all cub-like innocence at Kastain.

"Oh wow, I'll keep quiet if you promise me to never use such a facial expression on me again. It's disturbing to see it on a grown man's face."

"Yes." Kel celebrated with a little shimmy of his hips, and didn't the move just rub his cock against Corin in the most amazingly delicious way, eliciting a groan from both of them. Everyone else in the room just ignored them, going back to their own conversations. They really didn't want to witness more of their loved up behaviour.

"I missed you so much, baby. I dreamt of you every minute I was out of it. I dreamt I held you in my arms. It was what gave my body the strength to heal itself." Kel was holding Corin tight as he spoke.

"Those weren't dreams. You did hold me. I spent my nights beside you. I couldn't bear to be apart from you and it seemed to help. You have to know by now, I would do anything to help you recover. Trust me, it was no hardship to spend hours curled up in your arms with your body pressed close to mine. Although, damn, I think I'm suffering from a serious case of orgasm withdrawal."

"You want some help to fix your condition, babe?" Kel winked saucily at his mate.

"Fuck yes!"

Kel didn't even bother to verbalise a reply. He simply stood with Corin in his arms and walked to the bedroom door, Corin waving backwards to everyone as they went. At the last minute he changed directions to one of the other bedrooms, remembering he had shared with Dariux while they were both recuperating. Kel ignored the catcalls and comments their friends were throwing at them.

Corin looked over his shoulder. "Hey, you're all just jealous you're not getting any."

"You're damn right we are." Dax smirked as the bedroom door shut behind him. It was the last thing Corin heard before all his attention was firmly focused on the man who was gently laying him down on the bed.

Corin had a sneaking feeling this was going to be fast and oh, so perfectly satisfying. The teasing alone since Kel had sat down was more than enough to put him on edge. Add to the fact his hormones were making him horny as hell and he was sure this was going to be one hell of a ride.

"Baby, I need you." Kel was almost begging such was his desire for Corin.

"I need you too, Kel."

Once Corin was propped up against the pillow, Kel leaned down and unlaced his trousers, opening them up to reveal Corin's rock hard cock. It was already leaking precum in anticipation of the fun they would be having, his hips already starting to thrust at Kel. Damn, he really was desperate.

"Please, Kel, I thought I lost you. I need this. I need us. I have to feel you inside me. I, I, fuck." Tears were streaming down Corin's face at the intensity of his emotions.

"Oh, babe." Kel stopped dragging Corin's trousers down and simply hugged his mate. "I know. I feel it too. I never thought we would have this again. I honestly thought I was going to die towards the end of the battle. My only hope was you and the little one would survive and make it to Alix's."

"But we both made it," Corin sobbed. "And I should be happy. I don't know why I'm crying. Fuck, I hate these hormones."

"No, you don't. You have them because you're having our baby, so you don't hate them. You just hate how they are making you feel."

"Bah, I hate it when you're right."

"I know. Now just hold onto me for a minute and relax. You're safe, our little one's safe and I'm safe. Right now, nothing else matters." Kel held Corin and stroked a calming hand over his back. "Now, we have important things to discuss." Kel wanted to distract Corin from his current train of thought.

"We have?"

"Yes."

"Uh, like what?"

"Names!" Kel's smile was beaming so wide, excitement was alive on his face and he looked so vital in his happiness.

"Oh wow, I hadn't even thought about it. I haven't checked if it's a girl or a boy. I didn't want to spoil the surprise. Stars, handsome, we haven't even got anything ready."

"There's time."

"No, there isn't. My best guess was around six months for how long this pregnancy will last, but it's just a guess. With such an odd combination of genetics, there is simply no way to know. Stars, the baby could come anytime from two weeks on. We don't have a single thing ready, oh stars, Kel." Corin's breaths were becoming increasingly rapid. He was panting in an attempt to get air. His skin started to pale and he was shaking. "Um, Kel, I don't feel too good."

"Oh shit!" Kel quickly pulled Corin's trousers back up at the same time as he laid Corin down while also shouting for help. "Taynor! I need you in here now!"

The door burst open and in came Taynor with the rest of the guys hovering in the doorway trying to find out what was going on.

"What happened?" Taynor asked, immediately in doctor mode.

"I don't know, we were talking and then all of a sudden he just went funny." Kel was starting to get frantic at how off Corin looked.

"Corin? Corin, can you hear me?" Taynor even tried pinching Corin to see if it would provoke a response.

"Can't breathe, walls closing. Can't see, spinning." Corin was trying to talk through what little air he had, but his vision was becoming cloudier by the second as his vision dimmed. His body started to vibrate, muscles twitching with restless energy.

"His skin is clammy, he's sweating as well. Okay, Kel, I need you to hold him. Tight. Get on the bed and wrap yourself around him as much as possible. I need you to make him feel safe. Tate, go climb in on the other side of Corin. Wrap him up from the other side. You need to make him feel as secure as possible. You need to stop him moving."

Both men followed Taynor's orders to the letter. "What's going on, Taynor?" Kel asked even as he constantly tried to reassure Corin.

"He's having a panic attack. A bad one as well by the looks of it. The tighter you hold him, the better it will get. Right now it's a control thing. Corin is probably feeling as if things are spiralling out of control and he simply can't face any of it anymore. His body has gone into fight or flight mode. If you hold him so tight he can't move, you take away his control, while at the same time, you'll be making him feel safe. It will make him realise he can just let go. I think he's been holding too much in, too much back, from all of us, as you've been recovering. Now you're up and about, it was always going to hit him at some point. I imagine something just finally tipped him over the edge."

"We were talking about not having anything ready for the little one. Not a piece of furniture, scrap of clothes or anything. Then he started to look really odd."

"He's really so worried about everything?" Niko asked.

"I think so, although he's been hiding it." Taynor was positive he had been. "I've noticed small changes in his vitals every now and then. It was never enough to say anything, but I was keeping an eye on him."

"Well, not being ready is something we can fix. Leave it to us." Niko nodded at everyone to follow him out of the room.

Chapter Thirty Six

Once they were all back at the table, they quickly discussed what needed to be done. Soon, they were all off on assigned tasks, roping in anyone they could. The women of the clan were over the moon to help. Corin had saved so many husbands, fathers and sons that day, there was literally not one single family in the clan who hadn't been touched by Corin in one way or another.

Tir was working with his men at arms as they stripped the room next to Kel's bedroom. Once it was completely bare, the women took over and gave it a full clean. Others were sorting and washing clothes for the baby.

Niko, Kastain and the Avanti went to pay a visit to the local carpenter. There, they worked under his guidance to build some nursery furniture that would represent both Corin and Kel. While the men worked, the carpenter, Merin, carved into the crib itself. Under mutual agreement, the carving was a space scene on one end and their clan lands on the other. Merin worked hard alongside the group of friends. He was beyond honoured to have been chosen to help with such an important task. His apprentice, and son, Tebrix, worked on making a wooden mobile for over the baby's cot. By the end of the afternoon, the men stealthily carried it all into Kel's suite.

Dax stopped in the doorway, stunned at the changes that had been made while they were gone. The walls had been given a fresh coat of paint and someone had painted animals on the top of the pale yellow paint. It was incredible. The rocking chair he helped make sat in pride of place by the window, which held the perfect view of the courtyard. He could picture Corin sat there, whiling away the time as he fed the baby, watching the comings and goings of the keep.

The newly built dresser was soon filled with clothes that had been made and given by many members of the clan. The crib took pride of place in the centre of the room. Kastain's bookcase was already filling up with books for all ages, and the chests Bell, Hunter and Bray had worked on were lining one wall and being stuffed full of all manner of toys.

Tate had joined them in their efforts after he helped Kel settle Corin. He burnt a beautiful scene into a slab of wood. The scene showed a smiling Kel cradling Corin in his arms, who in turn, held a baby in his. There was a look of absolute joy and contentment on both their faces. Frankly, Dax was stunned at the skill and talent Tate demonstrated.

"Seriously Tate, it's an incredible piece of work. Where did you learn to do that?" Dax wondered if Tate had gone through some training or if it was a natural talent, maybe a mix of both.

"My grandfather used to work on a farm. He would spend his evenings whittling, burning and carving wood. From as soon as I could hold the tools, I would spend many an evening keeping him company and learning his craft. Those are some of my happiest memories." The look of loss and longing on Tate's face was difficult to see, but Dax made sure to keep his sadness for his friend off his face.

"Well, you certainly inherited his talent. They really will be stunned with everything. This room is amazing. I hope it helps take some of the pressure off Corin."

"I hope so. When I left, he was doing better, but still so worried about everything. Kel was making sure to keep the conversation light, but I know it only helped a little. It will be such a relief for him to see this, although, be warned, he is incredibly emotional, so expect tears."

"Hey, I almost have tears in my eyes from how happy I know this will make him." Dax sniffed and smiled at Tate.

"Roll on dinner, then we can show him afterwards."

Corin was horrified at what had happened. There they were, about to finally spend some quality time together, and he grade A lost it. He totally shut down, and wasn't that just embarrassing. He could barely even look Kel in the face. Oh, he knew he could argue it was his pregnancy hormones, but it didn't matter to him, all that mattered was he had completely broken down.

"Stop it, babe," Kel admonished his mate.

"What?"

"I know what you're thinking, and it's okay. It's not your fault, babe. You have been so strong for so long and eventually something had to give. Eventually there was always going to be a time when your mind simply said enough."

"I should be stronger, though. You don't see anyone else breaking down."

"Really?" Kel shot Corin an incredulous look. "So, we didn't witness Tate breaking down when Dariux nearly died? You haven't witnessed me lose it several times when I've thought I lost you? What about Tir? You think he isn't affected by all this? You think he isn't losing it in private at the thought of what could happen to Eliya? What nearly happened? He was distraught when she was kidnapped. I distinctly remember him punching a whole lot of things before crumbling to the floor in tears.

Breaking down isn't something to be ashamed of. It just shows you have simply been too strong for too long, and it's your mind's way of saying slow down, step back, take a break and rest. It's your soul saying it's time to focus on you. It's time to heal you. We all struggle. We are all trying to make sense of everything around us. Be kind to yourself, babe. Even when you feel your body and mind are weak, your soul shines strong. Of that I am sure."

Corin sighed as Kel held him close. "You really think I'm strong?"

"Oh, babe, you are one of the strongest people I know. We all have times when we feel like giving in. We all have times when we feel like we can't go one step further. But you know what? I've never seen you quit, no matter what life has thrown at you. No matter how many others around you have long since said 'enough,' you are still going strong. When life throws you down, I've witnessed you get up, dust yourself down, and keep going. I have never known anyone as strong as you are and it is my privilege and joy to have you in my life. It is a gift that I have been given to have you by my side and no matter how many times we struggle, no matter what we face, we can be strong together. If you are weak, I will stand strong and tall beside you. If I falter, I know you are there to guide me. We are a team. We work together, live together, laugh together and love together. You are my everything and don't think for even one minute I would have you any other way."

"Oh, Kel, I truly do love you. Thank you. Thank you for understanding me, for loving me. Thank you for supporting me and having faith in me no matter what." Corin simply held on to Kel, enjoying the comfort he provided.

"Now, I know a lot of people who are desperate to see you. They know you're okay, but I think they want the reassurance of seeing you with their own eyes. So, how about it? You up for some dinner?"

"I don't know if I can face them."

"Why? Because you showed you aren't some machine? That you care? Our friends, they love you. They need to know you are okay. They won't think less of you. Now, let's go put them out of their misery, hey?" With a quick kiss on the lips, Kel gave Corin no more time to try to find ways to avoid facing everyone. He simply took him by the hand and led him out of the room. Straightening his spine, Corin took a deep breath and walked through the door.

Tate knew Corin was going to feel tired, weak, embarrassed and uncomfortable. He shouldn't. "Doc, good to see you up and about." Tate walked over and gave Corin quick hug before sitting back down.

"Thanks." Corin smiled softly at Tate as he too sat down.

"Eat, babe." Kel put a huge plate full of food in front of him and as soon as Corin tucked in, conversation around the table resumed.

No one was looking at him funny. No one was treating him differently. Corin really did have some of the most amazing friends ever. It wasn't that they didn't care he was suffering, because they truly did. It was more they didn't want to make him feel uncomfortable, and they certainly weren't going to treat him any differently than before. Their dinner was a lively affair and they were happy. The only person they were missing was Dariux, but he was on the mend and they had hope it wouldn't be too long before he was awake.

"Seriously?" Hunter exclaimed. "Are you honestly, truly going to eat that?"

"What?" Corin pouted as Hunter's words jolted him out of his thoughts. "It's outstanding."

"No, it's nasty," was all Hunter could manage round the bile in his throat.

The other guys looked up from what they were eating and all of them wore similar looks of disgust to the one Hunter did.

"Um, babe, it's really is quite revolting." Kel motioned to the combination Corin had amassed on his plate. There was Melivian Stew, a spicy, earthy mix, to which he added Alsane root, which was a sour plant growing to the north of their borders. He topped it all off with crumbled Halicane, a sweet flower the clan children often snacked on. "That is one of the nastiest combinations I have ever seen, babe. Damn, even Eliya would balk at it and she eats everything."

"Hey, it's all your fault, so don't go blaming me," Corin mumbled around the delicious concoction he had made.

"How can it possibly be my fault?" Kel asked incredulously.

"Well, the way I see it, you knocked me up, so you gave me the raging hormones and off-kilter taste buds, therefore it's you who made me choose this truly incredible food. So, all in, it's your fault." Corin smiled sweetly as Kel spluttered, trying to find a way to come back with a witty response and failing.

All around them, their friends were laughing. Tir was almost doubled over, clutching his belly, fighting to get enough air into his lungs. "Oh man, sorry, brother, but he has you there and you know it. Damn, I love how he keeps you on your toes. Life is certainly never going to be boring when you two are about, that's for sure."

"Oh, shut it, you bastard." But Kel couldn't stop the smile spreading on his face as he watched his mate happily eating his weird and wonderful mix while laughing with their friends. Once again, it felt like everything was right in his world.

When Corin went to relax with a cup of tea, Kel stopped him. "Sorry, babe, we have somewhere to be first."

"Where?"

"Come on, just trust me, okay?"

"Pfft, you know I do, but it doesn't stop me wanting to know."

Kel simply shook his head and smiled, leading Corin along behind all their friends. All the way to his suite, Corin didn't stop pestering any of them with questions. Wow, thought Kel, his mate really didn't like not knowing what was going on. Once they were all in his suite, Corin looked confused.

"Okay, so it's your suite, Kel, but what are we doing here? You know I can't leave Dariux at the moment. So as much as I want to, I can't move in here yet." Corin looked at his mate apologetically.

"That's not it, babe."

"I'm confused."

"Well, our friends were worried about you earlier." Kel ignored his mate's blush, even if it did make him look incredibly mouth-watering. "They heard you say what was upsetting you so much and wanted to do something to stop you worrying."

"Still not understanding what's happening." Corin pouted.

Rather than say anything, Niko and Tir simply opened the double doors to the room adjoining Kel's bedroom. Corin took a couple of steps into the room, and his face relaxed, his muscles slack in shock. He was looking at the most beautiful nursery it had ever been his privilege to see.

Walking over to the crib in the centre, he lovingly ran his hands over the wooden carving. One side held a space theme. Looking closely, he could see part of it was a representation of the Terran solar system. A little spaceship was flying towards another system which he was pretty sure was the one that housed the Landran planet they were on. On the other side, there was a carving of Kel's clan lands with a little space pod descending. It was brilliant, incredibly detailed and perfect. Looking around, he walked over to the carving Tate had made. He ran his fingers over the figures carved there. Happy tears shone in his eyes at the beauty represented in the carving. Looking around, he was amazed at the chests, the clothes, the toys and books. How had they managed to get all this done? He walked over to the rocking chair, sitting in it as he felt weak with the emotions of it all. "When? How did you get all this done?" he asked no one in particular.

"Well, we knew it was upsetting you not having anything ready, so the entire clan worked together and got everything ready. You are loved within this clan, Corin. Never forget that." Tir smiled. "You have affected us all in one way or another, and this? This was a small way we could show our appreciation."

"It truly is beautiful and I can't thank everyone enough. It takes such a huge weight off my mind." Corin was smiling through the haze of tears in his eyes. Looking at Kel with all the love in his heart blazing in his eyes, he spoke. "Now all we need is to finally go through with the mating ceremony. I want it done soon, before the baby comes."

A small cough drew the attention of everyone in the room. "I, uh, have something to confess." Kastain wore a slightly guilty smile on his face. "I sent out some Riders and they are coming with a priestess tomorrow. Alix is already on his way. My men have been working with your clan members and everything should be ready for you two to go through with the ceremony in two days. As long as you want to?"

Corin launched himself as best he could from the rocking chair and enveloped Kastain. Screw protocol, this man was his friend and had done something truly special for them. Hugging Kastain tight, he let loose with a litany of thanks. "Thank you, thank you, thank you. This means the world to me. I was so worried about finding time to get it planned and now I find you've all given me not one, but two incredible gifts. You are the most amazing group of friends out there." Giving Kastain one last quick squeeze, he walked towards Kel with his arms wide. As Kel slid into them, he let loose a big sigh. "I can't wait to officially be your truemate. It's all I want. I want to pledge myself to you, tie myself to you, merge our lives together, completely and irrecoverably. What do you say?"

"Baby, any time, any way, every way, I want to tie myself to you too. You are my everything. It is a dream I never thought I would experience, being able to tie myself to you. I say yes, yes, a thousand times yes." He peppered Corin's face with kisses as he spoke before leading them both back to Kastain. "Words will never be able to say what I feel in my heart, but thank you. I will never be able to repay you for arranging this, for helping us, for coming to our aid, for standing by us through everything. You are an amazing King, an amazing man, but most importantly an amazing friend." He drew Kastain into their hug and squeezed tight. Turning to face everyone in the room, he spoke again. "I hope you are all going to be there, it would be our greatest wish to have those we love and care for surround us as we take this next step."

"Brother, you have nothing to worry about. Not one of us is going to miss it for anything." Tir smiled.

Just as the others started to speak, a guard came running into the room. Everyone in the room went to draw weapons that weren't at their sides. Muttered curses reigned as the guard panted, trying to catch his breath. "Dariux is awake." Those were the only words he needed to speak to see the group propel itself into action. Corin was slipping into doctor mode as he jogged as best he could at the front of the group.

Chapter Thirty Seven

The sight greeting the men had them all smiling and laughing. Dariux was indeed awake and propped up in the bed as Taynor monitored his vitals. Corin rushed to his side even as his eyes took in the wealth of data from the monitor. "How are you feeling?" he asked as he checked him over.

"Hey," Dariux's voice was husky, but surprisingly strong. "I'm in some pain, but feeling okay."

"Good, just hold still for a few minutes while we check everything out." Corin and Taynor worked in conjunction with each other, and with a shared nod of agreement, Corin spoke once again. "Well, things are healing nicely, there's no infection, by the looks of things, and you've managed to escape any serious long term side effects or loss of ability. You are a very lucky man, Dariux, and I literally owe you my life. I never expected you to take the sword for me, but I thank you. I would most certainly not have survived. It's just possible the baby might have, if Taynor had been quick enough to operate. So not just do I owe you my life, but the life of my baby as well. You really are a remarkable man who I am honoured to call my friend." Corin hugged Dariux gently as he spoke.

"Even if I hadn't promised Kel, I would do everything in my power to keep you alive. There was no way I was going to let them get you. You're an amazing man, Corin, and I would have happily given my life to save the two of you. Frankly, I have no idea how I survived. Your skill truly is remarkable. Thank you for saving my life." He hugged Corin back.

"Thank you for saving ours."

Kel was overjoyed. The man who had saved his family had pulled through. Despite his willingness, he hadn't paid the ultimate sacrifice and for that Kel was relieved. Dariux would never want for anything again. If something was in his power to arrange, it would be done.

Looking at Dariux, his voice was choked up, his throat closed with so much emotion he found he couldn't speak. He met Dariux's eyes, smiled and nodded. Dariux returned both, the silent communication between them conveying more than a thousand words ever could.

"So what have I missed?" Dariux asked.

As everyone was filling in Dariux, Tate was an emotional wreck. He stood rooted to the spot, a cascade of emotions threatening to overwhelm him. Everything he was feeling was hitting him with the strength of a battering ram. Relief, hope, acceptance, fear, helplessness, exhaustion and, most importantly, love. His eyes never left Dariux's face, soaking up the man like a child with a thirst for knowledge. As the men filtered out of the room to let Dariux rest, Tate simply stood there, his focus solely on his Ree. Corin was the last to leave. He stopped by Tate, touched him gently on the shoulder and whispered, "Talk to him, let him know how you feel. Embrace your love for him. Don't throw this away, Tate, please."

Tate never acknowledged Corin's words, but he slowly stepped towards the bed as Dariux's eyes tracked his every move. He sat on the edge of the bed and took Dariux's hand in his. The connection between them flared to life instantly. "I was so scared, Ree, I thought I lost you." Tears were running unchecked down his face. He never once acknowledged them.

"But you didn't lose me. I am still here and I plan to be for a long time, bab…" Dariux whispered words broke off before he finished, his eyes soaking up the sight of the man he loved with all his heart.

"It nearly destroyed me seeing you like that. I have no idea what this is between us. I feel so connected to you. I don't understand it. I can't deal with it. You make me weak. You make me scared. You make me a nervous wreck. You evoke so many feelings in me and they are overwhelming me. I can't concentrate. I can't sleep. I can't eat. I'm distracted and unfocused. I'm a confusing mess of emotions." Everything was laid bare by Tate's voice and eyes.

Dariux was stunned. "But I'm here. I'm safe. We have time to figure all this out. I know it's confusing. I know it's hard to understand, but I want us to try. I want to be with you, love you, live my life with you. Let us see where this journey takes us."

"I don't know if I can, D. It would break me to lose you. It's better I walk away now, before it happens." Tate stood up, a grim sort of determination on his face.

"Tate, babe, don't do this. Don't walk away from us. Stay, talk to me."

"I can't. I'm sorry. I just can't." Casting one last longing look at Dariux, Tate fled the room.

Slumping against the pillows at his back, Dariux's heart broke. What was the point of surviving this if he was going to lose the only thing he had ever wanted? Lose the only man he had ever needed, the only man he had ever loved. Damn Tate to hell. The man was stubborn and difficult and downright sexy. Dariux went to punch something in frustration before he realised he was too weak to even accomplish that. Instead, he simply slumped against the pillows as he let his thoughts consume him.

Corin and Kel exchanged concerned glances as they watched Tate run from the suite. "Want me to go?" Kel didn't want Corin having to run around the keep chasing after Tate.

"No, it's probably best to leave him for a little bit. I'll give him some time, then go and find him." Corin sighed. "I want for him to be happy, I just don't know how to get him through this and it's so obvious to us all they could be really happy together."

"I know, babe, but you have to let them sort this out for themselves as much as possible. Push them too hard and it will have the opposite effect. You need to let them do this themselves. Give them time. I have hope they will get there in the end."

"Shit, I just hate to see any of my friends suffer."

"I know, babe, but it's part of who you are. You care so much and sometimes it's going to hurt you, but don't change. You are perfect just the way you are."

Instead of chasing after his friend, Corin cuddled into his man and simply enjoyed his closeness as well as the companionship of his friends around him. A little while later, Tate returned. Corin sent him a questioning look to which Tate shook his head and mouthed, "later." Corin nodded, but he was damn sure there was going to be a later. He wouldn't let Tate run from this. It didn't matter if it took him a day, a week or a year, he would help Tate through this, help him find love and acceptance, at least of himself.

Kel was feeling horny and it was frustrating him. He wanted Corin, badly. He didn't want to say anything because he didn't want to pressure Corin after what had happened earlier. Yet the look Corin shot him said he wasn't buying him trying to hide his desire. Corin simply smiled at everyone and bade them goodnight, taking Kel's hand and leading him into his bedroom. Kel gulped at the look of passion that was written all over Corin's face.

Once the door shut behind Kel, he was slammed up against the door. Damn his mate was sexy when he was horny. Corin lowered himself to his knees in front of him and unlaced his trousers with his teeth, before pulling them down to his ankles. He had one moment to appreciate the lust burning bright in Corin's eyes before he was engulfed in Corin's warm mouth. Fuck, he was harder than he had ever been before. "Oh fuck, babe, fuck."

There was nothing gentle about it. Corin was consuming Kel's cock. He was sucking so hard his cheeks were hollowed out. Every part of Kel's cock was being touched by warm tightness. Corin pulled back to focus on the head. One minute he was dipping into Kel's slit, lapping at the precum there, the next sucking hard. Just as Kel was finding a way to combat the sensations, Corin deep throated him, swallowing around him. His bumps were swelling, increasing the friction on them. Kel couldn't stop himself. He started to thrust into Corin— he knew he should be gentle, knew he should hold himself back, but he was beyond having any measure of control over himself. His head hit the back of the door, then rolled from side to side, his hands fisted at his sides. "Oh stars, Corin, please."

Corin smiled up at his man, his own cock leaking in excitement at seeing Kel lose control. He refused to touch it though, if he did, it would all be over far too soon for his liking. Instead, he let the friction of his trousers against his bare length drive him slightly crazy. His entire focus narrowed to what was in his mouth. Corin could tell Kel was desperately trying to hold back and it was the exact opposite of what he wanted. Instead, he let Corin slide from his mouth with a huge pop, a trail of saliva dripping from the end as it mixed with his precum. He smiled wickedly at Kel before lapping it up with his tongue, then sucking out the extra hard.

"Babe, stop a minute."

Corin's eyebrows shot up in surprise. "Stop?"

"I'm worried about you. Please. As amazing as this is, can we move to the bed? I don't want you hurt doing this."

Corin smiled and grabbed the hand Kel extended to him. As they moved to the bed, they both stripped themselves, too horny to allow themselves to be distracted by each other's bodies. Once naked, Corin pushed Kel back onto the bed.

Damn, Kel really didn't know which side of Corin he preferred, the soft submissive side or the full on power top side. He was most definitely getting the power top today and just the thought of Corin anywhere near his hole made it clench in anticipation. He was feeling torn though, as no matter how much he wanted Corin to be inside him, he was desperate to feel his mate wrapped around his cock today. Unable to decide, he simply let Corin take what he wanted, what he needed.

Corin pushed Kel's legs back, bending him and stretching his cheeks wide. He took a moment to take in the beauty of Kel's hole. It seemed to twitch as if it was desperate for attention. He wasted no time in giving them both what they wanted and leant down, giving it one long lick to wet it, before hardening his tongue into a spear and diving in.

Kel's back arched at the immediate, overpowering sensations as Corin quite literally fucked him with his tongue. There was no gentleness, no slowness, just an honest hard tongue fucking and he loved every minute of it. He couldn't resist the driving need to thrust himself onto Corin's tongue, his head was once again thrown back in pleasure, eyes closed as he soaked up the sensations. He went to fist his own shaft but his hand was slapped away by Corin. Instead,

Corin wrapped him in a fist and pumped him, hard, twisting with each pull. Corin's other hand grabbed Kel's and guided one hand after the other to his own thighs, forcing Kel to hold on, keeping himself wide open. Once he was satisfied, Corin let go and moved his hand to Kel's balls.

The tugging on his balls was incredible in concert with the other sensations currently ravaging his body. Kel was desperate to prolong the moment, but nothing he could think of was halting the tremble that was starting in his body. He could feel the sparks begin in his spine as his balls drew close.

With one last tug, Corin let go of his balls and Kel had the brief hope it would be enough for him to gain control of himself. But it was not to be. In the next moment, he felt a small slap to his balls and that was it. The pleasure-pain was so intense his orgasm tore through him, hurtling out of him in stream after stream.

His body was rigid under the onslaught, his back arched and his mouth open wide as a silent scream tore from him— there was no sound as there was simply no breath left in his lungs. He next became aware of soft and gentle kisses being peppered over his skin as Corin lapped up the evidence of his release. His legs must have fallen to the sides, for which he was glad as his body was nothing more than a collection of spasms and shivers.

Once Corin finished licking Kel clean, he leant up and kissed him, sharing Kel's taste between them. Despite how horny Corin was feeling, the kiss was slow, languid and sensual. He really could just spend hours like this, simply kissing and revelling in the intimacy they shared, but soon his cock could be ignored no longer. Running his hand down Kel's body, he found his mate was already hard again. He got up and found the oil by the bed. Coating Kel in oil first, he then straddled Kel, using the oil on his own fingers to open himself up. He struggled to reach his hole, being pregnant, but managed to work his fingers slowly inside, determined to drive Kel crazy as he watched.

"Holy shit!" Kel watched in awe as Corin leant back, exposing himself for Kel. He couldn't believe how hot the sight was— despite the fact he had come already, he was back to rock-hard and weeping.

His eyes were trained on those fingers slipping in and out of Corin's greedy hole. He watched as Corin's fingers were almost pulled into his own hole, so desperate was he to be filled. It was too much for Kel and he slowly pulled on Corin's hand.

"No," whimpered Corin.

"Shh, baby, I've got you."

Kel lifted Corin up and positioned him directly over his cock. "Ride me, baby. I want to see you take, and control, your own pleasure. Let me see what I do to you."

"Oh Fuck!" Corin cried out as he sank down onto Kel in one long thrust.

"That's it, baby, fuck yourself onto my cock. Take it, however you need to. It's all about you, baby."

Corin's moaning was getting louder with each second. He was torturing himself on Kel's cock, his hips moving with a teasing slowness. As he felt Kel bottom out in him with every thrust, he twisted his hips, grinding his hole onto the base of Kel's shaft and the hairs there. A shudder went through him every time as the gentle scraping was driving his orgasm closer and closer. As his thighs started to burn and falter in their rhythm, he felt Kel take hold of his hips and start thrusting up into him. Letting his mate power into him, he let his hips rotate again and again. His hand reached for his cock and he began to let Kel's movement thrust him through the fist he had made.

"Oh fuck, oh fuck, I can't hold on, it's too much, I'm coming, Kel, oh stars!" Corin's body went taut as every muscle locked down, holding Kel's cock inside him. His insides rippled against those bumps, prolonging his orgasm while milking Kel. The intensity of his release dragged Kel with him, straight into his second orgasm of the night.

Corin slumped forward, his arms bracing himself on either side of Kel to protect the baby. He felt Kel gently slip out of him before he rolled them onto their sides. Soon enough, he was wrapped up in loving arms and it was the last thing he was aware of before he slipped into a rejuvenating sleep.

Chapter Thirty Eight

Morning found controlled chaos in the keep. People were coming and going as they raced to get everything ready for the ceremony. Taynor and Corin were working with Dariux, helping him get to a place where he could stay sitting and awake for long enough to watch the ceremony. Corin was prepared to postpone it to have him there, but Dariux was having none of it. A bond had formed between the two of them on that fateful day and they both instinctively knew their friendship would last a lifetime.

Tate made himself scarce after breakfast, not wanting to face either of them. Both Corin and Dariux let it go for now, but neither of them would let Tate leave it there. There were going to be some heartfelt discussions in Tate's future. It wasn't just about his relationship with Dariux but repairing Tate's soul.

It was afternoon before Corin got to see Alix. As soon as Alix had caught sight of him, he was enveloped in his strong embrace. "It's so good to see you safe. I was worried." Alix smiled as he drew back and looked at Corin's belly. "My, my, the little grandchild in there is certainly growing fast."

"Grandchild?" Corin prompted.

"Well, seeing as I see you as another son, I figured it meant the little one here was my grandchild. So I'm laying a grandfatherly claim to spoil them rotten."

"Oh, Alix, I would love you to be the grandfather." Corin sniffed as he hugged Alix tight. "Neither of us have parents left and I want my child to be surrounded by love, family and laughter."

"They will be, Corin. Never worry about how much your child will be loved. You have too many friends, and too many people who care for you, for it not to happen," Alix's voice sobered as he continued, "How is Dariux doing? We all owe him so much. He nearly paid the ultimate sacrifice for you two, and I want to let him know just how much it is appreciated."

"He's awake. It's going to be a long and slow process, but he will get there. There are so many people who will help him. Right now? I'm more worried about Tate."

"I saw him. He looks so sad. I will talk to him if I can. It might not help, but I will try."

"Thank you." That was all Corin could hope for, that someone could help his friend.

The priestess and her entourage had arrived safe and Corin was being kept away from all the arrangements. It was frustrating him like crazy, but he understood why. Kel wanted to make everything perfect for him after everything they had gone through. He couldn't manage to corner Kel. He needed to know what he had to do. He didn't want to make a fool of himself when they pledged to each other. The question was, if he couldn't pin down his errant mate, then who could he grab to help? Then it occurred to him, he had a captive audience in Dariux. The poor man couldn't exactly run away from him. He snorted as an image flared in his brain.

"What's got into you?" Dariux asked inquisitively.

"So, I was just thinking I could ask you for help to prepare for the mating ceremony."

"Of course you can, but I still don't see what's funny."

"Well, I had the thought you couldn't really refuse me seeing as you can't exactly run away. Then I had this picture of you try to hobble away from me, and me waddling after you. Let's just say it's an, um, interesting image!"

Dariux took one incredulous look at Corin then burst out laughing. "Oh stars, you've got me picturing it now. Ow, oh, it hurts to laugh this much."

"Shit, sorry." Corin still couldn't stop the laughing, especially when it turned to snorts as he desperately tried to control it, but those snorts just set the both of them off again.

That was how Alix found them. Tears streaming down their faces, arms wrapped around their bellies, bent double and groaning, they were laughing so hard.

"Fuck! Help, I need help in here!" Alix's horrified voice rang down the corridor. He had no idea what was going on but something had happened to both men and they looked in agony.

Dax, Kel, Hunter and Kastain had been walking down the corridor as Alix yelled. Seeing there were no guards at the door to the suite, they broke into a run as they heard Alix shout again. All three men drew their weapons in fear as they slammed the suite doors open and skidded into the room. They found Alix and the guards desperately trying to check and see what was wrong with both men, who in turn were desperately trying to bat the offending hands away.

"Oh fuck, oh fuck, it hurts, ow, ow, ow, ow, ow," Corin was chanting. He was attempting to breathe through the pain in his belly as he desperately tried to rein in his laughter. Only it wasn't really laughter for either of them, neither of them possessed enough breath to truly laugh. Instead, they were both silently shaking.

"Baby, baby, what's wrong?" When Corin didn't immediately respond, Kel was getting more agitated. "Babe, please, you need to tell me, you're scaring me," Kel begged.

It was those words that finally managed to sober Corin up. Taking a few deep, panted breaths, he wrestled control of his body. Managing a few even deeper breaths, he finally had enough air in his lungs to speak. "Oh stars, I'm sorry everyone, nothing is wrong. I promise. We were laughing so much it actually hurt. My poor belly is sore now."

"You were laughing? That was laughter? Stars, Corin, you made us worry."

"Oh, Kel, I'm sorry. Everyone, really, we're sorry." Corin felt deeply chastised.

"It was just too funny." Dariux was still clutching his belly. "Shit, it hurts." He moaned.

Corin immediately held his hand out to Kel who helped him up and he was by Dariux's side checking him out a second later. Corin was so intent on Dariux he didn't even register the fact more people had entered the room. He made quick work of checking over Dariux, making sure nothing had been damaged in their fit of hysterics. Once he was sure there was no damage done, he breathed easier. "I'm so sorry, Dariux, it was just too funny."

"Hey, Corin, it's fine, I was laughing right along with you and, stars, was it funny." He leant over slightly and hugged Corin to his chest. "It was just what I needed. I haven't found anything to smile or laugh about in a long time."

"So, now we know you two aren't actually dying, do you want to tell us all what was so funny?" Dax scowled, although he really was glad to see both of them happy. More than anyone else, apart from Tate, they had suffered over the last few months.

By the time Corin managed to explain it all, the entire room was laughing along with them. It was the laughter that prompted Corin to look around. He was sure he had heard the high, light laughter of a woman or two. On his right, his eyes landed on an almost ethereal woman. She was petite, with waves of long, vibrant red hair— it seemed to almost glow in the flickering light from the fire. Her eyes were a rich emerald green and her skin was pale. Despite her smaller height, she was curvaceous and her eyes held wisdom far beyond her years. She had laugh lines around her eyes and her smile was infectious.

"Hello." Corin smiled at her. For some reason, he felt at ease around her. There was no censure in her eyes, no hint of hatred, or disgust at his pregnancy.

She smiled at him, her eyes full of mirth and affection. "Corin, it is lovely to be here for you. I am Alesina, High Priestess of Ragarin. It is I who will be performing your mating ceremony. It is my absolute pleasure to see such a vibrant truemate bond. I know you have had a harsh journey to get to where you are, but life is complicated, it's messy, it's hard work and painful. But it is experiencing the harsher side of life which allows the greatest joys to be embraced. The difficult times are offset by moments of pure love and joy. And it is pure love that you and Kelin have and it's simply stunning in its intensity. It shines from your very pores."

Stunned, Corin could only just manage to mutter his thanks. His hand sought Kel's and held on tight, the simple connection grounding him in the moment.

"High Priestess, it is a privilege to have you here. For you to bless our mating is a gift we will always treasure." Kel bowed deeply in reverence as he finished speaking.

Alesina simply smiled at him before turning to Corin. "I know you are worried about the ceremony." She walked forward and grasped his hand. "Don't be, I will talk you through it. Mostly you just have to stand and look gorgeous." She winked as she spoke. "The most important part of it? Enjoy it. You must promise me though, if you find you are struggling to stay standing for it in your condition, then just let me know and we can have a chair ready for you." With a squeeze of his hand and a smile, she pulled away to take a chair by the fire. "Now why don't you join me and we will discuss what happens."

As he took a seat, Corin said, "Thank you for the kindness in offering the chair, but I want to go through the ceremony properly."

"My dear, you will. I offer the same to any woman who is pregnant. It is not necessary to stand, merely what normally happens. What's more, I would say you have no more than a week to go before the little one is introduced to the world." Her smile was radiant at the thought.

"A week? I was sure I had three or four. I made my best guess based on our combined genetics."

"Well, I would put you at what? Nearly six months?"

"Yes, six months is about right."

"I am blessed with being able to see certain things and this pregnancy was never going to be longer than six months."

While Corin was both nervous and excited at the prospect of the impending birth, he was also worried. "Will the baby be okay with being born so soon? I mean, Terran births are nine months."

"Oh my sweet, sweet man, the baby will be perfect. You need to stop thinking of yourself as only Terran. With such a mix of races in you, the pregnancy won't last beyond the sixth month mark. I'm sure of it."

"So I'm nothing more than a mutt." Corin grimaced as he was gently smacked on the head.

"You will stop any such talk. You are no mutt… You are unique and special. Trust in the fates, my sweet man."

"I'm sorry, I just worry." Corin's words were accompanied by a heavy sigh.

"There is no need, but it is understandable, and the worry you have? It is what will make you a good father. Worrying about your child means you will protect them, nurture them, guide them and love them. It means you will be there for them through every step of their lives, open and loving, caring and sharing in their achievements. You will support them, respect them and simply be there for them however they need it. You and Kel will make wonderful parents, do not ever doubt that."

"Thank you, Alesina. My only hope is our child will find love and happiness in their lives. I wish for nothing more."

"That is all you need to hope for. It is all any of us can ever hope for when we look to the future."

Kel was listening in on the conversation. Oh, his dear sweet mate had been so worried about so many things. He needed to stop him worrying. He needed to reassure him, be there for him. There was no need to be so worried. They would love and care for each other and their child. Soon enough, he was called away on some minor issue, but he knew he left Corin in good hands. As he walked past, he simply dropped a gentle kiss on his lips, accompanied by a gentle rub on Corin's belly. He pulled away with a whispered "I love you" before walking out the room.

The rest of the day passed quickly for them all. Excitement was building and a sense of celebration hung in the air. It was something the clan needed after the last few uncertain months. Yes, they had lost their Chieftain, but they still had both his sons, they had repelled an attack, with little lost, and now they had hope for the future with the upcoming birth of a new generation.

Chapter Thirty Nine

Breakfast was a subdued affair. It was simply Corin and his Avanti friends. Kel was separated from him and was with his brother and friends.

"You are sure of this, Corin?" Dax checked.

"Yes, dad," Corin teased, sticking out his tongue.

"Hey, I'm just checking on a friend." Dax gifted Corin with a mock scowl.

"You have to know we would do anything for you, Corin, and if it meant running, we would," Bell added.

"I know and I can't thank you all enough for being there for me. But this is what I want. Kel is what I want." He smiled as he mentioned Kel.

"Yeah, totally loved up," Hunter teased.

"You are sure you are happy to stay on this planet? With this clan? Even if we find a way to leave? If the Alliance comes to some sort of arrangement with the Conclave?" Bray asked.

"Staying is something I wanted to discuss with you all." Dax looked at each man in turn, letting them see how serious he was. "I have to be honest, I'm tired, tired of fighting battles that don't need to be fought, tired of chasing after people who are probably innocent, simply on the say so of the Council. We have been at this a long time, my friends, and I think it's time for me to leave. I am considering staying here. Despite everything that's going on, it's a great world and there are some amazing people here. Besides, I don't like the thought of leaving Corin here alone without us." Dax was hoping they would take his announcement well, but he just wasn't sure.

"Oh, thank fuck!" Tate pumped the air with his fist. They all looked at him in shock. "What? I feel exactly the same way. I'm fed up of the life we've been leading. It's lonely, tiring, and frankly, soul destroying. I will happily stay and make a life here on this planet."

Corin smiled. He was pretty sure who played a big part in Tate's decision to stay, whether he admitted it or not.

"I would like to stay as well." Hunter smiled as he thought of why he wanted to stay.

"Well, I'm staying with you guys, so I'm happy with whatever everyone decides," announced Bray, "but right now, I want to know what, or rather who, has put a smile on our man's face here?" He looked pointedly at Hunter.

"None of your business. If, and it really is a mighty big if, but if anything happens, you will find out when I'm ready to tell people."

Dax looked towards Bray. "That just leaves you?"

"I am stunned." The others all shot each other worried glances as Bray spoke. "Stunned to think you would believe I would want to be anywhere else but with you guys. You are family. Maybe not by blood, but by bond. We are brothers. I go where you go, it is as simple as that. If you stay, I stay. Besides, Dax is right. It's time for us to pass on the mantle to another team. It's time to at least take a break from the Alliance. Might I suggest we take a year here and then fully decide? Just in case it's not what we want in the end."

"A smart plan, but please understand, I can't leave Kel. He is it for me. He simply is my life."

"It's okay, Doc, we know and understand. While Bray is right, I have a good feeling this is going to work out for the best. Who would have thought a hellish trip and accident on the rust bucket Delphini would have led us here?"

Soon enough the men were laughing and joking around. The serious atmosphere from earlier was gone. They were attempting to dress in the outfits Tir and Kel provided for them.

"Seriously? How can anyone resist this amazing butt of mine?" Hunter turned round and shook his leather clad butt at them.

"Well, it is particularly bite-worthy." Dax winked. "Are you telling us someone is managing to resist the perfection of your butt?"

"I know." Hunter scowled. "It's unexplainable. I mean, it is a sexy little bubble butt, isn't it?" Hunter was trying to catch a proper glimpse of his own butt, a slight look of worry on his face.

"Oh, for fuck's sake, Hunter, your butt is divine. Now, can we finish getting ready so we can get Corin mated?" Dax rubbed his temples as he spoke.

Hunter pouted as he worked the leather armlets into place. The teasing continued as they got ready, the men simply enjoying being with each other and working to stop Corin's nerves getting the better of him.

Corin was nervous, but excited. He couldn't believe the day was finally here. They had all gone through so much since they crashed onto the planet it seemed like it was a lifetime ago. In the early days of him reaching Alix's clan, he had thought his life was over in some ways. He had loved and lost the man of his dreams. Not once had he even considered he would be where he was today. He rubbed the slight ache in his belly as he thought. He wouldn't change having the baby for anything, but his body was starting to feel the effects.

His back ached, his legs felt swollen and he was tired most of the time. He was distinctly unimpressed with the way he waddled everywhere and how often he needed to pee. He couldn't make it through a night's sleep without being kicked in the bladder. It was driving him crazy, but yes, in the end it would be worth it, so he would take whatever the pregnancy dished out. He knew this was the right decision, knew Kel was the man he loved with all his heart and knew he could see himself loving this clan as his own. As those thoughts enveloped him, a wave of peace washed over him and calmed him. A serenity he had never felt made him smile and he walked out of the room to see his friends waiting for him.

"Okay, look, get it out now. Go on, and laugh at me for the outfit!" Corin knew they wanted to. He would if the circumstances were reversed.

"It's not that, Corin," Bray smiled. "Honestly, you look, well, radiant. The happiness suits you." The others murmured their agreement.

"You don't think I look stupid in this outfit?" Corin looked down at himself. His leather trousers hung low on his hips, the leather ties resting under his belly. He wore a cream linen tunic with leather panels at the side and on the trim. It had been made especially for him by one of the clan seamstress so it complimented Kel's dress uniform and left his belly unrestricted, yet covered. It was a truly beautiful top and he was proud to wear it. His arms were adorned by thin leather circlets high up on his biceps and studded leather bracers. The ceremonial dagger he wore was attached to a belt at his hip.

The men in front of him differed in their outfits. As they didn't have access to their Avanti dress uniform, they wore the same leather trousers Corin wore and skin-tight leather waistcoats. They didn't wear the same bracers as Corin, nor the ceremonial dagger. Instead, like most of the warriors attending the ceremony, they elected to wear their swords at their sides. The Avanti also carried their pistols.

"Corin, you look handsome. Kel is going to be stunned stupid when he sets eyes on you." Bray smiled at the hopeful look on Corin's face. "Come on, let's go downstairs and get this party started." The men linked arms, Corin at the heart of their group, and left the room.

⤜O⤛

The war room had been decorated in neutral earth tones and with chairs along the walls, in a similar way to the banquet soon after their arrival. In the middle of the room stood a dais. It was there Corin and Kel would be bonded by the priestess, becoming mates forever.

Corin stood anxiously in a room off to the side as the clan and their guests made their way into the room. Tir popped his head in with Eliya. She looked adorable in a soft linen and leather dress which matched his tunic. "Unca Cori! We match!" She squealed when she saw him.

"We do, sweetheart. Do you like your dress, then?"

"It bootifel, I a princess" She twirled around, her hair flying out around her, the flower petals and gems in her hair twinkling and giving off a delicate scent.

"Would you like to walk in with me, little one?" Corin asked.

"Oh, can I, Papi?" She turned beseeching eyes onto her father.

Tir smiled at his daughter. "Only if Corin honestly doesn't mind."

"I would be honoured," Corin assured Tir.

"Yay." Eliya treated them all to her happy dance when Corin agreed.

"I shall leave you all here then and go and comfort my brother, who is busy pacing and worrying you won't be here. I think part of him still believes he fucked this up and you will leave him."

"Never. He is my heart and soul and I can't wait for us to be officially mated. But know this— in my heart, we already are."

Tir smiled at Corin before giving him a gentle hug and a whispered "good luck" before swiftly leaving the room to take his place beside Kel and Dariux, who had been positioned in a chair at the side of the dais so he could take a pride of place in watching them join together.

Carn popped his head around the door. "It is time, my friend."

"Thank you." Taking a long, deep breath, Corin turned to his friends. "No matter what happens from here on out you will always be a part of my family and will always be welcome here, to visit or to live."

Each man gave Corin a quick hug before taking up their positions outside of the double doors of the war room. One by one, they walked into the room and took up their positions on the dais to the left of the priestess while Tir, Niko and Dariux were to her right. Kel stood in front of her, his expression stoic and unrevealing. Subtle tells showed his nerves as his fingers tapped against the hilt of his sword, no doubt drumming out a rhythm only he heard in his mind. Those closest to the stage, and taking pride of place, were Kastain and Alix. The other seats running down the walls were filled with elders, friends, family and clan members. Once all the Avanti were in position, Eliya skipped down the room, twirling and dancing her way to the front. Smiles graced the faces of everyone who watched her.

Everyone knew what happened to her and they were relieved to see the little girl they knew and loved was still the same gregarious, beautiful girl she was before. As she made it to the end, she reached up on her tiptoes and pulled on Kel's hand. He bent down to her level and she gave him a big kiss before attempting to whisper, in a voice that actually carried across the room, "Don't be scared, Unca Kel, Unca Cori lubs you." After her declaration, she skipped off and jumped up into Kastain's lap who wrapped his arms around her as they sat and watched Corin enter the room.

Corin was a bundle of nerves. He was trying to concentrate on walking normally and not waddling down the aisle. Halfway down the aisle, he felt a twinge in his belly and drew in a harsh breath. His eyes caught Taynor's, conveying a silent message. Taynor's eyes widened in response, but he gave a discreet nod in response to Corin's subtle shake of his head.

Corin continued on, thankful no one else had noticed his temporary hesitation. Now was not the time to let anyone know what was going on. Making it to Kel's side, he looked into his mate's eyes. He was stunned at the depth of love he could see shining in them. His eyes glittered like stars as his eyelashes attempted to bat away the tears of joy collecting on his lashes. Kel took his hand and his whole body seemed to shudder with relief. "Hey, handsome. You look stunning." Kel truly did look incredible in his dress uniform.

"Babe, nothing could beat you for how gorgeous you look." Kel stole a quick kiss, much to the amusement of everyone there, before they both turned to the priestess.

As the ceremony went on, Corin could feel rhythmic twinges in his belly and they were becoming increasingly difficult to hide. He had to consciously prevent his hand tightening on Kel's. He refused to let the ceremony stop for anything. He would be mated and bound to Kel forever before their child was born. Trying to distract himself, he pushed all his focus onto what the priestess was saying.

"In my time of being priestess, I have heard many people speak of a love for the ages. People use the words to try to sway someone when they woo them. They use the words to try and justify their actions. They say things like, they were under the influence of true love and that made them act the way they did. They say because someone isn't their truemate, it's okay to cheat. It's been many years since we have seen such a strength of love as displayed by these two men here before us today. Their love is pure, it is honest, and it's painful and beautiful. It's hard work, yet easy at the same time. It's one half of a soul finding the other half, two souls uniting as one, their hearts beating to the same pace." Alesina looked at Kel and Corin, who only had eyes for each other as she spoke. The love radiating from them was both intense and beautiful.

"I have performed many mating ceremonies over the years, but yours is one I will perform with untold happiness in my heart. You are both incredibly special people."

She took Kel's hand as she continued. "Kelin, you were prepared to consign yourself to a life of misery and heartbreak to set your mate free, to keep him safe. You were prepared to pay the ultimate sacrifice for the man you loved. The fates took notice of such a selfless action. Even when you were so ill you were dying, you refused to drag him back into the chaos of your world. That is what a truemate bond is like. A love and sacrifice so strong, the other half of your soul is all that matters."

Next, she took Corin's hand. "Corin, you are an amazing man. The depth of compassion you hold for everyone is stunning. Even when everyone else about you is failing, even when hope is gone, you stand strong and true, you hold on when there is nothing left to hold on to. You have never once walked away from saving a life, no matter who they were or what they had done, or the cost to you personally. You are truly selfless and put others first. Even when you thought Kelin had rejected you, you went to him when he needed help. You faced down those who hate you to save a man who you thought didn't return your love. You didn't run and hide when you were in danger and because of your actions many people lived. Your courage is heartfelt, your compassion, strong, your skill as a medic undeniable. This world was blessed when the fates led you to Kelin and you have astonished even them with your actions."

She took in the looks of love and knew the fates had everything right.

"What you do not know is, while your ancestry provides the genetics to allow males to carry a child, it is extremely rare even for full bloods. The fates stepped in when they saw what was deep in your heart. A desire so strong, they knew it was the only way they could truly reward you for your actions. I know you will both treasure the gift you have been given."

She turned her focus to everyone else in the room with them.

"To those here today to bear witness to the joining of these two souls, I say this. Love is hard, love is beautiful, love is hope, it is pain, it is sadness and joy. Never turn your back on love. It is a gift that can only ever be given freely. It cannot be forced, it cannot be influenced by others who would try to harm it. Stand strong and proud of who you are today. Embrace love, embrace the chance at happiness, and you shall be rewarded.

"In the coming times, life will be hard. Only when we embrace what the fates guide us to can we rise above the darkness. Stand together as friends, family and lovers. Support one another, guide and defend each other, and you will succeed. There are challenges awaiting you all, and sooner than you think. Stand proud and strong, my friends, and you will not fall. You will not fail. Be true to yourself and those around you. But most of all, be true to love."

Alesina took their hands and joined them together. "Let these two ribbons, one white for the purity of Corin's compassion and healing, the other blue for Kel's strength and protectiveness, bind them together." Alesina picked up another, pale blue ribbon, intertwining it into the other two. "May your joining bring balance, peace and love to your lives." Lastly, she picked up a yellow ribbon. "May your child grow bathed in love and happiness. May those around you provide wisdom and hope, strength and companionship, happiness and peace."

Alesina took their joined and bound hands, passing them quickly through a flame burning on a bronze disc in front of her. "May the fires of Dalron cleanse you of fear and hate. May the Air of Tulion blow the ashes of fear and loneliness from your hearts." Their hands were passed through a swirling cloud of petals. "May the Earth of Naradin provide strength and resilience in times of need." Their hands were plunged into a chest of earth before finally Alesina dipped their joined hands into a ceremonial basin. "May the waters of Gerian bless you and heal you."

Letting their hands rest on the cushion on the table, she sprinkled oil over them before raising them in the air chanting in an unknown language for a minute. Then her hands rested over their hearts as she spoke once again. "Your love burns as strong as the wildfires of Dalron. May it traverse the breeze to ensnare us all. May those sparks ignite into a blazing quest for love, truth, happiness and peace. May that quest encompass us all in its beauty and righteousness. May your legacy be a hope for all that they may find their own truemate. May your child grow to be just and wise, uniting us as one. May your dreams come forth into the light and your nightmares fade into the dark. I am Alesina, High Priestess of the Ragarin, and I am here to bear witness to the love shared between these two men. I hereby bond these two as one. May your souls be united for all eternity and never put to sunder."

Alesina stepped back slightly as her hands lowered. "Congratulations, Kelin and Corin, you are now one." She bent her head, kissing each one on the cheek, before gently turning them to face their friends and family as a resounding cheer rent the air.

Just then, the doors burst open, the Conclave flowing through the door. The man at the front crying out, "Stop the bonding! Laird Kelin Tharn is pledged under oath to another and so must it be."

Chaos was upon them.

Chapter Forty

"**W**hat is the meaning of this?" Alesina demanded. "How dare you interrupt a ceremony sanctified by the Priestesses of Ragarin. You will explain yourselves. NOW!"

Corin was horrified. His perfect mating ceremony was being destroyed by whoever the hell this was who had just stormed the chamber. "Kel, what the fuck? Who is this?" As he spoke, a much larger pain rippled through his abdomen. Stars, this wasn't going to be good. His eyes caught Taynor's, a silent communication rapidly firing between them. He watched as Taynor turned to a guard and had a hurried conversation before the guard quietly slipped out of the room, unseen by anyone else in the room. Taynor nodded at him as he started to slowly move closer to Corin, not wanting to push the tense atmosphere over the edge with any sudden movements.

"This," spat Kel a moment later, "is the Conclave." His hand rested on the hilt of his sword. Seeing his Avanti friends move to flank Corin and Eliya was a relief. They must be protected at all costs. He was not about to lose everything now.

He couldn't believe the Conclave had turned up, not just with the entire Conclave guard, but also with squads of both Martellon's and Nestor's men. Since when had Martellon had so much sway with the Conclave? There was more going on than a simple attempt to take over one clan. He just had no idea what Martellon's end game was.

He felt, rather than saw, Niko and Tir step up to stand with him, a solid wall of muscle that stood in front of Corin, Eliya and the Priestess, blocking them from view. At the same time, Kastain and Alix also stood, walking towards the man at the front of the Conclave, whom he knew to be Chieftain Nestor, a friend and ally of Martellon. The three of them walked forward as one, standing just behind Kastain and Alix.

Nestor strutted forward, self-importance and arrogance written across his features. "As I said, Kelin here signed a pledge to mate with Teriva of the Farian Clan. That pledge negates any other pledge made after it." Nestor knew he had this clan exactly where they wanted it. "The pledge was witnessed by Martellon of the Farian Clan and we demand it be upheld."

Kel growled and was about to respond when Kastain stepped forward. "So, you are telling me the only witness to this pledge is one of the two people who would benefit from such a forced mating? What's more, your witness is the very same man who tried to take the Derin Clan by force. If, as you say, this pledge was made in good faith, then why would he need to try to take the clan by force? Why would he risk damaging the very clan his daughter was mating into? Not exactly sensible behaviour now, is it?"

"By force?" One of the other Chieftains of the Conclave spoke up. From what Kastain could see, it was Turian, an ally of his. "What is this force you speak of?"

"What I speak of is Chieftain Martellon attempting to take this clan by force, pulling weapons on the new Chieftain, ordering his warriors to attack. I speak of Martellon demanding the surrender of both Kelin and the clan to him. What's more, there is suspicion surrounding the death of Chieftain Damron."

"That is a lie!" screamed Martellon as he pushed through the assembled members of the Conclave, making his presence known. "If his death was suspicious, you need only look to his sons. It is they who would benefit from his death."

"Oh? Is this the same son who was lying on his deathbed through an unknown sickness? Or the son who was still trying to come to terms with the kidnapping of his daughter? Sorry, but I really can't see either of them masterminding such a plan. Can anyone else? So, try again with your accusations."

"Kelin was pledged to my daughter. We were to become united as clans. It was what Damron wanted. He promised me it would happen, no matter what Kelin wanted." Martellon was frothing at the mouth, spittle flying everywhere.

Gasps echoed around the chamber and Martellon looked around, confused as to why.

"Oh? So you are admitting this was a plan devised by you and Chieftain Damron? Not by Kelin himself?" Kastain challenged.

"Wait, no I never said that."

"That is exactly what you said, Chieftain Martellon." Alesina seemed to float down the dais steps as she spoke. "Do not try to lie to me. Do not try to lie to the Priestesses of Ragaron. We see far more than people think. We know far more. So I say again, do not lie to me."

Corin was only half interested in what was being said around them. There was now no question in his mind it was time for the baby to be born. The question was how long could he hold out before it became life-threatening? He could feel pain rippling across the skin of his belly and knew it must be the start of his skin opening for the birth. This was definitely not good. The only thought that brought him comfort was he and Kel were mated and there was nothing anyone could do to change it. He watched as the guard quietly returned carrying one of their med bags and made his way to Taynor. He tried to refocus on what was being said around him, ignoring the looks he was starting to receive from his Avanti teammates and Dariux. It was as if all of them could sense something else was going on with him apart from the chaos in front of them.

Turian spoke again. "What is this force which has been spoken of? What is the Conclave not aware of?"

"Martellon's men tried to take this clan by force," repeated Kastain. Silence greeted his statement for a moment before a concerto of voices swarmed around them.

"Quiet!" he roared. "Silence and I will explain."

As the voices settled, he filled in everyone present on the battle he had borne witness to. He left nothing out. Stunned faces greeted him at every turn of his face as he assessed the Conclave.

"Lies, I tell you!" Martellon was gesturing wildly, his fury escalating, his face red, so deep was his anger.

"If it is lies, then tell me, how is it rebuilding work still goes on around us? How is it the injured still recover?" He gestured to Dariux as he spoke. "How is it that in the cells below us there are around twenty of your men held captive and," —he paused for a moment, knowing this next point could tip the confrontation into violence— "and not just your men but your daughter?"

Pure rage descended on Martellon's face and he lunged at Kastain, dagger in hand. He was immediately restrained by Kastain's guards who had an iron grip on each of his arms.

"Yes, your daughter. Your daughter whom you abandoned to her fate when it became clear you were losing the battle. Your daughter, who has refused to be deterred from her steadfast belief you will make her mating to Kelin happen. Your daughter, who maintains that YOU arranged the mating, that YOU promised her she would have Kelin no matter what. That YOU wanted to control this clan. That YOU wanted huge amounts of power. Despite everything to the contrary, she still believes she will mate Kelin. In fact, why don't we bring her up here and see what she has to say?" Kastain nodded to his second in command, Jeksan, who immediately dispatched some of his men to retrieve her.

Alix stepped forward to recount his own version of events. "While I was not here for the battle, my son Nikoben and Dariux, his second, were. Dariux was charged with protecting one of our Offworld guests at all costs. Martellon was known to be targeting him. It was in that duty Dariux was almost killed. It was only through the skill displayed by the same Offworlder he survived. Why was this Offworlder targeted? Because he was who Kelin wanted as a mate. Martellon knew, as long as this man existed, Kelin would never bow down to his demands."

"No Offworlder is a mate to someone from this planet." Martellon scoffed. "They are of such little consequence. We would pay no attention to them. What you say is incorrect."

"Yes. Those Offworlders have no effect on life here on this planet, amongst our clans. So why the need to target him? He is not a warrior. He is a doctor. So tell me again why a squad of your finest warriors was sent to try and kill him?"

"You lie," sneered Martellon.

"I do not."

Just as Alix was about to speak again, Kastain's guards were dragging Teriva into the room. She looked as beautiful as ever. No matter what they felt about her, they had accorded her every luxury her station demanded. They were not one to abuse their prisoners. As soon as she saw her father, she launched herself into his arms, a dramatic wail echoing around the room.

"Daddy, Daddy, they held me captive. Why did you leave me, why? I did everything you wanted. I tried to get to Eliya, but I couldn't find her. I couldn't take her again. They had her guarded and hidden too well. I think they expected us to come for her again."

Horrified whispers swirled around the room at her statement, yet she seemed unaware of what she had revealed.

"When I couldn't take her, I tried to make my way back to you, but these men took me. They told me Kel was alive, but he wasn't going to be my mate." She literally stomped her foot. "Why, Daddy? You promised me you would make it happen. You promised me you would give me Kel no matter what it took."

"Silence!" demanded Martellon before a resounding crack echoed around the chamber as he struck his daughter across her face. She collapsed to the floor sobbing.

"Even your daughter speaks of what you deny," Alesina remarked. "Are you sure you still wish to deny what you have done? Do you deny you have attempted to kidnap Eliya during this battle? Do you want us to believe it wasn't your men who took her before?"

"I really don't care what you think, or believe, or say, Priestess," spat Martellon. "The simple truth is Damron signed a pledge giving Kelin to my daughter and it needs to be upheld."

"Ah, so you concur it was his father who pledged Kelin to you? Not Kelin himself?"

"It matters not!" jeered Martellon. "The pledge stands and nothing can break such a pledge." He was confident about that.

"Ah, but that is where you are wrong," Alesina announced. "There is something that trumps a pledge and that is a truemate bond." Excitement rippled through the gathered Conclave. The guests who had been at the mating simply sat there with smug smiles on their faces.

"Truemates?" stuttered various voices from the Conclave. There was no way to determine if they were friend or foe.

"That's not possible! Men and Offworlders cannot be truemates!" A voice rang out, its tone both defiant and sure.

"Ah, but they can. What is more, Kelin and his truemate have been blessed by the fates. Besides, it matters not what anyone wants now. The ceremony was completed, the men are bonded."

"No!" wailed Teriva from her position on the floor.

Corin paid no attention to the debate raging around him. His hand clasped his belly and came away drenched in blood. He looked up at Taynor who was already running to his side.

Tate reacted on instinct alone as Corin crumpled beside him. He gently lowered him to the ground as Taynor reached them. "Oh fuck!" he cried out as the other members of the Avanti turned horrified faces their way. No one else had noticed what was going on with Corin, they were too focused on Martellon.

Martellon attacked Kel. His squads, Nestor's men, the Conclave guards and all those warriors and guards who had been there to witness the mating ceremony, jumped into the fray. Kel reacted to Martellon's attack instantly. He dove to the left as the dagger cut through the air where his neck had been, whilst simultaneously drawing his sword. Ceremonial or not, this claymore was as sharp as his normal weapon. It was slightly larger and heavier, mostly due to the adornment on the hilt, yet Kel wielded it like it was a wooden training sword—with ease.

"You'll have to be faster than that to catch me unawares, Martellon," Kel taunted. He parried the next attack, almost taking Martellon's weapon with it. He watched as Martellon grappled with the hilt, trying to secure his grip. Stars, had this man ever fought in a battle before? He certainly didn't act like it.

"Fuck you!" Martellon made another desperate lunge at Kel. This time, he tripped on his own court robes.

Kel laughed at the arrogance of the man, wearing court finery to such a confrontation. "Are you ever going to learn, Martellon? You want to be a warrior? Act like one. Dress like one. Train like one. You're nothing but an arrogant old man who is desperate to gain whatever he can in the last vestiges of his life. You're no match for me. You never have been and never will be." Kel feinted to the right, before sidestepping to the left and driving his sword into Martellon's arm. A scream rent the air before Martellon was suddenly surrounded by his guards.

Fighting off three of the guards at once, Kel lost sight of Martellon. He took his frustration out on the guards, dispatching them with ease. He would have been embarrassed if these had been his men. No warrior should be beaten so easily. Stars, even their trainees were better. Once all three men were lying on the floor, out cold, he charged forward into the heart of the battle.

Niko gently scooped up Alesina and carried her over to the Avanti. There was no way he was going to allow a priestess to become injured. She smiled at him softly as he turned and dove into the battle to help his friends.

Taynor ripped open the tunic which was now soaked in blood. Corin's belly was dripping blood as it was splitting apart in an x-shaped pattern. Gently mopping away the blood, he noticed there was a lot less blood loss than they had anticipated.

Tate's training kicked in and he went about setting up a transfusion of fluids and painkillers. "Okay, Doc, we've got this. Just try and stay calm and we'll get this baby delivered soon. Just think, in a little while you get to hold your child." He smiled at Corin, trying to keep him preoccupied and not focusing on the pain, or the battle raging all around them.

Alesina knelt at his head and was gently brushing his hair back from his face as she softly comforted him. She felt Eliya burrow into her side. She gently lifted her and set her in her lap. Eliya's eyes were soaked in tears as she looked at Corin.

"Hey, hey, little one. It's okay, I promise," crooned Corin. "It's just time for the baby to come. I'm doing okay. Don't cry, honey, it's a good thing, I promise."

"You pwomise me, Unca Cori? You won leab me?"

"Oh, sweet thing, no. I won't, I promise. Now why don't you help me and start thinking of names for the baby, okay?"

"Owkay."

Corin was glad he had managed to distract Eliya as the pain was becoming intense. He looked around him trying to find Kel. He needed his man with him. When he couldn't see him, he started to panic, trying to get up.

"Whoa, slow down there, Doc. Now's not the time to go haring off." Hunter gently rested his hand on Corin's shoulder, stopping him from moving.

"Where is Kel? I need him here." Corin was starting to shake from fear. There was nothing that would keep Kel from his side during this, so he was sure something must have happened. Then his ears finally processed what was going on around him. "Oh, stars no. Please, no, no more fighting, no more injuries."

"Hush, focus on you, Corin. Do not fear, Kelin and your friends will be okay," Alesina assured him.

Corin turned his head to look at Dax, his eyes beseeching as he spoke. "Please, Dax, please keep Kel safe."

Looking around and realising there was more than enough people around their group for protection, Dax nodded as he stood. "I will," he vowed as he walked away.

Dax found Kel amid the chaos that had erupted. He was fighting two of Martellon's men. What surprised Dax most was the Conclave member, Turian, was fighting side by side with Kel, a manic grin on his face.

"Ah, stars, I haven't had this much fun in ages." Turian laughed.

Dax merely shook his head as he parried a blow aimed at his head. "You're having fun?" Dax asked incredulously.

"You bet I am. Sitting with the Conclave is boring. It is not a warrior's life. Nor one I wanted. Now this is what a warrior was born for." He grunted as the hilt of a blade connected with his hip but it didn't slow him down in the slightest.

Dax turned to Kel. "You need to go to Corin."

"I'm a little bit busy right now, Dax." Kel rolled his eyes. "As long as he is safe, I am needed here, protecting him and our clan."

"I get it, Kel, I really do, but damn it, you need to go to him. NOW! He's having the baby, and I mean right bloody now." He had to turn and lunge at the warrior behind Kel who was attempting to separate his head from his neck as Kel stood there stunned motionless.

"Damn it, Kel! Focus. Get your ass over to your mate!"

"Fuck, the baby's coming? Now?" Kel was shaking, fear and horror mingling together at the thought of what his mate was going through.

"Yes! Now shift your bloody ass over there, damn it! I've got this."

Kel didn't bother saying anything else, he simply turned and ran to Corin's side.

Turian was chuckling away as he fought beside Dax. "Stars, I didn't even know his mate was pregnant— now isn't that a surprise. Can't wait to see the look on Martellon's face when he realizes his plans of gaining the clan are completely shot to fuck!"

"Now you're my kind of friend. Let's go have some fun." Dax shot Turian a wink as they both roared and flung themselves deeper into the battle.

Corin looked up from a particularly painful contraction and saw Kel running towards him. A huge sigh of relief escaped his lips as he relaxed back panting. "You're okay," he whispered as he caressed Kel's cheek the minute he knelt next to him.

"I'm fine, babe. It's you I'm worried about." Kel took in all the activity buzzing around his mate.

Tate and Taynor were getting everything ready to look after the baby once it was delivered. Alesina was looking after Eliya, Dariux sat beside them on the floor. The Avanti, bar Dax, were standing in a ring protectively around the group having been joined by guards from Niko's, Kastain's and Kel's forces.

"It's going as we expected, Kel. He's doing okay. I know it looks scary, but it's going well." Tate tried to reassure Kel who looked distraught at not being able to help his mate. "Just keep holding his hand. The physical contact will help him, I promise."

Kel went one better and sat behind Corin, drawing him back into his arms, supporting his weight, holding him while trying to transfer as much strength as possible through the contact of their bodies. Kel felt Corin sigh and sag slightly into him. The vitals on the monitor beside them slowed slightly as Corin relaxed. Tate looked up at him and smiled, both of them glad to see the evidence of the comfort he was providing.

"So, Corin, how are you doing up there?" Taynor grilled him as he worked.

"How the fuck do you think I'm doing?" Corin's eyes were scrunched together as he spoke.

"Now, now, no sniping. I mean it, Corin. You're my best help at knowing how you're doing. I need to know what you're feeling. If you need me to adjust drug dosages. If you need me to put a blocker in for the pain. If you feel anything that doesn't feel right, okay?" Taynor tried to modulate his voice so as not to piss his patient off further.

"Shit, sorry, Doc. It just bloody hurts. I mean, I knew it would, but damn, I have so much sympathy for women now. Honestly, it feels as if my insides are being peeled away layer by layer, but I guess it's a good thing. What're my blood levels like?"

"Seriously? You want to treat yourself?" Kel knew his man was stubborn, but this was taking it to the extreme!

"I just want to help if he needs it, Kel. I'm not trying to take over."

"It's fine, both of you. Stay calm. This is just nerves talking. From what we read up, this stage should take about another ten minutes or so. I wish I could move you to the clinic, but I don't see how I can get you through this safely." He nodded towards the chaos surrounding them.

Hunter overheard and looked at Bell, who nodded. "Go, see what you can do to stop this. We need to get him to the med centre."

"Stay sharp, guys." Hunter threw up a small salute before running into the fray in search of Tir. As he pushed his way through the throng of fighters, dodging and deflecting various blades sent his way, he came to a conclusion— Martellon's men were aiming to kill, everyone else was aiming to disable their opponents. He could only hope it might mean this battle would be over soon. As he raced past Dax and Turian, he ducked and forced his blade into a swinging uppercut, landing the flat of the blade against the temple of one of Martellon's men who was about to stab Turian in the back.

The smile the man sent him was blinding. "I could kiss you, stud," he shouted, laughing as Hunter shook his head and ran on past.

He dodged past a subdued Nestor, who was bound on the floor shouting at anyone and everyone. He had four Conclave guards around him, preventing him from going anywhere. Teriva had been dumped by his side and was still wailing away like she was dying. He barked out a laugh as he overheard Nestor yelling at her to shut up.

He finally made it to Tir's side as he faced off with Martellon's men, Niko by his side. "You have got to stop this bloody fight, Tir."

Tir sent him a look which could only be described as a combination of duh and what the fuck do you think I'm trying to do. Hunter carried on, "Corin's in labour." Now he had the men's attention.

"Oh shit, where is he?" Tir demanded.

"On the bloody dais! We can't get him out. We have Alesina, Eliya and him under heavy guard."

"My baby girl is safe, yes?" Tir begged.

"You know she is." Hunter grasped Tir's shoulder briefly. "Each of us would die for her, but we really do need to stop this and get them all to safety."

"How?" Niko wondered.

"Oh, fuck this." Hunter suddenly thought. He set the firearm at his side to maximum blast and pointed it out the nearby window, making sure no one was in its path. He fired shot after shot. The sound rattled around the room, boosted by its natural acoustics, grabbing everyone's attention. In that moment, the entire battle stopped.

Niko took advantage of the silence and shouted. "Stop this now! Know you will not win this fight. Surrender and live. Conclave Chieftains and Lairds, we have innocent people in this room, women, children, those injured. What's more, we have an imminent birth happening. Stop this bloody battle now. To those fighting in support of Martellon, I say, the clans are better than this. We have never before risked innocent children and babies like this before.

"Look around you. See the women cowering in the corner? The children crying their hearts out? Be ashamed of yourselves, because I am ashamed of you. Imagine if they were your mates, your mothers, your babes, how would you feel? I say enough! Lay down your weapons and surrender. We are not trying to kill you, only defend ourselves. Look around you. You are severely outnumbered. Your Laird has fled already." Niko watched as the faces around him registered shock and surprise. "Martellon is a coward and a traitor. He has fled, leaving you all to your fates. Lay down your weapons and let the Conclave sort this out peacefully. What say you?"

A resounding series of clangs echoed around the room as weapon after weapon was laid down. Man after man dropped to his knees in supplication, heads bowed, hands held out in front of them as they surrendered.

A sigh of relief waved through the rest of the warriors as all of the enemy forces surrendered. For a moment, no one spoke until a scream rent the air. All heads turned sharply at the sound.

On the dais, Corin was in agony, his skin almost fully open. They knew on the next wave, it would time for them to get the baby out. Kel was crooning to him, wiping the hair off his face as Alesina used a cool cloth on his forehead.

"Okay, Corin? I'm sorry, but it's too late to move you to the med centre. We're going to have this baby right here. On the next wave, I'm going to go in for your baby, but you're going to have to lie down flat, okay? I need full access." Corin nodded and with Kel's help he was soon flat on his back with just his head resting in Kel's lap to maintain the contact that helped him so much.

Kel became aware of the lack of fighting around him. Catching Carn's eye, his eyes conveyed his question.

Carn leaned down and spoke softly. "They have all surrendered, but Martellon has escaped once again."

"Fuck!" Kel was pissed. He was really, really, pissed. He wanted to see Martellon under guard awaiting his punishment.

"Focus on Corin. We can get Martellon and his allies another day. Your mate and the babe are what matters right now." Carn softly smiled at Corin.

Kel nodded, returning his attention to the scene in front of him just in time to see his mate's skin open fully, allowing him to catch the first glimpse of his child. His breath stuttered in his throat as it failed to push past the lump that had formed. He couldn't believe what he was seeing. Corin leaned his head up and all eyes shone with focused intensity as they watched Taynor's hands slide inside and around the baby.

With gentle, yet strong hands, he lifted the baby out. Tate's hand went straight to the sac surrounding the baby and burst it with a gentle nick of his medical hook. He used a small device to gently suck any remains out of the baby's mouth and not a second later, a cry rose up from the little one. Cheers erupted from around the room. Celebratory murmurs could be heard from beyond the ring of men around them.

Kel's eyes were full of tears and love as they looked upon his child for the first time. He looked down at Corin to see the same love pouring from his mate. Catching Corin's eye, he vowed, "I love you. You are my everything and I could not be more proud of you than I am at this moment. We are fathers. Our little one is finally here." The last words came out as a choked and garbled mess, the emotion too much for Kel's voice.

Corin watched as the cord tying his baby to him was severed. The baby was on its own now and Corin would do everything to keep them safe. "Is it healthy? Is it a boy or a girl?" he managed to rasp out.

"Corin, Kel, you have a perfectly healthy and completely beautiful baby boy." Tate held the boy out to Corin and laid him gently in his arms. Tate looked on as Kel helped Corin sit up slightly as he wrapped his arms around the two most precious things in the universe. Their little family was now complete. The sheer joy and love emanating from them had every man around them sniffing back the tears. Alesina was chanting a blessing over them, even as she still cradled an excited Eliya in her arms.

Tir burst through the ring of guards and was stunned at the sight that greeted him. As he gently knelt down beside his brother, Eliya climbed into his lap, hugging him tightly.

"They habs the baby now, Papi."

"I know they do, sweetie. It's a little boy."

"He weally tiny." She scrunched her eyes as she peered at the boy.

Tir chuckled. "That he is, little one." Turning to the proud fathers, he said, "My congratulations to you. I am in awe of the perfect little man you have created there. The fates truly have blessed you. He's gorgeous."

Chapter Forty One

All of them looked down at the baby who was quietly looking up at his fathers. His eyes were a deep lilac and his hair was a rich brown. He had the cutest little mouth, which was already making sucking motions. "Uh-oh, looks like someone is hungry already." Tir laughed as Kel started to panic.

"Shit, we don't have milk ready, oh shit, oh shit, oh shit." Panic was written all over his face.

Alix laughed at Kel as he joined them on the dais.

"Hey, Alix." Corin smiled tiredly. "Will you knock some sense into my mate please?"

Alix laughed as he cuffed Kel on the back of the head. "Idiot, did the battle shake your brains loose? Zinarian men can feed their own little ones, look." He nodded towards Corin.

Corin gently lifted up the baby and placed him against his nipple. He could already feel slight changes in his pecs, and from what he had read about Zinarian Heritage, they wouldn't look much different from normal, at most slightly larger, but still looking the same as any other man. As he gazed down at his son suckling away, he brushed a finger gently over the delicate features on his face.

Chuckles rang out around them as the baby immediately started sucking down. His little fist was making clenching motions as though he would fight off anyone who tried to take him away from his daddy and his food.

"You've got a little warrior on your hands, Doc." Tate laughed.

"Just what I need." Corin smiled.

All around them whispers were passing from group to group as the happy news of a new heir for the clan swirled around them. Even members of the Conclave were smiling, the purity of birth enough to bring joy to anyone's hearts.

Kastain and Turian had been talking with some of the Conclave Chieftains and Lairds. As one, they all turned towards the dais.

"We have agreed, under the circumstances, there will be no doubt cast upon the actions of the Derin Clan or its supporters. The Conclave has decreed the truemate bond between Kelin and Corin stands. It is a right and just true bond and we believe it was through manipulation and deceit that Kelin was pledged to Teriva. There will be no consequences to the Derin." Kastain smiled at the audible relief echoing around the room.

"We would ask, however, that the Derin Clan aid us in our fight to rout out the disease working its way into our clans. We need to stand united if we are to prevent an all-out clan war. We need to stand united if we are to decide what is best for the planet when it comes to the Alliance. What say you, Tir? What say you, Kel? Will you stand beside us?" Kastain looked them directly in the eyes, hope shining there.

The two brothers looked at each other for a moment, a silent conversation passing from eye to eye. With a simple nod from Kel, Tir turned to the Conclave. "We will stand beside you. The Derin have unfinished business with Martellon. I ask though, how many clans, Chieftains and Lairds have sided with him?"

"Martellon, Nestor, Ricarno, Yidane, Clasnor and Vadarin, from what we have been able to gather anyway."

"Shit, that's a decent amount. It's going to be a long, bloody battle sorting this out." Tir was stunned at just how far the rot had gone through the Conclave.

"It is. We can just hope some will return, or the clans themselves do not support their leaders."

Alix stepped up to them. "You can count us in. We stand with the Derin."

"Thank you, Alix." Turian clasped his shoulder. "Now may I see this lovely new gift who has been born? Afterwards, I shall take the Conclave and leave you to some peace."

The men made their way over to Kel and Corin. Thankfully, Corin's belly was already closing, knitting itself back together with a speed that surprised everyone. Turian walked over and squatted next to the new family. "My apologies for what has occurred today. The Conclave was swayed by those we trusted. I am ashamed at the way we have behaved to you and yours. I would beg your forgiveness. It will be with a heavy heart I leave today, knowing my part in this has caused you pain and ruined your day."

Corin looked at the man. He could see genuine remorse on his face. "While I would have wished for things to go better than they did today, I have mated the man I love with all my heart. I have our child healthy and here in my arms. Nothing said or done today can possibly offset the joy in my heart at having them with me. Please, just promise me, Kel spends time here before being called away. We have been through a tough few months and I just want some peace and quiet to enjoy our time together."

"Do not fear. We will not ask for more than attendance at meetings for a while. The Derin have more than played their part in trying to end this." Turian took one last look at the new family in front of him. "You truly are made for each other and I wish you all the best. He is beautiful and a treasure. Laird Kel, take care of your family. I shall see you soon."

They all watched Turian walk away, summoning the rest of the Conclave around him, the prisoners escorted away under their ever-watchful guard. As one, they filed out, leaving the clan to pick up the pieces of what had happened.

The Avanti relaxed their stances, sheathing their swords. Corin was happy where he was, surrounded by the clan, his friends and new family. He decided not to move to the med centre just yet, opting to enjoy the celebration going on around them. The food that had been prepared for the feast later was brought out and a party atmosphere rose as the clan all sat on the floor, chairs, whatever they could find. Warriors mixed with the cooks, the gardeners with the squires, elders with the merchants. The clan had come together as one, to fight together, to celebrate together and simply be together.

Corin and Kel were content wrapped up in each other's arms. They had moved back to their suite, Corin having moved in fully now. Their baby was asleep in the crib, which was temporarily beside their bed. They both simply lay there staring at their son as he slept. "He really is beautiful, babe. I am so incredibly proud of you for giving us such a wonderful gift. I love you more than words can possibly say. You two are my very life. I have never been happier than I am now. I praise the fates for the day they sent you crashing into our planet, as now, I cannot possibly imagine my life without you in it."

"I love you, Kel. I am so glad we worked things out. There's just one thing that needs to be done."

"What?"

"We need to name him."

They both looked at their son as names ran through their minds.

"What about Chance? I know it's not a Derin name, but it's through chance I landed here, chance we met and it was taking a chance on love that brought us together." Corin smiled as he explained his idea.

"I love it. Chance it is." Kel kissed Corin softly before they both looked at their son. "Welcome to the Derin, Chance. Welcome to our family."

Cast of characters

$$\rightarrow O \leftarrow$$

The Avanti. Barin Alliance's Elite Warriors

$$\rightarrow O \leftarrow$$

Commander Daxin 'Dax' Rydoc. Squad leader, politically savvy. (Barinian)

Lieutenant Commander Tate Riven. Sniper, weapons specialist. (Terran)

Lieutenant Bellan 'Bell' Nimeri. Master Swordsman of the Kingdom of Tarin. Explosives specialist. (Tarinian)

Lieutenant Braylen 'Bray' Dasthor, Master Tactician, hand to hand combat specialist. (Dunfranian)

Lieutenant Hunter Escedas. Comms expert, engineer, tech specialist. (Havernian)

Captain Corin Talovich. Doctor, surgeon. (Terran, Barinian, Zindarian)

The Derin Clan

$$\rightarrow O \leftarrow$$

Chieftain Damron Tharn. Clan leader.

Laird Tirathon 'Tir' Tharn. Heir to the Clan, Damron's son.

Laird Kelin 'Kel' Tharn. Damron's son.

Lady Eliya 'Ely' Tharn. Tir's daughter.

Carn Dibren. Master at Arms. Master of Lairds Tirathon and Kelin Tharn's Guard.

Naris Vilinx. Head guard for Tir, second to Carn.

Alcorn. Head of Eliya's guard. Second to Carn.

Al'Feram. Doctor.

Herica. Medicine woman.

Salin. Warrior.

Frenkie. Warrior.

Vrastin. Officer

Merin. Carpenter.

Tebrix. Merin's son.

The Estrivia Clan

Chieftain Alixandr 'Alix' Dastria. Clan leader.

Laird Nikoben 'Niko' Dastria. Heir to the Clan.

Lady Alisia Dastria. Lady of the Clan, mate to Alix.

Dariux Valcorn. Master at Arms, second in command to Niko.

Lixiss. Mate to Lexin.

Lexin. Warrior.

Grace. Daughter of Lexin and Lixiss.

Pacin. Warrior.

Oster, Officer, warrior.

Alasandra. Trainee midwife.

The Farian Clan

Chieftain Martellon Lendinas. Clan leader.

Laird Calahoun Lendinas. Heir to the Clan.

Lady Teriva Lendinas. Martellon's daughter.

Other Important people

King Kastain Asceadies. Ruler of Landran.

Antares Caridian. Master at Arms to King Kastain and his personal bodyguard.

Alesina. High Priestess of Ragarin, spiritual leader.

Other Chieftains

Chieftain Nestor.

Chieftain Ricarno.

Chieftain Yidane.

Chieftain Clasnor.

Chieftain Vadarin.

Chieftain Turian.

Others mentioned in Avanti/Barin Alliance

Master Sergeant Vasiliy Gregonavic, Avanti, member of another squad.

Admiral Car'velac, Admiral Areshole. Alliance Senator.

Others

Aladain. Moon Goddess, believed to be the protector of the moons.

The Collective. Rulers of Tarin.

Glossary

➤O←

Agent B. Used to help a mesh slowly dissolve after surgery. Used as a temporary binding agent.

Alpha Dawn. Avanti code name. Assigned to Dax as squad leader.

Alsane root. Sour plant growing to the north of Derin borders.

Avanti. An elite group of warriors, work for the Barin Alliance.

(BAC) Delphini. Barin Alliance battlecruiser.

Barin Alliance Founders. Seven men who first founded the Alliance. Hereditary title also given to the heirs of the original founders.

Battleboost. A mix of painkillers, artificial stimulants and adrenaline.

Battlegel. Delivers slow release infection control, draws out impurities, numbs the area it's applied to and provide a waterproof cover.

Chieftains. Rulers of each clan.

Clan elders. Offer guidance to Chieftains. Respected and can be a great help to Lairds that take on the leadership of a clan early.

Clan gatherings. Celebrations. Normally around clan events such as a death or birth. Some clans hold yearly celebrations of festivals.

Claymore. Heavy two-handed sword. History shows it was used by Scottish clans. Also known as a great sword.

Conclave. Assembly of Clan Chieftains, similar to a Senate.

Curse words. Thank the moons, by the moons, stars, for star's sake.

Delta Sector. An area of the fifth universe, home to many planets. A thriving hub of races. Contains one of the roughest parts of the Barin Alliance. The Karinski Sector.

Deris flower. A sweet flower that has a blue stem and vibrant yellow flowers. Produces a honey like smell.

Earth Centari V. Part of the Terran system of planets. Corin's home world.

Escape pod/Pod. Two man or four man units. Equipped with everything needed for survival in a hostile environment. Rations, weapons, communication systems and basic medical gear.

Faronine pet. Small, purple and white. Short bushy tail, big, floppy ears, vivid green eyes, feline face, tiny paws. *(Talisel – Eliya's pet)*

Field injector. Delivers medicines directly into a patient.

Five Moons Championship. Tournament on Tarin to determine the Master Swordsman. Very prestigious.

Gold Rank Surgeon. The best of the best in the Medical Corps. Always talented in at least two surgical fields. Considered the leading authority on medical practices.

Halicane. A sweet flower clan children often snack on. Slightly chewy leaves that eventually dissolves.

Haril. Rolling thunder plains. Known as Thunder Alley, on the edge of Estrivian clan lands.

Jinties. Small flying animals. Softly curved wings. Colours vary, all along the colour spectrum. Males are larger than females. Hunt by dive-bombing insects. Sharp beaks and talons. Soft downy feathers all over.

Karinski Quadrant. Home to the Karinski station. Mostly populated by gas giants. Heavily polluted mining zone, mining everything from metals to chemicals. Contains few habitable planets. Those present often used for resistance and terror networks.

King. Ruler of Landran, highest authority.

Klaxon. A warning horn on-board Alliance spaceships.

Lairds. Heirs to a clan.

Mate. Life partner. Pledged to each other in a mating ceremony.

Matesickness. Consequence of refusing your truemate. Usually the denied party suffers very little. Sufferers slowly deteriorate, become completely bedridden, slip into a coma, it's likely sufferers will die from the effects.

Matesickness elixir. Created by Corin and Herica to combat the effects of Matesickness.

Mating bond. The connection shared between mates. Provides physical and emotional support. Proximity can ease illness symptoms or emotional distress.

Medical Corps. Barin Alliance group of medics who are also trained military personnel.

Melivian Stew. A spicy, earthy mix of Caman meat, from the Caman bird. Stew also contains root vegetables.

Mystic archives. Estrivia Clan records.

Nonnie. Nurse, nanny.

Offworlders. Someone born, or from, a different planet than your own. Often used as a derogatory term.

Order of authority on Landran. King – Conclave – Chieftains – Lairds – Ladies.

Ragarin. Order of priestesses. Spiritual, believed to possess a connection to the fates.

Refrinti. Beasts, cross between the lions and zebras of old Earth, mane of long jet black hair, short hair on body, silvery white and black. Silver eyes. Feline, height similar to horses.

Riders. Official messengers, fast mounts, under the protection of the Conclave. Carry a green banner with a white X on it.

Sunrise. Avanti code name. Assigned to Tate.

Tarmuk Tea. An aid to healing, stimulates the body's natural abilities.

Tremack people. Clan of mercenary shape shifters.

Truemates. Extremely rare. Chances of pregnancy are greatly increased if a mated pair are truemates. Soul mates. Many consider it a celestial gift, that there is a person specifically designed to be perfect in almost every way for them.

Valinian worm. A bright red worm. Small, no longer than a thumb. Carnivorous. Only found in the bogs on Peris Majoris, a planet in the Gamma sector.

Wrappings. Bandages.

Zinarians. Similar to Terrans in appearance. Pureblood Zinarians have natural tattoos.

Meet the Author

Hannah Walker is a full-time mum to two gorgeous teenage sons, and shares her home with both them, and a very supportive husband. They have always encouraged her to follow her dreams.

She has always loved books from her childhood years reading alongside her father, inheriting his love of Sci-Fi and Fantasy. She has combined this with her love of MM romance to write her Sci Fi series: Avanti Chronicles and Demonic Tales, as well as her fantasy series: Elements of Dragonis. She loves writing about complex worlds where the men love, and live, hard.

Welcome to the world of MM Sci-Fi and Fantasy.

Books by Hannah Walker

➤O❮

Corin's Chance

Book 1 in the Avanti Chronicles

Posted to some stars awful cruiser, Dr. Corin Talovich hoped to serve his time quietly and get on with his life, but fate stepped in and decided otherwise.

Crashing into an unknown planet was the last thing Corin expected. With only his friend, Lieutenant Commander Tate Riven, by his side, they face the unexplored world and new enemies bravely, leading them to the Derin Clan, where they're welcomed by the leader's son.

Kel isn't sure about the strange men, but he isn't about to send them away, especially when the bond between Corin and himself is something he can't ignore.

When another clan wages an attack, Kel is forced to make some hard choices which nearly costs him everything he holds dear. Together, with their allies, Corin and Kel fight, focusing on the future they desire, knowing failure not only dooms their love, but also those around them. Side by side, they work to destroy the evil threatening to keep them apart and becoming the family both men desire.

Tate's Torment

Book 2 in the Avanti Chronicles

When a rare day out goes disastrously wrong, the men have to fight for the survival of one of their own. Their actions spark an appearance by the Conclave, leaving the Avanti's future in the hands of those who choose to destroy them.

Tate will give up everything to save his friends, even if it means losing Dariux and a love he never imagined he would find.

With half the conclave determined to punish the Offworlders, they have to rely on new found friendships. The question is, will it be enough to overcome the trouble that seems determined to take them down?

Delphini: Damage Control

Book 3 in the Avanti Chronicles

When Dax and Bell crash land on an unknown planet they only have one objective— find their friends and fellow Avanti. Of course Bell needs to heal up from his injuries first, then they have to work out where to go. Their biggest problem is— they hadn't counted on the world they landed on being quite as large as it was.

Along the way they encounter hostile local warriors, incredible beasts and more than their fair share of problems. It would be fascinating, if they weren't so worried about their friends.

Dax has gone into damage control mode, as the commander of the Avanti it's his job, his duty, to see his friends and teammates safe and there is nothing that will stand in the way.

Bell, the calmer of the two, has finally found somewhere he can let his inner darintha beast be free and he's making the most of it, using his darintha senses to help find their missing friends.

Never forgetting their mission, the two embark on a journey that not only tests them to their limits, but also deepens the trust and friendship that being Avanti is all about. Together, they search for their friends, and fight for survival as only the Avanti can.

Once Upon an Ocania

Book 4 in the Avanti Chronicles

A short story

After their trip to Berinias is delayed, thoughts turn to both love and the future. Ocania, a day of love for mated pairs, gives the men a treasured day off. But with love in the air, all the Avanti seem to feel the pull, pushing some to go after those they want and try to fulfil their hearts desire.

May your journey be swift and uneventful, may you all get one step closer to your truemates and may good triumph over evil. Remember love conquers all.

Dax's Desire

Book 5 in the Avanti Chronicles

The Avanti have made their way to Berinias, the capital and heart of Landran society. Not only is it King Kastain's home ground, but it's the seat of the Conclave's power.

Dax finally gets to see Kastain in all his glory— regal, confident, powerful and downright sexy. As events unfold, Dax and Kastain realize everything happening with the Derin, with Martellon, Nestor and Teriva, is linked. Their enemies draw closer and the plots and machinations of the Conclave deepen. They just need to work out who is behind it all and what they hope to gain.

Kastain finds himself turning to Dax, the one person he seems to be able to count on more than anything. The bond between the two leaders is stronger than they expected, and they long for rare times alone so they can explore it. Instead their time is taken up trying to work out which Chieftains they can count on and who is attempting to undermine them at every turn.

When plots and betrayals run deep within the heart of the capital, who will succeed and who will pay the ultimate price?

Bell's Beloved

Book 6 in the Avanti Chronicles

Bellan 'Bell' Nimeri loved Niko Dastria with all his heart. Knowing Niko was his lifemate from the moment he set eyes on him was bittersweet. Surrounded by unknown threats, becoming more than friends wasn't an option. Besides, he didn't think Niko had the same feelings as he did. What's more, Niko would need to accept both sides of Bell's shifter personality, as he and his darintha are a team.

Niko has grown up, preparing to someday take over the role of Chieftain to the Estrivia Clan. His life has been good, surrounded by friends and family, but he's always longed to find his truemate. Meeting Bell is a dream come true, but coming from different worlds, he's not sure Bell is willing to change his life to make things work between them.

Faced with war and unseen enemies, Estrivia battles for its very existence. The two men cling to their friendship, emotions growing stronger until neither can deny what they feel. Finally together and with the world trying to tear them from each other's arms, they face the enemy head on, knowing the only chance they have of finding happiness together is to defeat the ones who would destroy everything they know and keep them apart.

Mission Most Mysterious

Book 7 in the Avanti Chronicles

A short story

The Avanti are bored.

On a rare and treasured break from all the chaos, Bray decides to embark on a mission most mysterious. Tate has always been known for the practical jokes he plays on his teammates and friends. It's time for some revenge. This time, the tables are turned and Tate doesn't know what's about to hit him.

Faced with confronting his worst fears, Tate struggles to make sense of the odd happenings around him. He swears not only are there ghosts in the palace, but they are out to get him.

Revenge is sweet, but the Avanti know that if Tate figures out what they are up to, there will be hell to pay. Still, watching him get a taste of his own medicine makes the risks worthwhile.

With his sanity on the line, Tate battles with everything in him to combat Bray's mission most mysterious.

Demons Don't Dream

Book 1 in the Demonic Tales

Being the Terran ambassador assigned to Kenistal, the Demon home world, is not a particularly easy posting. Caris Dealyn wants nothing more than to get this assignment done so he can continue searching for his missing Avanti friends. But first, he needs to solve the mystery surrounding the last ambassador's disappearance, while navigating the Demon court with all its whisperings of plots and betrayals. It's not such a bad job, if he could keep his attention on work and not on the prince who seems to distract him just by being near.

Prince Dasalin Kan'erkit is busy running the kingdom in his father's absence, but not so busy he doesn't notice the new Ambassador. Caris gets under his skin like no one else before, which is quite a feat considering Dasa's demonically tough scales.

The attraction between them is undeniable, and when events throw them together, sparks fly. They can't get enough of each other. But there are forces at work that wish to keep them apart. In a fight for their survival, the two must figure out which demonic faction is behind the plot and protect not only themselves, but the people they have both vowed to serve.

Booker's Song

Book one in Elements of Dragonis

Rillian Mascini is one of the most knowledgeable mages in the world. Spending his days and sometimes nights with his nose in a book has taught him magic and histories that few care to remember. He has a passion for dragons that pulls him to learn all he can about them, including their language. He is one of the last people left alive who can speak to the magnificent beasts.

Conwyn D'Aver is squad leader of the Dragon Riders. He will do whatever it takes to protect the dragons and people he has given his oath to serve. Nothing is more important, and when Neela, his personal dragon, is attacked, Conwyn is out for blood. He vows to find the threat and defeat it.

When an old spell book is found that gives a person the power to control all dragons, Conwyn will do anything he can to keep it from getting into the wrong hands, even if that means teaming up with the bookish Rillian to find a way to overcome the evil enemies who seek to gain the power.

Together with the dragons, the two men must find a way to protect everything they both love, but while doing so, they risk losing their own hearts to each other. As their enemies seek to destroy them, they learn that sometimes it takes love and trust to defeat the things we fear the most.

Coming soon:

More from the Avanti Chronicles.

More from the Demonic Tales.

More from Elements of Dragonis.

Made in the USA
Columbia, SC
15 June 2017